COCKTAILS AT KITTIWAKE COVE

Teresa F. Morgan

SAPERE
BOOKS

COCKTAILS AT KITTIWAKE COVE

Published by Sapere Books.

20 Windermere Drive, Leeds, England, LS17 7UZ,
United Kingdom

saperebooks.com

ISBN: 978-1-80055-303-3

For Gwen,

Thank you for letting me borrow your daughter's pretty name and for coming on a few quests — for research purposes of course! — to sample wine and cocktails. It's a privilege to have you as a best friend. You always make me smile and we have so much fun together. Here's to many more cocktails and mini adventures, and never a dull day! This book is for you. Xx

ACKNOWLEDGEMENTS

The research for this book has been fabulous fun — as you can imagine!

My love for cocktails started way back when I used to visit Gwen when she lived in Axbridge. We'd have a wild night out, acquainting ourselves with the only three watering holes in the village. The Oak House Hotel used to have a bartender who made cocktails. And we would sit in the perfect ambience of the hotel's bar sipping cocktails.

In the early stages of this book, Gwen and I took a trip to Cornwall, staying in St Austell, where we visited the local brewery as well as Knightor Winery for a wine tasting session. We even attended a cocktail making course with Scavi & Ray at The Mall, Cribbs Causeway. Sadly, they are no longer there. These mini adventures, as well as others, have helped and inspired the writing of this book.

I've collected some books about cocktails, too, but I would like to thank Anna for buying me as a birthday gift one year *Drink Me Now: 150 Cocktails For Any Emergency*. It gave me the inspiration to name each chapter after a cocktail, and most of them came from this book.

I would like to thank Majestic Wines in Weston-super-Mare for a superb wine tasting event (28th July 2018). Richard Marriott (Store Manager at the time of event) and his colleague (I never caught her name — sorry!) were fantastic hosts, holding an informative yet fun wine tasting evening for me and ten other friends. You made us all feel relaxed and welcome. And we may have got a little bit drunk!

And obviously, I would like to share my appreciation to those who attended the wine tasting event, which was imperative to my research. Ha ha! So, thank you: Andi, Leanne, Michelle, Simon, Anita, Bill, Diana, Jane, Gwen, and Ali for making the evening so much fun! We didn't all know one another, but the wine soon changed that.

I am always grateful to my RNA Chapter — Weston to Wells — for their tremendous support and encouragement, especially in my darker, self-doubting times. A special thanks goes to Fay Keenan, who gives me the kick (not literally) I need sometimes and helps with me (quite literally) not lose the plot! Thank you for your words of encouragement.

There are many people involved in the publishing of this book and I am truly grateful to all of you, even if I haven't named you. I always fear that I'll forget someone, or they may take offence that I've not thanked them, so if you are reading this, I thank you. Thank you for reading this book and supporting me as a writer. Without you, I wouldn't be here.

CHAPTER 1: GINGER RICKY

Rhianna Price stepped off the bus carrying a large rucksack and a holdall. Both were heavy, containing her most important possessions — her clothes and essential toiletries. Oh, and her cocktail recipe books. She couldn't leave them behind. But this wasn't a holiday. Oh, no, the rest of her worldly goods were tucked away in storage — back home — until she could arrange for them to be moved. Although could she call it that now? Where she'd come from — Bristol — was it still home?

It was a mid-March morning and the sun was shining, easing some of her fears that she might regret her hasty decision to up sticks and get out while the going was good. If it had been raining, she might have been tempted to step back on the bus. She fought to control the strands of blonde hair that had worked loose from her messy bun, pushing them out of her face as she took in her surroundings as the bus pulled away.

It was easier to face the wind, blowing north west off the beach. Daffodils bloomed in clumps on the small green by the bus stop, and pale yellow wild primroses were dotted about. The tide was out, revealing the long expanse of sand, but she could still hear the roar of the sea. Overhead, a seagull gave its familiar cry.

Kittiwake Cove. Her fresh start.

Rhianna took a deep breath, inhaling the invigorating, salty air, and let the sun warm her skin. It was just the tonic she needed.

Online, she'd booked a self-catering apartment linked to the local pub, The Cormorant. From when she'd last stayed in Kittiwake Cove, three years ago, she remembered the pub was situated up the hill to the left of the beach. She would have loved to have booked the five-star Kittiwake Cove Hotel, where they'd all stayed for Jen's hen party week. But that came at a hefty price, and she needed to be careful with money if she wanted to make a success of her new venture, and the apartment was within her budget. She'd booked it months ago, when she'd pressed ahead with her decision to leave Bristol and move to Cornwall. She'd been able to book the apartment for two months, until she was able to move into her new home.

She'd spotted a small starter home on the internet and after a Skype tour, had arranged a viewing back in December. It was on a small development on the outskirts of Kittiwake Cove and was perfect for her. Her offer had been accepted, and now she just had to wait for the surveys to be completed before she could move. She'd be taking over the lease of her business premises at the beginning of May and would need it ready to catch the bulk of the tourist trade in her first year. There had been nothing for her in Bristol, so she had decided not to wait any longer. She could do more research and preparation while living here.

Lifting the rucksack onto her back and picking up the holdall, she set off on the steep climb up the road which ran up the left of the bay towards The Cormorant.

As she entered, she noticed that the pub had changed quite a bit since the last time she'd been there. It looked newly decorated, with white walls contrasting the original beams exposed overhead. Weathered oak tables filled most of the floor, and there was a pool table situated at one end of the room. Surfboards, surfing photos, and silver surfing trophies were displayed around the pub, giving it a fun beach vibe. A large original brick fireplace housed a log fire ready to be lit.

The pub was deserted, and Rhianna desperately tried to catch her breath after the climb.

"Hello," Rhianna called out, as there was no one behind the bar. She dropped her holdall to the floor and as she slipped off the rucksack, she let out an unintentional groan, still breathless and hot.

A blond man in his early thirties wearing chef whites emerged from a doorway which Rhianna presumed led to the pub's kitchen.

"Hey, good morning, what can I get you?" the man said in a London accent. He was about the same height as Rhianna and had a friendly smile. His left arm was covered in a sleeve of tattoos and he wore a wedding band.

"Hi, I know I'm early, but I've booked one of the apartments, and thought I'd see if I could check in early. It said to collect the key from here," Rhianna explained, wondering if she should rummage through her rucksack for proof of her booking. "I'm Rhianna Price."

"Oh, yes, just a minute." He walked around the bar to another door which led off behind it and returned with a key on a large fob with a number 1 etched into it. "I'm Ricky, by the way, the chef as you can tell." He gestured to his clothing. "The boss has had to pop out, so I'll show you to the apartment. Let me take one of those bags." He grabbed the rucksack, the largest and the heaviest of the two bags. "Follow me."

Rhianna followed Ricky outside and along a path that ran around the side of the pub, and towards a white single-storey annexe which had probably been some sort of outbuilding originally. It was split into a couple of apartments, each with a large front window and a cheerful blue-painted door. Her apartment was the one furthest away. Outside the front door was the number one on a plaque with the name 'Oystercatcher' underneath it. She noticed number two was called 'Kittiwake'. Ricky unlocked the door and stood aside for Rhianna to enter.

The apartment was spacious, with large windows letting in plenty of light. The view wasn't spectacular, as it only overlooked the pub grounds and the road. There was a small bedroom with a double bed already made up, which felt comfortable as Rhianna briefly bounced on the edge of the mattress. The lounge area had a futon as a sofa, which didn't look so comfortable, but could be pulled out to make another bed. There was a small, modern kitchen-diner area and a shower room with a toilet. With laminate and tiled flooring throughout, the place looked easy to keep clean. It would do her until the house sale went through.

"You've booked it up until the end of April, right?" Ricky placed the rucksack in the lounge, resting it against a small coffee table to keep it upright.

Rhianna nodded. "Yes, I'm waiting for my house purchase to complete." She'd booked until the last Saturday of April, hoping she'd be in her new home by then.

"I think we already have bookings in May, just to warn you."

"I should be okay." Her solicitor had confirmed as much.

"So, you're not holidaying? You're staying for good?"

"For good. You could say it's a new start for me."

"Kittiwake Cove was a fresh start for me too. You'll love it here." Ricky lingered by the door, one hand shoved into his pocket. "Hey, have you eaten? I can make you a sandwich in the pub if you're hungry?"

As if on cue, Rhianna's stomach gave a loud grumble. It had been a long day already, and it wasn't even midday. She'd been up very early to catch the National Express to Wadebridge. Maybe after a sandwich, she would be better equipped to reacquaint herself with the town she'd adored as a child and get some groceries in. "That would be lovely," she said, smiling. "I'll lose some layers first." She unzipped her jacket.

"Any preference on the sandwich?"

"Ham or cheese will do."

"OK, how about I knock up a mean ham and cheese toastie for you? Get yourself settled in and come over to the pub when you're ready."

"Will do." Rhianna smiled, starting to feel she'd made her first friend in the area. "Thank you."

"No problem. Welcome to Kittiwake Cove, Rhianna."

"Hello! Ricky?" Rhianna called out as she entered the pub, not too loudly even though the pub was still empty.

"Hey." Ricky appeared, carrying two plates. "I fancied one too. Thought I'd make the most of the quiet time and join you." He came around the bar and placed them on a table in the middle of the pub. "You look a lot less like the Michelin man now."

Rhianna giggled. She certainly did with her layers removed. She now wore only a blue hoodie with bootcut jeans and walking boots and felt more comfortable for it.

"Take a seat," Ricky said, gesturing to the table. "What would you like to drink?"

"Would it be too much trouble to ask for a coffee? I've not had one all day."

Ricky returned with two mugs of steaming coffee on a tray with milk and sugar. He took his seat opposite Rhianna and emptied a couple of sugar sachets into his mug. He picked up his toasted sandwich. "Breakfast was a long time ago. The boss won't mind." He winked, then bit into the toastie, which was oozing with melted cheese. They ate in companionable silence for a while, and Rhianna devoured her toastie hungrily.

"So, what plans do you have today?" Ricky asked.

"I think I need to refresh my memory of Kittiwake Cove," Rhianna said, after licking melted cheese from her fingers. When she'd come in December to view the house she was buying, and to meet her mum and dad's friends, Sheila and Martyn, who would be passing her the lease of their premises, the day had been very short of daylight and she hadn't seen much of Kittiwake Cove.

"Oh, yeah, a new beginning."

"I'm in the middle of buying a house and I have a new business venture, but I don't take over the lease until May. I'm opening a bistro-cum-cocktail bar."

"Cocktails, eh?"

"Yes, they're my speciality. I'm a bit of a mixologist."

"You'll have to name one after me." He winked.

"Actually, there is a cocktail called a Ginger Ricky. It's dry gin, ginger and lime juice mixed with ginger ale. Oh, and pineapple and lime wedges muddled in."

"Brilliant! Shame I'm not ginger!" He pointed at his blond hair. "Anyway, I expect to see it on the menu."

"Oh, you will."

"I'll bring my missus. I'll tell her you named it after me."

Rhianna laughed.

"So, what will you do until then? May is two months away, you realise," Ricky asked.

Six weeks, precisely, thought Rhianna. "Research, mainly. I need to check out local produce and suppliers, that sort of thing." She picked up her coffee cup. "I want to use locally sourced ingredients where possible."

"Well, if you need any help, the boss was born and bred here, so I'm sure he'll help you out with the local stuff. And I know a bit too, as a chef, and having been here a couple years now. But Joe's probably your best bet."

Rhianna's heart missed a beat. *Joe? Surely not the same Joe? No way. It's a common name. It can't be the same Joe.*

Her Joe had to be in Australia. That's where he'd said he was going…

And knowing that she wouldn't have the complication of bumping into him again meant Kittiwake Cove could be the perfect fresh start she needed. Not only a career reboot, but a life reboot too.

As Rhianna finished her toastie, memories of three years ago drifted back. That week in Kittiwake Cove had been so much fun, and meeting Joe, her surf instructor, had been half the reason. He was handsome and witty, and an extremely good laugh. Above all, he was a free spirit, which had been great as a holiday romance… She wasn't the sort to have flings, sex with no strings, but Joe had been very hard to resist. God, she'd fancied the pants off him. He was nearly ten years older than her — in his mid-thirties while she was in her mid-twenties — which had appealed to her at the time too, the older man fantasy … and she'd never known sex like it.

But Rhianna knew she didn't want that kind of romance now. She wanted stability. She also needed to concentrate on her new business and building her future — and she certainly didn't need any man involved. Not for a long time.

In fact, after the way her ex-boyfriend Glyn had suddenly ended their relationship, leaving her cynical that soulmates even existed, she didn't want any romance in her life whatsoever.

She'd thought Glyn would be the one. They'd bought a house together, so next she thought marriage would come, and children… She'd met him at Jen's wedding, only four weeks after her fling with Joe. Glyn had been a friend of Jen's fiancé, and they'd connected quickly during the party, both joking they were the only Welsh guests. Her love for Glyn left Joe's whirlwind holiday romance behind as a distant but happy memory.

But just like that, Glyn had thrown away their nineteen-month relationship, not wanting to work at a problem when it occurred, like a normal couple should. It had started with a silly row. Rhianna could hardly even pinpoint what it had been about. Just the usual bickering when two people in a relationship live together. She'd come home to find his dishes not put away in the dishwasher and had made a stupid, throwaway comment about it not being the fairies who cleared up after him.

Her parents had been really supportive. When her dad heard his old friends, Sheila and Martyn were retiring from running their restaurant, he'd discussed taking over the building's lease with her. Knowing she was unhappy with life in Bristol, he'd encouraged her to make the step to move on, run her own business, agreeing to be a silent partner. Basically, lending her some of the cash she'd need to make this venture successful.

And once Glyn had bought her out of the house they'd shared together for only a few months, she would be free of him for good, too.

She dabbed her mouth with a napkin, finished her coffee, then stood up. "Thanks for that, Ricky. How much do I owe you?" She reached for her small handbag hung over the chair.

Ricky shook his head, stacking the plates. "No, this is on me."

"Thank you."

"Ah, the boss did the same for me when I first arrived, and I'm sure he'd have done the same for you, too, if he'd been here. It's what friends are for."

CHAPTER 2: BITTER SPRING

The sun was shining and a cold wind was blowing off the sea as Rhianna strolled along Kittiwake Cove high street to get her bearings. It contained all the tourist essentials, including a boutique, souvenir and surf shops, a Spar, a chippy and an ice-cream parlour. Happy childhood memories of family holidays spent here flooded back. Rhianna noticed there was also an art gallery called White Horses, which hadn't been there when she was a kid. It had been some tacky knick-knack shop back then.

A lane cut up the side, giving access to the back of the shops for lorries, and also leading to houses, holiday lets and a caravan park tucked in Kittiwake Cove valley. On the opposite corner of the entrance to this lane was a large building. One half of it was a shop selling surf wear and beach paraphernalia. The other half of the ground floor of the building, with the entrance facing the road and the beach opposite, was a café called Surf 'n Turf, which Rhianna thought was a brilliant name. The upper storey of the building was a restaurant called Oceans with a decked terrace and a conservatory. As of the first of May, she — and her dad, Gareth — would be taking over the lease of these premises.

Sheila and Martyn — who they had visited frequently during family holidays — had decided to retire completely. They had a son settled in New Zealand and wanted to spend some quality time with their family. They had run a successful business, but being seasonal, it was tough during the winter months. Rhianna knew this. Her mother and father also owned a restaurant near Newport. She'd inherited the chef gene from her father. But unlike her parents, whose restaurant was busy all year round, she knew she'd have to make the most of the summer to survive through the winter. However, she planned to capture weekend trade as well as opening up the restaurant for events and functions during the low season. During her brief visit in December, she'd seen the premises were large enough to host intimate functions. Small weddings, business or birthday parties — even Christmas parties. The opportunities were endless. The past few months she'd thought of little else. Her father had full confidence in her too. After Glyn's persistent criticism chipping away at her self-esteem — which she hadn't realised he'd been doing until she'd moved out — it was so important to her to have her father's support behind her.

Unfortunately, there was no living space within the building. She'd booked the holiday apartment as it had been her best option, as most rentable places had wanted six-month contracts, and Rhianna expected to be out before then.

After much heated debate, Glyn had agreed to buy her out of the house they had bought together in Bristol. It should all go through before her booking at Oystercatcher ended. This was her hope. Otherwise she'd be sleeping on the restaurant's floor.

For now, she was living on savings and some money her father had lent her. For the past eight months she'd worked hard and saved every penny she could, while sleeping on friends' sofas when it became impossible to carry on living under the same roof as Glyn. Once he'd agreed to buy her out, he'd made it very clear it was *his* house and no longer theirs. *His* spare room was no longer appealing, and she'd moved out. Her parents had suggested she move back in with them, but they lived nearer Newport than Bristol, and the commute would have been horrendous.

During the first couple of months after her break-up, Rhianna had felt totally lost, adrift in a city she no longer loved. It felt as if she was stranded in the middle of the sea in a small rowing boat, and she would sink at any moment. And then, a lifeline was handed to her with Martyn and Sheila wanting to retire, and her father keen to take over the lease. Rhianna began to hope, and gradually a vision of a new and fulfilling future emerged.

Now she felt determined. Over the next couple of months she would concentrate on research for her new business, and basically get her life back on track. A fresh start, and hopefully she could use the time to develop some interesting new Cornish signature cocktails. She'd packed her cocktail-making essentials including the shaker, jigger and muddler. She also wanted to sample local wines, to see if they'd be suitable for her restaurant.

In the Spar, Rhianna picked up some necessities and then browsed the wine and spirits section. Unfortunately, the Spar, being a large corporate chain, didn't stock many locally brewed spirits, and those they did stock were expensive because of the tourist clientele. She would need to do some research to find somewhere to source her cocktail ingredients more reasonably. But for now, she would just pick up a bottle of vodka and a bottle of gin. That would be quite enough, given that she didn't have a car and would have to carry her shopping up a very steep hill.

Another bone of contention with her — Glyn had convinced her to sell her car, saying they only needed one. But at least no car meant less expense. Once she had a better idea of her financial situation, then she could look into regaining her independence in the transport department. Until then, she'd just have to get by with the local Kittiwake Cove bus service.

As she unpacked her shopping back at the apartment, Rhianna realised there was one fatal flaw in her research plans. The apartment didn't have Wi-Fi. Luckily, her mobile had 4G — when she could access it, as the mobile signal wasn't great in Kittiwake Cove. But for using the laptop she'd managed to squeeze into her rucksack, this was going to prove a real stumbling block. She needed to Google and save so many things, which was much easier on a laptop than on her phone. There was only one solution — she would have to use the pub's Wi-Fi.

Rhianna waited until after lunch before strolling into the pub, laptop tucked under her arm, assuming it would be quieter now. Maybe Ricky wouldn't mind her using the Wi-Fi if she bought a cup of coffee or two. He was her new friend, after all.

Apart from an elderly man, sitting at a table nursing a pint of dark ale and reading a newspaper, the pub was empty. The lunchtime rush was definitely over. She couldn't see Ricky, but behind the bar, with his back to her, a tall, broad-shouldered man with wavy dark brown hair was busy filling the fridge with bottles of local beer. Alarm bells started to ring in Rhianna's head as he turned towards her.

"Hey, good afternoon, what can I get you?" He was in his late thirties and incredibly handsome — just as she remembered him, with floppy hair and hazel eyes. His skin was already lightly tanned, as if it were his natural colouring.

Joe. Shit! Why wasn't he in Australia? Surely he recognised her? She opened her mouth, but no words would come out.

"Everything okay?"

Why didn't he recognise her? Admittedly, her hair had been much shorter three years ago, and she'd been going through a phase of bleaching it white blonde back then. And with the stress of Glyn, she'd probably lost a few pounds.

"Oh, er, hi, I'm renting Oystercatcher. I saw Ricky earlier. I was wondering if you'd mind if I sit in here with my laptop?"

"Yeah, yeah, sure." He looked at his watch impatiently and sighed heavily. Considering the pub was empty, he looked stressed — for a man who she remembered didn't do stress. His whole facial expression was tense, with barely a smile. Maybe this was why he hadn't recognised her — he had something else on his mind. He hadn't even looked at her properly yet.

"I'll buy a coffee," Rhianna said as she pulled her purse out of her small handbag. "It's just that there isn't Wi-Fi in the apartment, and I want to do some research." She placed her laptop on a table near a window, so that she had a view of the sea.

"What would you like? A cappuccino?"

Did he guess, or can he remember? "Yes, a cappuccino would be fabulous." Then she frowned. "Is everything okay?"

Joe was heating milk in a stainless steel jug. Over the hissing of the frothing he said, "My barmaid hasn't turned up. Again." He raised his arm to look at his watch. "And I promised to take my mum to the wholesalers at three."

Ricky appeared from the kitchen. "Hey, Rhianna, all settled in?"

"Yes, thanks. Just need to use the pub's Wi-Fi," she said.

"Any luck getting hold of Seana?" Ricky turned his attention to Joe.

Joe shook his head. "No, and I don't know what to do."

"I can stand in for her, if you like?" Rhianna offered without thinking. "Obviously, you'd need to show me how everything works … like the till."

Joe finished making her coffee, spooned the froth on top and sprinkled chocolate over it. "Thanks for the offer, but…" He looked at her dubiously, frowning. She could see he wanted to take up the offer — his eyes kept darting to the large clock over the bar — yet maybe he didn't want to offend her. Then it dawned on her.

"I'm a trained chef, but I've also had plenty of experience working front of house," Rhianna quickly added to reassure him, "and for the last year I've been working in cocktail lounges. I know how to pull a pint. I wouldn't have offered otherwise. I'm also a fast learner."

"Yeah, boss, Rhianna's sound," Ricky added eagerly. Possibly because he didn't want to be left manning the pub all afternoon on his own. "And I'll be here, too."

"You were supposed to be going home for a few hours." Joe frowned at his chef.

Ricky shrugged. "I don't mind."

"Oh, right, OK." She saw the relief wash over Joe's face.

"Just pay me in coffee and the use of your Wi-Fi?" Rhianna asked, hesitantly. "It's hardly busy." She gestured to the empty pub.

"Oh, go on then," Joe said. "Come around quickly, I'll show you the till." He lifted the hatch at the end of the bar, and Rhianna joined him, her coffee abandoned. "I'm Joe, by the way." He held out his hand and Rhianna shook it, resisting the urge to say, 'I know.'

"Rhianna," she said instead, but still received no signs of recognition from Joe. He had to be stressed.

"All the prices are on there. Each member of staff has their own code to get into it, but as I don't have time to set that up for you, you can use mine."

23

Twenty minutes later, Rhianna had mastered the till, and where most things were behind the bar. She retrieved her laptop and set it up on the bar, typing in the Wi-Fi password Joe gave her.

"We're not serving food until after five p.m. now," he said, car keys rattling in his hand. "Ricky, go up to my flat and chill for a bit. Rhianna can call you if necessary, or ring me if you have any problems," he said to Rhianna. "And thank you." His voice was laced with gratitude. Before leaving, he pinned his mobile number by the till, but Rhianna was confident she could handle a quiet pub. She doubted she'd be overrun by tourists.

"Go on, Ricky. I'll be fine," she said, encouraging him to leave the bar and go and rest. She was dying to ask him how come Joe was apparently now the owner of The Cormorant and not living in Australia, but resisted the urge. "I'll call you if I need you."

Perched on a bar stool near the hatch, Rhianna sipped her coffee contentedly and started googling Cornish wineries.

She smiled to herself. Joe clearly hadn't recognised her yet. Maybe she'd have some fun and see how long it took him to realise who she was.

"Hey, what can I get you?" Rhianna watched as a tall, good-looking man in his early thirties walked towards the bar. She closed the window she'd been browsing on the internet, shut the lid of the laptop and walked around to the other side of the bar. She'd got distracted from researching local produce, and moved on to cocktail recipes, looking at ideas for different times of the day, and even for different times of the year. One called Bitter Spring had caught her eye. The combination of grapefruit juice and Aperol would make a refreshing afternoon beverage. She'd added it to her list of cocktails to test.

Turning her attention to the man, she noticed that he was covered in plaster dust, making his short, dark hair look grey. He had a younger, slightly scrawnier and shorter lad with him, who looked to be in his late teens or early twenties, and was similarly dressed in tradesman trousers with holster pockets and a black T-shirt and also covered in dust.

"You're new," the man said with a predatory smile, instantly putting Rhianna into defence mode. Although he was good-looking, his obvious arrogance made him unattractive.

"I'm sorry, I don't think we sell 'You're New'. Is it a bottled beer?" Rhianna pretended to look along the fridges with their glass doors, then smiled back. "Is it Cornish?"

He laughed and elbowed his apprentice. "Cute. And the joke."

Rhianna narrowed her eyes briefly. The man's idea of flirting was poor. "I'm just standing in while Joe had to dash out. He should be back soon. This isn't a permanent arrangement. So, what can I get you?"

"That's a shame. You certainly brighten this pub up. I'll have a pint of Doom Bar, and the kid here will have…" The man looked at the younger lad.

"Lager. A pint, please," he said, rather timidly.

Rhianna frowned. "Are you over eighteen?"

Without a complaint, the young lad retrieved his wallet from one of the many pockets on his trousers and showed her his driving licence, confirming he was over eighteen. Just. "Don't worry, I get asked all the time."

"That baby face, huh, Will?" The older man nudged him jovially.

"Thank you," she said, smiling at Will and handing back his driving licence. "Don't want to lose Joe his licence on my first shift."

"You said it wasn't permanent."

Rhianna started to pour the drinks. "You know what I mean."

"So, are you not staying long in Kittiwake Cove?"

"Oh, yes, just this —" Rhianna gestured to the bar — "wasn't part of my plan. I am moving here. I arrived today. I'm staying in one of the pub's apartments for now."

"Oh, in that case, I'm Nick," he said, holding out his hand over the bar. Rhianna dutifully shook it. "I'm a builder, painter-decorator — general tradesman. As you can see, we've been plastering today. I own a building company. And Will here is my apprentice; we call him the kid."

"I gathered. I'm Rhianna." She handed over both pints.

Both men remained at the bar, which made Rhianna feel that she should too. However, to avoid any small talk, she set about cleaning and refilling stock, even though ideally she wanted to be sat at her laptop.

Before long, another man entered the pub. Another imposing figure; taller than Nick and a bigger build, possibly in his early thirties too. He was handsome with sun-bleached blond hair, long on top but swept back. It made her think, *Surfer*. But instead of board shorts — it would be a bit cold — he wore beige khaki trousers and a blue polo shirt with a company motif embroidered on it. The shirt stretched over his well-built torso. The man had biceps. The way Nick looked at him, they'd clearly had a pissing contest at some point. The man glanced at Nick and gave him a brief nod.

"Hey, I'm Liam, Joe's gardener. Is he about?" Liam said. He had an Australian accent and piercing blue eyes.

"Oh, uh, no, he had to pop out. I'm just standing in — temporarily!" Rhianna said, straightening her back and nervously fiddling with her hair. The guy was so good-looking she could hardly speak.

"Rhianna's new in town," Nick said, sipping his pint.

"Yeah, I'm the new girl. Oystercatcher is my home for now." She needed to stop waving her hands around like an excited teenager.

"Welcome to Kittiwake Cove," Liam said, smiling. His voice was deep but soothing. He was so much less predatory than Nick. Rhianna liked him instantly.

"Can I pass on a message to Joe for you?"

"Yeah, just let him know I called in. He'll be able to see I've cut the lawns." Rhianna had thought she could hear the humming of a lawnmower outside earlier. "Tell him I'll be around weekly now, as the weather's picking up and the grass has started growing."

"Okay, will do."

"Nick," Liam said, with a curt goodbye nod.

"Liam," Nick returned. Rhianna could see the tension between these two. Will noticed it too, and quietly kept his head down, concentrating on his phone and drinking his pint of lager. "How's Tilly?"

"She's good, thanks."

"Send her my regards."

Liam politely waved his goodbyes and left the pub.

Rhianna couldn't help noticing the animosity between Nick and Liam. Those two had history. And maybe Tilly was it. It reminded her she had no idea who these people were. They were the locals and she was the newcomer in a small town. A very small town. So far, everyone appeared to know everyone.

She couldn't take her eyes off Liam's sun-bleached hair and broad shoulders as he made his way out of the pub. Lucky Tilly had certainly chosen the better man.

"Sorry, love, but he's taken." Nick must have noticed the admiration in her eyes.

"She is one lucky woman," she replied wistfully.

"But I'm free if you'd like to be shown around the town … or even discover other parts of Cornwall." Nick grinned, gesturing to himself. "Yours truly is free and single."

I wonder why. Rhianna held her tongue and plastered on a fake smile. "Thank you for the generous offer, Nick. I'll get back to you on that. I've only been here a day, and I'd like to get to know the place — on my own."

Rhianna was pretty sure the only place Nick wanted to show her was his bedroom. She had always thought herself a good judge of character — until Glyn. Now she had lost faith in men generally. Looking back on her relationship with Glyn, which she'd thought was good and made her happy, she now realised the extravagant gifts he'd given her were used for manipulation and deceit. For now, Rhianna was not going to get involved with any man whatsoever. Especially not Nick.

CHAPTER 3: BETSY

Joe parked up on the cobbled drive outside Trenouth Cottage, his family's farmhouse which was now run by his parents as a bed and breakfast. It was a large, L-shaped house with several chimneys, built of grey-blue granite, with a Cornish grey slate roof and white leaded windows. Its traditional Cornish farmhouse look had won it recognition by local photographers, and it regularly appeared on postcards. He had been brought up here. The front cottage garden was chock-full of spring bulbs, mainly daffodils, crocuses and early tulips that he'd helped plant with his father over the years. They'd gradually multiplied.

As he pulled up the handbrake, his mother jumped nimbly out of the passenger seat of his old green Range Rover. The vehicle was a classic two-door 1979 model. It guzzled fuel, but the old girl had been with him a few years now. And driving down the narrow Cornish country lanes, it didn't matter if she received the odd scrape or scratch. The four-wheel drive had been useful at times too — most memorably when towing cars off the beach when left in the car park at an ultra-high tide. Its most modern feature was the roof rack, which usually had a surfboard attached.

"I've heard from Heather; they're visiting this Easter as usual," Rose said, as she waited for Joe to lift the boot hatch to gain access to their shopping.

Joe insisted on hauling the heavier items into her kitchen. "I'll make sure I'm free. I'll have to jig my rotas around. Lizzie is reliable enough to be left in charge." He wasn't so sure about Seana. She hadn't showed up again today, and when he'd told

Rose about leaving the pub in the hands of Rhianna as they walked around the wholesalers, she'd frowned at him.

"You're mad, leaving the pub in the hands of a stranger," Rose had said.

"I know, I know, but for some reason, Rhianna doesn't feel like a stranger to me," Joe had replied. "And Ricky vouched for her."

"You're too trusting. Shame that doesn't extend to trusting someone with your heart." Rose had given him a reproving look.

And maybe she was right. Not about trusting someone with his heart, but he did need to return to the pub as soon as possible. For a start, it wasn't fair on Rhianna to be left on her own. She hadn't even been in Kittiwake Cove twenty-four hours. It was five now, but Ricky had stayed on the premises, so Joe felt confident his pub was in safe hands. But it would start getting busier with the locals and weekenders, being a Friday.

As for his mother's concerns over his love life, Joe enjoyed his summer romances with no ties, no fears of getting hurt. Life was easier this way, with no complications.

With the last of the shopping carried in and the bags dumped on the large oak table in the farmhouse kitchen, he left his mum to unpack it. She preferred to put the shopping away herself.

"Catch you later." Joe kissed her goodbye.

"Bye, love."

Joe parked up around the back of The Cormorant in his private parking area and could see Liam had been, as the lawns had been cut. Joe didn't have time for gardening, especially in the summer when he'd much rather be surfing, so it made sense to pay someone to keep on top of the pub's grounds for him. Soon the pub would be adorned with hanging baskets and tubs filled with summer flowers as the winter to spring flowers were coming to an end. He left Liam to manage it. Ironically, Liam was a surf instructor too. In the summer, the man couldn't have time to sleep. Gardening jobs picked up, and so did the surf-instructing. Well, Joe wouldn't have time to surf if he had to manage the gardens as well as a pub. That's how he looked at it.

"Hey," he called as he entered the pub, coming through the back door and through the kitchen, waving to Ricky, who had fired up the grill and ovens and was now preparing to cook.

"Hey, boss." Ricky waved, wielding a knife.

"Is the pub still standing?"

"Rhianna's a star. If Seana doesn't show up again, I'd give Rhianna the job. Seana's bloody useless as it is. She usually gets the food orders wrong."

He couldn't help but agree with Ricky. Only Joe, who was too soft for his own good, kept giving Seana chances. Her flaky attendance record was almost bearable now, but later, when the season picked up, he needed someone he could rely on. Someone who would pull their weight with the rest of the team.

Joe entered the bar area to find Rhianna pulling glasses out of the dishwasher, wiping them and placing them back on their shelves. The sight of her sandy-blonde hair tied back in a messy bun, with strands falling prettily around her face and her cheeks rosy from the heat of the dishwasher steam, made something stir inside Joe. *God, she's attractive.* He quickly put a lid on that thought.

"Hey, you don't need to do that," Joe said. "I'm going to need to pay you in more than just coffee."

"It's okay, it needed doing and I wanted to stay busy."

There were a few more customers in the pub now, only a handful, but even so — she'd had to serve them all. Joe noticed Nick at the bar, finishing his pint. Nick and Joe got on because Joe was the kind of guy who got on with everyone. Too laidback, his mum would say. However, he knew what the guy was like with a pretty woman around and hoped Nick hadn't given Rhianna too much grief.

He gave Nick a friendly smile but concentrated on Rhianna. She was certainly easier on the eye. *Lid on it, Joe. And why is there something familiar about her?* "Any problems?"

"No, no, the barrel went on the Doom Bar — luckily Ricky pointed me towards the cellar."

"Oh, sorry." Joe brushed a hand through his hair. "You could have left it off."

"I think it was easier to change the barrel than put up with the grumbles from some of your locals," she said softly, and he noticed a hint of Welsh in her accent.

"Right, well, I'm back now, so get on the other side of the bar, young lady. And what would you like to drink?" Joe didn't take no for an answer, ushering her through the hatch and onto the bar stool where her laptop sat closed on the counter.

"I could murder a glass of red wine."

"Then so be it," Joe said. "And choose something off the menu; I'll get Ricky to make you some dinner. What red would you like?"

"I'd like to try something local, if you have one?"

Joe looked along the shelf of his red wines. "There's this one. Carpe Diem Red by a Cornish winery. It's the cheapest of their selection. I don't have great demand for expensive wines in this pub." Tourists wouldn't buy it, especially not those camping.

"Oh, yes, that sounds great."

Joe reached for a large wine glass and didn't bother pouring to measure. He'd happily give Rhianna the whole bottle for saving his bacon today. He left it on the counter.

Rhianna took a sip of the wine and nodded. "Oh, it's quite light."

"Yeah, not sure why that is."

"Well, the cooler climates can't quite create the fuller bodied red wines you can get from, say, Australia, Chile…" Rhianna sniffed the glass. "Hints of red berry, maybe strawberry —" she sipped — "black pepper, spice." She grabbed her notepad by the laptop and started scribbling, turning the wine bottle to see the label and noting that too.

"How d'you know this stuff?" Joe watched, impressed. He had left his pub in capable hands.

"I'm a sommelier," Rhianna said. "Not quite to the standard of some, but I know enough. When I decided to move from the kitchen to front of house, I took some courses."

"Got a keeper there, Joe," Nick said, draining his pint. Joe took the glass away, gesturing for another, but Nick shook his head.

"If she's managed to keep you in your place, Nick, she is just that."

Nick chuckled, slapped Will on the back, and they both left the pub.

"How was he really?" Joe asked Rhianna.

"Manageable. He thinks he's God's gift … which really isn't attractive."

"He's a bloody good builder, though."

"He should stick to that, then. No wonder the man's single."

"He just hasn't found the right woman," Joe said, even though he didn't believe what he was saying. Joe had found the right woman, Alannah, a few years back now, but hadn't realised until she'd walked out. Unable to bear the pain and misery of a broken heart after Alannah left him, Joe had vowed not to put himself through that kind of anguish again. His summers were filled with holiday flings. The women came and went, and his heart remained intact.

Rhianna chose a beef lasagne off the menu and he took the order out back to Ricky. Not wanting to disturb Rhianna, Joe busied himself at the bar. A couple more customers had arrived, so he had to serve them. When Ricky called to say Rhianna's meal was ready, he took it over to her then topped up her wine from the bottle he'd opened.

"Oh, thank you," Rhianna said, shutting her laptop to make room for the plate before her.

"Look, I'm eternally grateful for today," Joe retrieved his wallet from the back pocket of his jeans. "Take this." He handed Rhianna thirty pounds. It was above the going rate, but she'd helped him at short notice, and had been on her own for at least three hours. And his pub was still standing. And more importantly, there were no complaints. With Seana, there would have been a grumble from someone, especially from Seana herself.

Rhianna shook her head. "There's no need. Honestly."

"No, I insist."

Hesitantly, her fingers clasped the notes. "Are you sure?"

"I'm always sure." Joe grinned. He had an overwhelming urge to sit and talk with Rhianna, for some reason he couldn't quite put his finger on. But he also knew he needed to stay clean away. Rhianna could not be one of his summer flings, especially if she intended to remain in Kittiwake Cove. He had a strict rule not to get romantically involved with anyone local. But she was new to Kittiwake Cove and needed a friend.

The phone started ringing, taking Joe's attention away from Rhianna. It was Seana with some ridiculous excuse, as if Joe had never been nineteen before. Joe could see straight through her.

"To be honest, Seana, it suits me." He was listening to how she'd been offered a fantastic job and had to take it. "I need someone more reliable, so I'll sort out the wages that I owe you and we'll part with no hard feelings. I can give you a reference if you need one." He'd be lying through his teeth if he did, but hey. Seana had done him the favour of not having to sack her. Easy-going-Joe had hated the idea, but businessman-Joe, who wasn't a pushover, would have done it eventually.

At seven-thirty, Lizzie, another member of staff who was much more reliable than Seana, arrived. She had two young children and liked to work the evenings. It made her feel as if she was having a night out and getting paid for it. She was in her early thirties and was sociable and bubbly. The regulars liked her. Now Lizzie was here to take over the bar duties, it meant Joe was freed up.

He cleared Rhianna's plate when he noticed she'd finished her dinner, and he saw her wine glass was almost empty. He returned with the bottle of wine and a glass for himself, too. "Do you mind if I join you?"

He didn't wait for a reply as he topped her wine up first. Naughty, he knew, but he wanted to get to know the new girl in town — as friends, of course. Luckily, she didn't refuse the wine.

"No, please do," she said, gesturing to the chair beside her. Joe filled up his glass and took a sip. He knew full well the pitfalls of owning a pub and how easy it was to drain the profits by drinking them, so he limited his drinking to weekends only — or special occasions. He'd seen enough alcoholic landlords in his time, and their unattractive beer bellies, to put him off. The pub paid for him to surf, which was his real passion. And it was much harder to stand on a surfboard with a beer belly.

"So how was your first day in Kittiwake Cove?" Joe said. There was something oddly familiar about her green eyes.

"Well, I didn't think I'd end up working behind the bar for the afternoon," Rhianna replied.

"Ah, yes, sorry about that. But actually, would you consider doing it more often?"

Rhianna frowned at him.

"Seana, the person who didn't show today, called to resign from her job, so I'm stuffed for a member of staff... I wondered if you'd fancy filling in?"

"Oh, no..." Rhianna chewed her lip, as if thinking it over, then hesitantly asked, "How long for?"

Joe hoped she'd say yes. In his mind he crossed his fingers, because if he did it physically it might look like he was begging. "For as long as you like, or if you don't want it permanently, at least until I fill the job. I'll pay you — properly. It'll have to be the going rate, though." He couldn't afford to pay above the minimum wage, plus he'd have a mutiny on his hands with his other staff members if they found out.

"Oh, I realise that." Rhianna took a sip of her wine. "How many hours were you thinking?"

"Seana worked sixteen hours a week — four shifts of four hours."

"Can I sleep on it? Tell you tomorrow?"

"Yes, of course."

The Cormorant was getting busier, and Joe had to return behind the bar to serve some customers. As she sipped her wine, Rhianna mulled over Joe's unexpected job offer. In some ways, she didn't need it, but for the next few weeks the extra money would come in handy. It would pay for her to live, so that she wasn't dipping into the savings she'd need for the business.

But would it be wise to work with someone she still found attractive? Rhianna mused as she watched him work. He hadn't recognised her yet, though. Which proved how insignificant she'd been to him. *Just another holiday fling.*

However, on the plus side, this would give her access to a bar, and keep her toe dipped in the water — so to speak. It was only sixteen hours a week, so she would still have plenty of time to work on her business. She would only be able to work until the end of April. That would give Joe plenty of time to find another member of staff. She would soon need to hire staff herself.

Even though her mind was made up to accept, she decided to stick to her decision to sleep on it and give Joe her answer in the morning.

After a while, Joe returned with another bottle of red wine. He turned his seat slightly, so he could watch the bar, but also chat with Rhianna. "Mum thought I was mad leaving the pub in the hands of a stranger," he said topping up their glasses. "But I said you didn't seem like a stranger…"

"Only strange?"

They both laughed.

Maybe he does recognise me? Should I put him out of his misery? There was an ease about Joe that Rhianna really liked. She'd liked it the first time she'd met him, standing in the cold waves with a surfboard tucked under her arm. It was possibly why she'd ended up in bed with him that very same night. *Must not happen tonight.* With the wine flowing through her veins, like a truth serum, Rhianna couldn't help herself. "You don't remember me, do you?"

Joe frowned, placing his glass back on the table. He scratched his head, fingers combing through his dark curls, as he stared at her. He had a hint of shadow on his face now, his stubble coming through, giving him a rough and ready look. "You do look familiar…" His eyebrows knitted together as he studied her face.

"I was here three years ago, in the summer, on a hen party week," she said slowly. "We stayed at the Kittiwake Cove Hotel." She waited, watching Joe to see if he was catching up. "Jennifer — Jen — wanted us to go on team-building activities. We did two days of surfing first, and…"

"I was your instructor?"

Rhianna nodded. It had been a fun — and exhausting — hen week fuelled with a great deal of alcohol. Jen had always wanted to do a team building type break, thinking it would bring her bridesmaids together for the big day, and so had booked them all on one. It had included two days of surfing instruction, where Rhianna had had the delight of meeting Joe. Single at the time, she'd been more than happy for some extra activity during the evening. He'd taken them out on beach barbeques and midnight walks. She'd spent most of her week in his bed rather than her hotel bedroom.

She could see he was still finding it hard to place her. Rhianna didn't want to think about the amount of women Joe had probably had holiday flings with. He'd been a player back then, and probably still was.

"I had much shorter hair, bleach blonde … and I've possibly lost some weight." She left off with stress. Hesitantly, she added, "You called me … Betsy?" She shrugged.

"Betty!"

"Oh, yes, Betsy's the name of a cocktail." Rhianna slapped her palm to her forehead. "At the time, I think you said my name sounded similar to an ex of yours. You'd been single a couple of years, you said." She wondered if that had been true, or whether he was just good at the player act. "At the time, I didn't really think our names sounded the same."

"Alannah." Joe didn't meet Rhianna's gaze, glancing out the window as he took another sip from his wine glass. He shrugged, then laughed. "I call all the girls Betty." Then he swallowed, his gaze leaving Rhianna's again. "God, that's sounds awful now I've said it out loud."

"I suppose you can't upset anyone by getting their name wrong." Rhianna laughed and Joe joined her, seeing she wasn't offended.

"That's it! It is the reason, I'm ashamed to say. Also Betty is a surfing term for a surfer's girlfriend, a fit surfer babe." He winked. "I can't forget that name."

"And you are a surfer." They tapped their glasses together, making a *ting*.

"I am. Gosh, this now feels really awkward." Joe rubbed his hands along his jean-clad thighs.

"Nah, it was three years ago. We can be friends. You didn't hurt me. I knew exactly what you wanted, and so did I — at the time. I lived in Bristol, I was single. You were single. It was fun." The wine really was opening her up. She had to stop drinking and soon. Hopefully the dinner she'd eaten would soak up some of the alcohol — it's why she'd chosen chips instead of salad. *Insist on an early night.* It had been a long day.

"To be honest, I'm shocked to see you here. I thought you were going to Australia?" Rhianna blurted out. The wine was really doing the talking now.

"I was," Joe said, his expression becoming sombre for a minute. He swirled the wine gently in his glass. "My brother's wife died, so I decided to stay. It devasted our family."

"Oh, I am sorry to hear that."

"I was worried about Mum, worrying about Sam… The pub became available… It just made sense." Joe remained silent, as if lost in thought. Then his expression changed, and smiling, he raised his glass to Rhianna. "And now you're here permanently? You've left Bristol behind?"

"Yeah."

"Any reason? Although, the sunset alone — and the surf — is enough of a reason. Obviously."

"Obviously." Earlier, from this very window, Rhianna had watched the sun dip down below the sea. Now it was dark, but the evenings would stay lighter a little longer each day. She remembered watching the sun set with Joe, and making love on the beach, three summers ago. She loved spring and summer. From the moment the daffodils started opening, Rhianna grew excited for the warmer, lighter months. "No reason, though. I just wanted to escape from the city." She couldn't confide in him about Glyn. It still physically hurt to talk about it. She didn't want her eyes to well with tears in front of Joe. She'd probably drunk too much wine now to hold in those emotions, so it was best to bury them. And fast.

"What about friends, family?" Joe wasn't helping, though, with his questions.

"They'll visit. And I can visit them. Mum and Dad used to bring me and my brother here when we were kids. They love it here too."

Joe went to pour more wine into her empty glass, but she covered the glass with her hand and shook her head. "I've had enough. I should really go to bed."

"Oh yes, you've probably had a long day."

"Yes, I had a very early start from Bristol." Rhianna yawned, trying to stifle it as much as she could.

"See you in the morning," Joe said, standing up as Rhianna did. "Do you need a hand with anything?"

Rhianna stumbled and Joe grabbed her arm to steady her. She shook her head. "No, I'll be fine." Without thinking, she kissed Joe on the cheek. Had to be the wine. But it wasn't the wine causing butterflies in her stomach. The whiff of his aftershave, the feeling of his rough stubble brushing her smooth skin caused a flashback to the hen party break, and the sex and fun she'd shared with Joe. Hoping she wasn't blushing, Rhianna said goodnight hastily and hurried out of the pub.

CHAPTER 4: SEX ON THE BEACH

With Joe's job offer still at the forefront of her mind, Rhianna took an early bus into Wadebridge the next morning. Flipping heck, she wished she had a car. The journey took twice as long, and she had to choose her seat wisely for fear of sitting on something sticky.

Wadebridge was the nearest town, and her aim was to explore and visit butchers, grocers, and delicatessens. She couldn't sit idly for the next few weeks; she needed to plan menus and decide on the cocktails and wine she wanted to serve. As the bus rumbled along the narrow country lanes, she pulled out her notepad from her rucksack and made a list of the things she wanted to achieve.

Visit local wineries. And breweries! Not everyone liked wine — and craft beer was the latest trend.

She had a to-do list for today, and then a more long-term list to remind her of jobs required before the grand opening. Things like signage, stationery, website... This list was endless. And daunting.

She couldn't resist grabbing a takeaway coffee as she mooched the small high street, and savoured the aroma of pastry and bread as she passed a bakery, its window adorned with different varieties of pasties. She felt it was a little early in the day to sample the Cornish ice-cream.

Finally, arms loaded with groceries and her rucksack also stuffed full, Rhianna waited for the bus to return to Kittiwake Cove.

The clouds were growing darker and greyer by the minute. However, it seemed the gods were on her side, because the rain didn't start falling until she was off the bus and walking up the path towards her apartment. After packing away her shopping and waiting for the rain to ease off, Rhianna called in at the pub to talk to Joe.

"Hey, Joe, are you there?" she called, entering by the side door closest to her apartment.

Joe appeared in the doorway that led to the kitchen. "Hey, just doing a stocktake. Come through."

Rhianna followed him, trying very hard not to appreciate how well he wore his Levi's. *Eyes up, Rhianna.* It had been lust at first sight, and she couldn't shake off the feeling that she still fancied him — even three years on.

The stainless steel kitchen, typical in most restaurants and pubs and all too familiar to Rhianna's old working environment, had boxes scattered on the metal worksurface, with a freezer door open. This soon brought her back to the here and now, shaking her out of her memories of how they'd bonked like crazy in that wild week. The sex they'd shared on the beach…

"Any thoughts on the job?" Joe asked, ticking off paperwork and returning a box to the freezer.

"Oh, er, yes, I'll take it," Rhianna said. *Stop thinking about sex with Joe.* "But I can only work until the end of April, and I only want the sixteen hours a week."

"Of course."

"You'd best let me know the shifts, so I can work on what I need to do around them."

"I tell you what, you go make us a coffee each, and I'll be out in a sec," Joe said, shoving another box away.

"Deal."

By the time Rhianna had heated the milk in the coffee machine and was spooning froth on to make the perfect cappuccino — one third coffee, one third milk and one third froth — Joe had returned to the bar with a notebook. She sprinkled chocolate on both cappuccinos and they took the coffees to a table in the bay window. Rhianna got the impression that Joe needed regular glimpses of the sea, as if to check it was still there. Even with it looking grey and miserable outside, the sight was still spectacular. The ocean didn't look so appealing today, but despite this there were a couple of mad — *dedicated*, Joe had corrected — surfers out there anyway.

Rhianna wanted to pinch herself. Could this beautiful place really be her home now? Would she find happiness here? Yes, if she kept Joe at arm's length as a friend. She very much doubted he'd changed his ways.

"Right, Seana worked two afternoons, Thursdays and Fridays, and two evenings, Saturdays and Sundays. Four hours each shift. Will that suit you?"

"I can't see why not." Rhianna blew at the froth on her coffee.

"If it's quiet in the evenings, and we close up early, I'll still pay you for the four hours. If it gets busy — which tends to happen closer to the summer — then I may need you to stay on. Easter Holidays can be busy. Licensing allows me to stay open later, but I don't bother unless there's a demand. The summer season is so short that I'd be stupid to kick out customers with money to burn."

"I'll be here already, and it's not as if I have far to travel home." Rhianna gestured towards the back door that led to the apartments. "Does this mean you want me to work tonight?" It was Saturday, after all.

"Up to you. You can start as soon as you like. It would really help me out."

"So, I start at…?"

"Half-seven okay?"

"Yes, that's fine — boss."

"You haven't told me what your plans for Kittiwake Cove are. Is it a big secret?" Joe put his cup down and relaxed back in his chair.

Rhianna shook her head. "I'm going to open a bistro and cocktail bar."

"Oh. I've got competition, have I?"

Rhianna's cheeks flushed. She'd feared Joe may see it that way. "I'm taking over Sheila and Martyn's restaurant."

"Oh, yes, I know. They're above the Surf 'n Turf café."

"That's the one." Rhianna explained her ideas to Joe, who nodded approvingly. How, after three years, could the two of them fall back in sync with one another so easily? She already felt at ease in his company. "Before moving here, I was working in a cocktail bar, and I just loved it. I got to use my chef experience, but by making drinks rather than food."

"Loved it so much you moved here?"

"As you said, Bristol doesn't quite get the same sunsets."

"True." Joe nodded. Rhianna drank the last of her coffee. "Oh… You've got…" He reached with his finger and wiped her top lip, his touch sending a jolt of pleasure through her. Shocked by her reaction, she feared her expression must have revealed this. "Sorry, you had froth on your lip."

She wiped her mouth, paranoid she looked like a kid drinking a milkshake and leaving a milky moustache. "All gone?"

"Yes." His hazel eyes stared right into hers. "So, where were we? You're opening a bar."

"Bistro. Serving cocktails," she said assertively, her eyes narrowing. "Just no idea what to call it yet." Joe nodded. His lips showed the hint of a smile, as if teasing her. Why did she feel this magnetic pull towards him? Did he feel it too? *Focus, woman.*

"We'll need to work on a name, then, if you're launching your business this summer."

"Yes, I will."

He tapped his nose. "I'll have a think."

"Right, well, I'll see you back here at seven-thirty, shall I?" Rhianna stood up, as did Joe.

She went to pick up both coffee cups, but Joe placed a hand on hers. The heat of his palm shot through her body and into her stomach. Electricity again. "I'll clear these. You go and enjoy the rest of your day."

Rhianna couldn't find words to speak, so she nodded. She needed to stop feeling like this around Joe. He probably hadn't changed from being the player he was a few years ago. But the sex had been so good … and she hadn't slept with anyone since Glyn.

No, no, no!

Rhianna returned to her apartment and grabbed her coat. She had arranged to meet up with Sheila and Martyn for a tour of the restaurant before it opened for the lunchtime rush on Monday — not that there was likely to be much of a rush on a Monday in low season. She had last visited in December, and with Sheila and Martyn being friends of the family, she had known the place since she was a child.

"Hey, how are you?" Sheila said, greeting Rhianna with a hug and a kiss on the cheek.

Martyn hugged her. "How are your parents?"

"They're good, both busy with the restaurant."

Sheila and Martyn were both in their late sixties, but still fit and able. Over coffee they went through the formalities of catching up. Luckily, Glyn wasn't mentioned. They explained how eager they were to make the most of their retirement — to travel and visit family while still young enough to enjoy it. Rhianna swore they looked more like they were in their late fifties. *Must be the sea air.*

Coffees finished, Martyn stood with a smile. "Come on, let's give you the tour."

They started in the kitchen, which was like The Cormorant's — spotless stainless steel and large enough to cater for the main restaurant, which could seat fifty comfortably. The bar was solid wood, with a rustic feel, as if it had drifted off the beach with the tide. Plus there were tables set for dining in the conservatory and outside on the terrace, when the weather was warmer and dry. The conservatory was an extension, expanding the restaurant but making it a separate area that could be used privately for small parties, while the rest of the restaurant could be left open for the general public.

Rhianna imagined all her options as she walked through the premises. The conservatory was a great idea, considering the unreliable British weather. With terrific views of the beach, it would make a great location for wedding ceremonies. She imagined draping white nets from the roof to create a marquee effect. White lights could also be incorporated. She wrote down a reminder to research getting a wedding licence. The whole restaurant, with its separate parts, could easily house up to a hundred for private functions, and with tables completely cleared possibly more. The venue had so much potential. Rhianna couldn't wait to get stuck in and put her own stamp on the place. She wanted to capture a coastal vibe, but in a classy, upmarket way so it didn't look like another beach hut café.

Lastly, Martyn showed her the attic. There was thick rope across the entrance to the stairs, which Martyn unhooked. "We dreamed of converting this into a roof bar, but never got around to it. It became more of a storage space," he said as he led the way up the narrow stairs tucked into the far corner of the restaurant. "It just needs a woodburning stove or something up the end there, and this would be one cosy den."

It certainly would. Rhianna was blown away. She hadn't realised this was included in the lease. If she looked past the boxes and old furniture cluttering up the space, this was one hell of a blank canvas.

The attic was floored with wood boarding, so they could walk on it, but proper flooring would need to be laid. Rhianna imagined limed oak laminate for ease of cleaning. People were bound to come off the beach with sand on their shoes. She'd need something hardwearing. The sloping walls were plastered ready for painting. There were a couple of roof windows, plus a dormer window, so the room was light and airy and you could look right out to sea as if you were in the clouds. She imagined a squishy leather sofa — if she could get it up the stairs — tucked in the alcove with a coffee table, surrounded with other comfortable chairs. The attic would make the perfect cocktail lounge for those wanting drinks but no food. Or it could be where guests could wait until their tables were ready. She could create a longer bar here, to allow seats along it. There could be tall tables and high stools. With her imagination running wild, she was going to have to keep an eye on her budget.

Over more coffee, they discussed what items would be included when Rhianna took over the lease. Some items they threw in for free, not wanting the hassle of getting rid of them. For other items, like the patio burners and the tables and chairs, Rhianna offered a price. It would make her start-up cheaper if she didn't need to purchase new large items. The tables might not quite suit her theme, but a sand down and a new wood stain would do the trick. She wouldn't need to change the interior of the restaurant too much. The walls just needed a fresh lick of paint. Rhianna couldn't wait to put together a mood board of her ideas for making the place her own.

CHAPTER 5: BEE'S KNEES

On Thursday, Rhianna was back behind the bar at The Cormorant. Joe was manning the kitchen, as he'd given Ricky the day off. An elderly couple had just placed a food order, so he was being kept busy. Rhianna was emptying the dishwasher and giving the glasses a wipe with a tea towel, mulling over cocktail ideas and the glasses she'd need to buy, when a familiar face entered — Nick, with his young assistant, Will, who was focused on his phone.

"Ah, just the person I wanted to see," Rhianna said, beaming at Nick.

He smiled back at her. "Music to my ears from a pretty lady," he said, placing both hands on the bar and leaning towards her.

"Don't get too excited. I wondered if you could recommend a painter and decorator, as you're a builder."

"Project manager," Nick corrected her. "So, you only want me for my contacts?"

"I'm afraid so."

"Are you sure you wouldn't want me for anything else?"

"What else could I possibly want you for?" Rhianna rolled her eyes and asked what they were drinking.

"Pint of Doom Bar, please, and a lager for the kid," Nick said. "I can do the decorating. Or my team can, anyway."

"And would you also be able to give me a quote for fitting a bar?" She placed Nick's pint in front of him.

"Yeah, sure. Does Joe know you're thinking of making changes to his pub?"

Rhianna laughed. "It's not for here. It's for my bar. I'm taking over the lease of Oceans from the first of May. Ideally, I would like the place ready before May half-term."

Nick sucked his lips as if in thought. "Yeah, should be able to do that, if I move some projects around. You'll need to get me in for a quote as soon as possible."

"I know. I'll have a word with Sheila and Martyn. I'm sure they'd be fine with that. It might have to be early one morning before they open."

Nick handed Rhianna his business card. "Give me a call. For anything." He winked, then took his pint over to a table by the window, Will following.

"I hope he's not flirting with my staff?" Joe said, close to Rhianna's ear, making her jump. His breath on her neck ignited memories she needed to keep buried if she were to remain professional with Joe.

She placed Nick's business card in her back pocket, then swatted Joe with the tea towel. "Don't do that. You scared me to death."

He chuckled and flinched at the whipping tea towel. He held his hand up. "Hey, just came out to tell you table three's order is ready." He winked, then returned to the kitchen.

Rhianna threw the tea towel over her shoulder and followed Joe to the kitchen to fetch the plates of food. Even in chef whites he looked bloody gorgeous.

The following Tuesday morning, Rhianna had arranged for Nick to visit Oceans before it opened. They'd discussed the changes she wanted to make so that he could provide a quote. To Rhianna's surprise, Nick had been nothing but professional and not nearly as overbearing as he'd appeared in the pub. A little flirtatious, but nothing she couldn't handle.

51

Joe had taken an interest upon learning Nick was quoting for her refit, and was now, on Thursday morning, marching her to the local Post Office which was situated inside Surf 'n Turf. Rhianna had some paperwork she needed to send back to her solicitor dealing with the house sale, so this suited her too. She hoped they were close to exchanging contracts soon.

A small corner to the left of the café entrance had been cordoned off with a single, old-fashioned Post Office counter. It was boxed in with a varnished wooden frame surrounding the glass. It possibly wasn't as strong as the modern-day fortresses Post Offices had nowadays, but it was enough for a sleepy town like Kittiwake Cove.

"Hi, Peggy," Joe said, smiling to the woman behind the glass counter. "Please can I withdraw some cash?"

Rhianna listened as they chatted, wondering where this was going and what it had to do with her new bistro. Peggy was a good-looking, smartly dressed woman, who appeared to be in her late fifties. Apparently, she'd been running the Post Office in Kittiwake Cove for over thirty years. She'd originally taken the job on to work around her three sons, and eventually she and her husband had bought the business, to keep a Post Office in Kittiwake Cove.

Peggy counted out the cash to Joe as he removed his debit card from the card machine.

"Peggy, this is Rhianna, by the way. She's staying in one of my apartments until she buys her house," Joe said. "From the first of May she's taking over Oceans."

"But I'm going to change the name," Rhianna added shyly.

"Oh, wonderful, well, you know where to get your change from, and you can do all your banking here," Peggy said, turning her attention to Rhianna. She had a warm smile, and as she propped her glasses on top of her head, she revealed pretty green eyes, making her look younger than her age.

"Oh, that would be useful."

"A lot of the smaller businesses here use us. Saves traipsing into Wadebridge. Come and see me, and we can sort something out."

"I will."

"Anyway," Joe said, looking at the two women, clearly amazed at how quickly they could get off topic, "Rhianna needs a quote for some building work. Have you got Oliver's number to hand?"

"I have his business card." Peggy retrieved a card from a folder underneath her desk. "He told me to keep some handy. He knows how I like to chat to my customers." She gave a chuckle as she pushed the card through the gap under the glass.

Joe took the card. "Thanks, I'll get Rhianna to call him." He handed Rhianna the card. On it read: *Oliver Rosdew — Carpenter, Painter, Decorator* — with his contact details.

Joe stood aside so that Rhianna could post her letter. Once they were done, she said to Peggy, "Nice to meet you."

"And you, dear. See you soon."

Joe walked out of the café, with Rhianna following. "Get a quote from Oliver, too. Nick's good at his job, but he'll give you a more competitive quote if he knows he's got competition." He shoved his hands in his pockets as the wind whipped up their hair. Rhianna wished she'd tied hers back. "Right, I'm going to call in on Mum and Dad, check if they need anything. Want to come?"

"Oh, no, now's not a good time. I need to get some bits from the Spar. I'll meet you back at the pub later." She wasn't sure whether she wanted to be introduced to Joe's parents and was puzzled that he had asked her.

Back in her apartment, her shopping packed away and the kettle boiling, Rhianna called Oliver's mobile number. It went to his voicemail, so she left a message, then made the most of her time ticking off jobs on her ever-growing to-do list before she started her shift at three-thirty. Sadly, this mostly involved housework, but she did manage to call suppliers and her solicitor.

The afternoon shifts passed more slowly than the evening ones, as the pub was usually quieter. Although it was nearly the beginning of April, the season was still slow. There was some passing trade of ramblers, sightseers and retired folk, but the season wouldn't truly pick up until May.

"Hi, the usual, babe," Nick said, with Will beside him. Rhianna was getting used to the sight of them both, either covered in paint or plaster dust. And being called 'babe'. "And I've got your quote."

He slid over a folded piece of paper. Rhianna pocketed it and continued to pour Nick's pint of Doom Bar and Will's lager. "Any questions, give me a shout. I've put my number on there. For anything…"

If Nick wasn't such an arrogant, overbearing, cocky guy, he'd be attractive. He was great eye-candy until he opened his mouth.

They remained at the bar, talking and watching the TV, as Joe usually kept the sports channel on. Will was his usual unsociable self, thumbing through his phone.

A few minutes later, two young women entered the pub. They chose a table and picked up a menu. They were both heavily made-up with immaculate hair, and Rhianna made a mental note to check they had ID as they only looked in their late teens. Rhianna remembered how at fifteen she would slap loads of make-up on to get into a club. And she had been successful. She noticed that underneath their coats they both wore navy-blue tunics, so she guessed they worked at the Kittiwake Cove Hotel spa. It would explain the perfect eyebrows and pristine nails.

Both women went up to the bar. "Are you serving food?" one asked.

"Yes, we are," Rhianna replied, knowing Ricky was in the kitchen warming up the ovens.

The two women placed orders for food, then ordered a bottle of the house white wine to share. Rhianna got the impression from their private conversation that they'd finished their shifts and neither had work the following day.

"I'll need to see ID from both of you," Rhianna said politely.

One of the women gave a huff. "You're new, aren't you?" Thickly lined black eyes with bronze eyeshadow stared at Rhianna, unimpressed.

"Yes, I arrived the other week." Rhianna smiled politely, concentrating on the proffered provisional driving licence. The woman's name was Imogen and her date of birth checked out, making her twenty.

"You must be the one staying with Joe, aka the professional fuck buddy." Imogen sniggered and winked at Rhianna suggestively.

"I'm staying in an apartment that Joe owns ... not *with* Joe..." Rhianna corrected sternly, trying to keep her voice low. She didn't need Nick, at the other end of the bar, hearing. And she couldn't be rude to the customers, however tempting that was. "He's certainly not my *buddy*. He's my boss."

The fact he had very definitely been just that three years ago was neither here nor there and wasn't any business of Imogen or her friend. But it was further confirmation that Joe was not into serious relationships, if he was the gossip of the town. She checked the other woman's ID. Clearly used to being asked, she carried her passport. She was only nineteen. But still old enough to drink alcohol.

"Oh, right, sorry... Just Joe... Well, you know what he's like," Imogen continued, more to her friend, regardless of whether Rhianna wanted to hear the gossip or not. She fetched their bottle of wine from the fridge and placed it in a wine cooler. "He's bloody hot, though. I would, if he asked me." The other woman concurred. "Just I'm not his type. Bit young..."

Rhianna didn't stop to find out what Joe's type was, which Imogen clearly knew. She quickly took the docket with their food order to Ricky in the kitchen.

Imogen had confirmed some of Rhianna's fears; Joe was definitely not boyfriend material. She needed to keep things between them strictly platonic, and lose the girly crush she might have developed for him.

Another man who looked in his early thirties approached the bar, really livening up the quiet pub this afternoon. The two younger women stopped drinking and gawped at him.

What was it with Kittiwake Cove? Every guy looked like a surfer. This guy had a slim, perfectly toned physique and sun-bleached hair. He was married, though — gold band, left hand, ring finger.

"Hey, are you Rhianna? I'm Olly — Oliver Rosdew. You left a message on my phone. Thought it would be easier to come see you." Then he acknowledged Nick standing at the end of the bar. "All right, mate?" They shook hands.

"Oh, hi, yes." Rhianna lifted the bar hatch and went through to shake Olly's hand. His grip was firm. He was tall, possibly taller than Joe. He had a hint of his mother in his handsome looks; definitely Peggy's son. "I wanted a quote for some renovations at Oceans when I take over the lease." Rhianna was aware that Nick was within earshot, but his expression gave little away. She was perfectly entitled to get another quote. But it was somewhat awkward, and she wished Joe was here to support her. "Sheila and Martyn said I can go along most mornings before they open, so can you do tomorrow?"

Olly didn't appear the slightest bit threatened by Nick. Clearly another laidback surfer. He ran a hand through his hair as he pondered. "Yes, sure, I can do tomorrow morning. See you there at eight a.m. I need to be at another job for nine."

Rhianna nodded. "That's great, thanks. See you then." God, why did it suddenly feel so hot in this pub?

She stared after Olly as he left. Rhianna had never thought she'd feel flustered around an attractive guy. Maybe her embarrassment was more because Nick had witnessed her asking another contractor for a quote. She didn't like confrontation. Realising Nick was looking at her, she turned towards him.

"He's married," Nick said.

"I know. I saw." Her cheeks flushed hotter still.

"I'm not." He beamed.

That's the cold water you need. "Nick, how do I put this nicely? I'm not interested. I'm not looking for a man."

Which was true. Only there had to be something in the water at Kittiwake Cove — it was sending her hormones doolally.

There was an itch to be scratched. It played on her mind that Glyn was the last man she'd slept with, and she wondered if sleeping with someone else would help erase the memory of him. Would it take away some of the hurt?

"Are you sure? Because I could see the way you were looking at him." Nick stood cockily, jutting out his chin.

Rhianna scowled, and walked around to the other side of the bar. Not for her safety but for Nick's. She felt like slapping him. "And that is exactly why I am not interested in you."

As Rhianna placed the hatch down, Nick rested his palm on her hand. Will had disappeared to the toilets — his half-drunk pint remained on the bar. She tried to pull her hand away, but Nick held it firm. He leaned forward, his voice low and predatory. "I promise, we'd have a lot of fun."

"Hey, what did I miss?" Joe entered the bar. Immediately Nick released Rhianna's hand and she jumped back, her heart thumping, and tucked a loose strand of hair behind her ear. "I just saw Olly. I gather you're seeing him tomorrow?"

"Yes, yes…"

"Hey, Nick, getting to be a bit of a regular. Hope you're not making my staff feel uncomfortable." Joe looked away from Rhianna, who feared she looked as flushed as she felt. Like a deer caught in the headlights. She couldn't be more relieved to see Joe. Will returned at that same moment too, and chugged down the remains of his pint.

"No, just advising Rhianna how married Olly is." Nick finished his pint and turned to Rhianna. "If he comes in cheaper than me, call me. I'll re-evaluate my quote."

They waited until Will and Nick had left before speaking.

"What was that about?" Joe looked sternly over the bar at Rhianna, who'd found a cloth to wipe the bar down with. She couldn't meet his gaze.

Shrugging, she said, "I don't know. I may have been a little speechless over Olly's good looks. It was like talking to a blond Henry Cavill."

"Just be careful of Nick. I know I'm bad, but he's so much worse. You really don't know where he's been. Just promise you'd make him wear triple thick condoms."

"Joe!" Rhianna's eyes widened, throwing the cloth down so that it made a loud slapping noise. Her face was flushed, more with anger than embarrassment. "I wouldn't sleep with Nick if he was the last man in Kittiwake Cove."

"Good."

"To be honest, I can't believe any woman sleeps with him. He may think he's the bee's knees, but he's hardly a charm a minute."

They both smirked, lifting the tension. Only briefly, because the next thing Joe said took Rhianna by surprise. She was glad she had her back to him when he said it.

"Yeah, but I can see why he wants to sleep with you."

CHAPTER 6: LUSH CRUSH

The next morning, Rhianna was up early to meet Olly at Oceans and show him what she wanted done. Martyn had let them in and provided them both with a much-needed cup of coffee. She took a deep breath and told herself to be professional. Olly was married and he, too, was a professional.

"I was thinking of having a bar built in the top-floor room, and turning it into a cocktail lounge." Rhianna looked at Olly questioningly. She wanted confirmation that her ideas weren't unrealistic.

"Yeah, it's the perfect blank canvas. You know what would be really cool? The bar could curve like a wave." He traced an S shape with his hand. "It could be wider at one end for serving the drinks and you could have stools all along it." Olly exuded trustworthiness, and unlike Nick, didn't see Rhianna as some conquest. What was even more attractive about Olly was that even if he knew he was sex on legs, he didn't act like it. He was modest and charming. His wife was one lucky woman.

He made Rhianna feel at ease discussing her ideas. "Yes, I'm liking the idea of it being a cosy beach hut, a snug — but with more class. I was wondering if a surfboard would make a good bar."

"Hmm … the problem with a surfboard is its curvature. Might find drinks not resting properly. We could hang a board over the bar, though."

"Oh, yes!"

"And it's the in thing to have them painted with beach scenes."

"Great idea; I could commission one of Kittiwake Cove beach." Rhianna wanted to fill the restaurant with local art inspired by the beach her bistro looked over. "I'll ask in the gallery."

"Tilly owns the gallery," Olly said. Rhianna recognised the name. Liam's girlfriend. "She'll know who can do that. Although my brother is an artist, so you could ask him."

The rest of the interior only needed decorating. She wouldn't change the layout of the other rooms. She'd already thought about possible colour schemes and shared her ideas with Olly.

"My brother Noah — the artist — is my painter and decorator. We usually work together on jobs."

"Great! And could you install a wood burner at the far end of the room?"

"You might want to get Nick to do that job. It's more his area of expertise. He'll need to get a flue put in. But I'm your man for carpentry." He beamed his Hollywood smile.

"Okay." Rhianna nodded. She'd already had a quote from Nick for installing a wood burner. Maybe getting him to do some of the work would keep him sweet.

After they'd finished, Rhianna waved Olly off, and her temperature cooled a degree or two. He promised to get a quote over to her as soon as possible with his availability in May and drop in some wood samples at The Cormorant.

The next morning, fresh from the shower, with her hair wrapped up in a towel, Rhianna heard a knock at the door. She hurriedly threw on some clothes. "Give me a minute," she called.

It was Joe.

"Hi," she said, a little flustered, but relieved she had got dressed.

"Olly just dropped this off." Joe handed her a white envelope.

"Thanks, do you want to come in? Fancy a coffee?" Rhianna said.

"Yeah, sure. How are you finding the place?" Joe stepped inside, closing the door behind him. He glanced around the apartment as he followed Rhianna.

The place was fairly tidy, but she still puffed up the cushions on the futon and tidied the papers on the table into a neater pile as she made her way to the kitchen area, worried that Joe might be taking notes. He was technically her landlord. Rhianna flicked the switch on her kettle and tore open the envelope. The quote was more expensive than she'd hoped.

"Olly creates great quality work," Joe said. He must have seen her expression. "He'll be better than Nick."

"Is Nick's work shoddy?"

"No, I didn't mean it like that." Joe leaned on the kitchen counter while Rhianna made the coffee.

Rhianna frowned. "Well, then it makes better business sense to get Nick to do all the work."

"Olly will have more creative flair with the bar — hence he's charging you more." He sounded stern. After meeting Olly, she'd talked to Joe about her ideas for the bistro. She had liked Olly's suggestions. The S-shaped bar had given her all sorts of ideas for her rooftop cocktail lounge. It made sense to work with someone local, too. She wouldn't know who Nick would get in to design the bar. "I'd prefer it if Olly did the work," Joe said as Rhianna handed him a coffee mug.

"Joe, this is *my* venture, *my* money..." *My bistro*. She scowled at him, although she wasn't sure how seriously he'd take her with a towel still wrapped around her head. His hazel eyes stared at her over his coffee mug as he drank, but he just shrugged and didn't try to argue. Rhianna hated the confrontation lurking between them. She agreed with him really, but she didn't like the way he was telling her what to do. "Look, I'll have to get Nick to do the stuff Olly can't do."

"If you have to."

What was Joe's problem with Nick? He'd been so laidback with him the first time she'd seen them together, and now it was as if he saw Nick as a threat. He couldn't possibly be jealous?

Ridiculous. She'd already said she wouldn't touch Nick with a paddle board oar.

"Well, unless you have someone else you can recommend at short notice, it has to be Nick." She had asked around in the town, and he did come highly recommended. "Hey —" Rhianna wanted to change the subject — "I need your help on local produce. There's a couple of places I'd like to visit, but I'm not sure if I can get there by bus."

"I'll take you," Joe said, his tone lightening. "I know a few places. It'll be good to make a day of it."

"Oh, right, if you're sure." Rhianna had been planning to be really cheeky and ask if she could borrow his Range Rover. But maybe going with Joe would be more fun.

Over the weekend, in between her shifts at the pub, Rhianna spent her time choosing wood samples for the bar, experimenting with cocktails and recipes and surfing the internet. She wasn't a keen shopper at the best of times, so it saved her so much time browsing the web. She searched for the equipment and furniture she would need, as well as thinking up new menu ideas. She had a to-do list the length of the bar she planned for Olly to build. Martyn and Sheila were great, allowing Olly to go in and measure up, as well as Nick for the jobs she was hiring him to do, so as soon as she took over the lease of the property, work could commence.

After a lengthy telephone conversation with her father, who'd recommended she went with what she truly wanted for the business, rather than opt for something just because it was cheaper, she'd taken Joe's advice and hired Olly for the carpentry and decorating. Her father had made her look at the long-term prospects of her business. She hired Nick to install a wood burner and oversee some other jobs under his project manager umbrella.

The next step was to work on the branding for the business.

"I've got some ideas I'm playing with, Rhee, but until you've thought of a name, I can't design anything."

Rhianna paced around her bedroom, hair damp, trying to put on clothes as she talked to Jen, her best friend, who happened to be a graphic designer and had agreed to create the logo for her bistro — if she could just come up with a name. She had her mobile on speaker. "I know, I know… I want it to be called 'The something Bistro'." As she buttoned her jeans Rhianna hovered over her phone, which lay on her bed. "I think."

"You were always indecisive. I'm surprised you moved when you did. I was thinking it would take you, oh, at least another five years." Jen laughed.

"Well, you know there was nothing left in Bristol for me."

Jen cleared her throat. "Excuse me." Rhianna could imagine the raised eyebrows.

"Except you, of course. I know I've left friends behind. But I needed a fresh start. I didn't want to work in Bristol anymore, and I decided I might as well get on with following my dream. It's your fault for dragging us here three years ago for your hen party," Rhianna ended lightly.

"Uh hum. It was *you* who suggested I should have my hen party in Kittiwake Cove — actually. If I remember rightly."

"Well, I put it forward as a suggestion, as I'd holidayed here as a kid and knew it was nice. It just happened to have the team-building adventure stuff you wanted to do."

"Yeah, I miss the surfing ... and the cute surf instructors."

"Hello! Happily married!"

"No harm in window shopping," Jen said with a chuckle.

There was a knock at Rhianna's front door. She glanced at her watch. It was probably Joe. He was earlier than agreed. "Look, I've got to go."

"Okay, send plenty of photos for me to work with, to get a feel for the place, and maybe I can visit you at the beginning of May to help you get the place up and running."

"Oh, that would be great. Talk later, bye!" Rhianna hoped she'd be in her new house by then. Jen could help with the move too. Oh, which reminded her, she needed to chase the solicitors...

After ending the call, Rhianna slipped the phone into her pocket as she answered the door.

"Ready?" Joe stood leaning against the wall outside. Freshly shaven, with wax through his hair to tame his curls, he was dressed in shorts — it was April, just — with a casual shirt. The night before, when she'd finished her Sunday shift, he'd suggested they take a trip out in the morning after she'd complained she was lacking inspiration for her restaurant's menu. Then, when she'd desperately thought she best head off to bed, as he was calling on her early, he'd insisted on pouring her a glass of wine.

"Not quite. You're early, you said nine." She shielded her eyes from the low morning sun.

"Sorry, I finished at Mum's bed and breakfast earlier than planned. Thought we could grab a coffee first."

"Give me five minutes." Rhianna left him at the door and dashed into the bedroom, brushed her still damp hair frantically, and with no time to braid it, tied it back in a ponytail. A quick glance in the mirror told her she'd have to do. There wasn't time to apply make-up, so she dabbed her lips with some lip gloss.

Joe's old green Range Rover was parked in the pub's car park, and she climbed in as he started the engine.

"Where are we going first, then?"

"Let's get that coffee." He smiled as he pulled away.

They headed towards Wadebridge. They got there much faster than Rhianna had when she'd travelled there by bus. Joe parked up and they strolled around a bit before finding a café, where they ordered coffees.

"Do you need anything to eat?" Joe asked, eyeing the delicious-looking cakes and pastries on the counter.

"No, I'm good. My muesli will keep me going a little longer."

They talked with the owner, who appeared to know Joe well. She was able to recommend food suppliers and local produce. She provided names of local farmers for meat, eggs, and even seasonal vegetables. Rhianna, kicking herself for forgetting to bring a notebook, tapped notes into her phone.

Another of Rhianna's ideas was to offer cream teas during lunchtime and in the afternoon, anything from traditional scones with clotted cream and jam, to champagne high teas which would include sandwiches and cakes. She intended to make the cakes and scones in house, but wanted to source the ingredients, like the butter, clotted cream and the jam locally. She was given a couple of contacts for those too.

This stop broke up their journey as they headed towards St Austell, where they sampled the Cornish ales, lagers and ciders at the town's famous brewery. Rhianna shook hands and made contacts, all the while wishing she had business cards of her own. But she couldn't get those printed until Jen came up with a logo, and Jen couldn't do that until Rhianna had come up with a name for her bistro. Jen was right. She was indecisive.

As they continued on their journey to visit a winery, Rhianna took in the glorious Cornish countryside, the terrific views and the quaint villages they passed through. She was able to sit in comfortable silence with Joe, the radio set to BBC Radio Cornwall. Now and then he would point out a landmark, and they talked nonsense, completely at ease with one another. Just like three years ago.

Off a narrow country lane, Joe turned left, into a gated entrance. They drove into a courtyard and parked up. Unbeknownst to Rhianna, Joe had booked them in for a wine-tasting session.

They were in a small group of about fifteen people, mostly tourists. The tour was led by one of the winemakers, a young man in his early thirties, who first showed them the polytunnels where the grapes grew, before taking them into the working winery, where the magic happened. The winery was housed in a large barn, where the stainless steel tanks towered over them. Standing beside a table laid out with a thicket of wine glasses, the young winemaker explained the picking, pressing and the process of fermenting the wine in the vats. For the wine-tasting itself, he was joined by the winery's owner, a stocky white-haired man in his late fifties. Here they sampled four wines and the winemaker explained the process and the grape used. The first wine they sampled was a white wine.

As she swilled it around her mouth and listened to the winemaker describing its fruity undertones, Rhianna imagined which dishes it could go with. Fish, chicken… Joe tipped the rest of his glass into Rhianna's.

"Driving, remember," he said with a wink.

By now, Rhianna's muesli had worn off. She feared she'd be drunk at this rate.

They went on to try a sparkling rosé wine, which Rhianna really enjoyed. She was more than happy to have Joe pour the remainder of his glass into hers.

"That's too good to be in my pub. No one will pay the price, even if it is worth every penny," he said.

The bubbles were fine, like a good champagne. It had been processed using the same method. This had to go on her wine list. She could imagine sipping this on a summer's evening, while watching the sun set over the beach. It would also work with her high teas. She could serve this instead of champagne. Her mind went into overdrive thinking about all the sparkling cocktails she could make, which were always popular with customers. *A Lush Crush would be perfect*, she thought, blushing as she looked at Joe.

The red was next. It had the same light, crisp tone as the two other wines she'd sampled. As she sipped, the winery owner explained that due to the UK's marginal climate, English grapes did not produce such a full-bodied taste as, say, a red wine like a Shiraz would have.

He continued by explaining that the winery's red wines were produced using the ripest of grapes and the result meant the body was light, yet the flavour was still dry. It was therefore the perfect accompaniment to a wide variety of foods. The winery wasn't trying to copy flavours; they wanted to create their own distinctive English character in their wines. Rhianna liked the flavours of the different reds, their lightness and crispness. She could still taste the hints of fruit and the elegance of their flavour on her tongue. These wines would be perfect for summer evenings. The winery's emphasis was on quality, not quantity, hence their wines were more expensive than average, but Rhianna knew they would be perfect to include on the more sophisticated end of her wine list.

The last wine was a complete surprise. Another white, which was sweeter … but not as sweet as a dessert wine. It would make the perfect aperitif. Rhianna felt inspired. And possibly a little light-headed.

"Did you enjoy that?" Joe said, as they were led out of the barn.

"Oh, yes, that was great. I haven't tested my sommelier tastebuds in a while."

"Fancy having lunch here?"

It was getting on for two o'clock. Her stomach grumbled. She doubted she could go on much longer without food. "Yes, why not?"

"Good, because I've already booked a table for us." Taking Rhianna completely by surprise, Joe linked his arm through hers and led the way to the restaurant.

Inside a converted barn, a waitress showed them up solid wooden stairs to the floor above and to their table laid for two. They were by a small window which looked out over a courtyard surrounded by old farm buildings and the original farmhouse opposite, which was now being used as the winery's offices.

The menu was printed on good quality, cream paper. There was a set three course lunch menu with some delicious-sounding choices.

"Are you having all three courses?" Rhianna asked.

"Of course." Joe rubbed his stomach. "The food's meant to be great here. And have a glass of wine, so you can get a taste for how it complements the meal."

Rhianna nodded. "Good idea." If she had the soup, it wouldn't be so filling, and she could probably manage dessert. There was crème brûlée on the menu. It was her weakness. It would definitely feature on *her* menu.

The waitress placed a jug of iced water on the table and two tall glasses. "Are you ready to order?" she said, taking out her notepad and pen.

Joe ordered the pork pâté, while Rhianna chose the leek and potato soup with cider, making a mental note that cider would be a great ingredient for some of her dishes — especially if sourced locally.

Having chosen the roast topside of beef for her main course, she decided to order a glass of the red wine they'd sampled earlier, to see how it worked with the red meat.

The waitress left the table and Rhianna, taking in her surroundings, said, "This really is a lovely place."

"Yeah, they hold weddings and parties here. I thought the whole place might give you some inspiration."

"Oh, it certainly has. Thanks for bringing me here, Joe."

The waitress served her wine, and Joe raised his glass of water. "Cheers," he said.

"Cheers." Rhianna sipped. "I feel guilty you're only drinking water."

"It's okay, it's more important that you get the full taste of everything going on here."

"Do you mind if I quickly write some notes on my phone? I'm worried I'll forget otherwise."

Joe nodded. "Of course. I don't want it to be a wasted journey."

The soup was divine, with a delicious hint of Stilton. Not caring that she was in a restaurant with a handsome man seated opposite her, Rhianna mopped up the last drops of soup with some focaccia bread. She didn't want to waste a thing.

"Was that good? How did they make it so green?" Joe asked, watching her with a cheeky smile. "I've never seen leek and potato soup like it. It looks more like pea soup."

"Oh, they would have added the green ends of the leek in at the end." Rhianna dabbed her lips with her napkin and sat back.

The main course was equally satisfying. The roast beef, which she had ordered pink, was succulent and tender and the red wine complemented it perfectly. And with Joe sat opposite her, she couldn't help thinking how much this felt like a date.

"It's only a month until you get the keys," Joe said, raising his glass of water to Rhianna's wine glass again — now half empty.

"I know. I really need a name for it."

"Any ideas?"

"I like the idea of it being called a bistro. But I haven't really got further than that. It's near the Beach… The Beach Bistro… I'm not sure." She shrugged.

"I'll have a think for you." Joe tapped his temple. Rhianna dropped her gaze to her glass, his hazel eyes and wicked smile sending her insides bonkers. She had a sudden flashback to three years ago and the fun intimacy they'd shared. But it wouldn't be good to go back there. Joe was a player. This summer he'd be finding his next Betty. She had to look at him as nothing more than a friend.

Next up was dessert. Rhianna couldn't leave a crème brûlée on the menu, however stuffed she was now feeling. She finished her glass of red wine, knowing it wouldn't mix well with something so sweet and creamy, and switched to water. As the waitress had cleared the main course plates, they'd asked her to take her time in bringing the desserts.

"So, tell me what brought you back to Kittiwake Cove?" Joe rested his elbows on the table, leaning closer towards Rhianna.

Should she tell Joe about Glyn? How he'd broken her heart so suddenly? One minute full of promises of a life together, then the next moment, driving off after some silly row. "I broke up with my boyfriend nearly a year ago. I moved out of the house we shared and to keep busy got a second job in a bar — that's when I started learning how to make cocktails. My parents have a restaurant and I've always dreamed of following in their footsteps, so I thought, why wait until I'm older to follow my dream? Dad inherited some money from a cousin and wanted to help me out now, when I needed it most."

"Good ol' parents. Mine certainly keep me on a more even keel now."

"*You*, sensible?"

Joe's eyes widened playfully at Rhianna's teasing tone. "Oi!" He screwed up his paper napkin and chucked it at her.

Rhianna laughed as she caught it and threw it back. Their laughter was interrupted by the waitress arriving with their desserts. Remembering their orders, she placed the apple and cinnamon crumble and a mini jug of custard before Joe and the crème brûlée in front of Rhianna. Silence ensued, with only murmurings of delight. Rhianna loved cracking the burnt sugar on her crème brûlée, and the texture of the sugar crunching against the smooth vanilla custard. She wished she could try the sweeter wine they'd tasted earlier with this dessert to see how well it worked. She mentioned this to Joe, who told her to stop eating and called the waitress back over.

"We don't want a whole glass, just a sample, to test with the dessert." He described the wine they'd tasted down in the barn and the waitress nodded, saying she knew the one. "She's opening a bistro, and is considering stocking your wines," Joe added. The waitress quickly returned with the wine they'd sampled earlier and handed it to Rhianna.

"Thank you," she said to the young woman. She narrowed her eyes at Joe once the waitress had left. "You didn't need to do that."

"You know yourself wine tastes different with certain foods. It'll be good to try it, then you can decide whether to have it on your wine list."

"You're not trying to get me drunk, then?"

"Would I?"

The sweeter white wine worked brilliantly with the vanilla of the crème brûlée. Rhianna even asked Joe to take a sip to tell her what he thought with his dessert. He nodded his approval, although did say it was probably too sweet for him. If she did include this wine on her wine list, it would be better to sell it by the glass.

Joe insisted on paying for the meal, despite Rhianna's protests. "My idea, my treat." Joe placed his hand over hers, and Rhianna felt a surge of heat up her arm. "Put your purse away."

"I can't let you pay."

"You can treat me next time." His smile reached his eyes as he stood from the table, gesturing for Rhianna to walk down the stairs before him.

Next time?

At the bar, Rhianna asked who she needed to speak to regarding the winery supplying her restaurant. The bartender fetched the winery's manager — and owner. He handed her a business card and shook her hand warmly, saying he would welcome a call from her soon.

CHAPTER 7: SALTY DOG

"Oh, look, the tide's coming in and the waves are clean. Fancy a surf?" Joe said, pulling into The Cormorant's car park.

"After all that food?" Admittedly, the car journey had rested Rhianna's stomach. It had taken nearly an hour to return to Kittiwake Cove, as Joe had stopped at a couple of places to show Rhianna the spectacular views. "And won't it be freezing?"

"Nah…"

"I don't have a wetsuit."

"I'll get you one. And a board, before you think of another excuse." He pulled up the handbrake, then nudged Rhianna. "Go on, it'll be fun."

"Getting wet and cold, surfing at the beginning of April, is not my kind of fun."

"If I remember rightly, you were quite good."

"You can't remember that. You don't remember anything about meeting me. Or do you?" She looked at him suspiciously. He gave a cheeky smile. "And actually, I was pretty crap." As soon as she'd managed to stand up on the board, she'd just as quickly fallen off. Her balance was terrible.

They both got out of the Range Rover, slamming the heavy doors, the view of the beach below them. The sun shone over the horizon, making the water look clear and tempting. But since it was April, and the sea hadn't had a chance to start warming up, Rhianna shuddered at the thought of how cold it would be.

"Come on, we've been in the car most of the day or sat on our bums somewhere, eating. The most exercise we did was walking around the winery."

"I don't have a swimsuit."

"Liar." Joe laughed. "Look, if you're going to live down here, you need to be hardened to the water. Not some wimp who only goes in during the summer."

Rhianna's eyes narrowed. "I am not a wimp."

"Prove it." Joe's hands were on his hips, goading her with a mischievous smile. He was very hard to say no to. Was that just her, or did he have this effect on everyone?

"All right," she said, sounding less defiant than she'd intended. "I'll go in with you."

"That's my girl. Go get your swimsuit on. I'll go grab you a wetsuit."

Rhianna didn't know whether she would be putting a wetsuit on down on the beach or in her apartment, but she donned her bikini — because that was all she had. She would need to invest in a swimsuit if this ended up being a regular occurrence, because it would at least be an extra layer in the water.

Waiting for Joe, she'd put her clothes on over the top and concentrated on brushing her hair and braiding it back so that it wouldn't get in her way while she surfed.

Joe knocked and had two wetsuits in his hand. He held each up to Rhianna, then said, "I think this one will fit you best, but keep the other just in case. They're both winter suits, so they're thicker and will keep you warmer." He also handed her some black boots made of the same wetsuit material.

"Are we walking down in our wetsuits?"

"Yeah, means leaving less on the beach then. I'll be back in ten minutes."

Inside the warmth of her apartment, Rhianna threw off her clothes and stepped into the wetsuit. Thankfully it was dry. She remembered stepping into damp wetsuits for her surf lessons three years ago. They'd soon warmed up, especially in the summer sun, but it still wasn't initially comfortable trying to don something wet and cold. She shuddered at the memory.

Struggling with the zip at the back, she remembered how impossible it was to do it up, even though it was designed with a cord on the zip so that you could. She'd have to wait to get Joe to zip her up.

She watched as Joe emerged from the pub, smiling. This did nothing for her nerves. It had been so long since she'd surfed. And so long since she'd been in the water with Joe. He looked amazing in a wetsuit; it emphasized the breadth of his shoulders and chest, and it didn't leave much else to the imagination as she watched him picking up his board. Then she blushed, because her wetsuit was probably doing the same. And she hoped Joe hadn't caught her staring.

Joe tucked the board under his arm, and they walked down the hill, along the pavement towards the beach. With his free arm touching her shoulder, Joe guided Rhianna onto the inside of the path, so that he walked closest to the traffic. She thought this was rather sweet and chivalrous of him. Glyn would never have thought of doing that. Joe walked barefoot as if he wore shoes, unflinching, whereas Rhianna wore the wetsuit boots Joe had given her. They were a little big, but they had rubber on the base which meant they were okay to walk on hard surfaces with.

"Nervous?"

"A little. You're making me go in the freezing cold sea."

"I'm not making you."

"No, but you'll think I'm a wimp if I don't do it."

Joe chuckled. "That's true."

There was a board beside the surf school's shed. Liam sat inside on a deckchair, reading. He wore jeans and a hoodie, his blond hair windswept.

"G'day, mate," he said to Joe, his Australian accent pronounced. "Rhianna." He nodded to her. She waved nervously. "Surf's good today. Perfect for beginners too. You're in safe hands with our Joe."

"Thanks," she said. She was more concerned about the cold than safety. And were Joe's hands safe?

"Did you want me to carry your board?" Joe offered.

Rhianna shook her head. "No, I can manage."

"Catch you later, Liam," Joe said. "I'll take the board back if you've locked up."

"No worries, mate."

Joe helped Rhianna lift the board and tuck it under her arm. It was more awkward than heavy. They walked down to the water, which luckily wasn't too far with the tide coming in, because her arm and shoulder soon started to ache with the board hooked under her arm. The sun, lower in the sky, was due to set around seven-thirty, so they still had a few hours.

Rhianna could feel the coldness of the water, even in the boots. "I must be mad."

Joe now also wore boots. "You'll love it."

Rhianna was about to walk into the sea when Joe stopped her. "Hey, some warm-ups first."

"Am I getting a surf lesson?"

"Maybe." He chuckled, mischief behind his smile.

For the next couple of minutes, Joe had her stretching and warming up her shoulders, then her legs through lunges, thigh stretches and rolling her ankles, then finally touching her toes.

"That should do it."

They strapped the boards to their ankles and then waded out. Rhianna moved more slowly than Joe, needing to acclimatise to the water. Joe was a fish. Or maybe he was a Labrador. He looked glad to be back in it.

"Come on, duck yourself under and get it over with — the quicker the better," Joe said, after emerging from the clear blue water and shaking his head like a dog would to remove excess water from its fur. "Don't think of it as cold, think of it as refreshing."

"Come on," Rhianna said to herself, watching Joe, "if you're going to live here and blend in with the locals, you've got to do it."

And she did. She quickly resurfaced, gasping for air, the cold shocking with the little trickle of water allowed in by the wetsuit. Would she really get used to this?

Rhianna hadn't surfed since she was last here. It took her a while to find her balance, paddling out on the board, but like riding a bike, it soon came back to her what to do. But when the next wave arrived, she slid right off the surfboard.

Joe was beside her. "Make sure you paddle with your board straight into the wave; that way it'll go through rather than tip you off."

Rhianna nodded, wiping water from her face, the taste of salt already in her mouth. She joined Joe, turning her back to the waves as they crashed around her. Now she was in the water, there was something exhilarating about it — if she forgot the cold. The buzz surfing gave was a similar thrill to being on a rollercoaster. God, she hated it that Joe was right.

She caught a few waves, not trying to stand up, happy to let the waves take her in, her body flat to the board. It was still fun. So low to the water, and the speed. Joe was one of those surfers who could travel along the wave and exit the surf as planned, swivelling the board, dropping back into the waves with technique, ready to swim out to catch the next one. He was rarely wiped out. *Show off.*

"Do you want to try standing up?" Joe returned to her, his wet hair swept back off his face and his eyes sparkling. She nodded. "Can you remember what to do?"

"I think so."

Joe guided her onto the sand to demonstrate, and made her try it.

Hands by her chest, she had to push up to her knees, keeping her hands on the board, then bring them to her waist while sliding one knee along. Then, she had to push off from her back foot to straighten up, twisting and lifting fluidly into the standing position in the middle of the board, keeping her knees bent and her arms outstretched for balance.

Easy. On the board on the sand.

"You don't want to try and stand up too quickly, or you'll come out of the wave. But you need to do it fast enough while the wave has the power to carry you." History was repeating itself; Joe was her surf instructor again. But she couldn't give in to her desires for him this time. Not now she wanted Kittiwake Cove to be her home. This was no holiday romance. "But you'll get to know the timing."

They walked back into the sea, boards under their arms, then pushing them through the surf as they got deeper. Rhianna tried to put what Joe had shown her into practice.

It took her a few attempts. She would get to the point where, about to stand up, she would lose her balance and fall off, tumbling into the water, with the board tugging on her ankle. Joe stayed close, encouraging her. He'd catch the odd wave, to keep moving and to keep himself warm. Rhianna, concentrating on catching waves and standing up, had forgotten how cold the water felt.

Finally, she caught a wave and stood up. She lifted her fists to rejoice. And fell off. Just like she used to. She resurfaced, laughing, Joe wading towards her.

He high-fived her. "You did it." Then he wrapped an arm around her shoulder.

"I'm bloody knackered, though," she said, huffing and catching her breath.

"One more wave, then we go in?" The sun was lower and there weren't that many other surfers left in the water. Not that there had been that many to start with.

"Deal."

An unbroken wave was approaching.

"This one. We'll get this one," Joe said, paddling on his board, turning into position. Rhianna tried to do the same. She knew he'd definitely catch it. She was going to have to work harder to do so.

She paddled with her hands, scooping water behind her, and felt the board get taken up with the wave, and then she rose to stand. "Whooo hooo!" she screamed as she surfed towards the shore. She caught Joe up on his board out the corner of her eye, fearing if she turned her head, she'd lose her balance.

She could hear him shouting, "Way to go, girl!"

She'd managed it! She'd stayed on the board!

The water shallowed, and Rhianna jumped off the board, fearing she'd fall off. Then, as if a silent message between them said 'race', she was lifting her board and running out of the water, trying to beat Joe to the shore. He caught her up and they both tumbled onto the dry sand, panting, their boards at their sides. Rhianna lay on her back next to Joe, looking up at the sky, laughing as she tried to catch her breath.

"Enjoy that?" Joe raised himself up on his elbow, turning towards Rhianna. He wasn't as out of breath as she was, proving how much fitter he was.

She twisted her head. "Yes, yes, okay, you were right."

"I'm sorry, I didn't quite hear that." He leaned closer, holding a hand to his ear.

"I'm not saying it again."

He moved closer still, leaning over her. "For the record, Rhianna Price, was I right, or was I right? You enjoyed it."

She pressed her lips shut and shook her head. He poked her in the ribs so that it tickled. "I'll never hear the last of it," she said, laughing as he poked again.

"Just admit it!"

"Stop, Joe, stop…" she giggled. "Okay… Okay… I give up!" She held up her hands. "You were right."

He stopped and smiled. Beautiful white teeth. Hazel eyes studying her. His hip touched hers. God, if he kissed her right then she wouldn't stop him. He leaned forward, and Rhianna held her breath, her chest still. Her lips parted. Joe gently brushed a strand of hair stuck to her cheek.

Then he did lean in to kiss her. Her eyes widened. Coming to her senses, she pressed her fingers, covered with sand, to his mouth. Her heart now hammered inside her chest.

"I don't think it would be a good idea, Joe." She shivered, and the spell between them was broken.

"You're right." Joe pushed back and got to his feet. "Let's get you home and warmed up." He held out his hand, and she took it, and he pulled her to her feet. For a brief moment they stood close together, before stepping out of each other's personal space. They unstrapped the boards from their feet and Joe wound the cords around the fins. Rhianna now felt weak from the cold and the exhaustion of surfing.

"Here, you take the front." Joe had picked up both boards at the back, lifting them under each arm. Rhianna did the same with the front. Joe followed as she walked up the beach. Liam had shut up the surf shed, so they continued, walking past Oceans.

"I still haven't thought of a name," Rhianna said.

"I'm still thinking on it," Joe replied as they headed up the steep hill towards The Cormorant, the sun setting on the ocean, leaving the sky pink behind them.

They dropped the surfboards on the square patch of lawn outside Rhianna's apartment. Rhianna was shivering now, although walking up the hill had warmed her up. Joe ran into the pub to get her door key and unlocked the apartment door. He ushered her in and unzipped her wetsuit. She pulled off the sleeves, not caring she was in her bikini. Goosebumps travelled over her body. She'd left a beach towel over the back of the sofa in the living area. Joe grabbed it and wrapped it around her shoulders. She struggled to get her feet out of the wetsuit. She sat on the ground and Joe pulled at each leg, until at last she was out of it.

"What do you want me to do with the wetsuit?"

"Give it a rinse in the shower, but you might as well keep hold of it for now, so you can go surfing whenever you fancy it. Just ask Liam for a board, or whoever is in the shed, and tell them Joe says it's okay."

Rhianna nodded, pulling the towel tighter around her, rubbing her arms to warm up.

"Right, I'd best get out of mine, and go and help run my pub." Joe headed towards the front door.

"Joe," Rhianna said, making him pause. "Thanks for today." She'd loved every minute of his company. By stopping him from kissing her, had she looked ungrateful?

"Anytime." He smiled, then closed the door behind him as he left.

Rhianna stood in the shower until she felt the heat had penetrated her bones. Now she fancied beans on toast — a real culinary masterpiece — in front of the telly, and she hoped to push Joe almost kissing her out of her mind.

Getting involved with Joe wouldn't work. He would only want a short-term relationship. And that wouldn't be enough for her.

CHAPTER 8: MARGARITA

"You have remembered Sam and Heather are coming to stay for Easter weekend, haven't you?" Rose said, as she took a cake out of the Aga. The sweet smell of freshly baked coffee and walnut cake wafted towards Joe as he came through the back door carrying a basket of fresh eggs he had fetched from the hens at the bottom of the garden. Joe didn't get to see his brother or sister often, as neither of them lived in Cornwall, but Easter was as important as Christmas for the Trescotts, and they always made an effort to get together as a family. "Your nieces will want to see you, if not your siblings."

"Yes, I have," Joe lied, as he placed the basket on the counter. How could he have forgotten about Easter?

"Great." Rose smiled. "So, you will try to be free? The kids are asking to go surfing." Joe remembered last year. Sam's ten-year-old daughter Chloe loved surfing. Couldn't get her father in the water, though. And Heather's little daughters would be a year older too, so they might enjoy the dip. Joe would be running a surf school just for his family. But he didn't mind. He loved kids. He really enjoyed being an uncle. But he'd never felt ready for the responsibility of fatherhood.

"Yes, I'll try. When's Easter?" Joe had a bad feeling he'd be asking Rhianna for a huge favour. Lizzie was great at her job, but she had more commitments than Rhianna.

It had been a good job Rhianna had stopped him from kissing her yesterday. What had he been thinking?

He'd wanted to carry on the fun they'd been having... That's what he'd been thinking. Act now and think later. That was his way. Always his way. He never learned. Not when it came to a beautiful woman.

And he had a rule: never sleep with anyone living in Kittiwake Cove. He needed to remember that.

"Next weekend," Rose replied.

"When do the schools break up?"

"This Friday, or at least that's what Sam said."

"Things will start to pick up at the pub, then." He'd better take a look at the staff rotas, see who could pick up more hours. Rose gently tipped the cake on to a cooling rack.

"Morning, Joe." Charles entered the kitchen from the hallway with a bundle of bedsheets in his arms.

"Hi, Dad."

"Will you give us a hand in the garden in a minute?" Charles walked down to the end of the kitchen, where there was a small utility room which held a large washing machine and tumble dryer.

"Yeah, sure." Joe kissed his mother, assuring her he'd be available for the Easter weekend, then followed his father into the garden after he'd finished loading the washing machine. Rose had a new arbour she wanted building, ready for the summer months.

Once Joe had finished helping his parents, he returned to The Cormorant to open up. While it was quiet, he checked through the rota for the following week, to see where he'd need to increase the staffing. Soon, he'd have to advertise for more staff to cover the summer period. He'd glimpsed Rhianna leaving her apartment this morning and hadn't seen her since. Why was this bothering him?

When Ann came in for her shift at twelve-thirty, he sat her down to talk through increasing some shifts, including over the Easter weekend. Ann was in her early sixties and preferred working the daytime shifts, as she grew more tired in the evenings. If Rhianna agreed to run the pub, she'd still need staff. Joe wouldn't be too far away; if an emergency arose, then he could easily drop everything and come running. But he did want to free up his time so that he could spend it with his family. He didn't see them often enough.

He was lucky he could be a free spirit. He wasn't ruled by school holidays — except where trade was concerned, obviously. Sam and Heather had given their parents grandchildren, so Joe felt the pressure was off him in that department. He wasn't sure he wanted it, either. He loved his nieces. He was great with kids. Other people's kids. But he feared he was too selfish to have kids of his own. It would mean making sacrifices. Joe wasn't sure he was prepared to do that. He admired those that could, though, like his siblings.

Ricky arrived at three-thirty and took over the kitchen, so Joe could lose the chef whites and help Ann with manning the bar. Not that there was that much to man. Next week would be different.

It was now raining outside, darkening the day so that it felt later than it was.

Nick came in via the side entrance, brushing rain out of his hair. "Is Rhianna here?"

"She doesn't work Tuesdays." Joe shook his head. "Is she not in Oystercatcher?"

"No, so I thought she may have been in here abusing your Wi-Fi."

"Pint?"

Nick shook his head. "No, thanks, not on a school night."

"Did you want me to pass on a message?"

Nick pulled out an envelope from his back pocket. "Yeah, can you give her this? It's a couple of quotes for the wood burners, just some different options for her to consider. I wasn't sure what size she'd want in there."

Joe nodded, taking the envelope. "I'll make sure she gets it." Joe needed to stop giving Nick a hard time about Rhianna. She'd made it quite clear that she wasn't interested in Nick.

"Thanks, mate." Nick left via the other door, and Joe put the envelope by the till behind the bar. Through the window he could see the rain falling at a slant, showing which way the wind blew. It was only five o'clock but it felt like it would be dark any minute, even though the sun didn't set until around seven-thirty at this time of year.

At five-thirty Ann left, her husband collecting her in the car as the weather wasn't improving. And not long after, Joe caught sight of Rhianna with a carrier bag held over her head, running towards her apartment. Tempted to run after her, Joe held firm behind the bar. She wouldn't appreciate being accosted as soon as she walked through her door. Besides, maybe she'd come over to see him.

She didn't.

Spying the envelope beside the till, Joe realised he had an excuse to go and see Rhianna. "Ricky, do you mind holding the fort for a bit?" It was seven o'clock.

"No, boss. The rain's scared off the punters." They'd only had two couples in, ordering food. Plus Don, the old man who always stood at the end of the bar for a pint.

Joe tucked the envelope into his shirt pocket and retrieved a bottle of red wine. "I need to see Rhianna. I'm on my phone if you need me."

"Okay, boss," Ricky said. "Is the wine to sweeten her up?"

"Something like that. I need to ask if she'll run the pub over Easter."

"Good luck, then."

Joe knocked on Rhianna's door. It had stopped raining, thankfully. Anxiety crept up into his chest, the kiss that almost happened playing on his mind. He should just forget about it — take on his usual casual approach. But he'd had so much fun with her yesterday. From enjoying a nice meal together, to her being prepared to don a wetsuit and surf. *She deserves more than you can give her.*

Rhianna answered the door, dressed in jeans and a thick jumper. Her hair still looked damp from when she'd been caught in the rain earlier.

"Hey," Joe said, holding up the wine. "Can I come in?"

"Of course."

Joe entered, shutting the door behind him. Due to the open-plan design, he could see the small kitchen was a mess with pots and pans on the hob, plates and bowls in the sink, and a chopping board covered with the remains of vegetable peelings. It made sense, because he kept getting wafts of different, mouth-watering scents.

"Sorry about the mess. I was trying out a recipe," Rhianna said.

"That's okay, I just needed to give you this." Joe retrieved the envelope and handed it to her. "It's from Nick."

"Oh, right." She placed it on the coffee table with a pile of other paperwork.

Joe looked around the kitchen. "Anything you wanted me to test?" he asked hopefully.

Rhianna laughed. "I should have thought of you. I only made a small batch. Tested some myself; I've frozen the rest."

"Shame," Joe said, shrugging. "Anyway, I need to ask you a favour."

"Is this why you've brought wine?" She eyed him suspiciously. She knew him well already.

"Could be."

"It's brightening up." She gestured outside. The sun was seeping through gaps in the clouds. "I was going to take a quick stroll to the beach."

"I'll come with you," Joe said; then he realised he might not be welcome. "If you want me to?"

"Yeah, I just wanted to take a look at Oceans for some inspiration." Rhianna put on her ankle boots and grabbed her jacket. "Jen's nagging me for a name for the restaurant." Rhianna locked up the apartment and they headed towards the centre of Kittiwake Cove.

"So, where have you been today?" Joe hoped this didn't sound nosey, and more like he was making conversation.

"Oh, I popped back into Wadebridge to get some ingredients. Bloody buses, though. I waited at the bus stop for an hour, and then it rained. I really need a car." Rhianna sighed. "But I can't afford one now. All my money needs to be poured into the restaurant."

"Hey, why didn't you say?" Joe said, arms swinging as they walked down the steep hill. He always felt it on his knees and had to take it slower — a sign he was getting old. "You can borrow mine."

"The Range Rover?"

"Yeah, I'll get you insured on it. I don't mind."

"Are you sure?" She stopped and stared at him.

"I trust you."

"You haven't seen my driving."

"That is true." Joe chuckled as they continued walking. "But as long as I don't need it, then you can borrow it. I'll give the insurance company a call tomorrow."

Rhianna smiled. "Ah, thank you, Joe."

They stood on the pavement, facing the beach. Behind them was Oceans.

"I thought if I came down here, it might inspire me to think what to call it." She kept turning, looking up at the building, then back out to the sea.

Joe breathed in the fresh salty air, the scent of rain on the tarmac still lingering, and he copied Rhianna, staring at the building, then out to sea.

"I'm thinking something to do with the beach, or the ocean … but it's already called Oceans."

"Keep the title simple." Joe shrugged casually. He'd tucked his hands into the pouch of his jumper, the wind relentless. "It's situated on the beach front … so why not The Beach Front Bistro?"

Rhianna clapped. "Oh, Joe, yes, I love it." Without hesitating, she grabbed his face and kissed him. Lips to lips. The lip balm she wore tasted of cherries. She pulled away, eyes wide. "Oh, god, I'm sorry."

He smirked mischievously at her mortified expression. "Shall we go back to the pub and celebrate?" he said, thinking it best not to make a big thing of the kiss, because he sensed Rhianna didn't want to either. He was very tempted to pull her back into an embrace and kiss her properly — like he'd wanted to on the beach yesterday.

They strolled back up the hill, towards The Cormorant.

"I left the bottle of wine in the apartment, but do you mind if we go back into the pub? I've left Ricky in charge," Joe said, catching his breath after climbing the steep hill.

"Oh, yes, sure," Rhianna said. "But I think we should toast the new name with a cocktail."

"Good idea. What were you thinking?"

"Well, you can't go wrong with a classic. Shall I knock us up a margarita?"

"Now you're talking."

Rhianna retrieved the red wine from the apartment, plus limes, tequila and the triple sec she'd need to make the cocktails, while Joe told Ricky he could head home. The kitchen was closed. The earlier rain had scared off any further punters.

The wine returned to the shelf, Joe allowed Rhianna behind the bar, where, grabbing the Herradura Reposado tequila, she added the ingredients and ice into his cocktail shaker. The thing rarely got used. Joe's clientele seldom asked for a cocktail. He didn't own margarita or coupette glasses, so she poured the two pale orange drinks into martini glasses (also rarely used) with salt on the rims.

They clinked glasses. "To The Beach Front Bistro," Joe said. Rhianna concurred, sipping her cocktail. The drink was refreshing and warming.

"I can phone Jen in the morning now. Think up menus, business cards, signage. Everything! Thank you, Joe." She chinked her glass against his again.

"You're welcome." After yesterday, Joe was glad to have Rhianna back in his company. But was he getting too attached to her? This little niggle in his chest, the fact she crept into his mind most of the time, wasn't healthy. This was so unlike him. Whatever these feelings were, they worried him. He hadn't felt like this in a long time … not since Alannah. "Hey, I've got a huge favour to ask you," he said, placing his glass down, remembering why he'd needed to talk to Rhianna in the first place. Professional reasons.

"Oh, there *was* a motive behind the wine." Rhianna rolled her eyes. Joe loved the hint of Welsh in her accent. "Not that we ended up drinking it." She raised her glass.

"No, no, no… I wanted to chat to you."

"Go on."

"My family are visiting this Easter, and I'd like to take a couple of days off from the pub, so I can spend time with them. I was wondering if you could work for me full-time over the weekend?" Maybe this would be a good opportunity to put some space between them. With Rhianna living on his doorstep, working in the pub, he was too used to her being about. And it had only been a few weeks. Spending time with his family would put his emotions back on the right track — at a safe distance.

"Oh, right."

"I'll pay you double!"

"You can't actually afford to do that," she said sternly.

"I can't ask Lizzie; she has commitments at home with the kids. Ann doesn't like long hours…" Joe said. "And as you're living on the premises, I just thought … hoped…"

"Joe, it's okay, you don't have to justify why you've asked me. You've been really helpful towards me, so of course I'll do it," Rhianna said without hesitation. "As long as you don't mind if I work on plans for the bistro during the quieter periods."

"Of course not. I'll get all the staff I can get in to help you."

"No problem."

They chinked martini glasses again.

"And you'll insure me on the Range Rover?" Rhianna asked, more hesitantly.

"Yes of course." Joe grinned. Then, without thinking, he asked, "So are you sore?"

"Sore?" Rhianna frowned.

"From surfing?"

She laughed. "Actually, I do ache in places I didn't realise I even had muscles."

When Rhianna had finished her cocktail, Joe suggested a glass of wine. She shook her head. "Sorry, Joe, I need to get to bed. I've got a meeting with Olly early tomorrow morning. And I think my kitchen still needs clearing." She stood up from the table.

"Understood. Maybe catch you tomorrow evening?"

"Yes, maybe."

"I'll be here," he said. "Thanks, Rhianna. I don't know what I'd do without you."

CHAPTER 9: THE BEACH FRONT COSMOPOLITAN

"Right, you've got my phone number if you need me?" Joe was in danger of wearing out the pub's carpet. It was eleven o'clock in the morning and Rhianna was behind the bar, a box of salt and vinegar crisps at her feet, ready to stock the shelves, while Joe paced anxiously around, not quite ready to leave. The Easter weekend had arrived; it was Good Friday, and Joe's family were staying at Rose and Charles's.

"Yes." Rhianna rolled her eyes as Joe continued to fret. The pub was his baby, and she also knew he was feeling guilty about asking her to work full-time over the Easter weekend, especially since she had her own project to be concentrating on. But he'd said she could use and abuse the pub, so she planned to work on the menu for the bistro during any down times. In fact, she couldn't wait for Ricky to turn up so she could pick his brain about dishes.

The first week of the Easter holidays had already brought a significant rise in the number of customers. Joe had even put up some of the prices on the pub's food menu. In the town, prices had also gone up, ready for the booming tourist trade.

"And I'll try to make sure I'm back before you close up tonight," Joe said.

"Okay, but don't panic. I'm quite capable of locking up."

"And remember there's a band playing here on Sunday evening."

"Yes, I know. You've told me a million times." Rhianna huffed.

"Any problems, Rhianna, promise me you'll call, or come and find me — you know how bad the network is around here." Joe had left the landline number of his parents' B&B by the phone behind the bar, and made her enter it into her mobile contacts.

"Joe, just go, will you? Your family will be expecting you. Everything's fine. I'll see you tonight."

"Okay, okay. I'm just so grateful that you're doing this for me."

"I know. You keep telling me that, but if you don't leave soon I may change my mind."

Rhianna watched Joe leave and heaved a sigh of relief. She had a long day ahead of her, but Joe had rallied the staff around to make sure she wasn't going to be stuck in the pub on her own. Ann would be in from twelve — an hour away — and Lizzie was due in at three-thirty to work until closing time. Rhianna had brought in her laptop and intended to make good use of any free time. She also planned to try out a couple of cocktail ideas. Jen was working on a logo for her bistro now. *The Beach Front Bistro*. The more she thought about it, the more she loved the name. She just couldn't believe how she'd reacted to Joe, kissing him like that, when the day before she'd stopped him. *Talk about giving the poor man mixed messages.*

But it had only been a quick peck. *On the lips.* As soon as she'd realised she was kissing him and shouldn't be, she'd pulled hastily away. Neither of them had mentioned it since, and that was probably for the best.

Before Rhianna could dwell on how good that brief touch of Joe's lips had felt, she got on with preparing the pub, giving the bar one last wipe down, emptying the dishwasher and stocking the nibbles behind the bar. She made sure the fridges were full of bottled drinks, from beers and ciders to juices.

"Good morning!" Ricky appeared behind the bar, ready to enter the kitchen.

"Good morning," Rhianna replied brightly.

"We ready to do this?"

"You bet." They high-fived one another.

A few minutes later, Ann arrived to start her shift, and gradually customers started arriving and ordering food and drinks. Before long, the pub was far busier than they had been used to in the past weeks. The holiday season was definitely upon them. At around three o'clock, the pub became quieter as the lunchtime trade tailed off, and Rhianna took a breather, as did Ricky, who was working the whole day. The Cormorant served food all day, and Joe usually covered the kitchen when Ricky wasn't available. But he hadn't wanted Rhianna to take that responsibility. Ricky used his downtime to shoot some pool and Rhianna blended strawberries and juiced lemons, limes and oranges she'd brought over from her apartment, ready to use in a cocktail she was experimenting with.

"Right, try this." Rhianna poured a measure of vodka, Cointreau and a blend of the fresh juices into the cocktail shaker with ice and shook vigorously. She was working on a cosmopolitan-style cocktail but experimenting with different fruits and replacing the triple sec with Cointreau. She poured the contents into three shot glasses.

Ricky immediately picked up his shot glass and knocked it back.

"It's not a shot. It's a cocktail. It should be sipped," Rhianna said to Ricky, who was nodding his approval. "Ann, come and try this."

"You're not going to get me drunk, are you?" The older woman approached hesitantly.

"It's just a single measure of vodka and it's mixed with juices, so it's not as if you're drinking it neat."

Ann, having heard Rhianna tell Ricky how it should be drunk, held the small shot glass delicately and sipped it cautiously, possibly worried it would taste disgusting. Rhianna watched her expression and she didn't grimace. Instead, she let out a satisfied, "Mmmm... Oh, that's nice," and nodded enthusiastically.

Rhianna topped up Ricky's glass, then took a sip from her own. She liked it. It would work frozen too. And if she used the locally produced vodka she had sampled while out with Joe, she could sell it as a signature cocktail in the bistro.

"It needs a name," Rhianna said. "It might have to be The Beach Front Cosmopolitan if I serve it in a martini glass."

"Sounds good to me." Ricky raised his glass and finished it. He hadn't grasped the concept of drinking it slowly.

Ann agreed, but her attention was drawn away to a couple of ramblers entering the pub.

Rhianna made some notes, then went into the kitchen to wash the cocktail shaker. Her heart sank when she came back and saw Nick standing at the bar. Ann was busy with the walkers, who had a map spread out on the counter on which she was pointing out landmarks.

"What can I get you?" Rhianna plastered on a smile. She never knew how she was going to have to handle Nick.

"A pint of Doom Bar, please."

"On your own today?"

"Yeah, I'm not working today."

"Oh, right," Rhianna said, as she placed his pint in front of him. "I suppose it is a bank holiday."

"Yeah, can't be all work and no play. Where's Joe?"

"He's with his family. He's left me in charge."

Rhianna hoped Nick wouldn't take this as an invitation to prop up the bar all evening and expect attention from her. She caught herself wondering what Joe was up to and if he was having fun with his family. She would love to be a fly on the wall, observing what he was like with his nieces. Her reverie was soon interrupted by Liam entering the pub. He looked noticeably washed out, despite his permanent tan.

"Blimey, what's the matter with you, mate?" Nick beckoned for Rhianna to pour Liam a pint of Doom Bar. There was no trace of the animosity Rhianna had first witnessed between the two men.

"Tilly's pregnant," Liam said.

"Congratulations!" Nick slapped Liam on the back.

"That's fantastic news," Rhianna said, though something felt off. She placed the pint in front of Liam and Nick paid.

"Is it?" He leaned on the bar, his shoulders hunched and his blond hair flopping in his face. "I mean, it's what we both want. But it's just too soon. I wanted to propose to her on her birthday, get married and do it all properly." Liam gulped down half his pint.

"You don't have to be married to have a baby," Rhianna said cheerfully. "It's not the nineteen-forties."

"I know, I know, but I'm old-fashioned."

Liam didn't look old-fashioned. He looked like he surfed every day, rain or shine. If they were re-casting *Baywatch*, he'd fit right in. He'd give Zac Efron a run for his money.

"Yeah, Rhianna's right, mate, you shouldn't feel terrible about this," Nick said, completely surprising Rhianna. He'd even placed a reassuring hand on Liam's shoulder. She was waiting for something arrogant to come out of his mouth, but for once he wasn't being a jerk.

"How many weeks pregnant is she?" asked Rhianna.

Liam shrugged. "She hadn't been feeling well for a couple of days, so she saw her GP."

"So, if it's early days," Rhianna said, trying the practical approach, "maybe you could propose to her and get married before the baby's born?"

Liam pulled a ring box out of his pocket. "Yeah, yeah, maybe that's what I'll do." He opened the box to reveal a solitaire diamond ring set in gold.

"When's Tilly's birthday?" Rhianna asked.

"Not until July." Liam stared at the ring, twisting it about so that it sparkled in the light.

Rhianna wondered if Tilly would start to show by then. She had no idea about these things.

"But you've already got the ring?" Nick asked quizzically.

"Mum brought it over at Christmas. It was my gran's."

"Well, don't wait for her birthday, then," Rhianna said. "Make a romantic night of it soon and pop the question. It'll be much more of a surprise. It's so predictable these days; birthdays, Christmas, Valentine's. Ask her now — if it's what you want?"

"Yeah, I agree with Rhianna. Just ask her to marry you and the rest will work itself out."

Liam finished his pint and stood up straight, a smile back on his face. "Yes, that's what I'll do. You're right, both of you. Thanks for the pint." He shook Nick's hand, nodded to Rhianna, and placed the ring in his pocket. "Not a word, either of you. Not till I've asked her."

"Our little secret." Nick tapped his nose. Once Liam had left the pub, Rhianna smiled at Nick and he high-fived her.

"Wow, Nick, you can actually be nice."

He tapped his nose again. "Don't tell everyone. I've got a reputation to uphold."

Rhianna laughed, shaking her head. "It's not a great reputation, you know that?" Nick shrugged. "But when I first saw you and him in this pub together, I sensed a certain animosity between you both."

"Ah, a misunderstanding. I'd been trying to … er … chat up Tilly." *Get in her knickers, more like.* Rhianna kept the thought to herself as Nick spoke. "Liam didn't like it. Never really trusted me after that."

"And so this evening, that was…?"

"Never kick a man when he's down, Rhee." She scowled, not sure she liked him calling her Rhee, and he quickly corrected himself. "Rhianna."

Joe sipped his bottle of Doom Bar, relaxing in his parents' garden with his family. There were six adults huddled around the warming embers of the firepit. It was getting dark and turning much chillier, but at least it was dry. His father, Charles, threw another log on the fire, causing it to crackle and spark.

There was plenty of laughter, but remembering the children had gone up to bed, they hushed their voices, then giggled quietly. While they all chatted, Joe silently observed his family and felt a deep pang of love for them. Rose was doing the same with a smile on her face, no doubt happy to have her three grown-up children back under her roof, even if it was only for the weekend.

This coming August would mark the third anniversary of his sister-in-law Jade's death. He remembered Sam's devastation over losing his beloved wife so young to colon cancer. Witnessing it had cemented Joe's certainty that he was better off living his life with no emotional attachment. If he did not love, he could not be hurt. That's why he now made it a rule not to sleep with anyone local, only with tourists. Jade's death had rocked his family to the core, and Joe had given up his dream of moving to Australia. He'd realised he'd be too far away in times of trouble. He wanted to be there to support Sam and his parents. Then, almost as if the universe was telling him he should stay in Kittiwake Cove, The Cormorant had come up for sale.

Sam now appeared to be coping well as a single dad. He even had plans to move to Portishead to be closer to Heather, their younger sister. He'd recently changed his job and was finding the commute from Swindon to Bristol meant it was difficult to make time for his daughter, Chloe. Heather insisted she could help him with the childcare and possibly be a mother figure to Chloe as she matured. At ten years old, Chloe was growing up to be a great girl, playing with her younger cousins like a big sister. She potentially could be a handful when she reached her teens, though, Joe mused. He wouldn't envy Sam then.

Heather and her husband Tom were still their strong united selves, and were devoted parents to their two mini-divas, Daisy and Scarlett, who were five and three. It would be good for Sam to have Heather close by.

Joe listened as Heather teased Sam about setting him up on online dating sites once he'd moved to Portishead. Surprisingly, his brother didn't completely object. This made Joe wonder: if Sam was open to finding happiness again, even contemplating loving again, after the devastation of his wife's death, should he himself start to believe that there was someone out there for him, after Alannah?

And why did his thoughts suddenly drift to Rhianna? He hoped she was managing at the pub. Subtly he checked his phone for messages. There were none. He needn't worry.

"You're quiet, Joe," Heather said, obviously noticing him deep in thought. She had always been the observant one.

Joe shook himself out of his reverie and smiled at his sister. He pushed his phone back into his jeans pocket. "Ah, just enjoying watching you lot. It's great to be back together again."

"I agree." Rose raised her wine glass.

"Are you dating, Joe?" Heather asked.

Sam leaned forward in his garden chair. "Yeah, anything to report, Joe?" he asked before raising his lager bottle to his lips.

"Nah, you know me." Joe shrugged and sipped his beer.

"There's a new woman in the village — Rhianna isn't it?" Rose said archly. Joe had talked to her about Rhianna, but not in *that* way. "She's working in the pub and Joe's been taking her out quite a bit."

"Not in that way, Mum! I've simply been helping her source local suppliers for her new bistro." Joe hated that he sounded more defensive than he'd intended. He'd never hear the last of it now. *Thanks, Mum.*

"Ooh, what's she like?" Heather asked, as Tom topped up her glass with Prosecco.

"She's nice."

"You'll never impress her if you just say she's *nice*," Heather said, frank as always.

"Heather, I don't want to, you know… She's just a friend."

"Yeah, yeah." Heather didn't sound convinced.

Joe stood, looking at his watch. "Right, well, I'd better dash. I promised I'd help Rhianna close up." It was coming up to ten o'clock. There was plenty of time yet before closing, but all of a sudden, the firepit felt too hot to sit by. He didn't like them probing him about his private life.

Tom approached, holding another bottle of beer. "Sit down, mate. Heather's only teasing. She loves you and wants you to be happy."

"I am happy."

"Of course you are." Tom slapped his back, then took his seat by Heather.

Joe sat back down. So much for an early night... Rhianna would manage another hour without him.

Nick finished his pint and said goodnight. The large clock above the bar read ten past ten. Rhianna picked up the empty glass as she nodded a goodbye. Lizzie, who'd been drafted in to work some extra hours over the weekend, appeared by her side with a mischievous smile on her face. Lizzie worked extremely hard, talked about her children mostly, and was great fun to work with.

"That man's been coming into this pub more and more lately," Lizzie said, giving Rhianna a nudge.

"So?"

"I think he likes a certain barmaid." Lizzie raised her eyebrows. "And it's not me. He doesn't come in during the week or on my shifts."

"It's a Friday — he usually comes in. End of the week and all that."

"Yeah, but he's usually gone by the time I start my shift. He's sunk more than a pint tonight, and he's spent the evening propping up the bar, watching you."

"Well, he's wasting his time with me," Rhianna said firmly. "Honestly, Lizzie, I wouldn't touch him with a bargepole. He's so full of himself."

Just then, an attractive woman around Rhianna's age approached the bar, wheeling a hand luggage sized suitcase, stopping Lizzie and Rhianna's conversation — to Rhianna's relief. The woman was dressed in an expensive-looking fitted trouser suit, and had bleached blonde hair tied back into a ponytail and precise make-up to match, making Rhianna think *flight attendant.*

"Hi, is Joe around?" The woman glanced along the bar as if looking for him.

"Oh, no, sorry, he's not here this evening. Can I give him a message?" Rhianna asked as Lizzie left her to serve a customer at the other end of the bar.

The woman gave a self-satisfied smirk, the effect heightened by her perfect red lipstick. Rhianna envied women who could carry off red lipstick. It made her look washed out. "It's okay, I'll show myself up."

"Oh, I'm not quite sure…" Rhianna tried to stop the woman lifting the hatch to the bar.

"It's okay, I'm Kerenza. I always stop over at Joe's when I'm in the area." Kerenza gave a suggestive wink. "He knows I'm coming."

"Oh, right, sorry, only he didn't say anything."

Kerenza frowned. "I messaged him a few weeks ago."

"He probably forgot." Rhianna didn't feel at all comfortable letting this unknown woman go through the bar and up the stairs to Joe's living quarters, but what could she do? She was clearly a regular visitor. And she didn't look as if she was going to take no for an answer.

"I doubt it." Kerenza shrugged at Rhianna's temerity in suggesting Joe could forget about her. "Anyway, I'm shattered. I'll go and warm up his bed." Before Rhianna could reply,

Kerenza let herself through to the back of the bar and headed towards the door leading to Joe's flat above the pub.

Rhianna watched her push the handle down on the case with a clunk and carry it up the stairs. She certainly was a stunning-looking woman, and all her actions had been confident and assertive. And she was going to be sleeping in Joe's bed… Jealousy knotted Rhianna's gut. But, she admonished herself, she had no right to be jealous. This was a prime example of why she should never get involved with Joe on a romantic level. He was a player, a cad. He flitted from one woman to the next — after all, she herself had once been one of those women.

And evidently, Joe still had women who visited his bed on a regular basis, no strings attached.

Finishing his whisky — Tom and Charles had insisted on opening a bottle, to keep them warm around the firepit — Joe said his goodbyes to his family, with the promise of spending tomorrow with them. Hopefully, weather permitting, they'd have a day on the beach. And depending on the waves, he'd take the children out surfing.

He made his way up the hill towards The Cormorant in the velvety darkness, the roar of the ocean ever-present; a sound he loved, giving him comfort as he walked. All evening he'd been thinking about Rhianna — he just couldn't seem to get her out of his head. Although he told himself it was just because he was worried about leaving her to manage the pub, he actually realised that the truth was that he missed her company. He liked being around her. Seeing Heather and Tom so happy, Joe couldn't help wondering what it would be like to have what they had together.

Could he see himself as the settling down type? Would he miss the summer romances? However much fun they were, with no commitment, no ties, no hurt, the winters were cold and lonely at times. And he wasn't getting any younger — as Heather had so bluntly pointed out. She'd tried to be tactful, but alcohol always made her speak before thinking first. But he loved her to bits, and he knew that she just wanted him to be happy.

The lights were on in the pub, and through the windows he could see Rhianna busily wiping down the bar.

"Hey," he called out as he entered, not wanting to give her a fright. He locked the door behind him. "Sorry, I'm back later than I expected."

"Hey, no worries. How was your evening?" Rhianna said, blowing a stray hair out of her face.

"Great, great, shattered now, can't wait to hit the sack." The few beers he'd drunk in the garden, with whisky on top, were taking their toll by now. And he knew he had to be up early the following morning.

"Oh, about that."

"What?" He frowned. Rhianna looked nervous and gestured towards the corridor leading to the stairs to his flat.

"Um, well, a woman arrived a couple of hours ago. Blonde. She said she had arranged to stay with you. She said she stayed regularly." Rhianna winced. "Kerenza?"

Kerenza. Shit, he'd totally forgotten about her. He ran a hand through his hair. Kerenza was not what he needed right now. She was a sales rep, and their agreement was that whenever she was working in the area and needed a bed for the night, she stayed with him, an arrangement that worked to their mutual satisfaction. Friends with benefits. But with Rhianna standing in front of him, his relationship with Kerenza suddenly felt sordid. He knew the sex would be good, but somehow, if he'd wanted to convince anyone he'd changed, it was Rhianna. But had he changed? And why? When had he decided to try and change? He had a rule, too, remember?

"I'm sorry, I couldn't stop her. She's gone upstairs to, erm —" Rhianna couldn't look him in the eye — "warm your bed."

Joe nodded. He couldn't meet her eyes either. An unexpected wave of shame swept over him. "Okay, okay, thank you. Look, you head off now. I'll finish off in here."

"Are you sure?"

"Yes, yes, and thanks, Rhianna." He placed his hand briefly on her shoulder as they walked to the back door. "I'm really grateful for your help this weekend."

"It's no problem."

He watched to make sure she reached her apartment safely, and she gave him a wave before she shut her front door. He locked the back door of the pub, pushing the heavy bolt across.

Why had he totally forgotten about Kerenza? And why did he feel so ashamed that Rhianna knew about her?

CHAPTER 10: MORNING GLORY FIZZ

Joe awoke to a mug of coffee being thrust in his face. His neck ached. He rubbed it, and as he came to his senses, he remembered why he'd slept on the sofa last night.

"Hey, why didn't you join me in your bed?" Kerenza stood over him wearing a man's white shirt, only a couple of buttons fastened, hinting at black lacy underwear underneath. Where had she found that shirt? Could it be his? It had to be.

Gratefully, he took the coffee and placed it on the table beside him. He'd slept in his boxers and a T-shirt, having decided the night before just to crash in the lounge. He usually slept naked, but hadn't wanted Kerenza to find him with his arse hanging out of the covers.

"I'd drunk a lot of beer. Wasn't sure you'd want me snoring beside you," he lied, still not ready to meet her eyes. He sat up, keeping the blanket over his lap to hide his morning arousal. He didn't want Kerenza thinking it was for her. Because it wasn't — it was just nature. The white shirt and the black lace wasn't helping, though. Kerenza had an amazing body. She was on the road a lot, but she took time to look after herself.

"Shame, I'd been looking forward to you joining me. Maybe we could make up for it this morning?" She perched seductively beside him and tenderly combed a hand through his hair. The shirt gaped open, and he got a close-up view of her magnificent breasts spilling over the delicate fabric of her bra.

Definitely not helping. He shrugged her off. "Sorry, Kerenza, you're more than welcome to stay here — but in the spare room."

"What have you done with the real Joe?" Kerenza cupped his face and stared into his eyes suspiciously. She felt his head as if he had a temperature. "Are you ill or something?"

"No, I'm fine. I just don't think it's a good idea." Again, he prised himself out of her grip.

"You usually think it's a fabulous idea." Kerenza frowned, trailing her fingers along his arm and pouting sexily.

"I've changed, that's all." He knew she wouldn't beg. It wasn't her style.

"You? Change?"

"I'm busy this weekend, my family are down, it's not fair on —"

"On who?" Kerenza stood up. "The pretty blonde downstairs last night? Who tried to stop me coming up here?" He could tell she was pissed off. The woman was a sexaholic. She probably had guys like him dotted all over the county. Country, even. Who knew?

And here he was, turning her down point-blank. Sex on a plate, no strings attached, with a beautiful woman to boot. "No, no, no … not like *that*." *You're in denial, Joe.* "Rhianna's just doing me a huge favour looking after the pub this weekend, and it wouldn't be fair on her if I spent the morning gallivanting around with you." This was true enough.

Kerenza huffed. "Okay, well I'll be out of your hair by Monday. You won't even know I'm here."

She stalked off, and over the rim of his coffee cup, Joe couldn't help admiring her slender, toned figure as she strutted towards the bathroom. Her long legs and pert buttocks were barely covered by the shirt and accentuated by a lacy thong. As if he wouldn't know she was here! How was he going to cope until Monday? Because he knew full well Kerenza would try her damnedest to seduce him.

Rhianna took a deep breath before entering the pub, psyching herself up for another long day ahead. She had bubbly Lizzie in this evening again, who always worked hard, and Ann in for the afternoon shift. Ann was a real mother hen and was great at giving out local information to the customers. It was only roughly four weeks since Rhianna had arrived, and she was already making friends in Kittiwake Cove. Ricky was a scream in the kitchen, too. They often compared notes about cooking, Rhianna usually giving Ricky some tips.

As she approached the bar, she could tell Joe was in a hurry. Even though he looked tired and stressed, he was still gorgeous, with his hair ruffled, and his aftershave smelt divine. He grabbed his keys and wallet, shoving them in his pocket.

"I've got to go, but you've got my number?" he said, waving his mobile phone, although Rhianna knew he rarely looked at it.

"Yes, sure."

He was out of the pub before she could say anything else.

"Hi, Joe. Bye, Joe," Rhianna muttered under her breath. "Great handover."

But Rhianna knew perfectly well what to do. To be fair to Joe, he had made sure she had as little to do as possible. It was just a case of manning the pub and keeping the customers happy. She could do that.

Kerenza appeared dressed as if it were July, not April, in denim shorts and a cut-off T-shirt. Okay, the sun was out, but Rhianna thought she was brave to risk shorts. She'd felt the cold wind just walking from Oystercatcher to the pub a minute ago. And didn't only thirteen-year-old girls get away with wearing T-shirts like that nowadays? Kerenza's feet were bare. She was wearing less make-up than yesterday, and it was quite a transformation from the businesswoman she'd appeared last night. She still looked stunning, though.

"Where's Joe?" Kerenza said, scrunching back her long blonde hair into a messy ponytail. Her T-shirt rose, showing off her midriff. Rhianna couldn't help envying her toned stomach.

"Oh, you just missed him." Rhianna busied herself, looking for jobs to do behind the bar, hoping to avoid small talk with Kerenza. But she'd already replenished the crisps and peanuts the night before when the pub had grown quiet.

"He moves fast. I obviously didn't wear him out enough!" Kerenza winked at Rhianna, then went back upstairs.

So, Joe had slept with her, as Rhianna had feared. She'd lain awake last night, trying not to imagine Joe and Kerenza entangled in bed together, fighting the jealousy swirling around inside of her.

A small part of her wanted to reignite the fun that she'd shared with Joe three summers ago. She wanted to feel it once more. But had it been fun precisely because there had been no commitment, no ties between them? Would it be fun again, if she slept with Joe? Or would it just complicate life in ways she was trying to avoid, after the disaster of Glyn?

Joe wasn't like Glyn, though. He didn't guilt trip Rhianna into doing things for him. After all, he was paying her to run the pub. Whereas, having had time to reflect, when she looked back at her nineteen-month relationship with Glyn, she realised it hadn't been as happy or as healthy as a normal relationship should be. She found it hard to believe that it had ended nearly a year ago now.

But she had proved to herself that she could live without him. She didn't need him to make her happy. Her happiness was down to her, and her alone. And even though at the back of her mind she feared her bistro venture would be a failure, as was only human, she was happier than she had been in months. And she was not prepared to let anyone, especially not Joe, wreck her hard-won emotional stability.

Hours later, after a busier than expected day, Rhianna said goodbye to Lizzie and Toby, thanking them for staying on and helping her clear up the pub. Toby was a university student, home for the holidays, and worked at the pub during the holiday seasons. The young man had a good sense of humour and was great with the locals. The reason for the hectic day was the sudden and unexpected appearance of the sun. In fact, it had had nowhere to hide, without a cloud in the sky all day. It had brought day trippers flocking to Kittiwake Cove, in addition to the holidaymakers already staying in the village for Easter. She'd briefly seen Joe returning for his wetsuit around midday, but otherwise she hadn't seen or spoken to him all day.

More than ready for bed, Rhianna was just about to head over to her apartment when Joe appeared, smelling of salt water with a hint of wood smoke. Even in his tired and ruffled state, Rhianna couldn't stop herself noticing how good he looked.

"Hey," he said. He came around the bar, picked up a glass and helped himself to a whisky. "Want one?"

"No, thanks, I'm exhausted. It's been heaving in here all day. I should be heading off."

"Please, stay. Don't let an old man drink on his own." Joe's eyes were glazed, showing he'd been drinking. He squeezed past Rhianna behind the bar, tortuously close, whisky on his breath, then went through the open hatch to perch on a stool on the other side.

"Kerenza's upstairs…" she said, hesitantly. She'd hardly seen Kerenza all day either, which had suited her.

Joe rubbed his free hand down his face and let out a groan. "Don't remind me. Please, stay, tell me about your day." Joe reached a hand across the bar and placed it on Rhianna's, his palm hot.

With a nod, reluctant to take her hand away from the warmth of Joe's, Rhianna grabbed a glass, scooped in some ice, and poured a measure of Baileys. She had been bought a drink during the day by a customer, so she might as well take it.

She sat beside Joe, both leaning on the bar. This way she didn't have to look him in the eye too regularly. She'd been standing most of the day, and now, stopping and putting her feet up, the tiredness washed over her.

"So, how was your day?" Joe asked, once Rhianna was sitting beside him. However busy he'd been today, she'd been in his thoughts — only because he felt bad about leaving her to run his pub. Obviously.

"Hectic." Rhianna sipped her Baileys. He watched as she licked her lower lip.

"I'm sorry. This is so unfair of me."

"It's okay. I could do with the money. And I did have a couple of quiet moments in the morning when I was able to do some work for the bistro."

"Really?"

"Yes, came up with a couple of recipe ideas, with Ricky's help. He was chief taster."

"Oh, good." Joe nodded. Curiosity got the better of him. He kept his gaze forward, staring at the optics. "Was Nick in?"

"Yes, he came in for a couple of pints. Why?"

Joe shook his head and shrugged nonchalantly. "No reason."

"So how was your day? You do look tired," Rhianna said, concern etched on her face.

He turned, wanting to take in her pretty face. He smiled. "I spent the afternoon in the sea with Chloe, teaching her to surf. Daisy and Scarlett came in for a bit, but they're still small. They got cold quickly. Whereas Chloe, you'd think she was my daughter. I couldn't get her out of the water." He gave an involuntary yawn.

"Sounds like she wore you out."

Joe chuckled, then took another sip from his glass. "Yeah. Tonight was nice too." Getting off his stool, he went and poured another shot of whisky, and gave Rhianna another Baileys. He felt guilty for leaving Rhianna to manage the pub on such a busy day and for getting back from his parents' house so late, having fallen asleep by the firepit. But he hadn't wanted to come back too early, as he was keen to avoid Kerenza as much as possible. Despite his tiredness, he wanted to sit and talk with Rhianna. "Heather told me she's going to set Sam up on an online dating website once he's moved. She wants to get him out more."

"Really? Does he know?"

Joe chuckled. "Not yet."

"Oh, Joe." Rhianna laughed with him.

"Thanks for today." Joe saw Rhianna's hand resting on the bar and took it, giving it a squeeze. Touching her felt so good. "I am grateful." He stood up. "Right, we'd better go to bed," Joe said. He realised he was still holding her hand. He let it go reluctantly. "You know I mean you in your bed, me in mine."

"Yes, Joe, I know perfectly well that's what you meant. After all, you have Kerenza waiting for you upstairs." She kissed him on the cheek and he caught the scent of her sweet, floral perfume. "Goodnight."

After Rhianna had gone, Joe stood rooted to the spot. Damn! He should have contradicted her. He should have put her straight, right there, but stupidly he had missed the opportunity of explaining that Kerenza was sleeping in the spare room. What an idiot he was.

He badly wanted his bed. He just hoped Kerenza wasn't already in it.

CHAPTER 11: MUDSLIDE

Easter Sunday dawned bright and sunny, and the lovely weather brought tourists and locals alike flocking to the pub. They had been run off their feet all day. And now Rhianna had the added stress of the band Joe had booked turning up at around seven to set up. They had cleared the tables from the bay window to make a stage area, and the four band members were busy assembling their drum kit, mics, guitar stands and PA system and doing sound checks.

Once again, Rhianna had not seen much of Joe, apart from a brief morning handover. It showed how dedicated he was to his family. She didn't doubt that, given the amount he helped his mother and father, and now he was prepared to drop everything to be with his brother and sister. It was admirable.

Plenty of regulars, including Nick and Will, entered the pub, adding to the congestion. Rhianna had never seen The Cormorant so busy.

Liam and Tilly arrived next, and by the smiles on their faces, and the sparkle on Tilly's ring finger, Rhianna knew what the gallery owner was about to say.

"Liam's just proposed to me! We've come to celebrate," Tilly said, excitedly showing off her ring. Liam and Nick shook hands, Nick giving him a discreet wink. Rhianna wondered if Tilly was aware that she and Nick were in on the big secret. Congratulations were offered generously all round.

"Let me get you both a drink," Nick said, pulling a twenty-pound note from his wallet.

"Oh, thanks, but I can't have alcohol." Subconsciously, Tilly rubbed her stomach.

"I'll make you up a mocktail so that you can have something special too," Rhianna said.

"Oh, great."

"Rhianna, get a drink for yourself." Nick handed her the cash.

She shook her head. "No, I'm all right, but thank you, Nick." What was going on? Had he forgotten to take his 'arrogant dick' pill? He was being friendly towards Liam, and attentive to Tilly. Rhianna had never seen him being so … *nice*. Was this just another tactic to get in her knickers?

"Take a drink. Even if you don't get to have it until after closing." Nick smiled.

"Okay, I will. Thank you." She took it for a Baileys. It had worked well as a nightcap with Joe.

Just as she was thinking of Joe, he walked into the pub, accompanied by two men and a woman who Rhianna assumed were his brother and sister and her husband. Rhianna gave him a smile as she rapidly made a mocktail for Tilly, remembering an old recipe from her days as a cocktail waitress, poured Liam a pint and ran everything through the till. Before he could reach the bar, Joe was accosted by Tilly and Liam, sharing their news, and he introduced them to his family. Rhianna, stuck on the other side of the bar, felt left out. But was it really her place to be included? And why did her stomach fill with butterflies every time she saw Joe? She had to get a grip.

"Rhianna, Rhianna, come here a minute?" Joe was calling her.

There were a couple of people waiting to be served, and Rhianna was torn between her duty to customers and wanting to see Joe.

"I got this." Lizzie appeared beside Rhianna and went off to serve the customers.

Rhianna wiped her hands on a tea towel, more from nerves rather than because they were sticky, and made her way towards Joe and his family.

"Hey, Rhianna, this is my brother Sam. And this is my sister Heather and her husband Tom." They all shook hands, nodded and smiled. The usual nervous introductions. There was no doubt Sam was Joe's brother, although he had shorter hair with more flecks of grey, and was of slimmer build and maybe an inch shorter than Joe. He definitely looked like a professional, in contrast to his surfer brother. Heather was a mix of the two, and as beautiful as they were handsome. Her husband was a mountain behind her. The Rock with hair.

"So, what would everyone like to drink?" Joe asked, clapping his hands together.

Rhianna took the opportunity to dive back behind the bar, and to the safety of serving customers. As she went to drop the hatch, Joe followed.

"I'll sort my family out. You carry on; it's way busier in here than I thought," he said, as they both reached for the same wine bottle in the fridge. For a moment their hands touched, a shock of warmth against the chill of the glass bottle. Even over the smell of food and beer, the typical pub smell, Rhianna caught the scent of Joe's aftershave…

In an effort to regain her composure, Rhianna turned and started serving another waiting customer as Joe poured his brother and brother-in-law's pints.

"Has it been this busy all day?" he asked.

"Yes, pretty much. The sunshine brings in the punters."

Rhianna noticed that Kerenza had appeared and was now propping up the bar alongside Liam, Tilly and Nick. She was wearing skin-tight black leather trousers and a black sparkly top, which accentuated her tall, slender figure. She was watching Joe, who, if Rhianna wasn't mistaken, was ignoring her, or pretending he hadn't seen her. Then, unable to ignore Kerenza's stare, he looked up and gave her a feeble smile before turning his attention back to pulling pints. Rhianna didn't know what to think. Surely Joe would treat the woman he was sleeping with better? She imagined such treatment from Nick, but not from Joe.

The band started playing, which raised the noise level, making it very hard to hear what customers wanted to order. It meant raising her own voice, and Rhianna could feel her throat getting sore. Joe stayed behind the bar most of the evening, helping to serve. They certainly needed the extra pair of hands. He stole moments to talk to his family, but he was soon back working beside her and Lizzie. Rhianna had never worked alongside him like this. As she learned to relax with Joe behind the bar, her guard dropped, and they started to joke and tease more. They were both too busy to pay attention to Kerenza's sulky looks. Rhianna couldn't understand why Joe seemed to be deliberately ignoring Kerenza. He didn't even appear bothered when she hooked up with Nick and they started dancing together as the band played a lively, upbeat Ed Sheeran song.

The music made it fun behind the bar too, because Rhianna couldn't help dancing, even if it was just tapping her feet or swaying her hips slightly. At one point she was bumping hips with Joe, then Lizzie, and singing along. She wasn't even drunk, just high on the music and the atmosphere, and the proximity of Joe…

The slightest touch from him, if they bumped into one another in the narrow bar area, or if he put a hand on her arm or shoulder to reach past her, sent her insides crazy. Every time he got close, the intoxicating smell of him played havoc with the rest of her senses.

The pub was so packed that even Ricky, after he'd closed the kitchen, came out to help, clearing tables of empty glasses and loading the dishwasher. Once the band had played their final song, the lights went up, and the pub gradually started to empty. Exhaustion was overtaking Rhianna now, and she wasn't sure how much longer she could stand on her feet. Joe said his goodbyes to his family and remained behind with Lizzie and Rhianna, clearing tables and wiping them down, ready for the next day. Rhianna had noticed Kerenza leaving with Nick, wearing his jacket. Had Joe noticed? Did he care? Rhianna couldn't believe he could sleep with a woman and then just let her go like that.

Now there was less to do, and the band were almost packed away, Joe let Lizzie and Ricky leave, bolting the side door behind them. The clock over the bar read midnight.

"Rhianna, you can head off now. I'll finish off. You've worked your socks off."

"Thanks for giving us a hand tonight, Joe."

"No need to thank me. There was no way I wasn't going to help. I hadn't imagined it would get so busy. In the summer, yes, but not Easter."

Rhianna scooped some ice into the cocktail shaker and measured out the Baileys Nick had bought her earlier in the evening. She'd had other drinks bought for her throughout the evening, so she figured they covered enough to make a Mudslide. She added vodka and Kahlúa and shook. Joe looked askance. "Don't worry, Nick bought me a drink. As did many others. And I think I need this to help me sleep. Even though I'm so tired, I don't think my brain will switch off immediately."

"Yeah, I know what you mean. I might join you. Sam bought me a drink and I never got to have it."

"Join me —" she gestured to the shaker — "or a whisky?"

"Whisky, please."

Rhianna retrieved another tumbler and put it under the whisky optic. She'd already noted from the night before that Joe liked it neat without ice. After pouring out her drink into a tumbler, adding some of the ice from the shaker, she sat down on the stool next to Joe. She could do this. Just be his friend.

"Tonight was fun with the band," she said. They chinked glasses, then sipped their drinks. The warmth of the creamy liquid sliding down her throat helped Rhianna start to relax.

"Yeah, you're a great little mover."

"So are you." Rhianna swirled the ice around her glass. "Joe…?"

"Yes?"

"Er, you do know Kerenza's gone home with Nick tonight?"

Joe shrugged. "She's a free agent."

"So, it doesn't bother you?"

"No, why should it?"

Rhianna frowned, shocked at his indifference and not knowing what to say. Maybe her morals were different to his? "But she's staying with you?"

"Yeah, but at least it might mean I get a decent night's sleep tonight."

Rhianna finished her drink, suddenly feeling the need for her own bed and not wanting to be around Joe any longer. Her delight in his company was replaced by anger. How could he so easily sleep with a woman and then discard her? Joe must have sensed her sudden haste to get away, because he grabbed her hand.

"Don't go yet."

"Sorry, Joe, I'm shattered. See you tomorrow." She snatched her hand away and headed towards the door.

As she let herself into her apartment, she reflected that the sooner she could move into her new home the better. She needed to concentrate on setting up her bistro and getting her life back on track. Joe would never be right for her.

CHAPTER 12: STORM AT SEA

Stifling a yawn, Rhianna strolled into the pub late on Monday morning ready for her last full shift of the Easter weekend. Kerenza was sitting at the bar nursing a steaming cappuccino and flicking through a magazine. Her suitcase stood beside her stool and she was dressed in a burgundy trouser suit, rather than the casual attire she'd been wearing over the weekend.

"Hey," Kerenza said, looking up at Rhianna. She closed the magazine.

"Hey." Rhianna walked through to the other side of the bar.

"Joe said I should talk to you before I leave. You're opening a bistro?"

Rhianna frowned. Had she been the subject of their pillow talk? "Did he?"

"Well, Nick actually mentioned it last night, and I asked Joe this morning."

"Oh."

"Joe said he was going to say something, but just hadn't had a chance. I'm a sales rep for a Cornish brewery. So, yeah, grab a coffee and we can run through a few things if you like."

"OK, I'll just check if Joe minds." Rhianna looked around for him.

"Don't worry, he suggested I talk to you now. He's cool. I think he's already got the pub ready for opening."

Rhianna made herself a latte, fancying a milky coffee and knowing it would keep her fuller for longer with a busy morning ahead of her. The two women sat at the table by the window.

"The brewery I work for is based near Penzance," Kerenza said. She'd opened a notebook and had her pen poised. "My job is visiting my customers as well as searching out new pubs and restaurants to drum up trade."

Rhianna nodded and listened, a little guilty she'd not properly spoken with Kerenza until now.

"I usually show my face regularly to discuss stock levels, highlight promotions, etc. I have other pubs like Joe's that put me up." She smiled mischievously as she said the last words. "So tell me a little about your bistro?"

"On the drinks side of things, I want to create some signature cocktails as well as sell locally brewed beverages like beers and ciders," Rhianna said eagerly.

"Sounds perfect."

"Joe did take me to a winery, and I was thinking of using them for some of my wines." When Rhianna gave the winery's name, Kerenza nodded approvingly. They soon became deep in conversation. Kerenza was a fount of knowledge, and talking business with her softened Rhianna's opinion of her. It wasn't Kerenza's fault she had a relationship with Joe that Rhianna didn't like. Sharing a bed with Joe didn't make Kerenza a bad person. Or with Nick… It just proved what both men were like.

"I think we'll be ideal for your bistro, as the brewery offers local bottled ciders and beers," Kerenza said. "We also supply some wines. We have a partnership with a supplier." Kerenza handed Rhianna a brochure.

"This looks perfect. I want to keep as much of my produce as possible, including the beverages, locally sourced." Rhianna eagerly flicked through the pages.

"We even produce a variety of gins." Kerenza pointed them out in the brochure.

"Oh, cool, loads of different flavours." Rhianna envisaged the fancy coloured bottles on display behind her top floor bar. They would help create a sophisticated and relaxed ambience for sipping cocktails and socialising.

After an hour, they shook hands with a deal in place for the brewery to supply a variety of gins, beers and ciders.

Wheeling her suitcase towards the door, Kerenza said to Rhianna, "Just give me a call if you need anything else." Then she looked at Joe, who was giving her a non-committal wave from behind the bar. "See you again, Joe."

"You are always welcome here, Kerenza," he said, smiling.

"I'll take you up on that, unless I get a better offer." Kerenza winked, then turned and headed out of the door.

Joe looked up at the clock behind the bar. It was nearly midday. "Shit, I didn't realise the time. I'd better head down to the B&B." He wiped his hands on a towel and grabbed his keys.

"Yes, thanks for hanging on while I spoke with Kerenza," Rhianna said. "I didn't realise it would take so long."

"No problem. I should have got you two speaking sooner." Was Joe miffed that it had been Nick who'd mentioned Rhianna to Kerenza and not him?

"It's okay, you've been busy with your family. When do they go home?"

"Tomorrow." He must have read Rhianna's expression of panic, because he quickly added, "Don't worry, I will cover tomorrow. I've told them there's only so much I can ask you to do."

"I've barely been here a month and I'm practically running your pub!" Rhianna said teasingly.

"And I will always be eternally grateful." Joe rested his hand on her shoulder and paused. Panic rose inside her that he might try to kiss her, but he just nodded and headed off, leaving Rhianna to manage his pub.

On Tuesday morning Rhianna awoke to her mobile ringing. She'd forgotten to put it on silent, even though she'd turned off all her alarms. After the bank holiday weekend, and an extremely late night closing up the pub, she felt she deserved a lie-in. She had the whole day to herself. That didn't mean she could laze around — there was the small matter of a bistro to plan — but she had been hoping for a longer lie-in than this.

It was Justine, her solicitor.

"Hello, Rhianna speaking," Rhianna answered blearily, seeing it was eight-thirty-seven on her phone. She should probably get up. Only it felt earlier than that to her body.

"Hello, Rhianna, it's Justine here. I'm just phoning to say there's been a problem with your house sale. Your buyers have pulled out, so that means the chain has broken down."

"What do you mean my buyers? Glyn's buying the house!" Rhianna shot out of bed.

"All I can say is I've been informed by his solicitor that he no longer wishes to proceed with buying you out."

"What! But what about the house I'm buying?" Panic rose within Rhianna.

"Well, I'll talk to the vendor's solicitors, to see if they can hold on until you get another buyer, then it shouldn't affect anything, but they can sell to another buyer if they choose."

Rhianna knew this too. At the time, the estate agent had stressed that the house had received a lot of interest, so she'd offered the asking price.

Her searches were done. Two weeks ago, Justine had informed her they'd soon all be ready to exchange. Rhianna now paced her bedroom, her heart beating rapidly.

"I don't understand what's happened." Rhianna rubbed her temples.

"You might need to talk to your partner about that."

"Glyn is no longer my partner! Hence he is buying me out." This had been going on too long now. Her left hand balled into a fist. Her temples ached with tension and she could feel the stress creeping up her spine. She couldn't afford to lose this house. She was shouting at poor Justine. It wasn't her fault. "I'm sorry. Please inform Glyn's solicitors that I expect him to put the house on the market immediately if he can't afford to buy me out."

She couldn't face phoning Glyn herself and asking what the hell was going on.

For the rest of the day, Rhianna tried her best to concentrate on the bistro: planning menus, testing recipes, phoning the job centre to advertise positions, all sorts of things that needed ticking off her to-do list. But later that afternoon, she received the dreaded telephone call she had hoped she wouldn't receive. It was from the estate agents in Cornwall, informing her that the vendors of the house she was buying did not want to wait as they could lose the house they were buying, and that another buyer had already been found. Rhianna had lost her new home.

"Hey, I would have thought you'd had enough of this place." Joe looked up to see Rhianna walking into the pub. He hadn't been expecting to see her at all today as she'd worked all weekend for him, but his spirits lifted upon seeing her. He'd missed spending time with her. He frowned; her face was pale and sombre. The redness around her puffy eyes meant she must have been crying. He felt a prickle of anxiety.

Before he could ask, Rhianna demanded, "A large gin and tonic. Please…" she added, as if remembering her manners.

Joe made her drink. He glanced at the clock: it wasn't even six. "Everything okay?" He could see from the glistening of her eyes that she was close to tears. "A little early for that. It is a school night."

"It's the Easter holidays," she retorted. "Care to join me?" He poured himself a glass of red wine.

"What's up?"

"What's up, you ask?" She took a large gulp of her drink. Her tone was laced with anger, bitterness and sadness. "My shit of an ex has pulled out of buying out my share of our house. So, in turn, the chain has broken down, and I've now lost the little house on the outskirts of Kittiwake Cove I was buying — nothing fancy, but it would have been home. My home. It would have been perfect."

"Shit." Joe drank his wine. "Why would he do that?"

"I don't know. One more way to try to control me? Bastard." Rhianna shrugged as a tear escaped her eye. She wiped her face. "So at the end of the month, when I am due to leave Oystercatcher, I have nowhere to live."

"Hey, I won't let you go homeless." Leaning across the bar, Joe rested a hand on her shoulder.

Rhianna bent her cheek to its warmth. Her eyes widened excitedly, her spirits lifting. "So, can I rent it for another month?"

"Ah, no," he said, grimacing. "It's booked from May onwards. That's the beauty of Kittiwake Cove; everyone wants to stay here." Joe watched her shoulders slump.

"Oh, what am I going to do? I can't sleep in the bistro … or I can, I suppose, if worst comes to worst. Nobody need know…" She exhaled with a groan. "I don't need this right now."

Joe could see tears forming as she looked up to the ceiling, taking a deep breath. He made his way round the bar and pulled her into a hug. "Hey, I have a spare room in my flat above the pub. You're more than welcome to stay there."

He'd said it. Without even thinking, he'd said it. He hadn't said 'move in with me'. That's not what she was doing. She would be staying in the spare room until she found a new home. He wouldn't see her go homeless. And at this very moment, Rhianna needed a friend and some hope that all was not lost. She pulled out of his embrace and shook her head. "No, I can't impose on you like that."

"Rhianna, you have enough to worry about with the opening of the bistro. Let me take one stress off your shoulders. You can work out where to live in your own time, then."

She frowned over her glass, holding it to her lips. "Are you sure?" Her beautiful green eyes still glistened. It made Joe's heart ache to see her so upset.

"Yes, of course. I'm letting you borrow my Range Rover; you might as well help yourself to my spare room," he said jovially. He wanted to lift the tension. "I'll worry when I start giving you my credit card." For a moment Rhianna remained solemn, but then a smile lifted her lips.

"Thank you, Joe. I don't know what I'd do without you." She hugged him. He wrapped his arms around her, reciprocating the hug. She felt so good in his arms. And she smelt amazing too, her floral scent now familiar to him. Too familiar; it jogged his memory back to *that* summer... Splashing around in the surf, sex on the beach under the moonlight. They'd had such fun together.

If he'd thought things had been difficult with Kerenza under his roof this weekend, they were going to get a whole lot harder once Rhianna moved in.

CHAPTER 13: RISING SUN

"Are you sure you don't mind letting me stay in your flat?" Rhianna said, carrying a cardboard box up the stairs to Joe's flat.

"For the umpteenth time, Rhianna. No." Joe sighed. He was in front of her, carrying another box. He turned to look at her, his handsome face stern.

It was early in the morning on the last Friday of April, and Rhianna's lease of Oystercatcher was at an end. Joe was helping her move her stuff into his flat.

Ever since accepting Joe's offer, Rhianna had been having doubts about whether it had been a good idea to accept, because it meant living even closer to Joe. But what else could she do? She wasn't in a position to make an offer on another property until she released the money from the house she owned with Glyn. And he seemed to be intent on blocking any progress on that front. Wait until she got her hands on him…

She couldn't bear to call him. The very idea left her cold. Was he doing this to retain control over her? Fearing she'd become irrational and shout down the phone, and he'd bully her back, she was letting her solicitor deal with it. That way it stayed in professional hands. If Glyn wasn't prepared to buy her out, he had to agree to put the house on the market.

Other B&Bs or holiday homes weren't an option either; she'd have to move around every few days or so, because most places had bookings already in place. And they'd be expensive now, at high season rates. If she thought about it too much, it depressed her. Her belongings would remain in storage for even longer. And to rent a property, she'd need to pay a deposit up front, and stay a minimum of six months. Staying with Joe was her best option short-term, and at such short notice.

As she'd packed her belongings, she'd been surprised how much she'd accumulated over the past six weeks. She'd only arrived in Kittiwake Cove with a rucksack and a holdall. Most of her newly acquired belongings were food. Or bottles of alcohol. "For testing new cocktails," she'd explained to Joe when he'd looked askance at the contents of the box he was carrying.

"You've got a pub right next door!"

"I can't use your booze to try out new recipes."

They each placed their boxes in the small kitchen. Joe's open-plan flat was clean and tidy, and a proper bachelor pad with minimal furniture and large flatscreen TV on the wall in the lounge-diner. Rhianna could see how the rooms followed the shape of the pub below. The only decorations on the plain white walls were some framed surfing photographs and a painting of Kittiwake Cove.

"Bathroom's there." Joe pointed in the direction of an open door, where Rhianna could see the white bathroom suite. The toilet seat was up. "And this is the spare room. Make yourself at home."

The room was larger than Rhianna expected, and was furnished with a double bed, a large wardrobe, a chest of drawers and two cabinets either side of the bed, all white painted wood. It looked like a bedroom in a showroom, with fewer cushions and ornaments. The dormer window let in plenty of light. The duvet cover on the double bed had black and white stripes, and the overall effect was very masculine, clean-cut and minimal, like the rest of the flat. A single picture of a surfer going through the tube of a wave hung above the bed.

"If you want to make it a bit more you, I don't mind. You can stay as long as you need to." Joe leaned against the doorframe. "Kerenza always says the flat needs a woman's touch."

Rhianna swallowed at Kerenza's name. It still gave her a stab of jealousy. "It's fine, Joe. I'm so grateful for your help."

"Well, you did help me with the pub, so I'd say it's the least I can do." He patted her shoulder. "I'll put the kettle on."

Rhianna emptied her holdall and rucksack, either hanging clothes or folding them and placing them in the chest of drawers. She placed her toiletries and make-up on top of the chest. It would do as a dressing table. Once organised, she joined Joe in the kitchen. He was leaning casually against the worktop, his legs crossed at the ankle, looking relaxed as always. His face was already tanned from surfing regularly.

"I can't believe this is my last weekend working in the pub," Rhianna said, taking the mug of coffee Joe handed her. She felt a flutter of anxiety. Very soon she would be running her own bistro. Mixed feelings assaulted her: apprehension that she would fail, mingled with the excitement of doing something for herself, on her own, following her dream — without Glyn filling her with self-doubt.

"Yeah, I know. I've organised cover. This time of year, everyone pops out of the woodwork wanting a holiday job," Joe said. He straightened suddenly. "Oh, but you're not working on Sunday." Rhianna started to protest, but Joe held up his hand. "Before you say anything, Sheila and Martyn are having a party at Oceans. A farewell retirement party for the locals. You need to come."

"Oh, I don't know." Rhianna was hardly local — yet.

"Of course you should; they're friends of your family, right? Besides, I think they want to hand the keys over to you."

Rhianna felt her cheeks grow pink. "Oh, right."

"But I didn't tell you that."

"What do you mean?"

"It's supposed to be a surprise. They've roped me in to bring you along."

"Oh."

The last thing Rhianna wanted to be was the centre of attention. She had declined Martyn and Sheila's invitation earlier in the week. She had thought, in all honesty, she would need to work in the pub to cover for Joe. But it would be good for business if she got introduced to the locals as the new business owner. They'd be her customers as much as the holidaymakers.

On Saturday morning, Rhianna drove out to Wadebridge. It was far nicer and saved her so much time using Joe's Range Rover, rather than taking the bus, even if she did crunch the gears occasionally. Up with the rising sun, Joe had wanted an early morning surf and said she was free to use it — as he'd strutted around the flat, wetsuit half on, his bare torso on display. Rhianna had given herself a mental shake and grabbed the keys without a backward glance.

Wetsuits need a health warning. The sight of Joe in black neoprene sent her hormones into turmoil. But she would have to get used to this sight now that she was living with him. The man was a surfer, for goodness' sake.

Rhianna knew that once she was handed the keys to her new premises, life was going to get incredibly hectic with the bistro, so she wanted to make the most of today to potter around Wadebridge's high street. It felt liberating and refreshing to have this freedom. Joe had asked casually about her plans for the day, in stark contrast to the interrogation Glyn would have given her, as if she didn't know her own mind — "*Are you sure you want to do that? You'd be better doing this… Who are you meeting? Do I know them?*"

Parking up, she pushed Glyn from her mind and tried to focus on her mission for today, which was to look for inspiration and find things to decorate her bistro.

First, she found a shop selling glassware. There were some miniature old-fashioned glass milk bottles that she particularly liked. Rhianna thought they'd make perfect posy vases for the tables, or she could use them for serving milk in. She placed an order.

In another gift shop she found wall plaques. One read, 'Life's Better in Flip Flops' and another, 'Let The Fun Be Gin' but 'I Don't Have A Problem With Coffee, I Have A Problem Without It' was her favourite. She picked out some she thought would be suitable for the bistro and the top-floor cocktail lounge.

Passing a surf shop, she chose a gift for Joe. She was well aware he was in her thoughts but tried to convince herself that it was simply because he had been so helpful and such a good friend. She just wanted to say thank you, that was all. Besides, sleeping with him could ruin their friendship, and she didn't want to risk that. Anyway, she'd already slept with him, so it wasn't as if she was missing out.

That thought didn't make her reasons for not sleeping with Joe any more convincing, because she remembered how much fun it had been.

You'll get hurt.

She gave her head a shake. Soon she would be running a restaurant. Would that make her feel more like a local in

Kittiwake Cove? She still felt like a tourist. If she could only find a home…

She walked past an estate agent, and wistfully browsed the houses advertised in the window. But there was no point looking until she heard from her solicitor that she could go ahead again.

Back in Kittiwake Cove, she parked the Range Rover in The Cormorant's car park and walked down the hill, breathing in the salty air and admiring the view. She wanted to call in on Tilly at her gallery, White Horses.

"Hey!" Tilly was standing at an easel busily painting and greeted Rhianna warmly. She dropped her brush into a jar of clear water, the paint swirling like blue ribbons of smoke.

"Hi, Tilly. I just wanted to look at some of your paintings and photographs. I'm looking for some artwork for the bistro." Rhianna took a closer look at the price of a watercolour she was admiring. Could she afford to buy original pieces like this? She might need her money for other, more important items.

"I was going to come and see you actually, Rhianna. I was wondering if I could hang some pictures in your bistro, with the price tag attached. Any paintings you sell, you can take a percentage of the sale."

"Oh, that sounds like a perfect solution. I'd love to buy some of your pictures for the bistro, but I'm not sure I can afford it yet."

"You can choose the ones you want in the bistro, the ones you think fit its ambience."

They happily perused pictures and paintings and agreed the percentage Rhianna would keep from any sales.

"See you tomorrow night at Sheila and Martyn's party!" Tilly beamed at Rhianna. She looked happy and glowing, and her slim figure was unchanged. No one would guess she was in the early stages of pregnancy.

"Yes, I'll be there, although it's for the local community and I'm not really a local."

"Don't be silly, of course you are."

Rhianna hugged Tilly, then walked happily up the hill back to The Cormorant.

The pub was quiet, so she was able to give Joe his gift straight away. "Just a little something to say thank you."

Joe pulled a light blue surf T-shirt out of the bag. The caption on it read: 'A bad day surfing is better than a good day working'. He gave an appreciative chuckle. "Hey, this is great. And true. But you didn't have to."

"I wanted to get you something. You've been so good to me."

They stood awkwardly, neither knowing what to do. Then, all of a sudden, Joe enveloped her in a great bear hug. "It's not a problem," he said, his breath warm on her neck.

Rhianna stayed in his arms possibly a moment too long. She caught his scent and felt the firmness of his body against hers, and once again she fought with herself; she could handle a fling with Joe. She could.

No. She could not.

CHAPTER 14: B-52

"Rhianna, are you ready?" Joe knocked gently on the spare bedroom door. Oystercatcher was now filled with holidaymakers. It felt strange not seeing Rhianna pop out from the door now. And she no longer worked for him. Last night they'd shared a nightcap in the pub in honour of Rhianna's last shift at The Cormorant.

But it wasn't goodbye, as she kept repeating, and they had toasted new beginnings.

He was relieved that having Rhianna under his roof appeared to be working fine. At least she didn't make things awkward, like Kerenza had, and parade around in her lacy underwear. However, it had only been two days. *Don't speak too soon, Joe.*

"Two minutes!" Rhianna called from behind the door. He could hear the hairdryer blowing. He walked back to the sofa and sat down. He was wearing his best jeans for the occasion and a casual short-sleeved shirt with a collar, which he kept running his hand around to ensure it was straight. He wasn't used to collars.

Sunday evening had arrived. Sheila and Martyn were holding a party at Oceans, to say a final farewell to the restaurant they'd run for nearly twenty-five years. Everyone in the town was invited to their retirement bash.

Rhianna emerged from her bedroom and he dropped the magazine he'd been idly flicking through onto the coffee table. He was speechless. Who was this stunning woman standing in his lounge? Rhianna always looked pretty, but with heavier make-up and her honey-blonde hair straightened and glossy, flowing over her shoulders, she looked incredible. She was wearing skinny jeans, which accentuated her slender legs, and a cream top with a floral print and a plunging V-neck to show a little cleavage. Joe swallowed. Suddenly, sharing his flat with Rhianna felt a lot more complicated.

"Will I do?" she asked, tucking a strand of hair behind her ear, an earring sparkling.

"Do? Of course you'll do." She looked amazing. He got to his feet, unable to find the appropriate words to tell her this. His tongue was tied. What words would be appropriate for a woman he had no relationship ties with and to whom he wouldn't want to give the wrong impression? He'd never seen her so dressed up. He felt slightly underdressed now. Good job he'd opted for shoes and not trainers, or worse, flipflops. She was wearing heels, which made her much taller. Not as tall as him, but her face was closer to his. "I can see me fending off half the men in Kittiwake Cove."

She laughed and nudged him playfully. "Don't be silly."

"Just please stay away from Nick."

"Now you're being ridiculous. Shall we go?" she said, fetching a small clutch bag and slipping her mobile phone into it.

It was a good job she didn't walk around his apartment this dressed up all the time. Who was he kidding? She looked hot in pyjamas. "Will you be all right walking down that hill in those shoes?" Joe said as they walked out of the pub, having said goodbye to Ricky, Toby and Lizzie, who were manning the bar for the evening.

"I'll be fine." But she grabbed his arm all the same. It felt nice, natural even.

But every time he imagined being more than just friends with Rhianna, kissing her, making love to her, he saw Alannah … following her dream and, in turn, breaking his heart.

Rhianna released Joe's arm once they were down the hill. She could see herself climbing back up it barefoot later in the evening. "You can give me a piggyback on the way home," she said, nudging him teasingly.

Joe laughed. "You might need to give me a piggyback later. Depends how much we drink."

They climbed the steel stairs up to the entrance of Oceans, Rhianna's heels clanging, to find the party in full swing. They were greeted by Martyn, smartly dressed in a suit with waistcoat and tie, holding a tray of drinks. With a smile, he handed them each a glass of Prosecco. Joe clinked flutes with Rhianna before they took a sip.

"I've got a surprise for you, Rhianna," Martyn said merrily. He looked to his right and before Rhianna could say anything, her mother and father appeared, their arms outstretched to hug her.

"Mum! Dad!" she said, surprise, happiness and love for her parents filling her whole being. Joe took her glass off her as she hugged and kissed her parents, exchanging greetings and questions. They'd arrived in Kittiwake Cove sometime this afternoon. She turned to Joe. "Did you know about this?"

"Mum might have mentioned something. They're staying at the B&B." Joe winked.

"You must be Joe. Rose has been filling us in." Gareth, Rhianna's dad, shook Joe's hand. "I'm grateful that you didn't let my daughter go homeless."

"Think nothing of it." Joe shrugged, then turned to Rhianna's mum, Beatrice, and greeted her with a kiss on the cheek.

"And how long are you staying?" Rhianna couldn't believe her parents were here. Suddenly, all the stress and worry over Glyn and losing the house faded into insignificance.

"Unfortunately, we can't stay too long. The restaurant needs manning," Gareth said. "We just wanted to see how our baby girl is settling into her new life."

"Ah, Dad! Let me introduce you to some of my new friends," Rhianna said, looping her arm through her father's. Tonight would give her an opportunity to see the premises at night, filled with people, and to get a feel for the ambience of the building.

There was a buffet laid out in the main restaurant area where Sheila was flitting about, toing and froing from the kitchen in a sparkly navy dress. She'd already caught up with Rhianna's parents, but stopped briefly to greet Rhianna and Joe, kissing them both on the cheek. She left red lipstick on Joe's cheek, and Rhianna gently rubbed it off, his freshly shaved face smooth under her thumb.

She awkwardly dropped her hand after, fearing people, including her parents, would think that as they'd come together, they *were* together.

The music was somewhat quieter here, which enabled people to chat while tucking into their food. There was a DJ in the conservatory, where a dancefloor was laid. Band equipment was set up, so it looked as if there would be some live music too. The sound spilled into the adjoining back room, which was laid out as a seating area with tables and chairs. The stairway to the top floor was roped off.

"I can't believe this is mine as of the first of May," Rhianna said over the din. "I'm a little nervous."

"You'll be great. This place will be amazing with your ideas," Joe replied.

Gareth concurred with Joe. He had every confidence in her. "Do you want another drink?" he asked. They'd all finished their bubbly.

"Yes, go on, please." Rhianna said. "We'll wait here." Gareth went with Joe to fetch more drinks, while Rhianna waited in the back room with her mother. From their table, they could watch the DJ and the people on the dancefloor in the conservatory.

"Hey, Rhianna, glad you came," Tilly said, approaching, holding Liam's hand. They chatted as best they could over the noise, filling Liam in on their plan to hang some of Tilly's pictures in the bistro.

"Hey, look who I found at the bar." Joe returned with a glass of Prosecco for Rhianna and a pint for himself. Gareth handed Beatrice her drink. They were accompanied by a younger man, somewhere in his late twenties but similar in looks and stature to Joe. "Rhianna, this is Tristan, my cousin. He's from the posh side of the family and runs the Trenouth Manor estate." Tristan, knowing he was being teased, played along, giving a royal wave before shaking Rhianna's free hand, then her mum's. "He's running his dad's estate now. Mum inherited the farmhouse, which she was more than happy with, and her older brother inherited the estate. Tristan has turned it around as a business, just as Mum has with the farmhouse, so they can afford to keep it. Tristan uses it for functions, business events, things like that. He also runs a team-building company, who use Liam and me for coasteering and surf sessions."

Rhianna nodded and shook his hand.

"Lovely to meet you," Tristan said.

"Hey, you know Tilly and Liam need a wedding venue," Joe said, tapping his cousin's arm.

"Yes, we met the other day." Tristan gave them a smile.

"And it's not that Trenouth Manor isn't lovely, but it's too big for what we want." Tilly sipped her orange juice coyly. "And out of our price range."

"Yeah, somewhere like this place would be more our thing," Liam said. He gazed around the room and into the conservatory.

"There you go, Rhianna, your first wedding event." Joe beamed at her. She spluttered on her drink.

"Oh, er…"

"Might be a good way to make ends meet, especially in the winter months," her father said in her ear.

"Oh my God, this place would be perfect. We could have the ceremony here and everything." Tilly jumped up and down excitedly, clapping her hands. She turned adoringly to her fiancé, and Liam nodded his agreement, wrapping an arm around her waist.

"I think I'd need to apply to the local council for a wedding licence." Rhianna had thought about weddings, but had wanted to get the bistro up and running first before thinking of it as a wedding venue.

"Well, Tristan can help you with all that, can't you, mate?" Joe said eagerly.

"Yeah, of course."

Rhianna spent the next hour discussing ideas with Tilly and Liam, with input from Tristan.

"When do you think you'd like to get married?"

"Around the beginning of June, I'll be twelve weeks. I'd like to get married before I start to show," Tilly said, looking at Liam, then back to Rhianna.

"End of June latest, then?" Rhianna frowned, but Tristan, ever confident, just like Joe, nudged her.

"It's doable," Tristan said.

"I don't even own the place yet!"

Tilly laughed. "Let's enjoy this evening, and arrange a meeting once you do own the place. We can decide on a date then."

Rhianna's nerves calmed and she nodded.

Joe and Gareth returned with more drinks for everyone, including another glass of bubbly for Rhianna.

"At this rate you will be giving me that piggyback," she said as she took the flute from Joe.

"I've got your back." There was a twinkle in his eye. He ushered two more people into the group of friends. "Rhianna, this is my mum and dad, Rose and Charles." She'd heard so much about them but hadn't met them yet. She could see where Joe had inherited his good looks from. He had Rose's hazel eyes and her bright smile, but his wavy dark hair was his dad's. Only Charles's hair was more silvery-white than brown now. Tristan gave Rose a kiss on the cheek and shook Charles's hand. Rhianna followed suit, though she gave Charles a hug.

"Lovely to finally meet you, Rhianna," Rose said. "We've heard quite a bit about you." Rhianna noticed the meaningful glance Rose gave her son.

"Oh?"

"How you saved my bacon running the pub," Joe interjected, giving his mother a pointed look in return. After the introductions, they joined Rhianna's parents around the table.

Needing to visit the loos, Rhianna made her excuses and got up from the table. She weaved her way through the crowds of people and found the refuge of the ladies'. The music and the noise of people became instantly quieter as the door shut behind her. Before leaving, she ran her fingers through her hair and touched up her lipstick. After a final check of her appearance, making sure she didn't have black smudges under her eyes, she left the restroom and returned to the throng of people. So many locals. She recognised some faces from the pub and the shop, but it showed how big Kittiwake Cove really was.

"Hey, Rhianna!" Someone caught her arm. She looked up to see Olly smiling at her.

"Hi." She smiled back.

"This is my wife, Rachel." They nodded hellos. Rachel, heavily pregnant, was rubbing a six-month bump of a stomach. "And this is my little brother, Noah, who'll be helping me out with your bar."

Noah was taller than Olly by an inch or two, so the 'little' wasn't quite true anymore, but Olly had told her Noah was a few years younger than him. He was just as good-looking as Olly. This Olly hadn't told her. Noah had scruffy blond hair, surfer style, like his brother's, and blue-green eyes, more striking than Olly's. He swapped his pint into his left hand, wiped his right hand on his jeans then nervously shook Rhianna's.

"Hi. Yeah, I'll be doing the painting and decorating," he said.

"The bar is coming along nicely. As soon as you get the keys, we're set to start work," Olly said, leaning in so that Rhianna could hear him. The band had started up. It was the same band that had performed at The Cormorant at Easter. A lot more people were on the dancefloor now.

"It's only a couple of days away!" Rhianna said, excitedly. Though internally, self-doubt ate away at her in a 'what the hell were you thinking?' kind of way.

She was chatting with Noah, Olly and Rachel when Joe appeared, holding another glass of bubbly. He greeted the Rosdews with a friendly smile.

"Come on, the band's playing. Let's dance," Joe said.

"Where are my mum and dad?"

"They're fine, they're chatting with my parents."

"Oh, that's okay then. Noah, want to dance too?" Rhianna asked, feeling Joe tug at her arm. He shook his head, and Joe swept her off, through the crowd and onto the dancefloor. It felt good to be dancing with Joe, bringing back the memories of their time together three summers ago. As Joe twirled her around, making her laugh more and more, she noticed faces she recognised. Nick was standing at the edge of the dancefloor drinking a pint, deep in conversation with a group of people. Liam and Tilly were dancing, although Tilly, being pregnant and sober, was maybe a little less energetic about it than Liam. Even Ricky and Lizzie from The Cormorant were strutting their stuff.

Rhianna looked at Joe quizzically, and he shouted in her ear, "I told them to close the pub early if it was quiet and to come along."

Late in the evening, when Rhianna was definitely feeling the effects of the Prosecco, the band stopped playing and Sheila and Martyn took the microphone and stood on the stage. Everyone fell silent, and gathered around the dancefloor. There were hushed voices and the scraping of chairs.

"Martyn and I want to thank you all for coming tonight," Sheila said, as she wiped a tear from her cheek. "It's been so lovely to have so many of our friends and regulars under one roof for the evening. We leave this place with great sadness, as we've had so much fun running Oceans, but it is time for us to hang up our aprons — although Martyn insists he's keeping his." Everyone laughed, and Martyn bowed. "And we would like to take this opportunity, if you haven't met her already, to introduce you to the lovely new leaseholder, Rhianna." Sheila beckoned Rhianna. Joe gave her a nudge, and she nervously walked forward, hating the fact that all eyes were now upon her.

Martyn handed her his microphone.

"This is Rhianna, everyone!" Sheila said.

"Hi," Rhianna said hesitantly, hating how her voice echoed through a speaker. "Um, I didn't really prepare a speech." Her gaze darted nervously around the room, looking for some familiar faces in the crowd. Her dad blew her an encouraging kiss. "It will be very hard following in the footsteps of Sheila and Martyn, but I'm happy to announce that I will be renaming this place The Beach Front Bistro and we will be serving a mix of great food and cocktails." There was a loud cheer from the crowd. "Hopefully opening May half-term — whenever the hell that is!" It didn't matter how much she spoke, her nerves did not improve. "Anyway, I look forward to welcoming you all, but let's not stop the partying for my sake. To Sheila and Martyn!" Without hesitation, she handed the microphone back to Martyn and dashed back into the crowd to Joe, who gave her a reassuring hug. Noah was standing next to him and gave her an encouraging smile, too.

The party continued until the early hours, with everyone dancing and singing along to old classics, from The B-52s' 'Love Shack' to 'Walking on Sunshine' by Katrina and the Waves. By now, both Joe's and Rhianna's parents had left together to go back to Trenouth Cottage. Rhianna was relieved that she didn't have to worry about her mum and dad, and more importantly, that they wouldn't see her drunk. Trays of shots had circulated at one point, including some pretty lethal B-52s which contained a measure each of Baileys Irish Cream, Kahlúa coffee liqueur and Grand Marnier. These were Rhianna's idea, inspired by the song.

Eventually the band took over from the DJ to play their final songs, and an encore, and then it was time to leave. As the last of the partygoers departed, everyone said goodbye to one another, hugging, kissing and wobbling on heels, feet too sore to want to stay in them.

Joe caught Rhianna around the waist as she swayed and Noah took her elbow to steady her. Rhianna was still clinging to Joe as they approached the door, where Sheila and Martyn, the best hosts ever, were saying their final goodbyes.

Sheila kissed them both on the cheek. Martyn shook Joe's free hand, and kissed Rhianna. "Has our Joe finally found someone to settle down with? You two make a great couple," Sheila said, winking at Joe.

"Oh, no —"

"We're not together."

Rhianna and Joe said it in unison, hastily letting go of one another. Then they looked at each other and laughed, as if the suggestion was patently absurd.

Rhianna teetered slowly down the stairs, holding onto the metal handrail, Joe and Noah hovering around her as if she was some frail old lady. Her feet were so sore. And maybe she'd had too much to drink. But not so much that she couldn't walk. At the bottom of the steps a crowd had formed, still saying their goodnights. Rhianna desperately wanted to take her shoes off. She'd made the mistake of taking them off to dance, and now her feet screamed to be set free again.

There was more hand-shaking and backs being slapped by the guys.

"Night, Noah." Joe held out his hand.

"Night. See you next week, Rhianna," Noah said, giving her a wave goodbye.

"Yes, gosh, next week. Bye, Noah!" She took hold of Joe's arm. "Please can we go home now?"

"Of course," Joe said, patting her hand.

"You don't fancy giving me that piggyback, do you?" she laughed. He leaned forward in front of her, arms out to catch her legs, and she hopped onto his back. But they both wobbled tipsily, giggling hysterically, and Rhianna could see herself falling off. She shrieked with laughter, tapping his back. "Put me down! Put me down!"

When her feet hit the ground, she said, "Oh, sod it," and took off her shoes. The tarmac wasn't too bad under her feet. Occasionally she came across a stone and gave a yelp. They had the steep hill to climb, but what kept Rhianna going was the thought of her bed. And how much she wanted it.

The pub was dark and all locked up. A security light came on as they walked around the back of the building, where there was a back door not used by customers. Joe let them in and they headed up the stairs to his apartment.

"That was such a good night," Rhianna said, pouring a glass of water in Joe's kitchen. She handed it to Joe and then poured another for herself.

"Yeah, it was great fun." Joe leaned against the worktop, tortuously close to Rhianna.

She could fall into his bed right now. But she didn't want a fling. Especially with Joe.

"Rhianna." He stepped closer, facing her. His lips were inches from hers.

Gathering some self-control and summoning a huge amount of effort to resist Joe, she placed her trembling fingers on his lips and shook her head. "Let's not ruin our friendship, Joe," she said in a whisper. "I want something long-term."

He watched her, his hand pushing a stray hair back behind her ear. Her heart rate quickened.

"Joe, even the phrase 'long-term' brings you out in a cold sweat."

His lips broke into a smile, and he shook his head. "Yeah, yeah, it does." He faked a shiver and chuckled.

She laughed too, free to breathe again. "I don't want to ruin a good friendship with you."

"No, me neither." Joe cupped her face, and with his thumb, rubbed her cheek. "Goodnight, Rhianna." He planted a kiss on her forehead.

"Goodnight, Joe."

CHAPTER 15: SOUTH FOR THE SUMMER

Rhianna awoke to the sound of Joe clattering around in the kitchen, then gently knocking on her bedroom door.

With her eyes barely open, she managed to groan, "Yeah." Her head hurt. Definitely a reminder she'd consumed too much alcohol the night before. And not drunk enough water.

"Would you like coffee? And a bacon sandwich?" Joe asked through the door.

Rhianna thought for a moment. Could she handle eating, or would that make her feel worse? She felt hungry, which probably didn't help the queasiness. "Yes, please. I'll be out in a minute," she mumbled groggily.

She checked her phone. It read: 09:05 a.m. She needed to get up — slowly, she realised as she moved. She shoved back the duvet and swung her legs over the side of the bed. Could she be bothered to change out of her pyjamas? They weren't all that flattering, but they weren't revealing either. She was very conscious she needed to remain that way around Joe. Yes, he had seen it all before, a long time ago, but she didn't want to give the wrong signals. Finding a hairband, she scrunched her hair into a messy bun and made her way out of her bedroom, moving gingerly, so as not to aggravate the headache she felt forming. Food and coffee would fix it. And some painkillers.

Rubbing her eyes, she watched Joe, fully dressed in jeans and a T-shirt, prepare the bacon sandwiches. He had a coffee machine percolating away. The smell of frying bacon and the aroma of freshly brewed coffee didn't make her feel queasy; it had the opposite effect, so she took this as a good sign. Her hangover wasn't too bad.

"Brown sauce or ketchup?" Joe asked. He appeared far more awake and spritelier than she felt.

"Oh, brown sauce, all the way."

"Agreed." Joe spread brown sauce over the wholemeal bread. "How's the head?"

Rhianna squinted and rubbed her temple. "Sore."

"Sorry, that's probably my fault, plying you with Prosecco." He handed her the bacon sandwich on a plate.

"Yeah, it couldn't possibly have been the shots." She took the plate to the table. There were two empty mugs waiting to be filled, a milk jug beside them.

"The shots were your idea!" Joe brought over the jug of coffee and poured.

They tucked into their bacon sandwiches hungrily. The combination of soft wholemeal bread, melting butter and crispy bacon instantly made Rhianna start to feel human again. Suddenly there was a loud banging at the back door, and a voice calling, "Are you there?"

Joe frowned at Rhianna and, reluctantly putting his sandwich down, got up. "I'd better go down and see who the hell that is."

Rhianna continued to eat her sandwich and sip her coffee. She could hear a commotion downstairs. There was the sound of excited female voices and then what sounded like a herd of elephants stomping up the stairs. *Not more sex-hungry reps like Kerenza, surely?*

The door opened and two women burst into the apartment. It took Rhianna's poor, hungover brain a second to catch up.

"Jen?" She frowned. She didn't have a clue who the other woman was.

"SURPRISE!" the two women shouted in unison.

"We went to Oystercatcher … woke up some holidaymakers, and they suggested we try the pub," Jen said.

"What? What are you doing here?"

"Surprising you, silly. Thought we'd give you a hand with setting up the bistro," Jen said, giving Rhianna a hug. "This is Lucy, my sister-in-law, Drew's younger sister. You probably met at our wedding." If they had, Rhianna couldn't remember, but then she was currently hungover and not functioning properly. "She asked if she could tag along, and I said you wouldn't mind the extra pair of hands."

Lucy waved. "Yes, I could do with some R and R, and when Jen said she was heading down to Cornwall, I begged her to take me with her."

"I did warn her this isn't a holiday!" Jen raised her eyebrows at Lucy.

"Coffee, ladies?" Joe asked. "There's a fresh pot." They both nodded. Rhianna emptied her mug for a refill.

"Aren't you going to introduce us, Rhianna?" asked Jen.

"Oh, sorry, this is Joe, the landlord of the pub. He's helping me out, as my house purchase fell through, by letting me stay here — in the spare room!" she added before Jen got the wrong idea about their sleeping arrangements.

"Yeah, I heard about Glyn," Jen said, frowning and giving Rhianna another hug.

"Joe, this is Jen, my best friend, and Lucy is her sister-in-law." Rhianna turned back to them. "So where are you girls staying?"

"Well, we were hoping to stay with you…"

"Oh, uh, but…" Rhianna didn't know what to say.

"Hey, it's okay, you're welcome to stay here," Joe said, handing them each a mug of coffee. "How long do you guys plan to stay?"

"About a week. That's how much time we've taken off work so far," Lucy said.

"I can't be longer than two weeks," Jen said. "That's all I can get off work, and besides, Drew will be pining for me to come back."

Rhianna looked at Joe, but he didn't look the slightest bit worried. He'd gone from one woman under his roof to three. He deserved a medal.

"Okay, ladies. Shall I help you get your things in?"

"Oh, that would be great," replied Jen. "Lucy's packed the kitchen sink."

"And you need a cement mixer for all your make-up!"

Rhianna giggled as Joe looked at her.

"Did I agree to this?" he asked.

"I'm afraid so."

While Joe helped Lucy and Jen collect their bags from their car, Rhianna quickly washed and dressed. It certainly was going to be cosy with the four of them in Joe's flat. Jen and Lucy left their bags in her room, while Rhianna put another pot of coffee on. "I'd better get ready to open up the pub," Joe said, and the three women watched him go into his bedroom.

With Joe out of earshot, Jen leaned closer to Rhianna and said, "I can't believe he is the same Joe you hooked up with during my hen party!"

"I never expected him to be here. I thought he'd gone to Australia."

"Have you two ... you know?"

"No," Rhianna said quickly and as quietly as possible.

"Bye for now, ladies," Joe said, reappearing from his room.

Once Rhianna was certain he was out of earshot, she continued, "We're just friends. He hasn't changed. He's not the sort to look for long-term relationships, and I don't want to make things awkward by sleeping with him, falling for him, and then having my heart broken."

Jen filled Lucy in about Rhianna's summer romance with Joe, much to her annoyance.

Lucy chewed her lip. "Oh, a player? He is rather gorgeous, though. I don't know how you resist."

"We're just friends, by mutual agreement. He's helped me out — a lot."

"Would you mind if I tried it on?" Lucy raised an eyebrow. "I could do with some fun."

Would Rhianna mind? Yes, she would. But she couldn't say that because then Jen would be like a dog with a bone, and not let it slide. "No … of course not." Rhianna swallowed down the lie, not meeting Lucy's eye.

"Lucy's just split up with her boyfriend," Jen said.

"Caught him cheating on me with another woman, more like!" Lucy interjected angrily. Her face had turned pink.

"Oh, I am sorry," Rhianna said, sincerely. Would it have been worse if Glyn had done that to her? It might have given her more closure. Sometimes, she still couldn't understand why Glyn had ended their relationship.

"Hey, can I use the bathroom?" Lucy said, getting up from the table.

Rhianna showed her where it was. As soon as the door closed, Jen explained in a low voice, "I'm sorry, Drew begged me to bring her with me."

"Was her relationship serious?"

"It's hard to say. She's always dating, on and off. She plays the players, as she gets bored quickly. But this one guy, they seemed serious. They'd been dating a few months. Maybe she thought she'd found the one," Jen continued. "She's pretty angry about it all. Look, if you have a problem with her going after Joe, I'll tell her."

Rhianna didn't have a chance to reply; they heard the bathroom door unlock and Lucy returned to the table. Rhianna didn't own Joe. So, if Lucy wanted to have a fling with him, well, they were both adults and nothing to do with her. Lucy's lack of commitment would probably suit Joe perfectly.

But perhaps she should sleep on the couch and let Lucy and Jen have her bed … then maybe it would defuse anything happening between Joe and Lucy … because deep down, Rhianna wasn't sure she could handle Lucy sleeping with Joe.

"Anyway, I'm not here to drag up my past. I'm here to have fun," Lucy exclaimed, carrying on her conversation from before her bathroom visit.

"Lucy, sleeping with Joe would mean sleeping with Rhianna's sloppy seconds," Jen said, screwing up her face. "We have a code, you know?" Jen must have sensed Rhianna's unease.

"With ex-boyfriends. Joe's hardly Rhianna's ex…" Lucy said. "He was a summer fling."

"Yeah, and it was ages ago." Rhianna didn't want to make a big thing of this.

Jen gave a shrug. And to Rhianna's relief, the topic of Joe ended.

Later that morning, Rhianna showed Jen and Lucy around Kittiwake Cove, before waving off her parents. They promised to visit her again soon.

Her father hugged her and said, "I'm always at the end of the phone."

"I'd stay to help, but your father thinks getting the bistro up and running is something you should do on your own," Rhianna's mother said softly into her ear as she hugged her goodbye. "He thinks we'd be interfering, and he wants you to make the restaurant yours."

Once her parents had driven away, Rhianna took Jen and Lucy to see the future bistro. Jen had worked on the logo and signage, so was very eager to see the place in the flesh. Sheila and Martyn were there, clearing up from the party and packing up the things they were taking with them. They were only too happy for Rhianna to show her friends around, and the three of them got stuck in helping Sheila and Martyn with loading boxes.

Jen and Lucy had said they'd come to help, and they were as good as their word. Rhianna was so happy to have Jen staying, even if she was accompanied by her slightly eccentric sister-in-law. It made her realise that she really wasn't that far from Bristol and the friends she had there.

At the end of the day, they returned to Joe's flat and Rhianna started cooking a hearty chilli con carne for them all.

"I'm so proud of you, Rhianna," Jen said.

"Why do you say that?" Rhianna looked at her in surprise, while stirring the minced beef.

"Because Glyn shattered your whole world, all your hopes and dreams, of marriage, children…" Jen said, dipping a teaspoon into the chilli to taste it. Rhianna shrugged. She wasn't yet thirty. But she had thought Glyn was *the one*. He'd made her believe he was, at any rate. Good grief, had Glyn made her cynical? Was there even such a thing as 'the one'? "I really think the more assured you became in the relationship, and the more you started to shine, the more it scared him."

"How do you mean?" Rhianna frowned.

"I think the relationship was very much on his terms. As you became more confident, thinking it was safe and that you were loved, you started to air things you didn't like, telling him he couldn't treat you like a doormat, and that's when things changed for him."

"Yeah, it's as if he didn't like it that everything couldn't be on his terms," Lucy added. She'd been filled in over the course of the day about Rhianna's disaster of a relationship. "So, he ended it. Rhianna, you don't need someone like that in your life."

"I never really thought of it like that," Rhianna said. "But looking back, I didn't get much of a choice about the house we bought. He talked me into it, but the house location suited him more than me." She could kick herself for how stupid and weak she'd been. But she'd been in love and had wanted Glyn to be happy.

"The man sounds like a total narcissist. You're better off without him," Lucy said.

"Thanks, guys," Rhianna said, smiling. She was starting to feel that way more and more. She was dwelling on the past less and less, and instead was looking towards the future.

Rhianna pulled plates from the oven, where she'd put them to warm. "Did one of you want to go down to the pub and see if Joe's free to join us?"

"I will." Lucy shot out of her seat and down the stairs before Jen could move.

"Are you really okay with her pursuing Joe?" Jen looked at Rhianna sternly as she helped lay the table with cutlery and wine glasses. A bottle of red wine stood open in the middle, to let it breathe.

"I don't own him. He's a just a friend, as I keep telling you." Rhianna placed bowls of grated cheese, sour cream, homemade guacamole and tortilla chips in the middle of the table. They didn't have time to continue the conversation, as Lucy returned with Joe.

"I've left Toby on his own down there as it's quiet. I told him to come and get me if it gets busy." Joe entered the kitchen area, where Rhianna was spooning fluffy rice on to the plates, followed by the steaming hot chilli. "Need a hand? Smells great."

"Take these two. They're all the same, and there's more if you want it." She left the large saucepan on the hob.

"Do you still surf, Joe?" Lucy asked as Joe poured the wine into each glass. Rhianna resisted rolling her eyes at Lucy, who'd obviously taken notes from her and Jen's conversations.

"Yeah, when the season picks up, I'll be out there every day giving lessons," Joe said. "You ladies should come out one day."

"Oh, that would be great," Lucy said. "I packed my bikini, just in case."

"Hey, remember why you're here," Rhianna said. "To help me!" She hoped her smile made her look as if she were joking.

Lucy chuckled. "You're all work and no play."

"I keep telling her that," Joe added. There was mischief in the look he gave Rhianna, then to her dismay he turned his attention back to Lucy.

CHAPTER 16: KISS IN THE DARK

It was the first of May, and Rhianna didn't waste a moment before getting to work on her bistro. She now had the keys and was up early letting in Nick and his team, followed shortly afterwards by Olly and Noah.

Nick was going to be installing a log burner at one end of the top-floor room, and would need to drill through the wall to install a flue. Olly would be fitting her new bar, with Noah giving him a hand with the heavy lifting. Rhianna was thrilled to see that the wooden S-shaped countertop really did look like a wave, just as Olly had promised. Before long, the top floor echoed with the noise of banging and drilling, overlaid with the din of the radio which had been the first thing to be plugged in by the workmen.

Rhianna got to work scrubbing the kitchen and cleaning the bar area in the main restaurant area, helped by Lucy and Jen. Jen had brought a Bluetooth speaker with her to link to her phone, so they had their own music, which helped drown out some of the noise coming from overhead. In between cleaning, Rhianna was on the phone placing orders, organising new staff or chasing supplies.

Once the log burner was in place, Nick would be laying the wood flooring she'd chosen. They were on a tight schedule to get the bistro ready by May half-term, but the men assured her it could be done. There were a couple of other guys working with Nick, one of whom Rhianna recognised as Will.

When Noah wasn't needed to help Olly, he set to work painting those areas unaffected by the dust being created upstairs. Rhianna, Jen and Lucy kept finding their eyes being

160

drawn towards him. Like his brother, Noah was extremely good-looking. Jen kept firing her fingers at Rhianna; it was their code for 'nice guns'. He certainly had lovely muscular arms, accentuated by the tight-fitting T-shirt he was wearing. Her friends were so distracting! Rhianna didn't have time to be all dreamy over Noah, but it did help distract her thoughts from Joe.

Noah was oblivious to the giggles of the three women, as he worked with headphones in his ears. With a roller, he applied white paint to the ceilings and a pale blue emulsion to the walls.

Rhianna found him easy to communicate with too, and she was able to discuss her vision for the bistro with him. "I want the cocktail lounge to have a beach hut feel, so even on the bleakest days my customers will think they are sat on a warm, sunny beach," she'd explained. Unsure of what colours to choose in certain areas, Noah had painted some samples for her. Once they'd dried, they stood together with a cup of tea each, discussing the options and assessing the different shades. He had a great eye for colour, so Rhianna let herself be guided by his expertise. After much deliberation, she chose a warm sandy yellow for the cocktail lounge, in contrast to the pale blues and creams she was using downstairs. She decided to keep the conservatory area a neutral cream so that it wouldn't clash with wedding and party decorations when she hosted private events.

The weather was fine, which meant that all the windows and doors could be left open. The wind had dropped, and there was real warmth in the sun. Summer was definitely around the corner, and it wouldn't be long until the tourists started arriving in their droves.

In the middle of the first week, Joe appeared one lunchtime, carrying a large brown paper bag. Rhianna hadn't seen much of him as, being so busy with the bistro till late in the evening, she'd been crawling up to bed even later than Jen and Lucy.

Jen was working on her laptop, finalising the branding and logo for the bistro, so Rhianna could order business cards, menus and other items. Jen was also setting up her website and social media. She had made her phone a Wi-Fi hotspot so that she could use the internet, as the Wi-Fi for the restaurant wouldn't be installed for another couple of weeks. Rhianna was going to offer free Wi-Fi to her customers. Hopefully they'd share her new bistro and what a great time they were having all over social media. It was free marketing, as Jen pointed out.

"Thought you ladies might need some lunch," Joe said, using the workspace in the kitchen to lay out some pasties and a large bag of salt and balsamic vinegar Kettle crisps.

"Did I hear someone say lunch?" Lucy ran in, removing her rubber gloves. The three women crowded around Joe. Breakfast had been a long time ago, and Rhianna's stomach rumbled at the delicious aroma of the hot pasties. If it hadn't been for the radio, the others probably would have heard the loud grumble.

"There's steak and Stilton, chicken and bacon, and traditional pasties. Take your pick."

"I don't mind what I have," Rhianna said, letting Lucy and Jen delve in first. "Which one do you want, Joe?"

He shrugged. "I can eat any of them, so you take whichever you want."

Rhianna chose a chicken and bacon pasty, and Joe chose a traditional Cornish pasty.

The four of them munched in silence for a bit, helping themselves to the crisps spilling out of the large bag. Between mouthfuls, Joe asked, "How's it all coming along?"

"Oh, I'll show you around in a minute, if you like?" Rhianna said. "Did you want to take the leftover pasties back home with you?"

Joe shook his head. "Feed some of your crew, keep them sweet."

"I'm providing them with endless tea and coffee," Rhianna said, rolling her eyes.

"Yes, that's my job. I have a conveyer belt running," Lucy said, nodding.

"Yeah, the old boy working with Nick, you know when he's thirsty; he's hinting it's a dry old caff!" Jen added. "Rhianna corrects him. 'It's a bistro,' she says."

"I only mumble it under my breath."

Lucy and Jen giggled.

"I know then to switch the kettle on," Lucy said.

"We're going through a packet of biscuits a day. But if it gets the job done quicker…" Rhianna said, smiling at Joe.

Once she and Joe had finished their pasties, she wiped her hands on a serviette. "Right, let's show you around," she said, gently tapping him on the arm.

"Bye, Joe!" Lucy called. Rhianna couldn't help noticing the smile he gave Lucy, which jolted her with a stab of jealousy. She told herself not to be ridiculous. But she'd been observing Lucy's flirtatious gestures and could see that Joe was lapping them up. Fortunately, the fact that all three of them arrived back at Joe's flat knackered each night meant that Lucy hadn't yet had an opportunity to find her way into Joe's bed.

Rhianna led the way up the stairs, and Joe followed. The top floor was a mess in comparison to the rest of the bistro, as that was where most of the work was being done, but after only a few days the transformation was already astonishing. The S-shaped bar was in place and Olly, covered in sawdust, was busy building shelves within it for storing glasses. Nick and his men were at the other end of the room installing the wood burner, and a plumber was fitting a long, low radiator along one wall.

After a quick chat, they left the guys to get on with their work and headed downstairs to find Noah in the conservatory.

"Hi, Joe." Noah put the roller down and shook Joe's hand. "What are you doing here?"

"Just thought I'd pop in and see how the place was coming along." Joe looked around admiringly.

"Noah, there's a pasty in the kitchen," Rhianna said.

"Ah, thanks," Noah said, giving her a smile.

"Don't shout too loudly," she said, "as there's only two left. Maybe take the other up for Olly?"

"Will do," Noah said. "Do you like this colour? If not, I can change it. Sometimes the paint looks different on the wall compared to the sample."

"No, no, it's looking great. I wanted a neutral colour, but not magnolia." Rhianna could imagine the pale golden yellow shade being the perfect backdrop for the weddings and parties she hoped to hold in this area. "What do you think, Joe?"

"Hey, I like it. But it's not up to me. The important thing is that you like it," Joe said.

"Yeah," Noah agreed, retrieving the roller from the paint pad. "And it's good you've seen it on this wall before I paint the whole room. Much as I enjoy being here, Rhianna, we do need to get this project finished before the end of May!" He chuckled nervously, and his gaze didn't meet Rhianna's.

"We should let you get on, Noah," Joe said, taking Rhianna's elbow. "Come on, Rhianna, show me the rest of the place."

Leaving Noah to his decorating, they continued their tour of the bistro. It felt so good to have Joe at her side, and to see her fresh start taking shape before her eyes, her dream coming true.

Joe was struggling to cope with three attractive women hogging his bathroom, and taking over his lounge and kitchen, but it made Rhianna happy to have her friends supporting her, so he put up with it. His flat wasn't quite big enough for four people, but it was only for a week.

It was Sunday evening, and Lucy and Jen had decided to stay an extra night as the next day was the early May bank holiday. As tonight was their last evening, Joe had suggested they eat in the pub, share a bottle of wine (or two), and drink a toast to Rhianna's success. The women had been so busy, they hadn't really had the chance to socialise together.

Nick and his team would not be working during the bank holiday, and Joe doubted Olly and Noah would be at the bistro either, so it would be good to make the most of the day and relax. If he could convince Rhianna.

Tomorrow, hangovers permitting, he'd take them all out surfing before Lucy and Jen drove home. They had been so busy helping Rhianna all week, they hadn't had a chance to dip more than a toe into the water.

Joe stayed out of the girls' way, in the safety of the pub, while they showered and got ready for the evening. They'd had another busy day at the bistro, and Jen and Lucy had insisted on giving it a final clean before they left.

Eventually, the three women entered the pub dressed more smartly than Joe had seen them all week, wearing make-up and heels. He showed them to a table he'd reserved by the window, from where they had a view of the beach and Pentire Point.

The sky was blue, the sun was still high in the sky and the sea was retreating, leaving a wet, shiny watermark on the golden sand.

"I think that's all my nails gone now," Jen said, holding out her left hand towards Rhianna while perusing the pub's menu.

"I'm sorry," Rhianna said. "I did tell you to wear gloves."

"I was wearing gloves!"

Joe poured Prosecco into four flutes, placing the bottle in an ice bucket.

They all raised their glasses and clinked them together before taking a sip. Joe had Rhianna on one side of him and Lucy on the other. Once they had all decided what to order, the conversation returned to other subjects.

"When are your parents next coming down?" Jen asked Rhianna.

"Probably when I open." Rhianna put her glass down. "Will you two come back and see the bistro once it's up and running?"

"Of course, try and keep us away." Lucy beamed. She caught Joe's eye and gave him a smile.

"We'll try to book some accommodation next time," Jen added. "We could make a weekend of it once you've settled into the swing of things. I'll bring Drew."

Joe had noticed Lucy's attention towards him during the week, and he'd tried his hardest to react appropriately. He hadn't encouraged her, but perhaps he hadn't exactly been discouraging either, because he didn't want to create an atmosphere by telling her outright that he wasn't interested. And what if she was just being nice, in a flirty way? Another time, another Joe would have leapt at the opportunity to have a fling with a beautiful woman. Lucy was certainly pretty, with dark hair, deep brown eyes and a vivacious personality. But attractive as she was, she was also a mate of Rhianna's. Although Rhianna had no hold over him, there was something in his gut saying, 'don't do it'. He didn't want to make things awkward with her.

Lizzie brought over their order of four burgers in brioche buns, with different toppings, sides of onion rings and sweet potato fries.

While they ate, the conversation mainly centred on the bistro and how well it was coming along. Interestingly, Noah was discussed quite a bit by the ladies, referring to how lovely he was.

"He's such a gent," Jen said.

"I'm sure he fancies Rhianna," Lucy said, eyeing Rhianna.

"No, he doesn't."

Joe watched Rhianna blush. He remained silent on the subject, only agreeing that Noah was a nice guy.

They had finished their drinks so Joe ordered another bottle of Prosecco. But by quarter to eleven, the long day they'd spent working in the bistro caught up with the three women, and they couldn't stop themselves from yawning. Joe knew they'd been up early.

"I think I'm going to head up to bed," Rhianna said, finishing her drink.

"Me too," Jen said. Her glass was already empty. "I'm the designated driver tomorrow, so I could do with a good night's sleep."

"You ladies go up to bed. I'll clear up here." Joe gathered the empty flutes. "I need to help Lizzie close up, too."

"Okay, see you in the morning." Rhianna got up from the table and gave Joe a quick hug.

Jen hugged him too, followed by Lucy. She clung tightly to him and gave him a kiss on the cheek.

"I'll see you in the morning," he said, gently releasing himself from Lucy and carrying the glasses to the bar.

Joe spent nearly an hour helping Lizzie clean up the pub, wiping down tables, closing the till and locking the cash away. He let the last of the customers finish their drinks. It was a bank holiday weekend, after all.

Sometime past midnight, he climbed the stairs to find the flat silent and in complete darkness. All three women were clearly asleep. Knowing the place like the back of his hand, he was able to make his way around the flat in the dark so as not to disturb Lucy, who's turn it was to sleep on the couch. He crept into the bathroom and only pulled the light cord once he'd closed the door. As he came out, he turned the bathroom light off and allowed his vision to adjust. Rhianna's bedroom door was closed. He could make out the shape of the duvet that meant Lucy was on the sofa.

In his bedroom, he didn't bother turning on a light. He stripped off, dropping his clothes where he stood and slid under the duvet.

His bed sheets were warm. He felt the hair on the pillow before the body that went with it. The body turned, reaching out for him. He couldn't make out the face in the darkness.

Old habits die hard — he'd removed his boxers and was naked in bed. And now he regretted it.

"Hey, hope you don't mind, but I want you…" The female voice was sleepy and hushed, so he wasn't sure who exactly was in his bed. Then her lips found his, and kissed him. It sent a stir to his groin.

He gently pulled out of this kiss, trying to see who was in his bed. "Rhianna?"

"No, it's me, Lucy," she whispered, brushing her lips once more over his. She snuggled into him further, her hand

168

caressing his chest. Bone tired, Joe found himself wrapping an arm around her as she rested her head on his shoulder. But he would have preferred Rhianna to be in his bed.

It wasn't as if he didn't like a woman in his bed. A part of him was enjoying her warmth, softness, and her scent.

But something told him this was wrong. Very wrong.

"Lucy, just cuddles. It's late, I'm tired, I've had a lot to drink, so have you..." he said softly, trying as diplomatically as possible to convince Lucy he wasn't going to have sex with her.

He lay awake for what felt like most of the night, until naturally he fell asleep, cuddling Lucy. But he kept his hands above her waist and encouraged nothing more than a cuddle, making sure her hands didn't stray either.

He just needed to wake before she did and escape from the bed. And avoid any embarrassing effects that the morning can have on the average man's anatomy...

With jealousy and trepidation, Rhianna had watched as Lucy arranged her duvet on the sofa to look as if she were under it, like a teenager sneaking out at night, before creeping into Joe's bedroom.

She'd giggled, "Don't tell him. Let me surprise him."

Rhianna wanted to say something. But she couldn't. She had no hold over Joe. What could she say?

However, it didn't stop her from lying awake listening, with Jen breathing softly beside her, clearly fast asleep. She heard Joe climb the stairs, use the bathroom, and go into his room. She didn't hear Lucy being turfed out of his room. Or Joe coming back out to sleep on the sofa. Which meant Lucy and Joe were sleeping together in the very next bedroom...

Why did it bother her? Joe wasn't right for her — he wouldn't want a relationship unless it only lasted the summer.

Maybe it was more that she had slept with Joe, and didn't think Lucy should be there, taking sloppy seconds...

Yes, that had to be it.

Nothing to do with still fancying the pants off the man and wishing she could rekindle what they'd had all those summers ago...

But if she did that, it was bound to end in tears. Joe was a player, and Rhianna couldn't risk jeopardising her fragile emotional equilibrium. Kittiwake Cove was her new home. She didn't need to create a set of awkward exes here too. It was a hell of a lot smaller than Bristol.

CHAPTER 17: BETWEEN THE SHEETS

Rhianna awoke before Jen. Carefully, she pushed back the duvet and crept out of the bedroom, shutting the door gently behind her. She found Joe, his hair tousled, wearing pyjama trousers and a T-shirt, filling the coffee pot up in the kitchen.

"Hey," she said, a little surprised to see him up. It was early, but Rhianna had been woken up by the sound of seagulls squabbling. The lighter the mornings, the earlier the birds started singing. Only a seagull cry was much louder and more intrusive. She wasn't sure she'd slept that well either, her mind on Joe, with Lucy in his bed…

"Oh, hey," Joe replied. He smoothed a hand through his hair, then spooned ground coffee into the filter section and turned it on. "Sleep well?"

"Yes, great." *Lying awake wondering if you were shagging my best mate's sister-in-law.* "I'll be glad to have my bed back to myself, though." The coffee machine started its gurgle. "You?"

Why the hell was she asking if he'd slept well? Should she make out she knew Lucy had gone to his bed? The sofa didn't look slept on.

"Yeah, the wine possibly helped." Joe retrieved a couple of frying pans and placed them on the hob. "Want some breakfast?"

Eggs would probably help, Rhianna thought. They'd drunk a fair amount last night. Not enough to give her a raging headache, but her stomach felt as if it needed settling. Probably the jealousy bubbling in her gut, more than the result of a heavy night.

"Yes, go on then."

"It'll set you up for surfing."

They worked together, frying bacon and toasting wholemeal bread. Joe even made fried bread. They weren't particularly quiet, and it wasn't long before Lucy was the first to emerge.

"Good morning," she said, rubbing her eyes. She was wearing a powder-pink silk nightie which barely skimmed her thighs and her nipples were visible through the soft material. Rhianna wished she would cover up — preferably with a bloody great black bin liner — but instead, Lucy headed straight for Joe, who was standing at the stove frying eggs.

She gave him a hug and a kiss on the cheek. Joe smiled at her and didn't push her away. Rhianna found she couldn't watch. She made an excuse and escaped to the bathroom.

Sitting on the closed lid of the toilet, Rhianna took deep breaths and tried to gather her thoughts.

Lucy was Jen's sister-in-law. But even so, she'd got to know Rhianna this past week, as friends … but not good enough friends to stop her sleeping with one of her exes, though. Clearly.

Could Rhianna even consider Joe an ex?

But it did confirm one thing; Joe wasn't the settling down type. True to form, he was still the player, the holiday romancer. First Kerenza, now Lucy. He wasn't into anything long-term. It would not be right for Rhianna to get involved with him.

And she couldn't, even if she wanted to … because ironically, now she'd be going after Lucy's sloppy seconds, even if she herself had slept with Joe first! Rhianna shuddered.

She stood up, flushed the loo to make it sound like she'd actually been doing something in the bathroom, and washed her hands. Looking in the mirror, she took one more deep breath, and then returned to the kitchen. Jen was up now, holding a cup of coffee, and Joe was plating up the food.

The four of them sat around Joe's dining table eating a full English breakfast. For a moment there was silence, apart from the noise of cutlery clattering against the plates.

Joe looked up and said, "So are you all up for some surfing?"

"Can we let our breakfast go down first?" Jen asked through narrowed eyes, still not fully awake.

"Of course, I just wasn't sure what time you two were going to get away."

"Shame we can't stay another day," Lucy said, looking directly at Joe. He smiled back at her.

Much as she loved her friends and appreciated the help they'd given her, Rhianna hoped they wouldn't stay another day.

"No, sorry, Luce. Drew wants me back — and I do want to get back to him. Didn't realise how much I'd miss him," Jen said, picking up her mug of coffee. "Plus, I do need to get back to work."

"When I finally get my house, you guys can come and visit again. There might be more room to put you up," Rhianna said.

"Yes, it is a bit crowded in my flat," Joe laughed.

"What do you mean? You've hardly known we're here!" Jen joked and they all laughed.

They cleared away the breakfast things and then got dressed, taking it in turns to use the bathroom. While it was Lucy's turn in the bathroom, Rhianna whispered to Jen, "Do you think they slept together?"

"Well, they clearly *slept* together." Jen raised an eyebrow.

"You know what I mean. Neither of them has said anything."

"Ask Lucy."

"No, you ask Lucy." Rhianna blushed. She couldn't bring herself to ask her. And she certainly couldn't ask Joe. It really was none of her business.

Yet she needed to know.

Joe had disappeared downstairs to get the pub ready for opening, while Lucy and Jen packed their bags.

Around midday, Joe appeared carrying two wetsuits for Jen and Lucy. Rhianna still had hers from the last time she'd surfed. "Let's do this; the tide's coming in and will be turning in about an hour."

"How do you know these will fit?" Lucy stared at her wetsuit, frowning.

Joe winked. "I've been doing this job a while. Trust me. They'll fit."

His two areas of expertise, thought Rhianna, *women's bodies and surfing*.

The three women helped each other into their wetsuits, pulling the rubbery material over their bikinis. Rhianna wasn't surprised that both wetsuits fitted Lucy and Jen perfectly.

"Well, I'll be damned," Lucy muttered to herself, admiring the wetsuit in the mirror, running her hands down the black neoprene material.

"Oh, I remember this from last time!" Jen said, extending her arms and bending her knees to stretch the wetsuit into place.

The three women were laughing and chatting in the lounge when Joe emerged from his bedroom wearing his wetsuit. They fell silent.

This man rocked whatever he was wearing.

"Do you need a hand being zipped up?" Lucy asked, making a beeline for him.

"No, I'm good thanks," he said, smiling.

Of course, Joe could put a wetsuit on in his sleep. That did not stop Lucy fluttering around him like a butterfly round a summer flower.

"Come on then, let's get this over with," Rhianna said, realising she didn't sound very enthusiastic. Joe picked up on it.

"Hey, you loved it the last time I took you out!" He gave her a playful nudge.

"I did, yes. But it's the cold water I'm apprehensive about."

She was also apprehensive about seeing Lucy and Joe in close proximity in the water. And whether she'd be able to bear it.

The four of them, looking like a strange set of Fantastic Four superheroes in their wetsuits, walked down to the beach. They made their way to the surf instructor hut, which Liam was manning. Lucy and Jen's mouths fell open at the sight of him.

"G'day, ladies," Liam greeted them. His blond hair was already bleached from the sun and the sea. "The water is perfect today."

"But still cold, right?" Jen asked suspiciously.

"You'll be all right once you're in the water." Liam beamed. A true surfer. It made Rhianna realise why Tilly and Liam were considering a surf theme for the wedding.

Joe chose a suitable surfboard for each of them.

"Hey, ladies, let me give you a hand," Liam said, putting a surfboard under each arm so that Lucy and Jen didn't have to carry them. Both women seemed dazzled by him, and followed him meekly down to the water's edge as if he was a hunky Australian version of the Pied Piper. Rhianna and Joe carried their boards together, Rhianna at the front, with the nose of each board under each arm, and Joe at the back. He took most of the weight, though.

The sun was shining down on them, warm on their faces, the wind was gentle, but down by the water's edge the breeze made it a degree cooler.

"Thanks, mate," Joe said to Liam. "See you in a couple of hours."

"Go catch some waves," Liam shouted back. "If in doubt, paddle out!" He waved, then jogged back to his hut, looking just like a lifeguard out of *Baywatch*.

"Tilly is one lucky girl," Rhianna said wistfully to herself. Then a wave took her by surprise, and she squealed at the sudden iciness of the water against her ankles.

Joe laughed.

"It's not funny." Rhianna scowled at him, but then couldn't help laughing.

Joe clapped his hands together, getting into serious surf instructor mode. "Right, some quick stretches, then I'll show you how to get up on the board."

After warming up by circling their ankles and stretching their leg muscles, Joe demonstrated how to get up into the standing position on the board and made the three women practise doing it themselves. Then he helped each of them to strap their surfboard to their right ankle.

They picked their boards up and slowly waded into the water, the waves breaking and the white surf crashing against their bodies as they walked in deeper. The water still felt cold, but their wetsuits allowed their bodies to get gradually accustomed to it and keep warm all the same.

Rhianna tried to remember everything Joe had taught her the last time: paddling in, turning on the board, getting ready to catch a wave. Joe gave Lucy and Jen more attention — rightly so, as Lucy hadn't surfed before and Jen hadn't since her hen party.

Joe was right, though; once you caught that first wave, you were hooked. You just wanted to paddle right back out there and catch the next one. Rhianna forgot all about the cold water, the shock of it trickling down her neck. It all added to the exhilaration and euphoria. She was happiest surfing in on her belly at first. Only once she was used to catching the waves did she attempt to stand up on the board.

After losing her balance and falling in several times, she finally mastered it, screaming "Whooo hooo!" as she rode the board in. She even had the balance to give a thumbs-up to Joe as she passed him walking back into the water with Lucy. She was certainly much more confident with her surfing than a few weeks ago.

Lucy and Jen both managed to stand up too. It was hilarious watching them get gingerly to their feet and then fall straight off. There was so much laughing and screaming, but the noise of the ocean drowned it out.

Once she was totally exhausted and unable to face another wave even if she wanted to, Rhianna let the last wave take her right into the shallow water. Jen was already out. Lucy paddled in, followed by Joe, who came in on a wave, standing up in true pro surfer style. He could probably stay out for another hour.

"Did you enjoy that?" Joe asked, as they untied their surfboards from their ankles.

"That was great. Good job Rhianna will be living here. We can come for cheap holidays in Cornwall," Lucy said, her breath heavy from the exertion.

"Got to find a house yet. And wait for mine to sell," Rhianna grumbled, making a mental note that she needed to call her solicitor again for a progress report.

"How was it, ladies?" Liam said, as they returned to the hut with their boards.

"I didn't realise I'd enjoy that as much as I did." Jen swept her hair back out of her face, her wet tresses clinging together like rats' tails. Rhianna was glad she'd had the good sense to tie her hair back.

"I'll bring the wetsuits back later," Joe said, exchanging a friendly slap on the shoulder with Liam. The four of them said their goodbyes, gathered their belongings and headed up the hill towards The Cormorant.

Lucy fell into natural rhythm beside Joe, so Rhianna held back and walked with Jen.

"I am starving," Rhianna said, holding her hand to her rumbling stomach.

"Me too. And before we leave, I'm having an ice-cream," Jen said.

"Mmmm… You can't beat a Cornish ice-cream."

The three women were perched on a picnic bench outside the ice-cream parlour. After peeling themselves out of the wetsuits, they'd warmed up in The Cormorant where they'd had lunch, before walking back into the village for an ice-cream — a well-deserved treat after all the surfing. As they licked their delicious ice-creams, they watched the pedestrians sauntering along the small high street. The sun was hot for early May, and the surrounding buildings sheltered them from the breeze coming off the sea, making it a lovely warm spot to sit in and soak up the seaside atmosphere. Seagulls eyed them cunningly from the rooftops.

A sadness crept over Rhianna. She was going to have to say goodbye to her friends. For the first time in the almost two months she'd been in Kittiwake Cove, she found herself starting to miss her life in Bristol.

"Hey, you've gone quiet," Jen said, picking up on Rhianna's mood.

"I'm just thinking how much I'm going to miss you when you go." Even her salted caramel ice-cream had failed to lift her spirits.

"Hey, we'll be back," Jen said, giving Rhianna a hug. "We're so proud of you."

Lucy concurred. "Not many people would dare take such a gigantic leap and follow their dreams."

"I needed a fresh start. Just hope I don't fuck it up."

"You won't. You've worked in the restaurant trade, you're one awesome cocktail maker, and you have a head for business. You can make this work," Jen said, tapping her ice-cream cone against Rhianna's as if raising a toast to her success.

Lucy joined in, then licked her lips as she finished her ice-cream. "Mmmm … I recommend you have Cornish ice-cream on the dessert menu."

Later that afternoon, they loaded Jen's car and Rhianna said goodbye to her friends. Joe came out of the pub to wave them off. Lucy flung her arms around him and kissed him. Was it Rhianna's imagination, or did Joe look somewhat sheepish?

"Make sure you text me when you are home. Have a safe journey," Rhianna called as Jen pulled away.

Jen tooted the horn and drove out of the pub's car park.

Rhianna followed Joe back into the pub. She still didn't know what had happened between Lucy and Joe last night, but it was a fair bet that they'd done more than just sleep together.

CHAPTER 18: SEA BREEZE

Rhianna worked busily at the bistro, using the kitchen as her office — finalising menus, ordering furniture, and planning Tilly and Liam's wedding party — with the workmen working noisily around her. She didn't have time to see much of Joe. They really only saw each other in passing first thing in the morning and last thing at night. She'd had meetings with Tilly and Liam to discuss flowers, their colour scheme and what type of evening they wanted. Tristan, Joe's cousin, had been very helpful, answering any questions she had over the phone.

"Hey, pop along to the house tomorrow, and we can run through some things," he'd suggested the previous day while on a call together.

With all the hammering and drilling going on at the bistro, Rhianna was glad of an excuse to escape the noise and the dust for a morning. Joe had lent her the Range Rover to drive out to Trenouth Manor. She was getting to grips with the gears now and didn't crunch them too often.

Everyone at the bistro knew what to be getting on with. At times she felt she was just in the way. The log burner had now been installed on a Cornish slate hearth, and Nick and his team were laying the wood flooring. Rhianna had chosen a limed oak herringbone parquet. It was hardwearing and good quality — it had cost enough! — and Nick assured her it would be an ideal choice for the top-floor cocktail lounge. She wanted the flooring to look like sand, and the pale blue painted walls to look like water, to create the seaside vibe she was aiming for.

Olly was putting the final touches to the bar, which was also oak and complemented the flooring perfectly, while an electrician was busy installing lighting around the bar. Her cocktail lounge was taking shape at last! The combination of natural wood, chalky blue paint and daylight streaming in from the roof window, created the perfect inside-outside look she wanted, to give her customers the feeling they could almost touch the beach. Also, she and Noah had now agreed on all the paint colours for every part of the bistro. Yes, she could definitely leave them all for one morning.

Turning into the drive of Trenouth Manor, Rhianna forgot about the bistro, and concentrated on the scenery before her. The estate was situated a little inland, further up the valley from Kittiwake Cove. Clipped and cloud-pruned hedges lined the drive, which after a while forked left to the stables, and right to Trenouth Manor. She took the right fork, which led to a gravel parking area at the front of the Victorian mansion.

Tristan came out of the front door as Rhianna was locking the Range Rover.

"Hey," he said. He was casually dressed in jeans and a checked shirt, sleeves rolled up as if ready to work. Although younger, he bore some resemblance to Joe: similar good looks and build, with the same dark hair but paler skin. But Rhianna noticed his darker, brown eyes as she met his gaze and shook his hand. "Found us okay?"

"Yes, not too bad. Joe put the address into his sat nav, and I was well away."

"Good. How is Joe?"

"Oh, surfing, as usual."

Tristan gave a chuckle and casually combed a hand through his hair. "Yeah, we could never get him out of the water."

Following the gravel path, he led Rhianna around to the back of the house, which appeared much larger, as it was built in an L shape. A wisteria in full bloom covered the south-facing wall, its lilac flowers radiating a sweet scent. The grounds were full of magnificent rhododendrons and magnolias, all gloriously blossoming. Birds other than seagulls were in abundance. A blue tit clung to a birdfeeder full of seeds hanging from a tree as a blackbird, carrying a worm, hopped along the lawn beneath.

Rhianna caught her breath. "It's absolutely stunning."

"I can't take the credit, I'm afraid. I have a couple of gardeners," Tristan said, leading her onto the lawn, which was freshly mown with perfect stripes. The grounds were beautifully maintained and landscaped, with scatterings of colour sweeping down the valley. "Look at that view. As you can see, we're not too far from the sea."

On the horizon, to the south-west, Rhianna could make out the ocean, gleaming a smooth sea-green where it met the blue sky. It was breathtaking. With the sun shining warm on her face, even with the gentle breeze off the sea, she shaded her eyes with her hand as Tristan pointed out various landmarks.

"I had to find a way to make money for the estate. Some of the land had to be sold off, some is rented to local farmers, but I've been able to utilise the rest for tourism." He gestured in another direction. "We have a glamping site over there, containing log cabins and yurts, and a campsite over in another field for those who want to camp the traditional way."

"Rough it, you mean?"

"Yeah, but the glamping appeals to those who don't want to drag a tent or caravan on holiday with them. It's already set up, with a proper bed."

"That would be my style of camping too, admittedly."

"Some of the cabins even have hot tubs."

"Now you're talking!"

Tristan led her past the wisteria, through the back door, and into a large kitchen. This was modernised now, but it still housed an Aga, warming the room.

"Coffee?" He pulled a mug down from a cupboard and placed it under a machine.

"I would love one."

Tristan ushered Rhianna into a grand dining room, and over coffee and a plate full of shortbread his housekeeper had baked, they sat at the large table discussing Tilly and Liam's wedding. Tristan shared what knowledge he had, passing local contact details on to Rhianna.

"I can't see me getting a wedding licence in time for them to have the ceremony at the bistro," Rhianna said, chewing the top of the pen. This had been worrying her for a couple of days now.

"I'd suggest to Tilly and Liam they get married at a registry office and hold the reception at yours."

"Oh, that's a good idea. But I'm not sure Tilly wants a registry office wedding." Rhianna frowned. She tapped the end of her pen on her notepad as she thought.

"I'll tell you what, as I got the impression they liked it here so much, but it was out of their budget, if they can do a weekday I'll let them have a small ceremony here at Trenouth Manor," Tristan said.

"Really?"

"For sure. Tell Tilly to ring me."

"I will." Rhianna couldn't keep her eagerness out of her voice. "Thank you so much, Tristan."

When they had finished their meeting, Tristan showed Rhianna around the rest of the downstairs. It looked like something out of an interiors magazine, and skilfully combined original Victorian furniture and features with modern touches. Upstairs was similar, with twelve glorious bedrooms, all with en-suite bathrooms, some of which had freestanding roll top baths. The mix of old-fashioned furnishings and contemporary worked so well. "The house gets hired out for functions and weddings," he explained. "A marquee can be erected on the lawn for even larger parties."

"I can see why Tilly and Liam liked the house so much."

"Yeah, and the nice thing is that guests can stay in the bedrooms, or at least some of them can. Oh, there's someone I'd like you to meet," Tristan said as they exited the front door and headed back out into the sunshine. He led Rhianna into a converted outbuilding near the front entrance, where a young woman was sitting at one of the three desks talking on the phone. Tristan explained that this was the estate office. Once the woman put the phone down, Tristan said, "Rhianna, this is Anya; she's my events coordinator here."

"Nice to meet you," Anya said as she shook Rhianna's hand.

"Anya, Rhianna has taken over Oceans in town. She's turning it into a bistro and cocktail lounge, and I'm advising her on hosting small events there." Tristan reached for Anya's business card off a pile on her desk and handed it to Rhianna. "If you can't get hold of me, then Anya will be able to assist you."

They left Anya to her work; the phone started ringing again.

"Are you in a rush? There's someone else you should meet."

Rhianna shook her head. The change of scenery was doing her the world of good. The past few days, all she'd seen was the interior of the bistro. Tristan walked Rhianna over to what used to be the stables.

"These are spaces rented out to small businesses," Tristan explained, as he showed her round the two long buildings which sat opposite one other with a cobbled courtyard in between. They joined at the end with an arch large enough for cars to drive through. In the middle was an old fountain, which would have been used for watering the horses years ago. The old stables were beautifully converted. "Some are used as offices, but most of them are workshops rented by local artisans. It's another way to generate an income to save the estate."

Tristan introduced Rhianna to each business owner. There was a potter, and a glassblower, some of whose pieces she'd seen in Tilly's gallery. There was also a jewellery maker and a woodcarver, who made ornate sculptures of animals. Rhianna purchased a heart-shaped plaque for the bistro. Lastly, she was introduced to a florist.

"This is Poppy," Tristan said. "She's organising the flowers for Tilly. Rhianna will be hosting their wedding party in her new bistro." Poppy stopped weaving an array of pretty flowers into the perfect bouquet to talk to Rhianna.

"Oh, brilliant." Rhianna recognised the name. "I'll probably be seeing you again soon." Feeling that she should return to Kittiwake Cove, having abandoned the bistro, she thanked Tristan and said her goodbyes. "I'm so grateful for all your help."

"Ah, anything for a friend of Joe's." Tristan winked and added, in a laidback way that reminded Rhianna of Joe, "It's not a problem. And I'm always at the end of the phone. Tell Joe he and I are due a pint."

Rhianna hopped into the Range Rover, rolling down the window. "I will."

Before she returned to the bistro, still feeling worried that the wedding licence was out of her control, Rhianna called in on Tilly at the gallery to discuss the ceremony, and put forward Tristan's suggestion. "I'm concerned I won't get a licence in time."

"Hey, none of this was planned." Tilly patted her stomach. "It sounds like a great idea. I really don't want to get married in a registry office, so I'll call Tristan."

"Yes, I got the impression he'd do you a good price."

Tilly nodded. "It can be our little secret on the day."

That afternoon, her anxiety over Tilly's wedding now lifted, Rhianna removed the dust covers from the stacked piles of tables in the middle of the restaurant area and started placing them how she wanted them.

"Hey, let me help you," Noah said, taking a table from her. He made it look so much easier to carry. "Where do you want it?"

Rhianna pointed and he placed the table in the spot. "I can do this if you're busy," she said.

"Nonsense. These tables are heavy. I'm waiting for a coat of paint to dry anyway. Let me help you." Noah grabbed another table. "And I'll only get in Olly's way." Rhianna showed him where she wanted it. With the larger tables, they lifted an end each. They chatted as they worked, Noah relaxing around her a little more now that Lucy and Jen weren't about. Between them, they shifted all the tables until Rhianna was happy with their position. Noah not only had an eye for colour, but also interior layout.

"Thank you," Rhianna said, once all the tables were in place. "You made that job ten times quicker."

"Anytime," Noah said. "Shall I go put the kettle on? Tea or coffee?"

"Oh, tea, please."

Noah left Rhianna numbering the tables using post-it notes. She sketched out the table plan, in case the tables had to be moved again, and so that she could draw up a chart in the kitchen for the waiting staff.

Noah returned shortly with two mugs of tea and handed one to Rhianna. "It's all coming together."

She imagined the tables laid with shiny cutlery, napkins and gleaming glasses. "Yes, it is," she said, grinning. They chinked mugs. Exciting times were ahead of her.

Early the next morning, as she was leaving via the back door of The Cormorant, Rhianna bumped into Joe. He had evidently just returned from surfing. He had mentioned last night that high tide was currently early in the mornings, so he was making the most of it this week and getting his surf session in before he had to get on with running the pub.

He was unshaven, and his wetsuit was unzipped with the top half peeled down, so his chest and arms were bare. His wet hair was swept back with only a couple of stray curls dropping forward on his forehead. Rhianna quickly quashed her thoughts of trailing her fingers over his damp, bronzed skin and through his hair. He dumped the surfboard he was carrying by the back door.

"Hey, what are you doing with that board?" Rhianna asked.

"It needs to go to the dump ... I mean, surfboard heaven in the sky." Joe patted the board as if it had heard him say it was destined for the tip.

"Why, what's wrong with it?"

"It's seen better days. There's a crack here." Joe ran his fingers along the edge of the board. "It's letting in water."

"Can't it be repaired?"

He shook his head, and Rhianna felt a drop of cold water fall from his hair onto her skin. "It's not worth repairing; it's an old board."

"Oh! Could I have it for the cocktail lounge, please? I want something to hang above the bar. Noah should be able to paint a design on it."

"Yeah, sure."

"Great. Thank you! I'll take it now."

"No, no, I'll bring it down later, save you struggling with it." Joe stepped in front of her to stop her from grabbing the board.

Without thinking, Rhianna gave him a peck on the cheek, savouring the salty taste of his skin on her lips and the brush of his stubble, then she happily made her way to the bistro. She couldn't wait to tell Noah she'd found a surfboard. They'd been discussing ideas only the day before while shifting the tables. He'd talked about his paintings, and she'd offered to display some of his work in the restaurant — through Tilly, of course. She didn't want to undercut the gallery.

Noah was already there, wearing white dungaree overalls over a tight T-shirt, covered in splodges and finger marks of paint. He was crouching down, recoating the skirting boards. She rushed over to him, unable to contain her excitement.

"Hey, Noah, you know we were talking about a surfboard hanging over the bar?" Rhianna said, dumping her bag down on a table, the scent of paint engulfing her.

"Good morning, Rhianna." Noah got to his feet, putting his paintbrush down.

"Oh, sorry, I'm so excited, I couldn't wait to tell you," Rhianna gushed. "Joe's bringing up a surfboard later; I thought maybe you could take a look at it and paint a design on it?"

"Yeah, okay," Noah said, not sounding too enthusiastic.

"I'll pay you, of course, for your time," Rhianna added quickly.

"Oh, sorry, my mind was elsewhere," Noah said, rubbing his left temple with his palm. Rhianna couldn't help her eyes being drawn to his wonderful, muscular biceps. "I won't need paying."

"No, I insist. And make sure you sign it. You can paint on a surfboard, can't you?"

"Yeah, of course."

"Brilliant. Right, let's get the kettle on. I gather there are a lot of thirsty workmen about, and I no longer have Lucy on the tea run." Rhianna grabbed her bag and made her way into the kitchen. Her laptop was where she'd left it. The guy from her telephone and broadband provider had been in earlier in the week, and she now had Wi-Fi. Things were coming together.

With all his staff in, Joe found a quiet moment after lunch to walk the surfboard round to Rhianna's bistro. He was relieved her friends had now left, as the flat had started to feel way too small. Plus, he'd managed to keep Lucy's attentions at bay as best he could without hurting the woman's feelings, but if she'd stayed much longer…

He was only human, after all.

But there were codes of behaviour, and now that he was older and far wiser, he knew not to sleep with the friend of a friend. Even if his relationship with that friend was purely platonic.

But it used to be far from platonic…

It had been hard with Lucy lying beside him not to reciprocate her attention. He didn't find her unattractive. It was just that Rhianna's presence, and Lucy being Rhianna's friend, didn't sit right. Just like it hadn't with Kerenza.

Why Rhianna's opinion mattered so much to him, he wasn't sure.

Because you like her.

Only he was too afraid to commit. Plus, Rhianna had enough on her plate, with the bistro, trying to buy a house… It was best not to complicate things. For now.

And he knew Rhianna wouldn't want just a fling. She'd want something more serious than a holiday romance. And that's why he didn't sleep with locals. *Remember!*

So why did he miss being around her? He missed her working in the pub, where he could spend time with her — laughing together, experimenting with cocktail concoctions and recipe ideas. He hardly saw her now. And when her bistro opened, he wondered if he'd see much of her at all, she'd be so busy building up her business.

And then, when the day came that she moved out, would he see her at all? Or would the best he could hope for be a brief meeting in the street?

He realised envy niggled within him. Joe didn't *do* jealousy. But the thought of Nick working around Rhianna, and even Noah … getting to spend time with her…

He'd seen how Noah acted around Rhianna. And that spiked his jealousy further.

Joe manoeuvred the board up the metal stairs and into the bistro. About to rest it against a wall, he thought better of it. Rhianna wouldn't thank him for marking freshly painted walls, and neither would Noah.

"Hey, Noah, Rhianna about?" Joe said, spying Noah working.

Noah was a very different guy to the predatory Nick. He was decent. A little shy and quiet… He wasn't the sort for one-night stands and holiday flings. No, Rhianna deserved a guy like Noah. He'd be a gentleman.

"She's in the kitchen." Noah pointed with his paintbrush. "Is that the board?"

"Yeah."

"What's wrong with it?" He put the brush down in a tray.

Joe knew Noah loved to surf just like the rest of them. Born in Cornwall, surfing was in their blood. "There are a few cracks, only hairline, but the board is old. It's seen better days."

"Oh, yeah, I can see." Noah traced his hands over the smooth, hard fibreglass material. It was the old-style board. Nowadays, boards were made with polyurethane or polystyrene foam covering the fibreglass for more buoyancy and grip. But the bare fibreglass would make a great canvas for Noah to paint on. He nodded his approval. "This will be perfect." Noah took the board out of Joe's hands.

"I'll just say hi to Rhianna." Joe thumbed in the direction he was going, and left Noah to continue decorating. He admired the transformation of the bistro, which was now looking cleaner and brighter. It felt bigger, but he was sure that was due to the fact the tables weren't laid out fully.

Joe found Rhianna in the kitchen, the radio blaring. She was standing by the oven with her back to him and was dancing to the song on the radio, singing along with the chorus. Joe coughed to get her attention, even though it would have amused him to watch a while longer.

Rhianna turned and blushed, her hand flying to her chest. "Oh, God, you scared the life out of me."

"I prefer Joe." He winked. She had a rather charming dusting of flour on her nose.

Rhianna looked unimpressed by his joke as she turned the radio down. "Ha ha ha." Joe realised the radio was turned up to drown out some of the noise coming from overhead. Hammering and drilling, men's voices, and the din of another radio. "This is a surprise; what are you doing here?"

"I came to deliver the board to Noah, remember?"

"Oh, yes, I forgot about that as soon as I started cooking."

"What are you cooking?" Joe approached her. The scent from the kitchen was divine. Freshly baked scones were cooling on a rack.

"Just practising some recipes. The great thing is I have the workmen to test them out on, and it means the food doesn't go to waste."

"I think I need to come and work for you," Joe said. He reached for a scone, but she slapped his wrist.

"Ha ha! You don't have the time with a pub to run, helping at the B&B and then surf instructing." She pulled a baking tray out of the oven, releasing a blast of heat.

"True." This was another reason why he hadn't seen a lot of Rhianna. He was so caught up with the summer season arriving, he didn't have enough hours in the day either. He looked at the tray. "What are those?"

"Potato cakes, to go with smoked salmon and cream cheese. Just testing out a canapé idea."

"Are you sure there isn't anything you need me to do? I could be your chief taster."

"I think you already do enough for me, letting me live under your roof rent-free. I'll bring you something back tonight. I'll try not to be too late."

Her smile alone melted his heart. He just loved — *liked* being around her.

"Firstly…" He grabbed a tea towel and dabbed at her nose, making her pull her head back and blush.

"What are you doing?"

"You have flour on your nose."

"Oh." She grabbed the tea towel off Joe and wiped her face.

"Okay, I'll let you get on." Reluctantly, Joe left Rhianna. He'd agreed to take some surf students out at two, so he needed to get ready for that.

"Catch you later. And thanks for the board."

CHAPTER 19: AFTER DARK CRUSH

Hours later, while Rhianna was elbow-deep in dough, her phone beeped. She wiped her hands to check the text, then scowled at the name of the sender, her good mood instantly shattered and a chill running down her spine.

Glyn. What the hell did he want?

She wished she'd deleted his number, as it would have given her great pleasure to ask who it was messaging her. She read the text, unable to believe what she was reading. Anger resurfaced within her; she hadn't realised he could still have this effect on her after all this time.

He wanted to see her, to talk things through, to get back together…

Oh, the audacity of the man!

Without a thought, she texted back: *I've nothing to say to you.*

That was a lie. She had plenty to say. She wanted to tell him how he'd torn her heart out, ripped it in two, crushed it and shattered her dreams in the process. She wanted the house sold so she could move on with her life and put her past behind her.

Please, Rhianna. I want to see you. Please come home.

I don't want to see you. Bristol is no longer my home. Just buy me out or put the house on the market.

I need to see you! Please.

I don't need to see you! I'm too busy for your crap. Get the house sold!

She inserted a couple of angry emojis, hoping this would emphasise her fury. She couldn't waste a day travelling to Bristol. She liked to be present at the bistro in case any of the men wanted her opinion or agreement on a decision. She couldn't afford to hold anything up. The renovation was pushing it as it was. She would be interviewing staff soon. And as usual, Glyn appeared to be refusing to listen to her. *Always on his bloody terms.*

Well, she wouldn't allow him his terms. Not anymore. If his intentions were to revive their relationship, he was in for a big surprise. And she certainly didn't want him coming anywhere near the bistro and tainting it. It was hers, and hers alone. And she knew he'd try working his charm; he'd find a way to interfere. Kittiwake Cove was her haven, somewhere he could no longer control her. She didn't want Glyn here dragging up bad memories when she was trying to bury them. And she didn't want to travel to Bristol to revive them.

Staring blankly at her phone screen, Rhianna was unaware she was crying until she wiped her cheek. At that moment, Noah walked into the kitchen.

"Hey, everything okay?" He placed a hand on her shoulder.

Rhianna shook her head, took a deep breath, and wiped her eyes with her fingers. "Yes, fine, just my bloody ex wanting to meet me." She sniffed. Blood thundered in her ears and her hands trembled; that was the effect he had on her.

"Are you going to meet him?"

"No!" she said, her tone laced with frustration. "Sorry, I didn't mean to snap at you. I've told him I don't want to see him; I just want the house we owned together sold."

"He really did a number on you, didn't he?"

"Yes, he did." Rhianna started sobbing, and Noah pulled her into his arms. His body was firm and muscular, radiating safety and warmth. It surprised her how much she liked the feeling of his sinewy muscles, how good it felt to be wrapped in his arms. He stroked her hair and she breathed in his scent: citrussy aftershave mixed with paint.

"Well, if he does show up, I'll have your back," he said, releasing her from the hug. His tone was serious, then he gave her a cheeky grin.

Rhianna laughed and patted his arm, trying to hide her embarrassment at enjoying his embrace. "Thanks, Noah, but I'll be okay."

"Of course, you will. You're stronger than you think."

Glyn was too much of a coward to actually face her, wasn't he? He much preferred the passive-aggressive approach.

"I think I need a drink." Rhianna made her way to the bar, where she had some bottles of alcohol stored for practising cocktails. Noah followed and Rhianna poured them each a shot of neat vodka.

"Feeling better?" Noah asked, wiping his mouth.

"Not really." She poured herself another shot.

Noah frowned. "Why don't you go home, then?" he said. "I can lock up."

As she knew she wouldn't be able to concentrate on anything, she nodded in agreement. She wrapped the dough in clingfilm, put it in the fridge and left the bistro earlier than intended. Carrying a food parcel for Joe, as promised, she climbed the hill towards The Cormorant with thoughts of Glyn darkening her mind.

"You all right?" Joe couldn't help noticing Rhianna's dark expression as she climbed onto a stool at the bar, placing a plastic box on the counter. He hoped it contained the food she'd promised him. Wouldn't that mean she'd been thinking about him? Rhianna looked as if she was chewing the inside of her cheek. She did this when concentrating or stressed, he'd noticed. Something was obviously troubling her; it was written all over her face.

"No, not really." She let out a deep sigh. At least she wasn't lying to him. "A gin and tonic, please. Make it a double." She slumped on the stool, leaning on the bar. "Oh, here's your food parcel." She pushed the box listlessly towards him.

"Thanks." Joe frowned. Her lack of enthusiasm worried him. He filled the balloon gin glass with ice, added two shots of Rhianna's favourite gin from the optic, then topped it up with a bottle of tonic and a slice of lemon. He placed the drink in front of her with the remaining tonic in the bottle beside the glass. "So, are you going to tell me what's wrong, or do you want me to guess? Problems with the bistro?" He'd have words with Nick if he'd upset her in any way.

Rhianna shook her head. She sipped her drink and remained silent. He could see she'd been crying; her eyes were bloodshot and glistened as if she was about to burst into tears at any moment.

"Whatever it is, Rhianna, I'll help you." He hated seeing her like this. He felt useless.

"You can't help me with this."

"Try me."

"It's Glyn." She glared straight ahead over her glass, focusing on nothing before her. She couldn't look Joe in the eye.

"What about him?" Joe watched her. All the colour had drained from her face.

"He texted me, saying he's sorry and wants to meet me. He says he wants me back." Her tone was bitter and derisive as she took another gulp from her glass.

"And you don't want him back?"

"No, he hurt me." She glared at Joe. "However much I loved him, however much I never wanted our relationship to end, he destroyed what we had. I've lost trust in him. Besides, I've moved here now."

But has she moved on? The thought popped into Joe's head. By the looks of her, he wasn't certain. "Hey, you're shaking." He noticed the slight tremor in her hands as she raised the glass to her lips. Without hesitation, he joined her on the other side of bar and gently placed his hand on hers to ease the trembling. Then, not letting go of her hand, he propped himself on the stool next to her. The pub was now quiet as it was getting late, though it wasn't yet dark.

"I don't know if I could face him. What it would feel like to see him again," Rhianna said.

"You don't have to meet him if you don't want to." Rhianna's hand felt cold under Joe's palm, so he rubbed it gently to warm her.

"I've told him I don't want to see him. I just want him to sell the bloody house." She looked briefly at Joe, then back at her glass, the bubbles rising to the top, curving around the ice. She rapidly drained her drink. Joe had never seen her so on edge. She withdrew her hand abruptly from his. "I'm going for a walk."

Before Joe could argue, or even suggest he go with her, she was out the pub door.

Rhianna didn't have a clue where she was heading, but she needed to walk, to clear her head. She wasn't drunk — she told herself — but the shots of vodka and now the large gin had given her that invincibility she needed to power on through this. And she wasn't sure being around Joe, who for all she knew had slept with both Kerenza and Lucy in a short space of time, was going to help her black mood.

She didn't get too far, finding herself on the beach. Even her alcohol-fuelled brain knew walking to the Rumps wouldn't be wise in the fading light. Maybe the roar of the ocean was all she needed: the sound of the waves crashing was calming. It had drawn her onto the sand.

Even though she was very happy with the bistro, and her plans, the feeling of wanting to be loved ate away her. She hated the weakness. She hated that Glyn had sowed this insecure seed in her.

Removing her flipflops, she walked towards the shoreline. She didn't know if the tide was coming in or going out, but she had to walk some way to meet the water's edge, which meant it wasn't fully out or in. The sun was low on the horizon, hidden behind clouds, but there was still enough light and her eyes adjusted to the semi-gloom. There were still some surfers and kayakers in the water. Remembering she was still wearing it, Rhianna stripped down to her bikini and, leaving her clothes with her flipflops by a rock, decided to join them in the water. She hugged herself as the briny wind whipped around her, the loose strands of hair flying about her head like Medusa's snakes. Maybe the coldness of the water would jolt her out of the doldrums that a single text from Glyn had brought on. How did he still have this power over her? Why did she let him still have this power over her?

She paused at the coldness around her shins, then ploughed on in. She wanted the water to be cold, to sting her, to make her shiver. Her hope was that it would numb her pain and thoughts, like it numbed her limbs. She needed the saltwater to wash away the salt of her tears.

Once her body had adjusted to the temperature, she swam through the surf, legs kicking, arms alternately scooping at the water, the coldness making her breathless. Giant waves would tumble over her, and she'd stand up, clearing the water from her eyes and spitting the salt from her mouth. Before long, she stood neck-deep in the water, unaware she'd swum out so far.

The sky was darkening now, and she realised she should head in. It was bloody freezing.

Suddenly, a large wave approached, about to break. As she went to swim in with it, something hit the side of her face, sending her under the water. Unprepared for the sudden ducking, her temple pounding, she took in gulps of seawater, making her choke and panic. Saltwater stung her eyes, her ears filled with the brine, deafening her, and she felt her body being dragged helplessly under by the surging waves.

"Toby, can you hold the fort, please? I need to go after Rhianna." For the past fifteen minutes, Joe had wrestled with himself over whether he should go after Rhianna or not. She was old enough to look after herself, he told himself. On the other hand, she was upset and could do something stupid. She had only drunk a double gin, so possibly nothing too stupid, but all the same, his gut wouldn't settle until he knew Rhianna was safe.

"Sure, boss."

Opting for trainers, rather than his flipflops, Joe jogged down the steep hill, narrowly avoiding slipping. He ran onto the beach.

"RHIANNA!"

With the light fading, he couldn't see the water's edge very well, especially as the tide was heading out; it was halfway down the beach. He ran towards it, looking around to see if he could spot Rhianna sitting on a rock, taking cover from the wind, which was bitter at this time of evening without the sun warming it through.

As he grew closer to the shoreline, he saw someone in a wetsuit struggling with a woman in a bikini, trying to help her out of the water. They were still thigh-deep.

"HELP!" the person bellowed, their voice carried by the gusts of wind.

Joe sprinted towards them, running into the white water, battling against its surges, and placing an arm around Rhianna's bare waist. He ignored the cold rush from the water as a wave crashed past them, pushing them forward.

Rhianna coughed and spluttered and retched.

"I didn't see her, I didn't see her," the man was saying. "I was on my way in."

"It's okay, it was an accident. I've got her."

The man's kayak came in on another wave and collided with the three of them, knocking them over, creating more confusion in the surf. The man grabbed it, as Joe stood up and scooped Rhianna into his arms, carrying her towards the beach.

"It's okay, I've got you," Joe said as he felt Rhianna's grip around his neck strengthen.

"Joe?"

Once they were out of the water, he placed Rhianna on to her feet, but still held her tightly. She was crying now, making her cough even more.

"It's okay, you're safe." He could see a bruise forming on her right cheek as he pushed her hair out of her face. Luckily, the skin hadn't split, or she would have needed stitches. "Just take slow, deep breaths."

"I'm so stupid." She stood and bent over, shivering. Goosebumps covered her body.

"Where are your clothes? We'll argue later about how stupid you are." Rhianna pointed in the direction of the rocks. She had flipping well gone for a walk in just a T-shirt and shorts; that's all she had to keep her warm, but at least they were dry.

"Is she okay?" The middle-aged man with the kayak approached. The failing light made it hard for Joe to make out his features. "I'm so sorry."

"It's not your fault," Rhianna said through her tears and coughs. Her teeth chattered. "I'll be okay."

Clothes on, Joe walked a shivering Rhianna as fast as he could towards the pub, thinking about his best plan of action. Would it be quicker for her to have a hot shower, or should he run her a bath? He needed to warm her up before going bat-shit crazy at her. This could have been so much worse. He felt sick thinking about it.

In the apartment, Rhianna opted for a shower, desperate to feel immediate warmth. Once she emerged, wearing her pyjamas and dressing gown, Joe, also wearing dry clothes, presented her with a mug of hot chocolate and a bag of frozen peas. Silently, he sat beside her on the couch, holding the peas to the swollen side of her face.

"You've got a shiner there," he said.

She remained silent.

"Rhianna, what were you thinking?" Joe said, unable to hold his tongue. "You scared me half to death."

"Sorry, I just thought I'd have a swim. I thought the cold water might jolt me out of my black mood," Rhianna said. Hot tears streamed from her eyes. She could no longer hold them in. "The vodka made me do it."

"Vodka? I poured you a gin."

"I had some vodkas at the bistro after I got Glyn's text."

"Rhianna!" He couldn't keep the sudden anger out of his voice.

"I wasn't drunk."

"No, just stupid."

"Ouch, ouch."

"Sorry." He'd removed the bag of peas and placed them gently back. "Just promise you'll never do anything as stupid as that again. You don't go swimming on your own at that time of night, and definitely not with a skinful of vodka inside of you!"

"It was only a couple."

"I don't care! Something could have happened to you!" In one swift movement, Joe handed Rhianna the bag of peas and shot off the couch and into his bedroom, slamming the door behind him. He needed to regain control of his emotions. What if she'd drowned? He'd rescued people out of the ocean plenty of times, and even encountered a few fatalities, which had always upset him that he'd failed to get there in time. But never had it made him feel like this. His stomach churned.

He hated the feeling that he could lose her. It made him cold, sick with fear. Just like it had with Alannah when she'd left. He needed to control his feelings for Rhianna. He was afraid his heart wouldn't recover if he fell for her.

CHAPTER 20: RED KISS

Even though Rhianna had arrived early at the bistro, she couldn't concentrate. As she kneaded yesterday's pastry dough, her left cheek throbbed with the swollen bruise, which was a nice yellowy purple, reminding her of last night's ridiculous antics. She'd left the apartment with the dawn chorus to avoid facing Joe. She felt so ashamed of her stupidity. Drowning herself in alcohol was one thing, actually drowning was another. Did Joe think she was suicidal? Because she was far from it.

"Hey, what happened?" Noah's worried expression said it all. He dropped the paint pots he was carrying and rushed towards her. She wondered if she should make a recording of her foolishness on her phone and play that, so she wouldn't have the embarrassment of repeating the sorry story all day. She'd arrived before any of the workmen. It was going to be a long day.

"I took a late evening swim and got hit by a kayak." She swallowed down the tears that were trying to rise in her throat. Only she could get caught out doing something as senseless as that. She would have got away with the late dip if she hadn't collided with a kayak.

"Why? What?" Noah's tone was panic-stricken. "For a moment, I thought someone…"

"Someone?"

Noah shrugged. "Glyn?"

Rhianna chuckled. "Glyn is many things, but he's not violent. Besides, he'll never come to Cornwall. Really not his style."

"But you're okay?" Noah placed a hand on her shoulder.

She nodded gently, unable to look him in the eye. "More emotionally bruised by my stupidity. Joe's fuming." Moving her head, let alone talking, hurt her bruised face.

"Why?"

Rhianna blushed. "He's the one who rescued me out of the water … and he hadn't realised I'd drunk the vodka, on top of the gin I drank just before I stormed off."

"Oh, Rhee, I'd be fuming too." Noah's eyebrows knitted together in concern, his hands landing on his hips. For some reason, Noah calling her 'Rhee' didn't irritate her the same way it did when Nick called her by that name.

"I'm sorry, okay? I didn't think. I thought I'd go for a walk, but then I thought a swim would clear my head, but instead…" She pointed to her bruise. "Don't worry, I've learnt my lesson. I won't do it again."

"Good."

Rhianna was relieved when Noah left her alone in the kitchen; she hated being under his reproachful gaze. If this was how Noah reacted, what would Joe be like? Would he ever forgive her?

She busied herself in the kitchen, trying to stay out of the way of the watchful eyes of the workmen. She was relieved Nick wasn't on-site today, as he was off quoting for another job, otherwise she'd have him to contend with as well. He might be less sensitive than Noah, but he was still caring in his own funny sort of way. After all, he was making every effort to get the bistro finished for May half-term.

Later that afternoon, Noah entered the kitchen for a refill of tea for him and Olly. Rhianna had baked, cooked, and dosed herself up on paracetamol to shift a headache, and he caught her rubbing her forehead as she stared at her laptop. She'd pinged off an email to her solicitor to chase Glyn about getting the house on the market.

"Rhee, why don't you go home?" Noah said as he flicked the switch on the kettle.

"Because I have so much to do."

"And are you getting any of it done?"

"No not really." Thoughts of Glyn and his texts still troubled her. "My head hurts."

"I should think it does. You look like you've gone ten rounds with Anthony Joshua. Go home. It can all wait until tomorrow. I'll make sure it's all locked up later."

"Okay. I'm hardly being productive. And I was in very early. Maybe I need some sleep."

Rhianna cleared the kitchen and with heavy legs — and heart — strolled up towards The Cormorant, wondering what Joe's mood would be like. She needed to apologise and thank him.

To her relief, he greeted her with a smile. "Hey," he said. He glanced at the clock on the wall behind the bar. "You're back early."

"I can't concentrate; think I'm going to relax in the bath. Is that okay?"

"Sounds like a good plan. Let me know if you need anything."

That didn't go so badly. Maybe I'm forgiven?

Back in the apartment, Rhianna ran a bath. Although it was her face that was bruised, it felt as if every bone in her body ached. Maybe the swim had taken its toll on her, or the few seconds of being thrown about underwater until she'd managed to resurface after the wave had passed over her. She remembered hands reaching for her, pulling her up, helping her to stand as another wave crashed past. The surges of water had been powerful.

She stepped into the bath filled with white foaming bubbles. The heat of the water soothed her body, the scent of lavender relaxing her. Bubbles covered her completely, so only her head and neck were exposed.

Two hours later, wearing a summer dress, hair dried straight, and a little make-up applied to draw attention away from her bruise, Rhianna made her way downstairs into the pub, feeling the need to be sociable.

She wanted Joe's company. She wanted to know they were okay, as friends, that he wasn't mad at her anymore. His good opinion mattered to her. She wanted to reassure him that she wasn't some dizzy blonde with a death wish. She hadn't done what she did to punish herself or seek attention. She'd just been in the wrong frame of mind and had not thought things through — which did make her look silly. This had not been her usual, sensible behaviour.

"Hey, feeling better?" Joe's face lit up with a smile again upon seeing her. She walked through the bar, and round to the other side to take up a stool.

"Yes, thank you. I thought I'd keep you company, even help behind the bar if you need me," she said.

"You sit right there," Joe said assertively. "Drink?"

"Orange juice, please." She was relieved he didn't push for anything stronger. Enough damage had been done last night by the effects of alcohol.

"Rhianna?"

Her blood ran cold as she recognised the all too familiar voice, and she nearly fell off her stool. "Glyn? What the hell are you doing here?" Her throat tightened, panic rising. Now she needed something stronger than orange juice. She looked for Joe. "Joe, I've changed my mind. A glass of white wine, please." Thankfully, he gave her a nod without questioning it. She glared at Glyn. "Why are you here?"

"I want to talk."

"But I don't."

"Rhee, please…" That's why she hated being called Rhee, she remembered. Glyn. He reached for her cheek. "What happened to your face?"

She swatted his hand away, unable to bear him touching her. "It was an accident," she said coldly. He didn't get to act as if he cared. If he cared, they'd still be together. He never would have hurt her the way he did.

Joe placed a large glass of wine in front of Rhianna and gave her a questioning glance.

"I'll get that," Glyn said to Joe, holding out a twenty-pound note and ordering a pint of lager.

While waiting for Glyn's pint to arrive, Rhianna took a large gulp of her wine. She was trembling with nerves; she needed to calm herself. She willed the alcohol into her bloodstream with each swallow.

Stay calm. Deep breaths.

She didn't want to get drunk, but she might need some Dutch courage to deal with this situation. She hadn't seen Glyn for months, but it was still hard to face him. She could see Joe sizing Glyn up but he remained silent, and kept discreetly in the background.

"Shall we take a seat?" Glyn said, after paying for the drinks. A sick dread resting in her stomach, Rhianna led him over to one of the tables near the bay window so that she could look out to the sea if she needed to. It would be a gentle reminder of why she loved Kittiwake Cove. It would calm her. She took a deep breath. She never imagined Glyn would come and find her in Cornwall. But now he was here, she'd let him say his piece, get the ordeal over and done with, then send him on his way.

Sitting opposite him, she studied his face. He looked the same really, but something felt different. His blue eyes that had once dazzled her looked colder now. His blond hair, wavy on top and parted at the side, didn't make her want to comb her fingers through it anymore. Perhaps the way he'd treated her had tainted her perception of him. Although he was undoubtedly as good-looking as ever, she realised that he didn't have a hold over her like he used to. She didn't find him attractive anymore, knowing what a shit he'd been to her.

"So, how are you?" Glyn asked. "Apart from the bruise." Rhianna didn't want idle chitchat. She wanted this over with. Her heart rate was starting to normalise; she could no longer feel it thumping against the inside of her chest.

"Great, thanks. Great."

"Apart from the eye, you look amazing."

"Look, Glyn, cut to the chase. What do you want?"

He placed his pint back down and leaned towards her. "I want to say I'm sorry. I want to start again. I want you back."

"Why? Why have you changed your mind?" Rhianna asked. She'd hear him out. But she would not go back.

"I made a mistake."

"Really?" she erupted.

"I still love you," he said, desperation in his voice.

She exhaled in disapproval, eyes narrowing. "You walked out on me."

"I regret that."

Rhianna rolled her eyes, and took another sip of her wine, willing herself to drink more slowly. Getting drunk would not enable her to deal with Glyn effectively. "It took you — oh —

all of a year to realise that!" She took deep, calming breaths, realising her anger was rising inside her chest.

"I've been doing some thinking. I'd never seen you like that, and I didn't know how to deal with it."

Rhianna saw Nick and Will enter the bar. Then Olly and Noah showed up. Great, she was going to have an audience. Maybe having some strapping men hanging around might be useful if it came to throwing Glyn out. Rhianna quite liked that fantasy playing in her head. Karma wasn't exactly karma unless you knew it had happened, or even better, you saw it happen.

"Glyn, it was a silly argument. I was angry. It's a normal thing between two people in a relationship living under the same roof. Occasionally we got on each other's nerves. I should have been able to air that — freely!"

"What do you think? Can we start over? Can you forgive me?" Glyn reached out to take Rhianna's hand, but she snatched it away.

She hoped what she was about to say came out right. She'd rehearsed it enough times in the mirror over the past months, her voice laced with venom, in case she ever got the chance to confront him. And now here he was. "I do have a few things I would like to say to you, Glyn." Rhianna sat back, folding her arms, and glared at him. She hoped her voice would remain firm and not betray any upset. "Firstly, you deceived me." Her tone was icy. "I can't understand how you could spend so much money on me, shower me with extravagant gifts, then dump me, just like that." She snapped her fingers in front of his face. "You manipulated me, you used me, you used those gifts to make me believe you truly cared. But you never loved me!"

"I did. I'm sorry," he murmured.

She scoffed. "You *used* me," she repeated, just in case the bastard hadn't heard the first time. "And when you were done, you just dropped me. So, the answer is no, I've moved on. I no longer love you." She wanted to tell him how she no longer believed in happily ever afters, but she didn't want to give him the satisfaction of letting him know he'd hurt her so badly. She swallowed down that thought. "I'd never be able to trust you with my heart again. The next argument, would you run out on me — again? I could never be myself with you; I could never show you my true feelings. However much I might once have liked things to go back to the way they were, because I believed we had something good, they never will. You ruined it. All of it. You were the one who walked out without wanting to work at what we had, you were the one who threw our relationship aside, discarding me as if I meant nothing to you. I can no longer trust you."

"Joe, where's Rhianna?" Noah approached the bar, his face expressing concern. His brother, Olly, followed him. Joe subtly pointed towards the two people he hadn't kept his eyes off for a moment. Even with a bruised face, Rhianna looked pretty, but he could see how vulnerable she appeared. God knows what that dickhead was saying to her.

"Oh, shit, this is all my fault," Noah said. "I didn't realise who he was until I'd told him Rhianna was at the pub. I thought he had something to do with her bistro."

Joe poured Noah and Olly a pint. But his focus was on Rhianna and her ex. Noah watched them too. Olly tried to reassure him that Rhianna could look after herself.

"Do you think she's okay? Should we help her out?" Noah was leaning against the bar, but like Joe, he continued to glance over towards the table in the window.

"Who's Rhianna with?" Nick joined the party at the bar.

"Her shit of an ex," Noah answered before Joe.

"And why has she got a bruise?" Nick persisted.

"Quiet," Joe snapped. Keeping his voice low, Noah filled Nick in.

Joe noticed Rhianna's face redden. She was clearly getting angry with Glyn. Her body language had shifted to defensive.

"Should I step in?" Noah started moving towards Rhianna and Glyn, but Joe shot around the bar, the back of his hand pushing against Noah's chest.

"No, mate, I'll do it." Joe knew he could be more intimidating than Noah. And Rhianna, living under his roof, was his responsibility.

Besides, this was his pub; if someone was going to get chucked out, he should be the one to do it.

"Rhianna…" Glyn tried to place his hand on hers again, but she folded her arms and leaned back in her chair.

"Please put the house back on the market — or buy me out — either way, I want to move on. I've lost a perfectly good house because of you." Her fist thumped the table. "You wanted this, now you've got it."

Rhianna finished her drink and stood up. Her heart pounded in her chest, adrenaline pumping through her veins. She'd said everything she needed to say. At least she hoped she had. She was always good at thinking of brilliant things to say after an argument.

About to walk away, she turned on Glyn once more. "You know, once you ended the relationship, I realised it had never been a healthy one. Why would you think I'd want to go back to that?"

Rhianna felt a hand slip around her waist. Joe's familiar scent engulfed her, like a safety net.

"Hey, honey, you ready to go?" Joe said. With the adrenaline making her feel wobbly, she was glad of the support and leaned into him. He kissed her gently on the lips, letting his mouth linger on hers for a moment. It sent a sizzle of pleasure right through her. But Joe pretending to be her new boyfriend, to rub salt into Glyn's wounds, was perfect.

"Yes." She kissed Joe back, playing along and noticing out the corner of her eye that they now had a bigger audience than just Glyn. Noah, Nick and Olly were all catching an eyeful. This would probably be around the village quicker than a seagull stealing a Cornish pasty. But if felt good rubbing Glyn's nose in it. She didn't need him. She could see all of it now. And it had been so satisfying being able to say the words to his face.

"Hey, I'm Joe." Joe held out his hand to Glyn nonchalantly. Glyn stood up and shook it reluctantly. "I'm Rhianna's boyfriend. She's just one in a million." Joe gave her another kiss and squeezed her closer. She liked the feeling of his hand on her hip. "When she said you wanted to meet up with her, I wasn't happy. But you showing up, uninvited like this, has convinced me she's clearly over you."

"I told you not to be so silly," Rhianna said, holding onto Joe tighter.

Glyn, dumbstruck again, looked at Joe and then Rhianna. She was pleased to see Joe was a couple of inches taller than Glyn too. Oh, karma at work was a beautiful thing.

"So, as I've been trying to explain, I don't want to get back together with you. I've moved on." Rhianna smiled smugly. Joe tightened his grip around her waist. He was so close. She relished in the warmth of his body touching hers, as if she was drawing energy and confidence from him.

"Come on, honey, let's go," Joe said softly in her ear, the warmth of his breath against her neck sending her hormones haywire. Rhianna shot a glance around the pub, seeing Noah leave with Olly, now reassured she was safe with Joe, then focused her attention back on Glyn, whose face had reddened.

Glyn smirked. "If she thinks she's better off with a guy who beats her, more fool her."

As if a switch had been flicked, Joe turned, rounding on Glyn. He'd released Rhianna and had Glyn by his shirt, nose to nose. "I would never hurt Rhianna. Get out of my pub."

Nick, equally lightning fast, pulled Joe away from Glyn, standing between the two men. Rhianna grabbed hold of Joe's arm, unsure if his anger was an act or real. It looked real.

"I think you should leave, mate," Nick said to Glyn, shoving him towards the door.

"Why didn't you say… I wouldn't have driven all the way here…" Glyn said angrily to Rhianna, clenching his fist. Nick stood firmly on guard to make sure he left.

"I didn't ask you to come, remember?" She squeezed Joe's hand tightly.

"I'll get the house sale moving," Glyn said tersely.

"Good, you do that."

They watched as Glyn left the pub, kicking the front door angrily on his way out.

Rhianna hugged Joe. "Thank you so much for that."

"It gave me great pleasure." He still hadn't let go of her. There was a slight tremble going through his body, so maybe his anger had been real. Rhianna did like how it felt to be held by him once more. His warmth, his scent… "Hey, thanks,

Nick." Joe didn't quite release Rhianna, but with his right hand he shook Nick's.

"Never seen you go for someone like that before; thought I'd better step in." Nick finished his pint. "Can't have laidback Joe losing his reputation." He waved and headed out of the pub.

The pub was quieter now, Rhianna noticed, and the remaining customers had gone back to their own business and took no notice of them. Joe returned his attention to her. Was he going to kiss her again? As if spellbound, his hazel eyes studied her, from her mouth to her gaze. Then he smiled. "Let's have a drink to celebrate!" To her disappointment, he let her go.

Joe fetched a bottle of Prosecco from behind the counter, popped the cork and poured them both a glass.

"To karma!" Rhianna chinked flutes with Joe. The bubbles hit the spot. She now felt calmer and much more in control. Glyn was out of her life for good. She'd stood up to him and told him so.

"So, what did that loser want?" Joe asked, after taking a sip of his Prosecco. Then he paused. "Hey, actually, it's none of my business."

Rhianna shrugged. She didn't keep secrets. At least she didn't want to from Joe. "He wanted me back, basically. But I can't trust him again, Joe. He ruined everything between us. I believed he was the one … and however much I missed what we had, he's destroyed it. His actions were always passive-aggressive. I wasn't in a healthy relationship. I realise that now."

"He's done you a huge favour. You deserve so much better."

Eventually, with most of the bottle of Prosecco finished, Rhianna waited while Joe shut up the pub. He locked the front door and then the back door, showing out Toby and thanking him for his hard work.

He perched on a stool next her again, and their knees brushed. They'd been edging closer and closer throughout the evening. They finished the remainder of the Prosecco fizzing in their flutes.

"Thanks, Joe, for your help tonight." She leaned forward and touched his knee.

He placed his hand on hers so that it remained on his leg. The heat from his palm sent a sizzle through her body. "Anytime. I had great fun kissing you." Joe leaned closer.

"That kiss did feel good."

"I know... In fact, I could easily do it again. But properly." Centimetres apart. Millimetres... Joe edged closer. She could feel his breath on her lips.

"Did you not kiss me properly earlier?"

"No."

The next thing Rhianna knew, Joe's mouth was on hers. She closed her eyes to savour the sensation. And then, Joe swept her off the stool and they stood, bodies pressed together, his tongue gently searching for hers as his fingers combed through her hair, cupping her head, tugging her closer.

She remembered he was a good kisser.

It started gently, as their tongues touched, but became more urgent, his hands trailing over the fabric of her dress. She reached over his shoulders and around his neck, pressing her breasts, stomach, and hips against him.

He pulled away briefly, only their mouths separating. "This is kissing you properly."

CHAPTER 21: STORMY WEATHER

Joe insisted they leave the empty bottle of Prosecco and the glasses where they were on the bar, and gently taking her hand, he led Rhianna up the stairs to his apartment. She kicked her sandals off once they were in Joe's lounge, standing on tiptoes to kiss him as he pulled her back towards him.

A tiny voice inside her head told her this was a bad idea. But her body craved him. The memory of the passion they'd shared three years ago rushed to the forefront of her mind, extinguishing the whisper of doubt. She wanted to experience it again. She let Joe lead her to his bedroom, where he carefully unzipped her dress, pushing the sleeves down her arms, and letting it fall around her ankles. Her fingers fumbled with the buttons of his shirt, desperate to feel his skin against hers. He helped her by undoing his jeans, and in between kisses she pulled them down so they fell to the floor.

Stripping his socks off, Joe eased Rhianna onto his bed, only their underwear separating them. He gently stroked her skin, kissing her, his lips trailing, following his fingers, sending her wild with desire for him, a moan escaping her lips. She ached for him, to be one again. Wanting, needing to feel his love anew. Skin on skin, every touch, kiss, caress, sent fire through her veins. Closing her eyes, she relished every hot, delectable moment, until everything became urgent, passionate, and impatient...

No words were spoken. Afterwards they lay together, savouring the sensations they'd just shared, as the ripples of pleasure continued to pulsate through them. In the morning, Rhianna would worry about what she'd just done.

Just savour how you feel now.

Joe brushed the stray hairs off her face and kissed her. He left the bed briefly to visit the bathroom, covering her with the duvet, but returned to spoon behind her. He stroked her hair and gently caressed her back, sending ripples of delight along her skin. Then he kissed her softly behind her ear. "Night, Rhianna."

"Night, Joe," she said, her eyes closed and her heart aching with a love she knew she should quash.

She fell asleep wrapped in the warmth of his arms.

Rhianna awoke in an empty bed. Her night had been peaceful, sleeping with Joe's arms wrapped around her. She must have slept deeply, because she didn't even feel him leave.

Had he left early to avoid any awkwardness?

She was naked in Joe's bed. And she needed to get up. Did she just strut naked from one bedroom to the other to get some fresh clothes, or her pyjamas? Or should she just put on the dress she'd worn last night?

Oh, God, what had she done? Was this going to make things awkward? Did he want a relationship? Or would he merely want her in his bed regularly — with no strings attached?

Last night, they hadn't discussed anything. They'd just slept with one another. No confirmation whether they were to do it again, whether he'd been thinking about her being his girlfriend. Nothing. Just sex.

Pretty amazing sex, though. She and Joe had always clicked on that front. It's as if he knew where all her best buttons were and how to push them in just the right order.

It did mean that Glyn was now no longer the last man she'd slept with. But would the fact that it was now Joe help her emotional equilibrium?

Rhianna pushed the duvet back and gathered up all her clothes. Holding them in front of her so that they covered her modesty, she decided nipping between bedrooms and changing into her pyjamas was probably the best option.

Out in the lounge, Rhianna couldn't hear Joe. He wasn't in the kitchen either. She zoomed into her bedroom, relieved not to be caught naked with her clothes dangling in front of her, threw on her pyjamas in record time, then headed for the bathroom.

She emerged fresh-breathed from giving her teeth a clean, and with her hair not looking like she'd been dragged through a hedge backwards, having brushed it and tied it back into a ponytail.

"Hey, there you are," Joe said, smiling. He was now in the kitchen, waiting for the kettle to boil. "I remembered I had an early delivery arriving, so I tried not to wake you. I thought I'd let you lie in a bit longer before I brought in some coffee." He seemed his usual casual self. As if everything was normal between them. He poured the boiled water into two mugs, stirring as he did so. He offered Rhianna a mug. He didn't kiss her or anything.

"I probably need to be getting to the bistro. It's less than two weeks till we open." Rhianna took the mug of coffee, warming her hands around it.

"Breakfast first, though?"

"Actually, I'll be baking and trying out some recipes. I'll eat there." She took a sip of her coffee and watched Joe place two pieces of wholemeal bread into the toaster. "Joe…?"

"Yeah?" He briefly looked over his shoulder then concentrated on getting the butter out of the fridge.

"About last night?"

"What about it?"

His tone was so casual, unconcerned, and he still didn't catch her eye. His response jolted Rhianna's own feelings. It had clearly meant nothing to him. Just sex. She needed to make him think it had been the same for her too. She shook her head. "Nothing … nothing, thanks again for your help with Glyn." Rhianna retreated quickly with her coffee, for fear she'd betray her emotions to him. "I'd best jump in the shower. I'll catch you later."

"Sure. No problem."

"Hey, look what's arrived," Nick announced, entering the kitchen where Rhianna was busy baking. "Wow, it smells good in here."

Rhianna may have been physically present in the kitchen, but her head was elsewhere, going over last night's events. "Oh," she said, startled at her train of thought being interrupted. She should have been thinking about new recipes or cocktails, but no, her mind was on Joe. By sleeping with him, she feared she'd made it too awkward for her to continue staying under his roof.

Nick was holding a large sign, well wrapped for its protection. It was the signage for her bistro. He was in today finishing up some final details. "Shall I hang it for you?"

"Would you mind?"

"Of course not, I'll add it to my bill." Nick grinned. "Get your ex sorted last night?"

"Yes, thank you. Karma well and truly administered also."

"You mean with Joe?"

"Yes, fantastic idea of his to pretend to be my boyfriend!" Why was Rhianna blushing? She turned and opened the oven, and was hit by a wall of heat and the smell of hot pastry. She hoped this would look like a good reason to be red and flustered.

"Yeah, we all saw him kiss you. To be honest, he's probably been dying for an excuse to do that since you arrived. I know I have." Nick laughed and raised his eyebrows suggestively.

Rhianna blushed even more. Now the kitchen felt as if it was on fire.

"I'll go hang the sign?" Nick thumbed behind him. "Want to come check where you want it?"

"Give me five minutes to get these out of the oven." She was baking some mini Cornish pasties and was intending to try them out on the remaining contractors. She was working on Cornish canapé ideas and didn't want them to get burnt.

Back in the kitchen, after telling Nick where the sign should go, Rhianna was busy trying out a recipe for a cocktail using a Cornish gin that Kerenza had sent her, when Olly came in, wearing grubby overalls with sawdust in his hair. When she saw him, she stopped shaking the Boston shaker she was holding, her hands cold from the ice.

"Wow, smells great in here," he said. "I've been dying to come down and see what you're making today. We could smell it in the attic, even over the odour of paint and wood wax."

"Thank you." The pasties were cooling on a rack on a far counter. She had shot glasses lined up. She didn't want to get inebriated with the alcohol, so thought she could share out the cocktail with everyone. It shouldn't affect their work, a small sip, or their ability to drive. "You can try one in a minute. And a shot of the cocktail I've just finished making." Using a strainer, she slowly poured out the cloudy tangerine-coloured cocktail into the shot glasses.

"Noah and I wanted you to come and take a look at the finished work." Olly beamed at her. Rhianna never ceased to be bowled over by his amazing smile.

"Oh, great. On time too." She handed a shot glass to Olly, and took two up with her, knowing Noah would be upstairs too. She followed Olly up the stairs, being careful not to spill the drinks. She stopped at the entrance of the room. "Wow, this looks fantastic. Thanks, you guys."

"Nick and his team obviously helped."

"Oh, yes, I know."

Rhianna stood awestruck for a moment. Everyone had worked so hard for her. She wanted to pinch herself. Her cocktail lounge in the attic was complete, except for the furniture, which was due to be delivered in the next couple of days. With the flooring laid, the wood burner in place, and the walls painted pale blue, it just awaited the finishing touches of sofas, tables and chairs. The beautiful new wave-shaped bar was polished, with the painted surfboard hanging over it, on which Noah had painted her bistro logo and a coupe glass with a slice of orange garnishing the rim, against a backdrop of the sea, surf crashing. At the far end of the room, the wall with the wood burner had been decorated a darker blue. She knew blue would give a cooler feel to the room, which would be perfect in the summer. In the cooler months, the orange tones of the scatter cushions she planned to have on the sofas would warm it up. She'd chosen some orange chairs, too. Now the room was finished, she couldn't wait to start stocking the bar. She had boxes of glasses to unpack, and Kerenza was ready to supply her with the booze.

Noah was just finishing up in the corner, pressing the lid back on a can of paint. Rhianna handed him a shot glass.

"Thank you, you two," she said, raising her glass.

"Cheers," Olly and Noah said in unison, then they each knocked back the mini cocktail. Both men nodded appreciatively. She could see their tongues running over their teeth.

"Is it okay?" Rhianna asked. She thought it tasted great, although on second thoughts perhaps there was a bit too much lime. She wondered if it might be too sweet for her male companions. "I'm hoping it'll be a refreshing cocktail to sip while watching the sun set."

"Is it orange juice?"

"Tangerine juice, actually. It's based on a cocktail called Stormy Weather, but I've tweaked it slightly and used a local Cornish gin." Looking outside at the dark grey clouds looming ominously on the horizon out at sea, coupled with her worry about the complications of sleeping with Joe, the name of the cocktail felt particularly apt.

"Never heard of it," Olly said. Rhianna took the empty glass off him. She didn't want him putting the sticky glass down on the new bar.

"Nice, though," Noah said, giving a reassuring smile.

"Possibly one for the ladies, though?" Rhianna asked, looking at both men's expressions. Their eyes said it all. "It'll be served in martini glasses. Not shots. With a spiral of orange rind to garnish."

"Oh, yeah, Rachel would love this," Olly said. "Once she's had the baby, obviously." He clapped his hands together. "Right, I'm going to pack up my tools. We're finished here."

"Help yourself to a mini-pasty in the kitchen. I need to hear your thoughts on those too."

"I'm going to miss working here. All this free food to sample."

"Rhianna, have you got a minute…?" Noah asked.

"Yes, sure." Rhianna followed him over to the area with the wood burner.

"I was wondering if you'd like me to paint a mural over in this corner? There's great light from the roof window, and when the sofas are in place, it might just finish this area off."

"Oh, I would love it, but I'm not sure I have enough funds for something so elaborate."

Noah shrugged. "We could come to an arrangement with payment. It's something I'd like to do for you, if you'd like me to."

"What would you paint?"

"You've seen my paintings in Tilly's gallery, right? Do you like them?"

"Oh, yes, they're great." Like Tilly, he painted seascapes, but he also painted surfers in the ocean waves.

"Well, I was thinking you could have a wave on this wall, with a surfer riding it." He traced a wave with his hands. "I didn't quite have the room on the surfboard, but while I was painting that, I came up with this idea."

"Oh, yes, one of your paintings but on a larger scale," Rhianna said excitedly, then frowned. "But can you get it finished by next weekend, though? I'm opening on the following Thursday, remember, for the locals to give the staff a test run before half-term week starts."

"Yeah, I've painted the image I'm thinking of plenty of times. I could knock it up pretty quickly," Noah said. "The surfer could even be holding a cocktail glass with the bistro's logo on it."

"Okay, great. Just remember the sofa will sit here, so set it high enough so it's not obstructed by the furniture."

"No problem. I'll just let this wall dry, then I'll prep it."

"Fantastic. You're a star." Without thinking, Rhianna kissed him on the cheek.

Noah reacted by gently touching her arm as Rhianna pulled away, blushing at her brazen mistake. His skin had felt hot on her lips.

"Rhianna…" He reached for her again. "I was going to ask you out, for a drink…"

"Oh."

"But now I guess you're with Joe…"

"Oh, erm, I'm not with Joe." Rhianna's gaze dropped to the floor, feeling the heat rise to the surface of her cheeks. *Was she with Joe?*

"But last night? The kiss…"

"Oh, he just did that to get rid of Glyn for me." Rhianna giggled nervously, shrugging her shoulders nonchalantly. *And the sex, why had the sex happened? Not something to trouble Noah with.*

"Oh, right." Noah nodded thoughtfully.

"But a drink sometime would be nice." God, the word 'nice' sounded so lame. "Lovely, I mean it would be lovely, but I'm really busy right now. Really busy. And usually as soon as I finish up here, I fall straight into bed — on my own…" Oh God, why did she just say that…? "So yes, bistro to bed, to sleep, usually, as soon as I finish up here…" Rhianna could feel the words tumbling out of her mouth and not making much sense. She must sound like a right bumbling idiot.

"Eat, sleep, bistro, repeat," Noah said, chuckling. He really was a sweet guy.

Sweet, do guys like being thought of as sweet? "Yes, that's it." Rhianna nodded, trying to control her thoughts. "So maybe a rain check?"

Noah shoved his hands into the pockets of his overalls. "Yeah, sure. I understand."

225

Rhianna couldn't help noticing how disappointed he looked. She always found Olly the chattier, more outgoing of the two brothers. Noah was quieter, even shy, and tended to let Olly do all the talking. But perhaps this shyness, she now realised, was because of her. He liked her. "Honestly, Noah, this is nothing personal, but my mind really is focused on the business at the moment."

"Hey, these pasties are fantastic." Olly appeared at the top of the stairs. "How many was I allowed to have?"

"Well, save one for Noah, and Nick, at least." Rhianna was glad he'd defused the situation. "Right, I'd best get on." She smiled at Noah.

"Yeah, I'll set to work on the mural."

"What mural?" Olly approached his brother. Rhianna left them to talk, and made her way back downstairs to the haven of her kitchen. She just wanted to concentrate on the menus and not the men trying to complicate her life. Testing more recipes helped her concentrate on the bistro and blocked out all thoughts of Joe … and the night they'd just spent together.

CHAPTER 22: KIWI SMASH

"Is something troubling you, Joe?" Rose pulled a cake from the Aga, the heat warming the kitchen and filling the air with a sweet vanilla aroma. She baked for pleasure, but also supplied a coffee shop with cakes, and Joe even had one from her every weekend to offer in the pub.

"No, no…" Joe was sitting at the large kitchen table, stirring the cream around in his coffee. "Just a late night." Once Rhianna had left for the bistro, he'd headed over to the bed and breakfast to give his parents a hand. It being May, they'd seen an increase in guests, mainly young parents with pre-school children, and therefore not limited to when they could holiday. The full onslaught of tourists was yet to come, and very soon Joe would find himself busier on the beach, leaving the pub in the hands of his trusted staff.

Should he trouble his mother with his thoughts about Rhianna … and how he could have screwed up their friendship? He had an open and honest relationship with his mum; she'd always encouraged it. But how open should a man in his mid-thirties be? *Hey, Mum, I slept with Rhianna… No, don't say anything.*

"Late night, huh? Goes with the trade. I told you so when you bought that pub."

"Rhianna needed support when her ex-boyfriend turned up out of the blue, and we stayed up late afterwards, chatting about it." *Not a complete lie.*

"Oh?" Rose tipped the Victoria sponge out of the cake tin and onto a cooling rack. Joe eyed her warily, expecting her to question him further. It was easy to forget that your parents were older and wiser. But instead, she simply asked, "How's Rhianna getting on with the bistro? She opens next week." She had a saucepan of strawberry jam boiling on the stove, which she went over and stirred. She liked making homemade jam for her breakfasts at the B&B. "We've had an invite to her opening night, everything half price for locals. Your dad has booked a table."

"Yeah, she wants to give the staff a test run."

"It's a good idea. Are you going?"

"Yes, of course. I said I'd lend a hand if it got busy."

"Oh, shall I get Dad to amend the booking? Table for three?"

"You don't want me cramping your style. Besides, you two could do with a night out together. No, I'm fine. I've booked a table with friends." He was going with Tilly, Liam and Tristan.

Rose opened the door of the dishwasher and steam rose out of the gap. Joe helped her empty it, placing the crockery on the large oak Welsh dresser that matched the kitchen table. "And how are you getting on with Rhianna living under the same roof as you?"

"Great."

A couple of weeks ago, Joe had stupidly let slip that he had dated Rhianna three years ago when she was here for a hen party. Rose had hinted at a rekindling of their romance, but he'd managed to deflect her with the whole 'we're just friends' line. Which they were, of course.

"She's the first woman you've shared your apartment with since Alannah, isn't she?" Rose said, handing Joe a warm stack of her best plates to be stored inside the Welsh dresser. Rose kept her best crockery — the Denby — for family and friends, and used cheaper plates and bowls for the bed and breakfast guests, because they were more likely to get broken. She used mismatched vintage crockery which she picked up from flea-markets, car-boots and charity shops.

Joe rolled his eyes. His mother was always so keen to play Cupid. Especially with him. Sam and Heather had escaped her mild meddling, because they'd found love. She'd have a field day if he confessed to sleeping with Rhianna last night.

"Mum, Rhianna and I are friends. Just friends."

"It's probably the best way." Rose patted Joe's shoulder.

"What do you mean by that?"

"Well, best you get to know each other as friends first." Rose tucked a strand of white hair that had escaped from her bun behind her ear. "It worked for me and your dad."

Joe kissed his mother on the cheek, feeling it was time to leave before she put him under any more scrutiny, and headed out of the farmhouse. The sun was doing its best to shine through the clouds, and when it did break through it warmed his skin. The breeze was picking up, though, taking the edge off the sunshine. On the horizon a storm was brewing. He hoped that once it had passed over, the warmer weather would return and hold out for the May half-term. Good weather meant plenty of beach visitors, which boosted the town's business for everybody. The holiday season was short.

Walking past the bistro, Joe thought he would call in. He didn't want to leave things awkward between him and Rhianna. He had more than enjoyed their night together. But he thought it best not to make a habit of it. He wanted her to trust him, especially as they were living together, albeit temporarily. He hadn't offered her his spare room so that he could get her into his bed. Getting to know Rhianna more over these past couple of months and talking to her last night after they'd seen off her ex, he knew she wanted something more stable than a holiday fling. Those were things of the past. Kittiwake Cove was no longer her holiday destination, it was her home. Plus, this Glyn idiot had really screwed her over. The last thing Joe wanted to do was to hurt her further.

As he climbed the metal steps, Joe noticed that The Beach Front Bistro sign now hung in place near the entrance. Nick was descending a ladder with various tools in his hands.

"Nick." Joe nodded.

"Joe."

"Rhianna about?"

"Yeah, you'll find her in her office — the kitchen."

Thankful that Nick had made no comment about the previous evening, Joe made his way through the restaurant area to the kitchen at the back. Noticing that Rhianna was talking to a young woman, Joe knocked on the open door before entering.

"Hey, Joe, this is Yasmin. She's my new cocktail waitress. She's going to manage the bar up in the attic," Rhianna said.

Joe shook Yasmin's hand. "Nice to meet you."

"She's originally from Berkshire. She's got plenty of experience, working in cocktail lounges in Newquay."

"Bit livelier there," Joe said.

"Yes, but I think I'll prefer the quieter, classier nightlife of Kittiwake Cove," Yasmin said, smiling, looking from Rhianna to Joe nervously, as if still in her job interview. "But I'm used to the pressure of working in a busy environment."

The timer beeped on the oven and Rhianna fetched oven gloves off the counter, pulling out a tray of golden miniature pasties.

"They smell great," Joe said, reaching for one.

Rhianna slapped his hand away with a click of her tongue. "You can try one in a minute once they've cooled." With tongs, she gently placed them on a wire rack. "I made some earlier, which Noah and Olly polished off. But I thought I could start making some batches to freeze." Rhianna slipped off her oven gloves, then beckoned Joe to follow her. "While they cool, let me show you upstairs. Come along, Yasmin, come and see where you'll be working." Rhianna sounded excited. Joe was pleased for her. Everything was coming together.

The attic looked amazing, complete apart from the furniture. The bar had a large pile of boxes stacked beside it.

"This looks fab," Yasmin said, her dark eyes wide with wonder. Joe couldn't agree more. In the corner, up by the wood burner, he spied Noah still painting. He thought all the work had been finished.

Rhianna made to approach Noah, but he stood up and came towards them.

"No, no, I don't want you seeing it until its finished," he said to Rhianna.

"Oh, okay."

"I can always tweak it if you don't like it." Noah must have noticed some of the apprehension on Rhianna's face. Joe was intrigued.

"What are you painting?" he asked Noah.

"A mural. You can come and take a look. Though there isn't much to see yet."

Noah led Joe over to the wall he was working on, while Rhianna started talking to Yasmin about unpacking the boxes by the bar. Joe could see the outline of a wave, a surfer within it. It looked like something Noah usually painted, and Joe knew it would look impressive on the wall.

"It'll look great."

"Rhianna will like it, won't she?" Noah asked.

"Of course she will." Joe slapped Noah on the back.

"Hey, Joe, while you're here, I just want to ask you something. Make sure I'm not treading on anyone's toes, after last night." Noah wrung a rag in his hands and couldn't quite meet Joe's gaze.

"Last night?"

"You kissed Rhianna, but she said it was nothing, you were pretending to be her boyfriend to get rid of Glyn. Right?"

Relief washed over Joe. "Oh, yes, that's right."

"Well, I asked Rhianna out for a drink," Noah said tentatively. "Was that okay?"

A jolt of shock passed through Joe, but he quickly recovered himself. Did he have an issue with Noah dating Rhianna? He didn't own her. She wasn't his property. And however much he liked her, it wouldn't be fair to put Noah off. Joe knew he couldn't offer Rhianna what she wanted. "Yes, sure, mate. Rhianna and I are just friends. What did she say?" Intrigue filled him, jealousy licking at his gut.

"Oh, she said yes, but she wants to concentrate on the opening of the bistro first."

Joe stuffed his hands into his pockets, rocking on the heels of his trainers. "That's sensible. Hey, but good luck. She's a beautiful woman."

"Yeah, I know." Noah glanced over at Rhianna, then smiled nervously back at Joe.

Joe patted him on the shoulder. "Right, I'll leave you to it."

Joe went back to the bar where Rhianna was. For a moment, he got to observe her unnoticed. Her sandy blonde hair was tied back messily, with loose tendrils falling around her face. She was wearing denim shorts, revealing her slender legs, which were starting to bronze with the sunshine. She always had a smile on her face and a positive attitude. Yeah, he could see why Noah would be smitten.

"Ah, Joe, let's see if those pasties have cooled. You can tell me what you think of them." She tried lifting one of the heavy boxes, but Joe quickly stepped in and lifted it onto the bar for her. "Thanks." She looked into his eyes, pausing. Then she turned away, breaking the moment. "Yasmin, can I leave you here a moment? I'll pop back up in a sec."

"Sure."

Back down in the kitchen with Rhianna to himself, Joe devoured a miniature pasty, giving her his verdict on it while she worked at preparing another batch. The pasties tasted great. The beef was tender, there was the right amount of pepper, the pastry wasn't too dry or too hard. The only thing wrong with them was their size.

"Why so small?" Joe asked, licking his fingers after he'd finished a beef and ale pasty and was eyeing another on the cooling rack.

"I want to serve Afternoon Teas." Rhianna placed a mug of coffee in front of him and pushed over a draft of the menu. She hugged her own mug. "A range of Afternoon Teas, from classic Cornish cream teas with scones and a pot of tea, to lavish High Teas with Champagne. These pasties will be for the Gentleman's Afternoon Tea. And to keep it local, I thought I'd serve pasties, rather than steak sandwiches. It'll all be served on Cornish slate platters." She showed him the platters stacked ready in the cupboard. "A mini burger, a miniature pasty, and a Yorkshire pudding served with a small piece of tender beef."

"Ah, I see. Or perhaps a mini piece of fish if you want to mix up the meat options?"

"Oh, yes, I did think of that. A small piece of the catch of the day, on a couple of chunky chips."

"And what were you thinking for the evening?"

"Oh, I'll show you." Rhianna grabbed her manila folder, and as she came to stand next to Joe, she took out some pieces of paper. Among the aroma of pasties and cooking smells, he caught the scent of her perfume. It brought back memories of last night: Rhianna in his bed, his skin pressing against hers… *Focus, Joe.* Rhianna continued, "I've bought this high quality paper to print the menus out on — the colour is called champagne. I've set up a small office near the kitchen. I just prefer to be working in here for now, while testing menu ideas."

The menu choices looked great. There were options for everyone.

"I'm going to change the menu as the seasons change too, and have different menus for different days."

"Looks great. My mouth is watering looking at it. Have you got a chef?"

"Yes, but I'm likely to be in the kitchen too, until we're fully up and running and I can assess whether it's viable to hire more staff."

"Makes sense." Joe nodded. Another piece of paper caught his eye. "Oh, what's this?"

"This is the cocktail menu — drinks to recommend with the dishes."

Some of them he recognised, the popular classics, others he didn't. "Kiwi Smash? I've never heard of that one before."

"It's delicious! Gin based, one for the summer when kiwi fruit is in season. I'm trying to put some different ones out there."

Joe approved. "Will the cocktails down here be the same as upstairs?"

"Pretty much. I need to see how it works logistically," Rhianna said, packing away some of the papers back into the manila file. "Yasmin's got the experience to make any cocktail. And I know loads too. Between us, we should manage if we get a special request."

"Don't overstretch yourself."

She laughed. "I'll try not to. But it's going to take a lot of hard work to get the bistro off the ground, and to make sure it makes money."

"You'll do it." Joe grabbed her hand and gave it a squeeze without thinking. He let go just as quickly, the warmth and the softness of her skin reawakening the sensations of last night.

"Thank you."

For a moment there was silence, as they both finished drinking their coffees. There was still the elephant in the room — the amazing sex they'd shared.

"So, Noah's asked you out?" Joe couldn't believe the words had escaped his mouth. Some part of him wanted to hear how Rhianna felt. Did she like Noah?

"He told you?" Rhianna didn't catch his eye. Joe nodded nonchalantly when she did look at him. "He did, yes, but I said I needed to wait."

"You should have a drink with him. He's a nice guy." Joe shoved his hands into his pockets. *What are you saying? You need your head examining.*

"Really, you think so?"

"Sure." He shrugged his shoulders. He was trying to play it cool. He was trying to look as if it didn't bother him. *Friends, we're just friends.*

"So, last night?" Rhianna held the folder against her body defensively.

"A bit of fun?" Joe said, hating himself for even suggesting he wasn't taking it seriously. But what could he offer Rhianna?

"Yes, of course it was."

"It won't happen again. I mean, living under the same roof, I don't want there to be an atmosphere, or any awkwardness between us."

"No, me neither."

"I think we both just had a bit too much to drink. You needed comforting, I wanted to help." Rhianna was nodding at him. He could see her swallowing, hopefully not swallowing back tears. He would never want to hurt her. "Rhianna…" She looked at him, green eyes shining. "I don't think I can offer you what you deserve."

She nodded. And in a hoarse whisper she replied, "I understand."

Rhianna couldn't watch Joe leave. Opening cupboard doors at random, she took out ingredients with the idea of baking more batches of food, things she could freeze in advance. But her thoughts were whirling inside her head. She couldn't concentrate as she stared blankly inside the cupboards. She had a list of jobs to do, and now she'd forgotten what they were.

She could feel her eyes prickling, and she blinked and swallowed, hoping to hold in any tears. But she knew if anyone came into the kitchen right now, her shining eyes would give her away.

What had she been expecting from Joe? A declaration of love?

Of course not. The evening they'd shared last night hadn't been any different to the evenings she'd shared with him here three years ago: flirty, sexy fun. No strings sex.

Well, if Joe reckoned she should date Noah, then she damn well would. Once the bistro was up and running — of course. She wasn't going to let any man get in the way of her life and her career. Or her happiness. The bistro had to be a success. Her future depended upon it.

She swallowed, relaxing the tension gathering in her throat. Coming back to her senses, she remembered Yasmin, and dashed back up to the attic.

Yasmin had emptied most of the boxes containing different types of glasses: cocktail glasses, wine glasses, champagne flutes, tumblers, and shot glasses. The empty boxes were even sitting neatly flat-packed in a pile on the floor in front of the bar, ready for recycling. Rhianna already had a great feeling about Yasmin. In her interview, Rhianna had learned that Yasmin was born in Slough, Berkshire — but she told people Windsor because it sounded posher — that her grandparents were originally from India, and that she had studied at Plymouth University. However, she'd dropped out of university — much to the disapproval of her parents — but stayed in the West Country, first in Devon and then in Cornwall. Yasmin had only spent an hour at the bistro, but was already working hard and becoming invested in making Rhianna's dream a success.

"I'm sorry, I got talking to Joe and totally forgot you were up here," Rhianna said.

"Hey, I understand. For an older guy, he's rather hot." Yasmin, at only twenty-three, perceived Joe as 'older'. Then she whispered, "But he's hot too," gesturing to Noah, who was closer to both Rhianna and Yasmin's age, in his mid-twenties. Luckily, Noah had plugged in his earphones to listen to his music and was unaware he was being admired. In fact, he was so absorbed in his painting that he'd probably forgotten that Yasmin and Rhianna were there. He was singing along to a George Ezra track by the sounds of it, with not a bad voice either. Yasmin and Rhianna looked at each other and stifled their giggles.

Because the bar downstairs already had lines for beer barrels, Rhianna had decided not to have a tap in the upstairs bar. It would be expensive, for one thing. Up here she wanted to offer local bottled beers and ciders, a selection of wines and spirits, but predominantly, she hoped people would come to the bar for the cocktails. And it wasn't as if a pint couldn't be brought up.

Cocktails weren't supposed to be chugged back in a busy, bustling club with loud music and wall to wall people. They needed to be sipped and savoured, enjoyed in a relaxing environment. She wanted the ambience to be perfect for people to chat with friends. The music would be low, the atmosphere tranquil. She had ordered comfy sofas and chairs, and there would be a mixture of low seating and high stools round high tables nearer the bar. Yasmin was in total agreement with Rhianna's ideas, and had even suggested a waitress service on quieter nights, so that the cocktails would be brought to the customer, rather than making them lurk at the bar waiting for them. This bar would have to cater for the restaurant downstairs for some of the more complicated cocktails if customers wanted to order them with a meal. Yasmin had bar and cocktail-making experience, but what she didn't know, Rhianna was prepared to teach her.

As well as plenty of shelving below the bar, Olly had installed racks above the bar, on which to hang wine glasses and stemmed beer glasses upside down. They created a fabulous chandelier effect with a spotlight positioned above them. The other day, Nick's plumber had installed the ice machine — important for making cocktails — and a new glasswasher. Both were ready to use. The ice machine didn't need turning on yet, but Yasmin had already learnt how to work the glasswasher, putting the glasses once through and wiping them with a tea towel so they gleamed, before placing them on the shelf. Rhianna already loved this woman. She'd wanted someone to take responsibility for running the upstairs bar, and Yasmin was already proving to her that she'd picked the perfect candidate.

The line of fridges with glass-fronted doors behind the bar were empty, but stock would arrive soon to fill them. Olly had created a worktop above the fridges, the surface matching the S-shaped bar, where spirit bottles would stand. Mirrors were fitted, and lighting installed to display the various gin and vodka bottles. The cocktail lounge was taking shape. The furniture was due to arrive tomorrow. Rhianna's nerves fluttered for a moment, anxiety creeping in. Would this work? Would her bistro be a success? Would the tourists of Kittiwake Cove even want cocktails?

"I thought I'd put the glasses where I feel they logically should go. I won't know until we start serving customers if it works or not. Then I'll jig it about if I need to," Yasmin explained. She placed another pristine glass on a shelf and smiled at Rhianna. "If you've got things to be getting on with, I'm fine here." Rhianna had decided to give Yasmin some freedom in how she wanted to set the bar up. She would be working up here the most.

"Yes, okay, I'll get on in the kitchen. Make a note of the hours you work, and I'll square you up with your wages."

Later that day, as Rhianna was clearing her kitchen, having kept busy and managing to push all thoughts of Joe aside, Kerenza arrived with part of the order Rhianna had placed with her.

"I haven't brought it all. That'll come on your delivery. But I was in the area and wanted to see how things were coming along. And you did say you needed to have a selection of spirits early to test out cocktails." Kerenza dropped a heavy box on the kitchen counter and the contents clunked.

"I did." Rhianna wiped her hands on a towel and approached the box.

"I've got another couple of boxes in the car."

"Ah, thank you. I appreciate the visit. Are you staying locally or heading home?" Rhianna's mind instantly went to Joe's bed. Kerenza lived further south in Cornwall.

"Yes, I've somewhere to stay nearby." Kerenza gave a mischievous grin.

"So, let's show you around." Rhianna changed the subject quickly, grabbing the box and heading for the attic with it, Kerenza following. She couldn't help noticing the flirtatious glances passing between Kerenza and Nick, which made her think that Nick was possibly her stopover for tonight. It reassured her to think that Joe wasn't Kerenza's only option. Though why should it bother her? Joe had said himself last night had only been a bit of fun.

"Hey, Yasmin, this is Kerenza; she works for Cornish Coves Brewery." Rhianna put the box on the bar with relief, as it was deceptively heavy, making her biceps ache. "They'll be supplying some of the local Cornish brands of gin and vodka I want to use in the cocktails, plus locally brewed beers, ciders and wines."

After the two women shook hands, Kerenza looked around, and even went over to where Noah was working. Rhianna stayed away, as she knew he wanted her to only see the finished result.

"It looks impressive, Rhianna. Liking your vision here." Kerenza returned to the bar, where Rhianna was helping Yasmin empty the box of spirits, displaying them on the back bar. The different shapes of glass bottles, and the subtle shades of the spirits and liqueurs added a touch of decadence to the décor.

"It'll be so much better with the furniture in. It echoes in here at the moment."

Nick helped the women retrieve the other boxes from Kerenza's car and placed them on the bar in the restaurant for Rhianna to unpack.

Nick left with Kerenza, saying he'd be back in the morning. Olly had already gone and Noah packed up at about five, and so Rhianna suggested Yasmin get off too. But she herself carried on finding jobs to do, not wanting to be idle, and not quite ready to face Joe.

CHAPTER 23: PORNSTAR MARTINI

Over the next couple of days, Rhianna's life became manic, as she oversaw the arrival of the furniture and the stock deliveries, not to mention cooking, baking and staff introductions.

Nick continued working a couple of hours each day at the bistro, undertaking any last-minute jobs, like hanging the paintings and photographs that Tilly was supplying from the gallery, all marked with sales information, and the knick-knacks Rhianna had purchased to make the bistro her own — signs like 'There's Always Time for a Cocktail' and 'Let the Fun Be Gin'. None of his workmen were about now, having all been assigned to other projects of Nick's — projects Rhianna suspected he'd probably put on hold so that he could get her job finished, which she was very grateful for, otherwise she may not have been opening her bistro so soon.

Nick and Noah were very helpful, lifting the heavy sofas in the attic, positioning the coffee tables and chairs, and moving the dining tables in the bistro to match the plan Rhianna had created and stuck up in the kitchen with table numbers. Yasmin, keen to help, assisted Rhianna with the finishing touches to the bistro and cocktail lounge, styling the sofas with cushions and setting the tables with tealights and cocktail menu cards. Rushed off her feet, all thoughts of Joe were easily pushed to the back of Rhianna's mind. She barely saw him in the evenings, as she would get in late and take herself straight up to bed. It seemed that they'd settled back into their old friendship, as if their night together had never happened.

It was Tuesday afternoon. Rhianna's opening night was only two days away. She'd decided that a Thursday would be the best day, rather than a Friday when tourists would start to arrive, and might want to try out the bistro. Everything was pretty much done. She had arranged for all her new staff to come in for some training. She wanted to run through the layout of the bistro, the menu and the cocktails, to ensure the restaurant would run smoothly on the opening night. She also wanted this time for the staff members to get to know one another. They were due to arrive in another twenty minutes.

"Hey, Rhianna, got a minute?" Noah poked his head round the doorway of her small office. She was sitting at her desk and the printer was busy churning out the lunchtime menus on embossed champagne-coloured card. He looked very different than usual. Rather than his customary overalls, he was wearing mid wash denim shorts and a pale blue T-shirt with a surf motif on it. His blond hair was clean of paint and even styled with wax.

"Yes, sure." She stood up and joined him.

"I've finished the mural. Come see," he said.

Rhianna followed him up the stairs to the cocktail lounge.

"Oh, wait." At the top of the stairs, Noah stepped behind Rhianna and placed his hands over her eyes.

"Now I can't see where I'm going!" She gave a nervous laugh.

"Just keep walking in a straight line. I'll guide you."

Noah's strong hands were warm against her skin and smelt of soap. His body was torturously close too as, keeping her eyes covered, he guided her towards the end of the room. Her body temperature rose a notch, responding to this not unwelcome close proximity, and she feared it would give her away.

"Stop," he said. Rhianna halted, relieved she hadn't bumped into anything, and the ordeal of walking blindly — with Noah so close — would be over soon. "On three, you can look... One, two —" She took a deep breath just as he said, "three." He released his hands and she opened her eyes. He remained standing close behind her.

In front of her was Noah's mural. It depicted a handsome surfer, wearing board shorts, on a cream surfboard, riding in a huge blue wave tipped with white surf. He was holding a cocktail. On the martini glass was The Beach Front Bistro's logo. It looked brilliant.

"Oh, wow, Noah, this is amazing, thank you, thank you, thank you." Rhianna turned and hugged him, kissing him on the cheek. He reciprocated the hug tentatively, his body touching hers where she'd thrown herself at him, his hands cupping around her back and holding her close. It felt ... different.

"Hey, Rhianna!"

Rhianna released Noah and stepped back quickly, removing herself from his personal space, awkwardly placing her hands behind her back, like a child caught in the act of doing something naughty. They both turned in the direction of the male voice, but Noah remained at Rhianna's side.

Joe appeared at the top of the stairs. "There you are. It's quiet at the pub, so I wondered if you needed a hand here?"

"Oh, right. No, I'm good, thanks. I have my staff arriving soon for some training." She beckoned for Joe to come over and he walked towards them, giving Noah a nod, his gaze remaining fixed on Rhianna. "Look at Noah's mural." Rhianna grabbed his arm and pointed.

"Yes, it's great, isn't it? I saw it the other day." Joe winked. Of course, everybody had been allowed to see it except for Rhianna. "Are you pleased with it?" he asked.

"Yes, more than pleased. It's given the cocktail lounge something extra."

Noah stood quietly, not saying a word, just smiling modestly. If Joe had ruined the moment between them, Noah didn't give anything away.

"Well, if you don't need me," Joe said, "I think I'll go catch some waves. This painting certainly makes me feel like taking a dip."

"Yes, thanks for the offer. Catch you later," Rhianna said, waving Joe off. She turned back to Noah. He combed a hand through his hair.

"Shame you're not free now, we could go for that drink," Noah said. His green eyes almost pleaded with her to make herself available.

"Yes, sorry, I still have things to do," she said guiltily. She would love to take Noah up on his offer. She truly was grateful for all his hard work too. "But like I said to Joe, my team are arriving soon, and I want to get to know them." Rhianna puffed up the cushions on the sofas near the wood burner to give her hands something to do. "But I haven't forgotten. Just let me get the bistro up and running first, yeah?" Rhianna had mixed feelings about Noah. She didn't really know him all that well. But then that was all the more reason why she ought to go out for a drink with him. A relationship with Joe was out of the question. He'd pretty much said so himself.

"Of course." Noah smiled. "Well, that's me done for the day, so Joe's idea of a surf sounds like a good idea to me, too."

"Enjoy," Rhianna said. "And thank you for this wonderful mural. Don't forget to send me the invoice." Why she said that she wasn't sure, only she wanted Noah to know that she wasn't expecting a freebie. But judging by his gorgeous, cheeky smile and the shrug of his shoulders, she reckoned she wouldn't be receiving an invoice.

Rhianna arranged what she needed in the cocktail lounge, stopping briefly to admire the mural Noah had painted which brought a smile to her lips, before going downstairs to await her staff. Yasmin, the first to arrive, waved cheerily, then the others filtered in.

The newly hired waiting team were: Willow, a fresh-faced young woman, wearing no make-up (and still looking pretty, lucky thing), somewhere in her twenties; Vince, a tall young man, also in his early twenties, starting to lose his teenager scrawniness, his complexion still not clear; and Holly, in her mid-forties, wanting something to work around family life. Curtis, Rhianna's newly hired chef, was a stocky man in his thirties, with plenty of experience working in prestigious restaurants in Padstow and Newquay over the years. His blond hair was starting to recede, so he kept it very short. She hoped he would do most of the cooking, so that she could be present front of house as much as possible.

After the introductions, Rhianna handed out the uniforms she'd purchased, opting for black shirts with the bistro's logo on the pocket for the waiting team. She'd agreed these could be worn with black skirts, trousers, smart shorts or jeans — weather depending. She wanted her staff to look smart, but casual, too. Approachable and friendly. And comfortable on the hotter days of the season. Obviously, she had chef whites in abundance for her chef. They each had a name badge too.

All sitting around a table, Rhianna ran through the menus and schedule, and then explained her vision for the bistro and her expectations of her team. "I'm sure we'll have some teething problems, but together we should be able to overcome them. Any questions?" They all looked at each other and shook their heads. Rhianna stood up, clapping her hands. "Right, now for the fun part of the training! Let's make some cocktails!" She had laid on some canapés, and with the help of Curtis, carried them up from the kitchen to the cocktail lounge.

Although natural light still flooded in through the window, Yasmin set about lighting tealights on a couple of tables, and Rhianna switched on the lamps she'd purchased, to create the perfect cocktail ambience. There was now a pile of logs that Liam had provided, stacked by the wood burner for decorative effect, and ready to use in the colder months. Everyone admired the striking mural. It really made people stop and stare, filling Rhianna with pride for Noah. A large wooden fruit bowl that Rhianna had bought in a shop in Wadebridge now sat on the back counter, piled high with lemons, limes and oranges, and a couple of passion fruits, the fruit needed to make her cocktails. The berries — strawberries, raspberries and blueberries — would remain in the fridge below the counter.

Rhianna and Yasmin stood behind the bar, while Curtis, Vince, Holly and Willow were perched on the four high-backed faux-leather barstools opposite. Rhianna started making one of the cocktails on the list, a Pornstar Martini, talking them all through what she was doing, and explaining the ways to make a perfect cocktail. Although she and Yasmin both had experience in making cocktails, she wanted to go through some of her list to ensure nothing needed tweaking — The Beach Front Bistro's signature cocktails, especially. She thought the six of them could sample the cocktails, too. It was a good way for everyone to get to know each other — a team-building session before the bistro opened in a couple of days.

She poured the cocktail she'd just shaken into a couple of coupe martini glasses. Yasmin did the same, as she'd been creating the same cocktail, so there was one for each of the other staff. Prosecco was poured into shot glasses on the side and slices of passion fruit garnished the cocktail. They'd left notes and recipes behind the bar, marking up a cocktail menu to be used until they could make the cocktails blindfolded. There was a little left in the shakers, so she served this to Yasmin and herself in shot glasses.

Rhianna and Yasmin sipped their cocktails and took notes. They'd served up their first Pornstar Martini, one of Rhianna's favourites, and usually a hit in cocktail bars. Rhianna explained to her team that there was no wrong or right way to drink this cocktail. Some preferred to sip a little of the cocktail to allow room to add the Prosecco, lessening the sweetness of the drink, while some preferred to drink the Prosecco after they'd finished the passion fruit-based cocktail. Typically, ladies tended to enjoy this one more than gents, as it was possibly too sweet for them.

She then taught them how a gin and tonic should be served, and various other cocktails. She did not want her customers receiving a sloppy excuse of a drink. Likewise, she gave them all training on the coffee machine downstairs.

At ten in the evening, Rhianna locked up the bistro, hugging each member of her team in turn. The next time she'd see them would be Thursday evening, ready for the opening night.

A little lightheaded from the alcohol she'd consumed, and the steep climb up the hill, Rhianna walked into The Cormorant, to find Joe working alongside Toby. The pub was quiet now, at this time of night.

"Want a drink?" Joe asked as she approached the bar.

Rhianna shook her head, still out of breath after her hike. She wasn't drunk, but she'd certainly tested enough cocktails tonight. Her head was light, almost dizzy, her reactions sluggish. "No thanks, I'll just have…" What did she want? "A hot chocolate."

"Shall I put a shot of rum in it?"

"No, no, please don't. I need to be up early again tomorrow."

"Cream and marshmallows instead, then?"

"Oh, go on then."

Minutes later, Joe appeared with the hot chocolate generously topped with cream and marshmallows elegantly served in a glass mug with a handle, like the sort used for liqueur coffees.

Toby served a couple at the bar while Joe emptied the dishwasher and talked to Rhianna. "Are you ready for Thursday?"

"I think so. Tomorrow will be just more baking and prepping for the day, so we don't run out of food." Rhianna started to spoon some of the marshmallows off with the cream. "It's only the evening à la carte menu we're serving. We're opening from seven."

"You'll be fine. I'll help if you need me to."

"Your table is booked for seven-thirty. You'll do no such thing."

Rhianna sipped her hot chocolate, wiping cream from her nose every now and then, as she spoke with Joe about her plans. It certainly seemed that as far as Joe was concerned they had reverted to 'friends' mode, their night together seemingly forgotten. Maybe Rhianna needed to forget it too. She didn't want to ruin the friendship she had with Joe; she valued it too much. But she didn't want casual sex with him to become a habit either, otherwise she'd start feeling used. The last thing she wanted was any awkwardness with Joe, considering he was someone she would see regularly — especially as she still couldn't afford to move out of his apartment. Keep Joe at arm's length and everything would work out fine.

He was just so damn hot. That was Rhianna's problem. There was nothing more frustrating than fancying someone you couldn't have. But maybe that feeling would fade…

She needed to get her hormones in check. Maybe dating Noah would help. Noah was a good bet for a happy future, a lasting relationship — unlike Joe, who would bolt as soon as it got too heavy.

CHAPTER 24: SURF RIDER

Thursday evening arrived, and Rhianna's nerves vibrated through her whole body. She hoped none of her team would notice how nervous she was. She'd run a restaurant before, she'd been head chef in a kitchen before, but she'd never actually owned the business. That took a certain edge off the job. When she'd worked in restaurants in the past, it had always been important to her to serve up the best possible food with the best service. Rhianna had always taken pride in her work, even in kitchens she'd hated working in. But the difference was that back then she got to go home at the end of her shift and not worry about the business side of things.

She had her entire team in this evening, including Holly, who was going to work mainly during the day. She wanted everyone on board tonight. Even if it meant they were overstaffed and they were standing around twiddling their thumbs, she didn't care. She wanted the opening night to go well.

Rhianna had her blonde hair combed back into a neat ponytail with her face lightly made up, and was wearing the same black Beach Front Bistro shirt as the rest of her team. They all looked pristine. She couldn't have been prouder of them. Now she prayed they would perform as well in their roles as they'd claimed during their interviews. She already had confidence in Yasmin and Curtis, but she was yet to see what the others could do. She had been blessed with a warm evening, with a gentle breeze, so she could give her guests the option of sitting outside if they wished. The tables outside had also been laid. The glass balustrade, which protected the decking area from the wind, had been polished, so there wasn't a mark on it.

Rhianna checked her watch, then with a deep breath, she said to her waiting team, "Shall we do this?" It was almost seven o'clock, when the first customers were due to arrive.

Curtis was already busy in the kitchen. The other four nodded. Yasmin checked her radio and earpiece. Rhianna wore one, too, and so did Vince. She only had the three, so not enough for everybody. The idea was that Yasmin could be contacted up in the cocktail lounge with orders for cocktails for the restaurant when required.

Rhianna took another deep breath, then made her way over to the main doors and opened them up. The candles were lit on the tables. Everything was ready for the guests. She had a podium with the restaurant's bookings diary lying open. They were going to have a full house tonight.

Rhianna swallowed down her nerves, reminding herself that Glyn was no longer around, chipping away at her self-esteem. She was surrounded by positive, supportive people. She could do this.

The first of the guests arrived — locals she'd seen in the pub occasionally but didn't know. Rhianna welcomed them and checked them off on the booking sheet, and Holly showed them to their table to take their drinks order.

Next to arrive was Joe, with Tristan, Tilly and Liam.

"We're early, but we thought we'd check out the cocktail lounge," Joe said as Rhianna greeted them.

"Oh, Yasmin will be delighted. You know where to go."

Joe winked. "We do. See you in a bit."

Rhianna couldn't believe how fast her heart was pounding. But after half an hour, her anxiety calmed as she watched Willow, Holly and Vince efficiently taking orders and serving drinks. Rhianna mucked in too, when she didn't need to be at the door. Checking her first customers were happy with their meals and the service, she was able to recommend wines and cocktails, and soon started to feel at home in her role; with her rustiness worn off, she was back to doing what she did best. It felt great overseeing her own restaurant. She also checked on Curtis, and gave him a hand in the kitchen when necessary. But he appeared to have everything under control. Tonight was going to be a good test to see what menu choices were the most popular, so she knew whether to adjust it slightly.

Rose and Charles arrived. "Hello, how's it all going, dear?" Rose asked, as she greeted Rhianna with a kiss on the cheek.

"Great. I'm a little nervous, though."

"Nonsense. I'm sure you have it all under control," Rose said reassuringly, still holding Rhianna's arm. "How are your parents?" It did occur to Rhianna to wonder whether her mother and father would turn up and surprise her again. But her dad had said something about taking her mum away, and that they'd be down once she'd got into the swing of things with the restaurant.

"Great, thanks. They said they'd come down in a few weeks."

"Maybe I'll give them a ring, to check if they want a room soon." Rose winked, and Rhianna smiled. The woman had a twinkle in her eye, just like Joe. He might look like his father, but he had his mother's charm.

"Would you like to sit inside or outside?" Rhianna asked.

"It's not often the evenings are this mild," Charles said, wrapping an arm around his wife.

"Yes, we'll make the most of it and sit outside, al fresco," Rose agreed. With his arm gently resting on Rose's back,

Charles followed her out onto the decking, where Holly escorted them to a table.

Bursting with pride, Rhianna took a minute to observe her busy bistro. There was the gentle hubbub of chatter and laughter, and cutlery clattering. Vince was very attentive, topping up wine glasses as he passed tables and checking that customers were enjoying their meals. Rhianna's gaze settled on Noah and his family. He was seated with Olly and his wife Rachel, and another couple who she assumed was their other brother and his partner. The three brothers all looked very similar — sharing the same good looks. Rachel was sporting a growing bump, being close to seven months pregnant now. Rhianna made her way over to their table to check on them.

"Rhianna, splendid job," Olly said as she approached. "We're going to check out the cocktail lounge afterwards."

"Yes, you haven't seen it all stocked and ready for use, unlike Noah." She smiled at Noah, who was looking at her.

"This is our middle brother, Matt, and his girlfriend Jane."

"Nice to meet you." Rhianna exchanged pleasantries with them. "Is your mum coming tonight?" She was referring to Peggy in the Post Office, who she had agreed to do her banking with. The Post Office being situated below the restaurant meant that she often bumped into Peggy.

"No, she's babysitting Kacey, our two-year-old. She said she's got plenty of time to try it out," Rachel said, before Olly could reply. He had his mouth full. Rhianna could see that he'd chosen the roast beef with shallots and the red wine enriched gravy.

"Dad's bringing her here for their anniversary in a couple of weeks," Noah said.

"Oh, fab!"

"Food's great, Rhianna. I can't really comment on the cocktails yet." Rachel rubbed her bump.

"You'll have to get Olly to bring you back once the baby is born." Rhianna checked they didn't need anything, then left them to enjoy their meal.

Rhianna decided to show her face in the cocktail lounge, bringing with her a platter of complimentary canapés she'd prepared earlier. Yasmin was busy shaking a Boston shaker, pouring the sunset-orange liquid into two coupe glasses through a strainer to hold back on the ice, a creamy froth forming on the top. Two shot glasses were filled with Prosecco. Pornstar Martinis. After the staff meeting, she and Yasmin had tweaked it to make it a signature cocktail for the bistro, confident it would become a popular request. Yasmin placed the glasses on a silver tray and took them over to a table. Rhianna placed the platter of canapés on the bar, paper napkins beside it, to allow customers to help themselves.

"How are you getting on?" Rhianna asked when Yasmin returned with the tray carrying empties.

"Great. I can honestly say the cocktail lounge is a winner!" Yasmin said, grinning. "I hope you don't mind, but I've put a tips jar behind the bar. I keep getting tips. We can split them between all the staff, including the chef, later."

"That's a great idea. Vince has one behind the bar downstairs too," Rhianna said. "I brought up some canapés; hand them around if you like."

From where Joe was sitting, with Tilly, Liam and Tristan, he watched Rhianna busily working, attending to tables and customers, her neat ponytail swishing as she walked. They'd tried the starters, except for Tilly, who insisted on saving space for dessert, and were now tucking into the main course. Before being seated at their table by Willow, they'd spent some time in the cocktail lounge admiring the transformation of the attic. Tilly had had to make the most of the mocktail list while the three men had enjoyed the alcoholic choices. When they'd seen Surf Rider on the cocktail menu, of course they just had to try it. The locally sourced vodka-based orangey cocktail was served in a rocks glass each, over ice, with a little froth on top. It was quite refreshing, although maybe a little sweet, but it made a good aperitif.

Rhianna appeared beside them, automatically reaching for the bottle of red wine on the table and topping up their wine glasses. The men had chosen to share a bottle of red together. Joe recognised the label; it was from the winery where he had taken Rhianna wine tasting earlier in the year.

"Everything all right with your meals?" she asked as she topped Joe's glass up last.

"It's great. Compliments to the chef," Tristan said before Joe could.

"I will be sure to pass them on." Rhianna placed the bottle back in the centre of the table.

"Is everything running smoothly? It looks as if it is," Joe said, keen to keep her attention, yet conscious he shouldn't hold her up for too long. The bistro was busy.

"Yes, yes, I think so. We had a mix-up with a couple of tables earlier, but that might have been Willow's first-day nerves muddling her — and my bad handwriting on the plan out in the kitchen."

"Ah, but we're all locals tonight, so you shouldn't get any grumpy customers."

"No, everyone has been so supportive. I definitely don't regret my move to Kittiwake Cove." She pushed her ponytail back off her shoulder.

"I'm glad to hear it," Joe said.

The others around the table all concurred, raising their glasses to toast Rhianna.

"Rhianna!" Vince was calling her from the bar area. She waved to indicate she was coming.

"Right, sorry, I'd best get on. I'll try to catch up with you again later."

Trying to concentrate on the rest of his meal, Joe watched Rhianna walk off in the direction of Vince.

Tilly excused herself and got up to go to the bathroom, placing her napkin by her plate, leaving the three men sat around the table.

"You haven't taken your eyes off Rhianna all evening." Tristan placed his knife and fork together, having finished his main meal, and reached for his wine glass. He observed Joe quizzically. Joe was relieved that Liam stayed quiet, finishing his roast beef.

Although Tristan was eight years younger than Joe, they had always been close, possibly because they were similar in nature and opinions. He wasn't quite the settling down type either. But it was more due to being busy with the estate and being rather fussy when it came to women.

"I just want to make sure she's not having any problems. I said I'd help out if she needed." Joe lifted his wine glass to his lips and tried not to follow Rhianna's every move, concentrating on his companions at the table. The sip of burgundy liquid warmed the edges of his tongue before sliding down his throat, and it revived memories of when Rhianna first arrived and when he took her wine tasting. They'd had so much time for each other then. Now he barely saw her.

"Yeah, yeah," Tristan said dryly. "It must be hard sleeping under the same roof with a pretty woman, too, if I know my cousin."

"Rhianna sleeps in the spare room…"

"Afterwards…" Tristan teased.

Joe looked at him sternly. "She doesn't get into my bed."

"So you get into hers?"

"No!"

"Oh, come on, Joe, aren't you tempted?"

Joe wasn't going to divulge that they had shared one night together. He didn't want his cousin putting two and two together and making five — thousand. Rhianna was a friend. A good friend. And he didn't wish to jeopardise that. However, when he watched Rhianna and Noah's attentiveness to one another, a sudden jealousy spiked in Joe that he'd never experienced before. But he told himself it would be unfair to lay claim to Rhianna and stop her from being happy. Her future was not with him.

"No, I am not *tempted*." A white lie. Never harmed anyone. Besides, it was none of Tristan's business.

"Well, if you're not tempted, then maybe I am." Tristan smiled, his white teeth gleaming. "She's got a great personality and great legs…" The black skirt and the black kitten heel court shoes certainly accentuated her slender, tanned legs.

"Oh, not you too." Joe threw his cloth napkin onto the table.

"Oh, so there is something there."

"No." Joe had to think quickly to justify his answer. "Only, I've already warned off Nick, and besides, you'll have competition from Noah."

"Nick's no competition. But Noah might be." Tristan drummed his fingers on the table in thought. "He's the settling down type."

"Exactly. And that is what Rhianna is looking for."

"How do you know?"

Joe clenched his fists in frustration, quickly hiding them under the table. "Because I do. She lives with me; we do talk, you know?"

"Ah, so that's why you haven't gone there. She wants scary territory." Tristan nudged Joe subtly. "All joking aside, Joe, I'm only messing with you. You shouldn't let a great girl like Rhianna slip through your fingers. What if that scary territory isn't so scary after all?"

Huh! thought Joe. *Tristan is just as scared of that territory, so what does he know?*

Tilly arrived back from the bathroom, kissing Liam and sitting down. "What did I miss?"

"Nothing, darling, just boy talk." Liam winked at Joe and Tristan.

As the evening drew on, Rhianna gave Vince the task of lighting the patio heaters. Even though it was a warm May evening, as soon as the sun dipped on the horizon, the night air cooled. It was still light past nine o'clock, giving her guests the view of a perfect sunset. Someone was looking out for her tonight, because everything had gone well without too many hiccups. There had been nothing that couldn't be easily rectified; that was the whole reason for having a trial run. To iron out any teething problems.

The final tables had been filled, and all main courses served. Only desserts were being ordered now, so Curtis tidied the kitchen and prepared for tomorrow. Many of her guests remained at their tables, drinking and chatting. Some had retired to the cocktail lounge. It was exactly the ambience Rhianna wanted to create. A place where guests could make a full evening of it, and not feel pressured to leave their tables too early. With the weather right, Cornwall could be just as relaxing and exciting as a foreign destination.

Rhianna's smile remained plastered on her face as she tried to ignore the dull ache forming in her feet due to wearing heels. What had she been thinking? Flat shoes from now on. Even her lower back was starting to complain.

Rose and Charles were still outside; they'd moved their chairs, so they were next to one another, snugly seated under a patio heater. Rhianna fetched a navy-blue blanket from a chest by the patio doors and handed it to them.

"How was everything?" Rhianna asked, as she cleared their dessert plates.

"It was wonderful. Well done for all your hard work; it's really paid off," Rose said, leaning into her husband, and covering them with the blanket. "Your mum and dad will be proud when they visit."

"Thank you." Rhianna hoped this too. "Is there anything else I can get you? Coffee? With a dash of something in it? Or an espresso martini to finish the evening?"

Charles gave a little chuckle. "Not sure about the cocktail, but yes, a brandy coffee would be lovely." Rhianna looked at Rose, who had picked up the drinks menu.

"Oh, I think I might try the espresso martini." Rose looked up from the menu card. "Let's try out your cocktails!"

"An espresso martini is another of my favourites," Rhianna said, smiling. She could probably do with one now, too. Over the radio, she placed the order through to Vince at the bar, then carried on checking the rest of her customers were comfortable.

As the restaurant quietened, Rhianna let Holly leave, followed by Willow, no longer requiring their services. They'd wiped down tables and set them ready for the next day. Curtis had packed up around ten p.m. Rhianna and Yasmin emptied the tips jars and stored the money in Rhianna's office. She'd had a small safe installed under the desk. They would count it up the following day — both felt dog tired, with sore feet. It was agreed that the tips would be split between all the staff, including Curtis. He might not get to talk to the customers, but quality food coming out of the kitchen meant fewer complaints. She wanted her staff to work as a team and be rewarded fairly for their efforts. She'd worked for too many companies where she'd felt she was only a minion, and her effort wasn't appreciated. It was important her staff enjoyed their jobs and felt valued. She wanted them to greet customers with friendly smiles and mean it. Repeat custom was going to be imperative to Rhianna's success.

It was nearly midnight when she locked up after all her final checks, and walked down the metal steps that led to the pavement. To her surprise, Joe was sitting on the low wall opposite, the sound of the ocean behind him. The tide was high.

"Hey," she said.

"Hey, I didn't know if you'd need a hand, but I didn't want to impose on your territory." He got to his feet. "So I thought I'd at least walk you home."

"You couldn't carry me, could you?" Rhianna slipped off her shoes, giving each set of toes a rub.

Joe chuckled. "You know I'm crap at giving piggybacks. Anyway, I know the perfect treatment for sore feet." He grabbed her hand and led her onto the beach. The cool sand between her toes felt good. *So good.* Some of the street lighting and the half crescent moon lit up the beach enough for them to find the edge of the water. They didn't have to walk too far either, as the tide was in. Joe slipped his socks and shoes off too. As a wave came in over her feet, only ankle-deep, Rhianna gave a squeal.

"It's freezing."

"But good, right?" Joe paddled with her. He'd rolled up his trousers. He'd looked really smart this evening, wearing a checked shirt. He'd actually dressed up! Could it possibly be he even owned a tie? Rhianna doubted that, but at least he could smarten up when required. He wasn't always in shorts and flipflops.

"Yes. I think so. My feet are going numb," she said, crunching and stretching her toes into the wet sand underwater.

"That's the idea." Joe chuckled. "The cold saltwater will help. I promise."

"Then you give me a piggyback home."

"I can … but you'll have to hitch up your skirt." She couldn't quite make out his facial expression, but his tone hinted mischief.

"Okay, point taken. I can walk it," Rhianna said. "Flat shoes from now on, though. And trainers or flipflops for walking home in." This evening had made her realise that even the smallest heel on a shoe was not a good idea when you were on your feet all night.

"Why'd you wear them?"

"I wanted to look the part. But flat shoes will have to look the part from now on."

"You did look nice tonight."

"Thank you." Rhianna wasn't sure where to take that compliment and wanted to change the subject. "Let's head back; my legs ache too, and I'm not skinny dipping." Not a great change of subject. She feared it would remind him of that awful night. Her bruise had faded, but had the memory?

"Shame." Joe chuckled, his tone light. Clearly it had, or maybe Joe didn't want to broach the subject either.

"You can. I'll hold your clothes."

"More like run off with them."

"Never!" she replied jokingly. Rhianna stepped out of the water and they started walking back off the beach. Rhianna let her now numb feet dry naturally within the soft, cool grains of sand.

"How do you think it went tonight?" Joe asked. Rhianna was relieved he had changed the subject. She was bursting with excitement with how well the bistro had run tonight.

"Well, judging by the tips jars, my team were amazing. No major issues, fortunately. Thank you, God." She looked up to the sky and moved her hands into a prayer position as best she could while still holding her shoes. She wasn't one hundred percent sure the Big Guy existed, but someone had definitely been looking out for her this evening. "I think I might need to find someone else to work in the kitchen with Curtis, because I don't have the time, and I love being front of house." At one point, she'd even had to mix a few cocktails because Vince hadn't quite got the hang of it. Again, first-day nerves. He'd worked in a pub and for a restaurant chain but had never made cocktails before. Rhianna had been in her element, though, back doing the things she enjoyed, and all for her own benefit. It was so amazing to think that it was her own business. She was the boss. "Did you enjoy the evening?"

"Yeah, it was great. We had a cocktail, the food was wonderful... Great evening, apart from my cousin teasing me—"

"What was Tristan teasing you about?" Rhianna frowned.

"You."

"Me?"

"But I told him we were just friends."

"Yes, just friends." Rhianna made her voice sound as cool as Joe's.

Holding onto Joe's arm with one hand, Rhianna dusted off her feet, one by one, but couldn't bear to put her shoes back on, so she hobbled up the road barefoot. As usual, Joe walked on the outside, closest to the road. Fortunately, the pavement didn't have too many stones on it, and she made it back to the pub slowly, giggling as Joe teased her about her slow pace. It became a natural distraction from what they'd previously been talking about.

"It's all right for you; you're used to walking up this road without shoes." Joe often walked up and down the hill barefoot in his wetsuit, to save leaving much on the beach. "You must have hard soles."

"I hope you're talking about my feet?"

"Well, you're not all heart, are you? Otherwise you'd be carrying me up the hill…"

"Right!" With that, Joe hauled Rhianna over his shoulder in a fireman's carry and Rhianna squealed as she was turned upside down. His hand temporarily found her bum as he steadied his hold of her. He did have his left hand full, carrying his shoes. He swayed and stumbled slightly as he adjusted to the weight over his right shoulder, which made Rhianna panic he would drop her.

"Put me down! Put me down!" She was talking to his backside, and laughing. So was he. She used her free hand, the one not carrying her own shoes, to slap him.

"Okay, okay…" Thankfully, after much giggling, and a bit of swaying, Joe placed Rhianna back on her feet.

"Thank you." She swatted him, and he laughed harder. Rhianna winced as she trod on a stone.

"You all right?" He touched her hair lightly, a loose strand stuck to her lip.

"I've been on my feet all evening. My calves ache, as well as my feet," she said, trying to discreetly brush the stone from the ball of her left foot as well as the hair out of her mouth.

She was used to being on her feet all day and night, including at the pub. But maybe the initial stress and constant worry that things might go wrong at the bistro had exhausted her too. She felt mentally drained as well as physically. Her body ached for her bed. She was fantasising about her head hitting the soft pillow and closing her eyes.

"Not far now. Come along, Hop-along."

She slapped him playfully again.

The Cormorant was dark and all locked up. Only the light over the back door was on.

"Who locked up?" Rhianna asked, relieved to finally be back at the pub. She was gasping for breath after the steep climb. Surely she should be used to that hill by now?

"I got Toby to do it. Ricky said he'd stay on, too." Joe inserted the key into the back door, and they made their way up the stairs into Joe's apartment.

Thinking of her sandy feet, Rhianna said, "I think I'll have a quick shower, then go straight to bed. Early start, tomorrow."

"Me too," Joe said, shoving his hands into his pockets. "Goodnight, Rhianna."

"Goodnight, Joe."

Clean from her shower, Rhianna lay in bed. Tired as she was, her brain could not quite switch off. She checked her alarm on her phone twice, to make sure it was set. She couldn't afford to oversleep. She needed to be up and out, preparing for tomorrow.

But she could not stop thinking of how successful tonight had been. And of Joe waiting for her... She thought of their laughter, how at ease she felt being in his company.

Friends. Just friends.

CHAPTER 25: PINK FLIRTINI

May half-term week proved very busy. And the customers were tougher to please than the locals of Kittiwake Cove, but Rhianna's team worked hard to keep them all happy if the tips jars were anything to go by. During the week, people she knew had dined at the bistro who'd been unable to visit on the opening night — Ricky and his wife, Nick with some business colleagues by the looks of things, as he footed the bill. Kerenza clearly wasn't in town.

It was now Saturday and they'd been open just over a week. Rhianna looked down the list of bookings and was surprised to see Joe's name. A table for four people at seven-thirty. He hadn't said anything earlier that morning. Maybe he'd forgotten to mention it.

When Joe arrived, he was accompanied by three people. Rhianna had made sure she'd be by the door upon his arrival. He was casually dressed in a navy-blue polo shirt with a surf motif and faded jeans. He greeted her awkwardly with a kiss on the cheek. The heat of his lips shot tingles of electricity up her neck.

"Hey, Rhianna, this is my sister, Heather and her husband, Tom. And this is my brother, Sam. You met them briefly at Easter."

"Oh, yes, of course; lovely to meet you again." Rhianna shook each of their hands in turn. Back then, she hadn't taken as much interest in them as she did now, her feelings for Joe having grown — *into a stronger friendship, of course.* She remembered Sam, who was clearly older and more formal than Joe, and took more after their father, Charles. He was wearing dark jeans and looked comfortable but smart in a casual collared shirt. Not something you saw often on Joe.

Rhianna recognised Joe's younger sister and his brother-in-law. Heather had a closer resemblance to Joe than Sam, particularly the way she laughed and some of her mannerisms, and she had a similar twinkle in her eyes, inherited from their mother. Rhianna could not forget Heather's husband, Tom, who stood beside her. She still thought he could be The Rock's body double, only with more hair and possibly fewer tattoos. Okay, maybe he wasn't quite as massive as Dwayne Johnson, but he was an impressive physical presence.

Rhianna showed them to a well-positioned table at the front of the restaurant, with a view of the beach from the window. After some initial chat, she ran through the specials and gave them wine recommendations, but left them for a few minutes to make their choices.

Walking away from the table, she realised that she was shaking with nerves. For a silly, brief moment, she'd pictured herself with Joe. She'd imagined these people as her extended family.

"Did you want me to see to Joe's table?" Vince broke Rhianna's train of thought, thankfully.

"No, no, I'll look after them tonight, if you don't mind?" Rhianna wanted to give Joe and his family her full attention — for all the right reasons. He was a mate. Nothing to do with wanting him to notice her.

What had got into her today?

Noticing the menus resting on the table, Rhianna took this as a sign they'd chosen their meals. She dug her notepad out of the small pocket in her black apron and headed over to the table.

"Have you decided what you'd like to order?"

They opted for an English sparkling wine, as Heather didn't wish to drink alone.

"Too much red wine makes me queasy," Heather explained.

"You mean you get drunk quicker, darling." Tom nudged his wife teasingly.

"I took Rhianna to the winery, near St Austell, and this was on the tasting menu," Joe said to the group, smiling up at Rhianna as he told the tale.

"We are going there on Joe's recommendation," Heather said.

Rhianna collected up the menus and returned with complimentary bread and butter. The restaurant was busy, and it would be unfair of her not to help her staff, so she found herself unable to sit and chat with Joe's family as much as she'd have liked.

She noticed some commotion with Willow at one of the tables at the back of the conservatory area and made her way over.

"Willow, is everything okay?"

It was a table for two, and the gentleman, a portly fellow with red cheeks somewhere in his late fifties, was glaring at Willow. Apparently, he'd wanted his steak rare and was complaining about it being tough. He prodded it aggressively. Rhianna quickly intervened, asking Willow to take both plates to the kitchen and service their table with more bread and olives while they waited for their fresh meals.

They walked out to the kitchen to have a word with Curtis.

"I swear he said medium," Willow was grumbling. She showed Rhianna her notepad and there it was.

"He's here to get a free meal. You get them all the time. Sometimes there is a genuine mistake, and that's fair enough, but I'm pretty sure he's trying it on. Well, he won't get a free meal, but the correct one he supposedly ordered." Rhianna winked. "And he can't complain his wife's meal had to go cold while she waited for his to be served again."

"Oh, I wondered why you took her plate."

Rhianna tapped her nose. "I've been doing this long enough now."

Rhianna gave her orders to Curtis to prepare the two meals from scratch again. Rhianna hated the thought of wasting good food, but she'd learnt a long time ago the reputation of her restaurant would keep people returning, and with today's social media she couldn't afford for the bistro to be bad-mouthed, whether justifiably or not, in its first weeks of opening.

Willow returned to the table with olives and bread. However, Rhianna, seeing that Curtis was up to his eyes in orders, slipped on an apron, and set about helping him with things that would make his life easier, and would get this meal out quicker.

As predicted, later that evening, Rhianna noticed Willow once again having problems with the table. The man was loud, too. Rhianna wanted to nip this in the bud. It was ruining other people's enjoyment of the bistro, disturbing its ambience.

"Can I help you, sir?" Rhianna said. "What seems to be the problem?"

"My steak — it's on the bill."

"Yes, because I replaced it with another. In fact, I replaced both meals." She'd personally made sure both meals had been made to perfection, so he had nothing to complain about.

"Well, I don't wish to pay for it."

"Was there anything wrong with the other steak?"

"I had to wait for it."

Rhianna looked at Willow. "Did he eat the steak?"

"The plate was clear." Willow shrugged.

"Excuse me." Joe appeared by Rhianna's side. "I'm sorry, I couldn't help hearing the commotion." He gave Rhianna a sly wink. She wasn't sure if she was grateful or not for Joe stepping in. But he did have a way of calming situations. "Madam, was everything to your liking with your meal?" He turned to the wife, his surfer charm on full, with his best million-dollar smile.

The woman blushed, patting her lips with the cloth napkin. "Oh, yes, yes, it was delicious."

"Dot!" The man growled at his wife.

Joe turned to him. "And did you eat all of your meal, sir?"

"Yes, he did. His plate was clear." Willow found her confidence now Joe was there. His smile obviously worked on her too.

"Well then, sir, you should pay for what you ate. If you're not happy with the service, then, by all means, don't leave a tip, but if you've eaten the food, it should be paid for. You wouldn't dream of filling your car up with petrol and driving off without paying for it — would you?"

The man's face grew redder. "No but —"

"This is a business, after all, and Rhianna is trying her hardest to make it a success. The bistro has only been open a week; it is bound to have some teething problems."

Joe crouched down to the level of the two people seated, closer to the wife, so she could probably smell the spicy and woody scents of his aftershave. "Wouldn't you agree, madam?" He patted her left hand. She looked a little flustered, clearly not used to a handsome man giving her attention.

"Yes, yes, pay the bill, Jeff, and let us get out of here. Stop making a scene!" Maybe Joe's presence also gave the wife confidence to speak up. "Every time we go out for a meal..." She screwed up the napkin and placed it on the table. Willow had already brought their jackets over. The man threw the cash on the receipt wallet and mumbled something about keeping the change.

Rhianna showed them out of the bistro, praying she never saw them again. This was the downside to owning your own business. Not all customers could be sweetness and compliments, but it grated on her that her staff hadn't actually done anything wrong. In fact, she'd done everything she could to fix a problem of his own making, because Willow had shown her the notepad with his order, and she had definitely noted that he wanted his steak medium.

She hadn't realised Joe was standing next to her, watching them descend the stairs.

"You always get one," he said.

Rhianna grabbed his arm before he returned to his table. "Thank you for your help, Joe, but I was handling it." Rhianna could feel her cheeks flush red as heat rose to her face and her nerves jangled with the confrontation. She was standing agonisingly close to Joe, trying to keep their conversation private. She didn't want to appear ungrateful, but she did have to handle these situations herself. She was the boss. And Joe wouldn't be in the restaurant every evening to stick up for her.

"Yeah, well, sorry," Joe shrugged. "I couldn't sit there and watch that arsehole take advantage."

"It's part of the deal, though, with owning my own restaurant. I'm going to get arseholes occasionally. I've got to deal with them, unless you're here every night, guarding me like a Rottweiler."

"Bah, I'm more like a playful Schnauzer." Joe winked.

A bloody Labrador, with the amount of time he spends in the water. But Rhianna kept that thought to herself.

Joe's fingers brushed her arm briefly, then he headed back to his table, where Rhianna could tell he was filling his family in on his heroic actions.

"Whoop, whoop, the old git left us thirty-two pence!" Willow said. She'd taken the cash to the till behind the bar and held the coins in the palm of her hand, showing Rhianna, like a proud toddler.

Rhianna laughed at the silly face Willow was pulling. "Put it in the tips jar. Look after the pennies and the pounds will look after themselves … or something like that."

"Yeah, my nan used to say that all the time." Willow dropped the coins into the tips jar.

"Mine too."

"What was that all about?" Heather asked Joe as he sat back down at the table and took a long sip from his wine.

They had all been tucking into their desserts when Joe left the table to go to Rhianna's rescue. And now he wondered if he should have left well alone. Rhianna was right; he wouldn't always be here to bail her out, but with the bistro being in its early stage, he wanted everything to run smoothly for her. He found it very hard to resist the instinctive protectiveness he felt for her.

"Just someone trying to pull a fast one. You get them all the time. They'll look for a fault with their food even when there isn't one, just so they can get a free meal." Joe picked up his spoon and resumed eating his dessert. He wasn't really a sweet-tooth man. But everyone had opted for three courses, so he'd followed suit with an artisan Cornish vanilla ice-cream, which was more mush now.

"Oh, that's ridiculous!" Heather frowned, sipping her wine.

Sam topped up his sister's glass. "It does happen. I go out with colleagues a lot, and there's always one who will find something to complain about."

"It must bring the whole evening down," Heather said.

Joe listened, but his thoughts were on Rhianna. He couldn't stop thinking about the night they'd shared after the confrontation with Glyn. And what it would be like to have Rhianna in his bed every night.

Then the thought of commitment, of trusting someone again with his heart, set his anxieties off. After Alannah, he'd vowed not to get close to another woman like that. Just enjoy the fun, not get bogged down with the other stuff.

However, looking at Heather with Tom, they didn't appear bogged down. Okay, occasionally, their marriage was not as rosy on the inside as it appeared on the outside. They had their moments, when he'd catch Heather and Tom bickering about something. Usually about their daughters, Joe's nieces. Sam and Jade had been the same, before she'd fallen sick. But it must be quite something to have someone to share your life with, that solidarity, knowing that when you came home from work you had someone supporting you, helping you, sharing the burden of problems, sharing the fun of adventures, sharing a bed... If he wanted that — which he wasn't sure he did — would Rhianna be the woman to do it with?

"Shall we grab a cocktail?" Heather said, patting Joe's arm. Their wine glasses were empty, as was the bottle, but the night was still young — especially for those who didn't get out much.

"Yes, yes, you need to see Rhianna's cocktail bar." Joe stood.

"Wait, we need to settle the bill," Tom said, laughing at Joe and Heather's eagerness.

"It's okay, I'll sort it with Rhianna. We can set up a tab. Head up to the attic." Joe pointed in the direction of the stairs that led up to the cocktail lounge. He found Rhianna busy making coffees behind the bar in the restaurant. The machine gurgled and hissed as she frothed milk. "Hey, is it okay if we go upstairs and add drinks to our bill?" Joe leaned against the bar.

"Yes, sure, tell Yasmin table twelve." Rhianna nodded, pulling the milk jug from the steamer, wiping the pipe with a cloth.

"Come join us when you're finished." The restaurant was emptying out now.

"Yes, give me twenty minutes. Willow and Vince will be able to handle this floor without me now."

"Great." Joe made his way up to the cocktail lounge to find Heather already sipping a pink cocktail garnished with a wedge of lime. Sam and Tom were still waiting for theirs. There was a hint of coffee in the air, which made Joe think his brother and brother-in-law had opted for espresso martinis. Behind the bar, Yasmin slammed the glass into the metal part of the Boston shaker and started shaking hard, the ice rattling and condensation forming on the tin. The noise was part of the ambience of this room. Rhianna and Yasmin had nicknamed it Shakers and it had stuck.

There were still a few people milling around, seated at various tables, chatting and sipping cocktails, but the leather sofas beside the log burner were available, so Joe put his order in with Yasmin for a whisky sour and Yasmin confirmed she would bring the other cocktails over. Joe made his way to the sofas.

"Oh, wow, look at that mural," Heather said, nudging Tom.

"Noah, a local artist painted it," Joe said, sitting beside his brother on the sofa. "Some of his work is in the gallery."

275

It was nearly half past ten when Rhianna appeared, as Yasmin was taking their second order of cocktails. She'd untied her hair and put some lipstick on.

"Hello," she said. Joe jumped up and fetched a tub chair from an empty table nearby.

"Let me get you a drink." Joe gestured from Rhianna to Yasmin.

"Yes, boss, what would you like?" Yasmin stood, pen poised, smiling.

"What are you having?" Rhianna asked Heather.

Heather frowned, looking at Yasmin questioningly. The wine and the cocktails had made her tipsy. Yasmin answered for her. "She's having another Pink Flirtini."

"It was delicious! I enjoyed it a bit too quickly," Heather said, raising her empty cocktail glass.

"Oh, yes, I'll have one of those too," Rhianna said to Yasmin, then frowned. "Do you mind doing it?"

"Of course not. Now sit yourself down, you've been on your feet all day. You were here way before me this morning." Yasmin headed back to the bar.

Joe returned to his seat by his brother on the sofa, as Rhianna settled into the tub chair. He didn't have to try too hard to include her into the conversation, as his family were eager to ask her all sorts of questions, from where she got her cocktail ideas to queries about the food.

When Yasmin brought over the tray of drinks, Rhianna thanked her, then touching her elbow, said in a low voice, "Hey, clear up what you need to do, then head off. I'll sort this lot out."

"Would you like me to bring the bill over?" Yasmin asked.

"Oh, yes, maybe we should do that now," Sam said, fishing out his wallet from his jeans pocket. Tom did the same.

Joe nodded to Yasmin. "Print off the bill for us, thank you."

Rhianna shook her head. There was no rush. "You don't need to pay the bill yet. I can sort it later."

"No, no, there's been a few times where I've walked out of a pub almost forgetting to pay the tab. I'd feel better if we settle it now," Sam said. "While I can remember. These cocktails are potent."

"Besides, we'll never hear the last of it from Joe if we forget to pay," Tom said.

"It wouldn't be the first time you left me to foot the bill!" Joe pointed at Tom then Sam, who pulled innocent faces, shrugging their shoulders.

"Didn't Jade drag you two back into that restaurant in Padstow?" Heather said, giggling. "I still remember her face."

There was raucous laughter from the men. Rhianna felt a little lost at the joke, clearly something that had happened in their past. Wasn't Jade Sam's wife who'd died? Rhianna knew then she liked Joe's family unit. They were obviously close. What would it be like to be a part of this family?

The bill paid, Yasmin headed off, as Joe's family were the last party of people in the lounge bar. Rhianna started making the cocktails, having insisted Yasmin go home. She'd checked with Willow and Vince downstairs, and all was in order. Vince locked the door after the last of their customers had left, too. And once they'd finished wiping tables and laying for the next day, they headed home.

One in the morning approached when eventually everyone agreed they really should head home, for fear of bad headaches the next day.

"The surf will sort you out," Joe said.

"Ha! Tell that to Daisy and Scarlett." Heather was holding onto Tom for support. A mixture of cocktails and heels, and a long day, Rhianna presumed. She was feeling the same, only thankfully she had flat shoes on.

Heather kissed Rhianna and thanked her for the lovely food and delicious cocktails, with murmurs of hoping to see her again soon.

They showed Joe's family out, but Joe waited with Rhianna while she checked the restaurant over, making sure the ovens and all the lights were switched off, and Joe checked the toilets to make sure that no one was left in there asleep. It had been known to happen in some of the establishments he'd worked in over the years — Joe even checked the loos at The Cormorant on the busier nights.

Joe shoved his hands into his pockets as they climbed the hill towards to pub. "Great food, Rhianna, and fantastic cocktails, I must say. My family had a really fun night."

"Oh, that's so good to hear."

"They really like you, you know."

Rhianna kept looking straight ahead, afraid to catch Joe's eye. What could he mean? Usually that was the sort of thing a guy would say to a new girlfriend meeting his family or friends for the first time, wasn't it? "I like them too. You're really lucky to have such a great family."

"Yeah, yeah I am."

They finally reached the back door of The Cormorant, where an outside light was shining, moths fluttering around it, and Joe fumbled with the keys. Rhianna realised he was drunker than she'd thought. He dropped them, then wobbled as he bent down to pick them up.

"Here, let me." She picked them up, marginally less unsteady than him. She was certainly tipsy, though; four cocktails in a short space of time did that to you. She had eaten well, but it was a long time ago now.

She had a long day tomorrow too. At this rate, she could see herself knocking up a Bloody Mary to kickstart her day.

She decided not to give Joe the keys for fear of him dropping them again. Their hands touched as she searched for the correct key to the back door. Joe was standing very close to her; she could smell the whisky on his breath, mingled with his aftershave that she'd become rather fond of.

"Rhianna," Joe said huskily. His hand was winding its way around her back, trying to tease her closer to him.

"Joe?" Rhianna replied suspiciously. She made the mistake of making eye contact with him. The soft amber glow of the lamp above them was the only light, and even though it wasn't that bright, it provided enough light for Rhianna to see the lust in Joe's gaze.

"I was thinking…"

"Not too hard, I hope." Rhianna tried to make a joke, hoping to break the tension.

Joe stepped closer. His mouth was inches from hers. He gently pulled her towards him. "What if we were friends … with benefits?"

Rhianna woke up from the spell. She'd been like one of those moths drawn to the light. But as if the lamp had been abruptly turned off, she'd escaped from Joe's bewitchment. "Joe … I don't think that would be a good idea." She stepped closer towards the door, turning her back on him. She couldn't get the key in the lock fast enough! She needed her bed. Her own bed. Alone. *Long day tomorrow.*

"But think of the fun we could have, without the hassle of what a long-term relationship can bring — no arguing, bickering, no let-downs…" Joe continued, leaning casually against the wall, still gazing at her. He ran his fingers along her hairline, tucking loose strands behind her ear, and gently brushing along her neck, teasing her. His caresses sent a surge of electricity down her spine. God, he knew how to turn her on. If his lips touched her skin, she'd be lost.

Desperately, she struggled to get the key in the lock. She feared her cheeks were as pink as the raspberries in the Pink Flirtini cocktails she and Heather had drunk. "But that's all part of a relationship, Joe, and if you can't be honest with someone, and tell them occasionally you're not happy, then you shouldn't be with them." The key turned and the door opened. Rhianna hissed a *yes* under her breath. Joe shut the door and Rhianna handed him back the keys, dropping them into his palm so their skin didn't touch. She still didn't trust herself.

She could have one more night with Joe… *Just one more night…*

"I want a relationship, Joe, eventually, like your sister has. I want that…"

Not just one night.

"I'm sorry, I'm sorry." He kissed her temple. "Whisky's gone to my head. You're right… I'm not right for you… I couldn't give you what you deserve."

Rhianna watched him climb the stairs. She wanted to shout at him but held her tongue.

You are right for me. If only you'd open your bloody eyes and realise it. And stop being so afraid of commitment.

CHAPTER 26: WOO WOO

"Mum! Dad!" Rhianna squealed in surprise upon seeing her parents enter the bistro, shrugging off the hoods of their raincoats and wiping their feet on the doormat. Water dripped from them, as they'd made a run for it up the stairs in the pouring rain. Her father closed the door firmly behind him to stop the wind blowing into the restaurant with a bitter blast. Today looked more like February than June.

"We thought we'd surprise you." Beatrice kissed her daughter's cheek as Rhianna hugged her.

"And it's easier to get away midweek, now the schools have gone back," Gareth added, hugging Rhianna too.

"Unfortunately, you've chosen the week the rain's decided to set in." Rhianna took both their jackets, gave them a good shake and hung them on the coat stand by the door. "Have you booked? If not, I'm sure we can make room." Even though it was midweek, the bistro was fully booked. Apparently, there were locals coming from Port Isaac, Wadebridge and Padstow, as well as tourists wanting to try out the new bistro in town.

"Of course we've booked. Just under Mr and Mrs Jones." Beatrice chuckled. Being in the restaurant industry themselves, they knew the importance of booking.

"Oh, yes, I did wonder whether that might be an alias. But then Jones is a common surname." Rhianna looked down her bookings list and crossed through the name.

"It's great to see it's so busy," her father added, his shrewd business head still firmly in place. "I love the changes you've made."

281

As Rhianna showed her parents to their table, she had so many questions to ask them. The view outside was bleak today. She hoped this weather would pass in time for Tilly's wedding.

"Where are you staying?" Rhianna handed them both a menu now they'd dried off.

"At the B&B," Gareth said.

"Rose and Charles's?" Rhianna asked.

"Yes," Beatrice confirmed, smiling over the menu. "They're such a lovely couple. How are things with Joe?"

"Great." Rhianna was intrigued by the question. She hoped her expression hid her suspicion. Were both sets of parents gossiping about their *relationship*? "He's been a star, letting me stay at his."

"I get the impression from Rose that *you're* the star," Beatrice said, looking quizzically at her.

Rhianna frowned. What could her mum possibly mean? Rose obviously had the wrong idea. Joe clearly hadn't told his mother he wanted all the fun, and none of the commitment.

"Any news from Glyn?" Her dad's tone hinted at disgust. "About the house?"

Rhianna sighed. "No, not yet." Another job on her list: chase her solicitor.

Rhianna checked on her parents regularly throughout their meal. She'd told Vince she would settle their bill. She'd recommended a Cornish red wine to accompany their meal, knowing her father would like it. Maybe he'd consider using the winery to supply his restaurant.

Having tried and tested three courses, her father pushed his dessert plate away and said, "You've done a grand job, Rhianna. I'm proud of you."

"Not sure I'd have managed it without your support," she said, blushing.

"And to turn it around so fast." Beatrice grabbed Rhianna's hand, giving it a squeeze.

"I've had a great deal of help from the locals."

"The food was delicious." That meant a lot, as her father would always be her harshest critic, being a chef and restaurant owner himself.

"I'll pass on the compliments to Curtis, the chef." Rhianna bowed. "Right, come up and see Shakers! I'll knock you up a Woo Woo, Mum, your favourite."

"Shakers. What a fabulous name," Beatrice said, following her daughter slowly, as she observed everything around her. "Not too many cocktails, dear. I don't want to get too wobbly."

It gave Rhianna enormous pride to show her parents around the bistro, and thanks to her staff working so well together, like worker bees, she was able to spend nearly an hour chatting with them and catching up over cocktails.

"It's good to see you so happy," Beatrice said, when she came to say goodbye, Gareth holding out her coat for her. She looked at Rhianna seriously, her eyes glistening.

Rhianna nodded. "Yes, I am, Mum. I'm very happy. The bistro is everything I hoped it would be, and more."

And who knows, maybe a wonderful man would enter her life when the universe was ready.

For the next few weeks, once her parents had returned home, Rhianna did not know her arse from her elbow. The bistro kept her frenetically busy. She usually fell exhausted into bed at Joe's apartment long after even he had finished at the pub. Sometimes she found him waiting up for her, but most of the time she got back so late that even he, the quintessential night owl, had already gone to bed. His bedroom door would be closed, with only a lamp left on to welcome her home. If she was honest, returning so late might also be deliberate on her part, to avoid seeing him. To avoid being reminded how strong her feelings were for him, as he clearly didn't feel the same way. She needed to get the stupid idea of them being a couple out of her head. It would never happen.

He wanted to be friends with benefits, remember.

Even with the kids returning to school after half term, June remained busy. Rhianna found someone to work in the kitchen with Curtis. Oscar would be finishing catering college for the summer soon and looking for work during the holidays, so he could gain experience. Due to his age, Rhianna could pay him the minimum wage, rather than hiring someone with more experience. This would enable her to stay front of house during opening hours and keep her staffing budget low. The chefs were included in the distribution of the tips, so this would boost his wages. He would work evenings until college finished, then when the summer holidays started, Rhianna could increase his hours. As far as she could tell, Curtis and Oscar worked great together. Curtis was happy to share his experience and teach Oscar, who was willing to learn a trick or two of the trade.

Rhianna got into a routine of closeting herself away in the kitchen early each morning, baking scones, cakes and some bread, although she also had some delivered by the local baker in Rock. With the success of the evening, she now opened at lunchtime with her menu of afternoon teas, which went down a storm with the tourists.

In the late afternoon, she would hand over the kitchen when Curtis arrived and stow away her chef's whites. The staff had got into a routine, and Rhianna had been able to work out a good rota, knowing when her quiet periods were, and when she needed all hands on deck. During the summer, she would have the bistro open seven days a week, but as soon as September arrived, she had decided she would close on one of the days. Mondays or Tuesdays would be a day off for all her staff that way — including herself.

Apart from successfully avoiding Joe, she hadn't managed to fit in a drink with Noah either. She didn't have time, being at the bistro every night. At such an early stage, she couldn't afford a night off. Anyway, she didn't want a night off. She loved it so much. This first summer was so important in getting her business off the ground. Her love life was the least of her worries. And she really didn't want to complicate anything with anyone right now.

In her quieter periods, Rhianna got on with the preparations for Tilly and Liam's wedding — which was only a week away now. She had agreed numbers, table plans, colour schemes and menu choices with them. Both Tilly and Liam had been in, testing food at the bistro. Their official marriage ceremony was going to be held at Trenouth Manor — a secret Rhianna and Tristan were keeping for Liam and Tilly, plus the very close family invited to witness the two marrying. Rhianna had applied for a wedding licence for the bistro, but even if she was granted one it wouldn't arrive in time for Tilly and Liam's wedding. She really hoped to be able to hold ceremonies there one day.

Tristan's events coordinator, Anya, was a mine of information, and Rhianna had regularly called on her expertise in the run-up to the wedding. Tristan had recommended a catering company through which she could hire additional staff for the evening.

One Monday evening, Rhianna was chewing the end of her pencil, deep in thought, when a knock at her office door startled her.

It was late. The bistro was dark. Rhianna was alone.

"Joe!" she exclaimed with relief.

"Sorry for startling you. Toby is managing the pub, so I thought I'd pop out and walk you home. Or maybe I should have just brought your pyjamas and a sleeping bag?"

"It's Kittiwake Cove, not the middle of Bristol. I'll be quite safe walking home." Rhianna chuckled, then frowned. "How did you get in?"

"The door was open."

"Hmmm... I must have forgotten to lock the door." Yasmin had been the last to leave tonight.

"So how is it all going? You've become a stranger at The Cormorant."

"I know, I know, I'm sorry." She stretched, tiredness creeping through her body now she had stopped to think about it. Her shoulders ached from hunching over her desk. "But I do have some good news."

"Oh." Joe took the spare seat in Rhianna's tiny office. He was wearing denim shorts and flipflops, and one of his favourite surf T-shirts. It was so worn it had holes in the seams around the underarms. The sun had come out today, not that Rhianna had seen much of it.

"Yes, I got news from my solicitor today that we have a buyer for the house — finally — so the selling process is back on track! Now I can start looking for houses and putting an offer in. Hopefully, I'll be out of your hair soon."

This news had relieved Rhianna today. Maybe the best way to get over her attraction to Joe was to move out. Because it still wasn't fading.

"Oh," Joe said, hesitantly, his expression briefly showing surprise. Then in good old Joe fashion, he masked it with a smile. "There's no rush. Concentrate on the bistro for now."

"I know, but I am living under your roof, rent-free. Abusing it, too, by literally crashing there. Which I'm eternally grateful for."

"I don't mind. It's not like you leave the place in a state."

Rhianna continued to suck her pencil. "Although, to be honest, I'm not sure when I'll even find the time to look at houses —"

"See, no rush —"

"But tomorrow I'll put a call in to the estate agents in Wadebridge."

Joe sighed. "If you insist."

"Hello!"

Another voice called out, surprising both Joe and Rhianna, who shrugged at one another.

Noah appeared in the doorway. "Oh, hi, Joe."

"Hi, Noah."

"Hi," Rhianna said much more enthusiastically than Joe. What was his problem? She thought he liked Noah. But he was reacting as if Nick had walked through the door.

"I saw there was a light on and thought I'd check if you were okay, Rhianna."

"Oh, yes, everything's fine, thanks, just going through some paperwork before I head home … to Joe's, I mean."

"And I can walk her home, Noah. You can head off," Joe said, plastering on a smile. Wasn't Joe the one who'd told Rhianna she should go for a drink with Noah? And now, judging by his reaction to Noah, Rhianna could tell he wasn't happy about it. Or was she misreading it all? Joe was usually so laidback and easy-going.

"Why don't you both get off home? I'll be fine making my way back to the pub by myself," Rhianna said, looking from one man to the other. Why did her office suddenly feel so hot? Was it the testosterone levels or was it just a warm evening?

"No, I'll wait, or maybe —" Joe stepped closer — "I'll insist you finish now and leave it until morning." He took the pencil off Rhianna and placed it on the desk. He was agonisingly close; she could smell the scent of saltwater, his aftershave and a hint of beer. Rhianna was very conscious that Noah was watching them too.

"Joe!"

"He's right, Rhianna. You're working yourself to the bone. Get some rest. It's late," Noah said, leaning on the doorframe. He was dressed in clean fitted jeans and a T-shirt, but flecks of blue paint still highlighted his blond hair. He glanced at his watch, making Rhianna look up at the clock on the wall. Goodness, it was nearly midnight! Yasmin had left around eleven, after the last customers. Being a weeknight, it had been quieter. Until the school holidays in July, the weekends were the only busy, rushed-off-your-feet days.

Both men were looking expectantly at her. Joe had his hands on his hips, in his 'I'm not taking no for an answer' way. Noah looked equally uncompromising.

"Okay, okay, I'll stop now." Rhianna closed her laptop and turned off the printer, as Joe fetched her cardigan from the back of her swivel chair. He held it out, insistent, and with an eyeroll, she weaved her arms through the wool sleeves. She gave everything one last check, closed the office door and locked it. Then, with both men following, she checked that everything was switched off in the kitchen. Ushering them both out the front door, she then locked up the bistro.

Awkwardly, with Joe watching, she gave Noah a hug and kiss on the cheek, thanking him for his thoughtfulness.

"Remember, I'd really like to take you out for a drink," Noah said softly.

"Yes, yes, I know. Maybe pop by tomorrow evening and I'll try to get away from the bistro earlier. Being a Tuesday, it's usually quieter."

Noah nodded. "Okay, see you tomorrow." He walked off the other way, hands in his pockets. She'd sensed an air of disappointment initially, but her invitation to meet him tomorrow had obviously made him confident enough to let her walk home with Joe.

With Joe by her side, she headed up the hill towards The Cormorant, deep in thought. They were both sober, so a repeat of the awkwardness of the other evening wouldn't happen. The plus side of moving out of Joe's would be not having to climb the damn hill every evening. However, considering Kittiwake Cove was at the bottom of a valley, her new home was likely to also be up some sort of hill. She should start looking for somewhere, once the madness had calmed after Tilly and Liam's wedding, because she couldn't stay living under Joe's roof forever, not if she wanted to put down proper roots in Kittiwake Cove. And move on with her life.

If things worked out with Noah, how awkward would it be bringing him back — or any other boyfriend, for that matter — to Joe's apartment?

CHAPTER 27: NEGRONI

As agreed, Noah turned up at the bistro around eight o'clock the following evening. Rhianna had checked with Yasmin whether she could go off duty early, and Yasmin had said with a frown, "Erm, you're the boss."

"Thanks, Yazz." Rhianna really liked Yasmin. Not only did she shake the perfect cocktail, she had a good head for business too. Rhianna could trust Yasmin to look after the bistro in her absence.

However, she did wonder where she and Noah should go for their date, because it would be awkward going to The Cormorant. Since it was a pleasant evening, she decided to suggest sitting outside on the terrace at the bistro as an option.

"I know I should get away from this place, but I'm wondering if it's best we have a drink here?"

"I think you should get away, even if it's just for a couple of hours. And maybe away from prying eyes," Noah said. Kittiwake Cove was a small town, and Noah came across as a very private man. He waved his car keys. "I don't mind driving; we could head to Wadebridge. This might sound like a daft question, but have you eaten?"

Rhianna shook her head. "Nope, too busy to think about eating."

"Come on, then." Noah took her hand, and led her out of the bistro to his black pickup truck. It had a hard top over the flatbed. Rhianna could see all the tools of his trade and paints in the back.

The drive to Wadebridge took only twenty minutes. Noah parked up and showed Rhianna into a quaint pub serving food until nine p.m. They had half an hour to choose off the menu. Trying not to be distracted by the décor of low beams and antique brassware dotted around, they chose their dinner. Rhianna opted for the pub classic of hunter's chicken, and Noah chose the catch of the day on the specials board.

"Although I think I've got the best catch today," he said, looking at Rhianna. His green eyes looked darker in the dim light of the pub.

"Careful, you're starting to sound as corny as Nick."

"Oh, sorry, I take it back!" Noah laughed. "I'd hate to be compared to Nick."

"Don't worry, if you were anything like him, I wouldn't be sitting here."

The evening was pleasant enough. Noah and Rhianna had plenty to talk and laugh about, telling each other anecdotes from their past. The whole first date stuff of getting to know one another. He talked about his brothers and she told him about her life in Bristol, avoiding the topic of Glyn, and her enthusiasm for the perfect cocktail.

"Did you want to go back for a cocktail now?" Rhianna said, the words leaving her mouth before she'd truly thought about the possible implications. She liked Noah, but she didn't want to lead him on. Yet, she was really enjoying his company, and it felt too early to end the evening. And too soon to judge whether he was right or wrong for her.

"Sure."

The Beach Front Bistro still had a few patrons left in the restaurant. Rhianna showed Noah outside onto the balcony and fired up one of the patio heaters, thinking it was a shame to be stuck inside on a such a glorious summer's evening. The darkening night sky was clear, the wind had dropped since yesterday and the stars were emerging.

"What cocktail would you like?" Rhianna asked as Noah took a seat.

"Oh, you're the expert. I'll let you choose. But I should be buying." Noah reached for his wallet. Rhianna placed her hand on his to stop him.

"I'll get these. You don't have to drive?"

"No, the truck's parked up for the evening now."

"Okay, I'll be back in a sec."

Rhianna dashed up to Shakers, pleasantly surprised to find it busier than the restaurant. After some deliberation as to what to choose, she placed her order with Yasmin, who agreed she should return to her date and she would bring the drinks down.

When Rhianna returned to her seat beside Noah, he took her hand. His hand was warm, his thumb circling her palm.

"Beautiful, isn't it?" Rhianna said, referring to the evening, her mind racing, wondering what next, a shy awkwardness falling between them. Should she kiss Noah tonight? What was first-date etiquette? Did she want him to kiss her? And why — for the love of God — couldn't she get Joe out of her head?

"Yes, it is," Noah answered, looking Rhianna in the eye, sending her even further off guard. He certainly was very attractive.

He edged closer, then sat back as Yasmin arrived. She carried a tray with two ice-filled rocks glasses containing a dark orangey-red liquid, the colour of dark honey. An orange twist garnished each glass.

Noah looked at the glasses inquisitively. He stirred the ice round with his straw and took a sip. "It's delicious; what is it?"

"A Negroni — gin, Campari and red vermouth. It's really an Italian *aperitivo*, but I think it works well after dinner too,"

Rhianna said, sipping her drink through the straw, savouring the warm earthy and spicy notes of the cocktail.

Noah put his glass on the table. "Rhianna, this has been lovely. I hope we can do it again." Now they were alone again, he leaned towards her, his head inching closer to hers.

"Yes, yes…" Rhianna wasn't sure she wanted to do it again. Did she have time to do this again? She put her glass down too, for fear of dropping it. The way Noah was looking at her, his eyes intent, she could feel a kiss brewing. She remained still, unable to withdraw from his magnetic pull.

He cupped her cheek gently with one hand and kissed her, his mouth gently on hers, her lips naturally parting with his, letting his tongue touch hers as the kiss deepened. Rhianna allowed herself to relax into the moment, enjoying the sweet caress. When they pulled away, she could feel her heart beating nervously within her chest. There was no doubt it was a great kiss, an amazing kiss, but all she could think of was Joe.

Why, oh why, was she thinking of Joe? Noah was a catch. Handsome and a perfect gentleman too, and, unlike Joe, not a commitment-phobe.

But why was she struggling to get past this?

Noah was an attractive man in more ways than one, yet Rhianna couldn't quite put her finger on why she just didn't fancy him.

"How's Rhianna getting on with the bistro?" Rose asked Joe as she pegged out washing on her rotary line, positioned in her garden to catch the morning and afternoon sun.

The longest day was nearing, and there was real warmth in the air, which even the wind was failing to lessen today. All Joe could think of was how perfect it would be to get in the sea — he was running surf lessons later. A group from London were staying in Kittiwake Cove for team-building activities booked through Tristan's business. Usually when it was high pressure, the surf flattened, but it would be perfect for training newbies today.

"Great, I think. I rarely see her." With the season picking up, Joe had called in to help his mother and father early in the morning before the pub needed his full attention. Ricky was in more now with the busy season, so there was nothing he couldn't handle if a delivery arrived. Joe was putting away the lawnmower. Charles was further down the garden, tending to the chickens and his vegetable patch.

Tilly and Liam's wedding was approaching, so he'd hardly caught sight of Rhianna, except for the evening with Noah … an image he wished he could erase from his memory.

Rose removed a peg from her mouth. "I suppose she must be so busy getting the bistro off the ground."

"Yeah, either that or she's avoiding me."

"Why'd you say that?"

Joe shrugged. After the evening of cocktails with his brother and sister, when he'd crassly suggested being friends with benefits to Rhianna, he felt she'd distanced herself from him.

And then he'd seen her on the balcony of The Beach Front Bistro with Noah. What was worse, he'd caught sight of them kissing. That had felt like swallowing a gallon of icy, salty water.

But he was to blame. He'd okayed it with Noah, and even encouraged Rhianna to go on a date with him. Sometimes he was just so stupid.

"Let's have a cuppa, shall we? I can sense you want to tell me all about it." Rose finished pegging out the last of the sheets and they walked into the kitchen.

Joe wasn't sure he wanted to tell his mother about it, but could see she would insist that he did.

There was a filter coffee machine already on the go, the jug half full. Joe fetched two mugs from the dresser and poured two coffees for them.

Back outside, sitting beside one another on the garden chairs around the table on the patio, they stayed silent for a moment, absorbing the twittering of the birds on the feeders dotted around the garden, and allowed the sun to warm their faces. Joe almost believed he'd avoided his mother's interrogation, until Rose asked, "What's really the matter between you and Rhianna?" She had snagged the biscuit barrel from the kitchen and was crumbling a half-eaten digestive biscuit, scattering it a few yards in front of her flip-flopped feet. A friendly robin and a couple of house sparrows dared to retrieve the crumbs.

"There's nothing the matter. Rhianna may be moving out soon. Her house has sold, which means she can start looking for another property."

"You don't sound too happy about it. I thought you'd be glad to see her move out. Cramping your style a little, isn't she?" Rose was teasing, Joe could tell. "I mean, she's probably the longest you've ever had a woman live under your roof … since Alannah." Rose glanced at him over her coffee cup, as if to gauge his reaction.

"Mum," Joe frowned. "I'm just concerned about her, that's all. She doesn't need to rush out and buy a house; she's got the bistro to concentrate on this summer. Besides, Nick and Noah have been showing interest in her." He tried to make it sound casual, as if he was sharing gossip with a friend. There was no jealousy. Joe didn't do jealousy. He picked at some non-existent fluff on the arm of the canvas chair.

"So, really you're concerned about her love life?" Rose frowned at Joe. "That's why you don't want her to move out?"

"No … but luckily Nick's lost interest." Nick seemed to have been less flirtatious towards Rhianna over the past few weeks — possibly because he had realised his attentions were wasted on her. Joe also knew Kerenza kept Nick's bed warm with her visits from time to time. Joe wasn't jealous about that either. He was happy for Kerenza to move on. That had been their deal in their relationship. "I had warned Rhianna about him."

"And what's wrong with Nick?" Rose said, frowning at Joe over her coffee cup.

She knew full well what was wrong with Nick. "He's a womaniser, a player. Rhianna deserves better. He'd only use her."

"Pot calling the kettle black."

"I am not as bad as Nick. I do actually respect women."

"Good to hear I did something right," Rose said with a smile. "And so, Noah. Dear, sweet Noah?"

"He asked her out for a drink. Even asked if I was okay with it, and I said yes. Stupidly."

"Why? Is he not good enough for Rhianna either?"

"Because … because…"

"Oh, Joe, if you are in love with her, you need to tell her!" Rose sounded exasperated suddenly, as if she'd lost patience with him.

"I'm not in love with her."

Rose raised her eyebrows. "She's probably thinking you're the same commitment-phobe guy she met three years ago and doesn't want something that won't last. Which means she would never date Nick, so you have nothing to worry about there."

"I know that."

"However, Noah is the kind of guy to treat her right."

"I know that, too."

"So what is the real problem here, Joe? Only you can work it out," Rose said. She patted his arm and her tone softened. "Joe, my darling, you've never been right since Alannah left you, as if you're afraid to get hurt again. I used to think that maybe with all these women, you'd find the one. One that would make you happy and you'd settle down. And now, I think you've found her."

"Who?"

"Rhianna, silly. Look at you. Jealous as hell, you are."

"I'm not jealous!"

"Really?" Rose laughed. "Nick was rattling your cage when she first arrived, and now Noah's doing it. A little jealousy isn't a bad thing. It might make you wake up! For heaven's sake, Joe, if you don't tell her how you feel, she won't know. Would it be so bad to try and settle down with one woman?"

Joe shrugged. The thought of telling Rhianna he loved her petrified him. What if she didn't love him? And did he love her? Truly love her? He had thought after the sex they'd shared he'd have got her out of his system. But it had seemed to only make matters worse. He wanted her more than ever.

"It's not easy," Rose continued. "Me and your father have had our fair share of rows. More when we were younger, especially with you kids playing us up. Oh, how we bickered. But now, I have a companion. Okay, sometimes we still get on each other's nerves — that's life. But I have someone to chat to always, about the silliest of things. We *get* each other. We're great company together. You have to remember our bodies will fade, but our minds won't — well, hopefully they won't — don't book me into a home yet, will you?" She winked at Joe while chuckling. He laughed back. "And we get to cuddle before we go to sleep —"

"Mum." He frowned. He didn't want to think about what his parents got up to.

She waved him off. "We comfort one another now. He's my Dempsey, I'm his Makepeace. We're a team."

"I don't know. What if Rhianna isn't the one?"

"There is no way of finding out unless you try. Look at Sam, he is coming around to the idea of dating again, maybe with Heather's help." Rose chuckled at Heather's determination to interfere. "He didn't think it was possible to love another woman after Jade."

"I'm not like Sam." Joe wished he was, though, sometimes. To take that leap of faith and put his heart back on the line and under another woman's spell. Sam had a strength he feared he did not.

"I know you're not. You're very different. You've always been more laidback in your approach to life. Sam was always the builder, the engineer, painstakingly taking time over his Lego or Meccano, and you'd come in from the beach and destroy it all." Rose laughed, reflecting on the memory of their childhood. A silence fell between them for a moment. Joe wondered guiltily if he should go and help his father, still hard at work, rather than sit drinking coffee with his mother. "Is this about Alannah?" Rose finally asked. The question he feared the most. Was it?

Joe remained silent. He couldn't bring himself to confess. Not even to his mother.

"I do remember." Rose rubbed his arm affectionately. "A few years ago, you were besotted with a certain Betty who was holidaying here for a week. Out of all the women, she did seem to have captured your heart." Was she talking about Rhianna, back then? Even when they'd had their fling, Joe hadn't been able to get enough of Rhianna. When she'd returned home, there had been a dullness; he'd missed her. But another holiday fling had soon come along… "And now that Betty has returned to you, you're getting a second chance. Can't you see that?"

"Rhianna?"

Rose looked at him sternly. "You need to follow your heart, Joe —" she tapped the centre of his breastbone — "and not be afraid to make the same mistakes as you did with Alannah. Maybe you and Rhianna are meant to be." Rose sipped her coffee. Silence fell upon them again, as if she was giving him time to process what she was telling him. Joe's head spun: love, fear, revelation… "And maybe Alannah really wasn't meant to be. Have you thought of that? Life has a way of working things out. But Alannah only followed her dreams because you wouldn't show commitment, Joe. She could have followed those dreams with you, but you wouldn't let her. And Rhianna will do the same if you're not careful."

"I'm afraid I'll hurt her," Joe said.

"You won't. Not intentionally. As far as I understand it, Rhianna's dreams are here, in Kittiwake Cove, just as yours are now. She's putting down roots here," Rose said, looking at her son earnestly. "You're not intending to return to Australia, are you?"

Joe had thought about it. But over the past few years, owning The Cormorant, helping his family, balancing life with the beach, he had lost interest. Despite the more reliable weather over there. "No, I'm staying here."

"Then you're never going to find out if you two are right for one another unless you give it a try."

"What if she doesn't feel the same?"

"You'll never know if you don't ask. But I have a feeling you'll be surprised. Or are you afraid *you'll* get hurt?"

He sighed. "Maybe."

"Joe, you're not a coward. You have no other fears — I mean, you tackle the waves every day, you'll cliff jump as part of the coasteering. You've rescued people from the ocean in your coast guarding days. But one woman leaves you terrified?"

Joe smirked. When his mother put it like that, it did sound ridiculous.

"Your heart will survive the knock if she doesn't feel the same." Rose stood up. "You're not getting any younger, Joe, and eventually your good looks will fade."

"Gee, thanks, Mum."

She patted his hand. "I'm here if you need me to lend an ear, but I'd better get on. Your dad's down there working his socks off, and I'm lounging about sipping coffee."

Joe stood with his mother. "Me too. Thanks, Mum," he said, his tone serious. "I will think about what you've said."

"I hope so."

Joe kissed his mother on the cheek, called a 'cheerio' down the garden to his father, then headed back to his pub. Nothing like work to distract him from his thoughts. Maybe in the surf session he would find his next holiday fling.

But did he want that?

·

CHAPTER 28: CHAMBORD KIR ROYALE

The day of Tilly and Liam's wedding arrived — the twenty-first of June, the summer solstice — the longest day. When Tilly realised it would be better to hold it midweek to keep the costs low, she'd picked this day. She'd also joked with Rhianna that it might mean that Liam would never be able to forget the date of their wedding anniversary. Plus, at such short notice — they'd turned it around in just over six weeks — photographers and florists had already been booked for the weekends, so had limited availability. It was peak wedding season.

Unbeknownst to their guests, apart from the close family and Joe as best man, who had been their witnesses, they'd officially married that morning at Trenouth Manor.

The dancefloor and stage had been laid in the bistro conservatory, where the ceremony was also being held. Rhianna had attached bolts of white netting to each of the roof beams to make it look like a marquee, with soft white fairy lights hanging amongst it. Tilly's chosen colour scheme was a soft lavender, which would be the colour of her two bridesmaids' dresses. The flowers, provided by Poppy at Tristan's estate, were pale yellow, cream and lavender, and each table was decorated with a beautiful centrepiece. Rhianna had been up early, arranging the tables in the layout that Tilly and Liam had chosen. Little wedding favours, traditional sugared almonds, were placed with each name card. Lavender ribbons were tied in various places where the netting was gathered.

Rhianna had found white bunting online, too cute not to buy. She'd bought enough to hang outside along the balcony and upstairs in Shakers. Her bistro had been transformed into the perfect wedding venue.

The photographer was a local known to Tilly, who used her gallery to exhibit his work. He was taking candid pictures of all the small details as well as the wedding party. Rhianna hoped to buy some of those photographs so she could use them to promote future events and weddings.

While Rhianna made the finishing touches with her staff, ready to serve the wedding breakfast, the ceremony took place. She paused and watched some of it, but with the extra staff to monitor, she wanted this to be perfect for Tilly and Liam.

Tilly was wearing a pale cream chiffon ruched floor-length wedding dress which fitted just below her bust, then fell A-line, or princess style. The design had been cleverly chosen so that if her waistline had expanded slightly, it wasn't noticeable. Her bust was accentuated by a heart-shaped neckline. She looked like an elegant, magical fairy, with her honey-blonde hair curled and tumbling down her back, flowers dotted through it. No one would guess she was fourteen weeks pregnant. The fifty guests were all gathered around the stage, watching Liam and Tilly exchange their unofficial vows. With the limited space and set up for dining afterwards, it had made sense to have the majority of the guests standing, with some seats for those who couldn't be on their feet for too long. Rhianna, with the help of Tristan, had found a metal arch that stood prettily behind the couple, entwined with flowers and white fairy lights, in place of an altar. Joe, who looked unrecognisable in a dark grey three-piece suit, stood beside Liam, holding the rings, and Tilly's father stood beside her, to give her away.

A magnificent three-tier cake, decorated using the same pale yellow and lavender colour scheme, had been delivered the night before and stood to the right of the stage, ready to be cut. On top were two figures of the bride and groom, moulded out of icing. They looked cute and cartoonish, like Mr Men and Little Miss characters. The groom held a surfboard while the bride had a paint palette in her hand.

Tilly had got every detail of the wedding perfect. Rhianna had admired how she'd organised it all so quickly despite bouts of morning sickness, when most brides had a year or more to plan their wedding. Rhianna hoped one day she too would have an intimate wedding like this, surrounded by close family and friends. The sun was shining, with not a cloud in the sky, and even the wind was behaving, being no more than a gentle breeze. Everything looked beautiful, and Rhianna's bistro made her proud.

Later, selected locals were invited to the evening reception, featuring the band and the buffet Rhianna had planned with Tilly. Liam would apparently eat anything, so Tilly had selected the menu for the canapés. Rhianna planned to hang up her apron and join in the party during the evening — her dress was hanging on the back of her office door in readiness — but for now, as the ceremony ended, she concentrated on handing a glass of Kir Royale to all the guests.

"We need to serve the guests a cocktail of sorts, to be keeping in with The Beach Front Bistro," Tilly had said when planning the drinks. Rather than Crème de Cassis, which felt more autumnal being a blackberry liqueur, Tilly had chosen to use Chambord instead. Rhianna had done a special deal with her local winery for the Cornish sparkling wine they were using. A fresh raspberry floated in each glass as a garnish.

Once the guests had their drinks, the next step was to get them to take their seats, ready for the wedding breakfast. Tilly and Liam were going to have speeches beforehand, so then the nerve-racking bit would be out of the way, and everyone could eat their food stress-free. It made sense; Rhianna remembered Jen saying that Drew didn't taste any of the delicious food served up at their wedding breakfast because he'd been so anxious about giving his speech.

"Hey, it looks fantastic in here," Joe said, coming up alongside Rhianna and throwing her off course. He took a couple of flutes off the tray and handed them to guests. "Sorry I couldn't talk to you earlier." Rhianna had been so busy, and so had Joe as part of the wedding party, that this was the first time she'd got close to him. Too close for comfort. He smelled divine and, wearing a smoking hot suit, he looked gorgeous. It even looked like he'd run some wax through his hair. Liam, being Australian, didn't have much family attending, only very close relatives, so he'd asked the guys he ran the surf school with to be his ushers.

"That's okay. We've both been busy." Rhianna had to swallow hard. Joe scrubbed up so well in his suit, with a lavender cravat and a pale yellow rose pinned to his lapel. The sight of him actually made her go weak at the knees, so she had to tighten her grip around the silver tray of cocktails she was carrying and concentrate on keeping both feet firmly on the ground for fear of wobbling.

"I'll catch up with you tonight," Joe said, leaving her side. She was almost relieved. It enabled her to concentrate on her job now.

The father of the bride made his speech first, sounding choked up, proud of his little girl becoming a magnificent woman, then Liam stood up and told some great jokes, helped by his Australian accent. Rhianna's heart melted, as did every other woman's, as he spoke of his love for Tilly, and how he would do everything to make her happy and to protect her and the baby. Then Joe stood up. Rhianna could see he was nervous. He took a sip of his Kir Royale.

"I have only known Liam a couple of years, but he shows incredible patience with his coaching, great skill in his surfing — he's almost as good as me!" The guests laughed. "And he's not a bad gardener on the side, either." In true best man tradition, Joe went on to tell a couple of quick anecdotes to embarrass the groom, before explaining how they'd become good friends, and then his tone became serious. "Liam may have made some mistakes, but what is paramount about this guy, and blatantly obvious, is the love he has for Tilly. This beautiful couple are Kittiwake Cove royalty. And now, you'll be relieved to hear, my speech is coming to an end. I am also relieved, I can tell you." Joe chuckled nervously. Rhianna could see beads of sweat on his forehead. His hand was trembling slightly as he picked up his glass. "I would like you to raise your glasses, to toast the happy couple; to Liam and Tilly."

Everyone raised their glasses and cheered, "To Liam and Tilly."

Rhianna watched Joe sit back down and dab his face with his napkin. She knew he wasn't one for big speeches and being in the spotlight, so she felt proud of him. But with the speeches over, and the wedding breakfast about to begin, it was her turn to get to work and not fluff it up.

The wedding breakfast went without a hitch. The extra hired staff were a godsend, and they were able to get everyone served at practically the same time. The guests were now taking a breather either out on the terrace, or around their tables

305

while they were being cleared, and the happy couple had more photographs taken. Then everyone gathered again for the cutting of the cake. Rhianna had had the good sense to put it on a trolley, so afterwards it could be wheeled into the kitchen for one of the tiers to be cut for the evening.

Rhianna could see the first evening guests arriving and left Yasmin in charge while she slipped into her office and changed. Ideally, she would have liked to shower, but she didn't have time to slip back to Joe's, so a 'shower in a can' had to do as she sprayed deodorant under her arms. She hoped a fresh squirt of perfume would also remove any kitchen smells she may have picked up from the day. She sneaked off to the ladies' loo to use the mirror to touch up her make-up and tidy her hair. She pulled her ponytail out, gave her hair a brush and shake, dampening it with a little water to remove the kink, and hoped she would do. Why did she care so much about her appearance?

Joe.

And Noah would be there.

But she wasn't interested in Noah. She'd realised that as soon as she'd kissed him the other night. And Joe wasn't interested in her. Not in the way she would like him to be.

She was kicking herself. It would make her life so much easier if she could fall for Noah. Her feelings for Joe would fade into the background. Noah was who she wanted Joe to be: a dependable man not afraid of commitment.

Maybe she should give Noah time? Maybe her feelings for him would grow?

Even so, regardless of her love life dilemmas, Rhianna was not one for attending a party half-heartedly. She liked getting dressed up. She liked making an effort. She intended to have fun tonight. Having not had a chance to get to the shops in

Truro, she'd picked something out at the boutique next to Tilly's gallery. A floaty evening dress cut above her knees, with a bit of sparkle. The neckline possibly plunged a little lower than she normally dared. Back in her office, she slipped out of her flats and donned her black heels.

She poked her head around the door into the kitchen. Curtis and Oscar were busy preparing the canapés for the evening, assisted by Vince. They'd put a table opposite the bar to set them out buffet style for the guests to help themselves.

"Everything okay here?" Rhianna asked.

"Yes, boss. Go and enjoy yourself," Curtis said, steam escaping as he opened the oven.

Rhianna headed up the stairs to help Yasmin, who was opening Shakers for the evening, lighting candles on the tables. Some of the flower arrangements from the tables had been taken upstairs, and with the bunting Rhianna had hung from the roof, Shakers was ready for the wedding party. The cocktail lounge was going to be the quiet space for guests to retreat to, away from the music and the crowded atmosphere below.

Music played to get the party atmosphere going while the band were setting up, having had to wait for the wedding breakfast to finish. They were a local band — again, a contact supplied by Tristan — and they sung popular rock and pop songs by big acts like The Rolling Stones, Kings of Leon and Ed Sheeran. Something to get everyone dancing, old and young alike. Tilly and Liam's first dance would be accompanied by the band.

"Hey," Noah said, bumping into Rhianna as she came down the stairs from Shakers.

"Hey." Rhianna jumped. She paused on the last step. Noah looked as handsome as ever. Surely there was no reason why she couldn't fall in love with him?

"Wow, you look amazing," he said.

Rhianna blushed as she smoothed her hands down her dress nervously. "Thank you."

"I'm hoping I'll get a dance later," Noah said, smiling at her. He touched her elbow.

"If you don't mind your toes being trodden on."

"Can I buy you a drink first?" He held his hand out.

She placed her hand in his. "Yes, that would be lovely."

Joe looked for Rhianna as the music started. He was dying to loosen his tie, but felt he'd better wait a little longer, until he saw another usher or even the groom take his off. Liam couldn't get rid of his tie just yet. They were going to announce the first dance soon. The band wanted to warm up first, and it looked like the happy couple were busy with family and friends, trying to talk to everyone, and this became harder with more guests arriving. Rose and Charles were among them, and they made their way over to their son.

"How did the wedding go?" Rose asked. Joe could tell she was admiring his outfit. "Don't you look dapper."

"Thanks. It was beautiful," Joe replied.

"And have you spoken to Rhianna?"

Joe shook his head. "No, I haven't had a chance."

"Well, go and find her." Rose gave him a gentle nudge.

The conversation with his mother the other day still played on Joe's mind. Maybe he needed to take that leap of faith and tell Rhianna how he felt. When he'd led the surf lessons later that day, there had been a couple of attractive women, and one had been single. But all he could think about was Rhianna. Holiday flings were not his style anymore. He kissed his mother, letting his parents head to the bar to buy a drink.

He caught sight of Rhianna as she was descending the stairs from Shakers, and his heart leapt. She'd now changed into an evening dress, revealing those slender legs he so admired. He started making his way over but with a jolt, he saw Noah approach her and the two of them become deep in conversation. Then he watched as Noah held out his hand, and Rhianna took it.

There was that spikey feeling again. *Jealousy.* Joe wasn't used to it. He hated watching another man flirt with Rhianna.

"Ladies and gentlemen, the bride and groom are about to take their first dance," the lead singer of the band announced into the microphone, dominating the room as everyone fell silent and started to clap.

Joe turned his attention to the dancefloor, where Liam and Tilly started to dance as the band played their favourite song — 'Just The Way You Are' by Bruno Mars. After a while, because the song was an upbeat tune, other couples started joining Tilly and Liam. Joe searched for Rhianna in the crowd, to see Noah leading her onto the dancefloor.

Noah was a hard man to compete with.

CHAPTER 29: BELLINI

Rhianna couldn't escape Noah for a while. But she was determined to give him a second chance and not base her decision on one night. A couple of glasses of fizz inside her and she was starting to relax, and trying not to stress too much about her staff and the bistro. Noah helped, tugging her back onto the dancefloor when the band started singing another song, making her laugh more. It was to be the last one of their first set, and they slowed the pace down.

Rhianna giggled as Noah moved to dance closer to her. His hand rested on her hip, while the other took her hand. He was a good dancer. She'd had a lot of fun so far, and the evening had only just begun, really. But she gulped at how close she was to him now; she could see the flecks of hazel in his green eyes when the lights caught them. She caught the citrus and spicy scent of his aftershave. Her body stiffened. If he kissed her now, everyone would see. Joe would see.

Why did she feel guilty?

"Hey." To Rhianna's surprise, Joe appeared. Her panic increased. Had thinking about him made him magically appear?

"Joe!" Rhianna said, possibly more excitedly than she should considering she was dancing with Noah. The fizz was taking effect. She felt as though she was doing something wrong, even though she wasn't.

"Can I cut in? Please?" Joe addressed Noah, then smiled at Rhianna.

"Oh, yeah, sure," Noah said, reluctantly releasing Rhianna from his arms. Joe fell into his place, but he pulled her even closer than Noah had dared. Rhianna didn't know whether to relax into his hold or not. He felt so familiar; his scent alone sent tremors of delight through her body. She wished Noah made her feel like this. It would make life so much easier.

They danced silently for a moment, staring and smiling at one another.

"I've been dying to dance with you all night," he said.

"The night is still young; besides, you could have come and asked me."

"I did, didn't I?" Joe gestured by tapping her hip and squeezing her hand. The heat of his palm against hers sent tingles up her arm.

"Well, you could have asked sooner if you were so desperate." Rhianna moved closer. They weren't so much dancing now, more swaying to the music. Their concentration was more on their words. Thank God the music was loud, otherwise the whole room would probably hear Rhianna's heart hammering.

"I needed to get things straight first." His breath on her ear sent goosebumps down her spine. Her body always responded to his touch. Damn, how it betrayed her.

She dared to ask the question, her brain trying to take over from her heart. "Joe, what are you up to?" She eyed him suspiciously. Her throat tightened. She really didn't want Joe ruining a good evening by making another silly proposal about being friends with benefits.

"I need to talk to you. Before I lose my bottle." His face was so close to hers now, their noses almost touching, his lips inches from hers. If he kissed her now, everyone would see, including Noah — who she was sure was watching them like a hawk. God, she really didn't want to hurt Noah. Especially when Joe's intentions were probably not honourable, in the sense that he wanted the fun, but not the relationship. How had she got into this mess?

"Are you drunk?"

"No." He frowned.

"Shall we go and talk, then?" She chewed her lip.

"Let's grab a drink first." Joe tugged her off the dancefloor, but didn't let go of her hand. In fact, his grip tightened. Not to the point he was crushing her fingers, but she knew he didn't want to let her out of his grasp. They passed Nick, Olly and a heavily pregnant Rachel, among others, and he just waved and strolled through, ignoring his friends.

"Hi! Bye!" Rhianna joked, passing them.

Vince was serving at the bar. Rhianna ordered another glass of sparkling wine and Joe asked for a beer. Then, taking her hand, he led her outside onto the terrace, where the patio heaters were now lit. On the horizon, the sun was setting, the sky an orangey-pink, but it wouldn't be dark for another hour yet.

They chose a free table with a bench seat and sat down close together, Joe straddling the seat so he was close to her. He took her hand, his thumb circling her palm, and for a moment he watched this movement, rather than meeting Rhianna's gaze.

"Joe, what's this about? I don't want to miss the party, and, well, I was dancing with Noah..."

"You dancing with Noah has been killing me all evening," Joe mumbled. Then he looked up. His hand cupped her cheek. "You're the most beautiful woman I've ever known. And I can't watch you with Noah, or with any other man for that matter, Rhianna. I realise now, I'm..." He dragged a hand through his hair. Rhianna's heart quickened. Joe talking seriously scared her.

"Joe?" she urged.

"I don't know how to say this, but, well, there's only one Betty for me, and I want her in my life — permanently."

Had he met someone on the beach? Was this Joe's way of telling Rhianna he'd found someone else? But he'd just said he'd hated watching her with Noah. What was this all about? A sadness started to ball in her chest. "You've met someone?" she said weakly.

Joe shook his head. "No, Rhianna... I'm in love with you." He stammered out the confession hesitantly. Rhianna wasn't even sure she'd him heard right. His thumb brushed her cheek.

"What did you say?" Rhianna's throat tightened with tears.

"Oh, please don't make me say it again." He chuckled.

"What? I don't understand. Are you trying to tell me you've met someone?"

"No, silly, I love *you*." This time, Joe said it more loudly and assertively, so that another couple nearby turned their heads in Joe and Rhianna's direction. "I love you!"

Rhianna straightened up in her seat, taken aback by Joe's confession. She wiped her face. The lump forming in her throat had released with a trickle of tears. Tears of happiness, relief ... not sadness.

He loved her.

"Oh, God, I love you, too," she said.

"Oh, thank fuck for that." Joe cupped her face and kissed her. As the kiss deepened, they edged closer and closer together so that their bodies pressed against one another. The twisting was making Rhianna's lower spine ache, but she didn't care.

Then her brain, determined to ruin the moment, thought of something. Joe caught her hesitation. She released herself from his arms.

"What's wrong?" He frowned, stroking under her chin.

Rhianna shook her head. "It's silly, but I need to know … about Kerenza … and Lucy… Did you sleep with them?"

"No!" Joe sounded aghast. "I haven't looked at another woman since you set foot in Kittiwake Cove!"

"You haven't?"

"No!" He shuffled closer. "Rhianna, don't move out. Live with me, properly. I don't want to waste another moment not having you in my life." His hands held her head close to his, their foreheads almost touching.

"Joe? Are you sure?"

"Yes! I've wasted too much time already as it is." He kissed her again.

"Okay, okay, we can maybe discuss the finer details tomorrow, but should we get back to the party? It is Tilly and Liam's day, after all." Rhianna could see people on the dancefloor, the disco music playing as the band took their break.

"Yes, yes, we should. But come here first." Joe pulled her into a hug, holding her, stroking her hair and kissing the top of her head. "Let me have five minutes of you to myself."

"In Wales, we call a cuddle a *cwtch*." Rhianna's voice was muffled, her head held against Joe's chest. She could hear the steady beat of his heart, even with the music blasting out.

"What?" He gently pushed her away so he could look her in the eye.

"*Cwtch*," she said, but when he still looked puzzled, she continued, "Rhymes with butch, pronounced kutch."

"I want to do more than kutch you." He tugged her closer again, pulling her into another kiss. His fingers swept lightly over her bare shoulders, sending tingles down her spine.

Reluctantly, she pulled out of the kiss, fearing they'd need a room soon at the rate the electricity was passing between them. Through the glass, Rhianna saw Noah at the bar. He was laughing, thankfully, with his brother Olly. "Oh, bugger, what am I going to do about Noah?"

"I'll talk to him."

"Maybe I should too. I wasn't sure he was right for me anyway. Oh, I don't want to hurt him. It'll break his heart."

"He'll get over it. Time heals. I've realised that now." Joe pushed strands of hair from her face. "And he's a good man too. It'll be fine."

"I hope so."

"I know so." Joe's gaze became intent on her again. "I won't let anything get in the way of us being happy. I promise."

"Joe, you know I'd like to get married, one day, even have children…"

"I know, I know…" Joe's hand nervously combed through his hair. "One day at a time, my darling. I've only just announced I love you… Do you know what that's done to my nerves?"

Rhianna giggled. "I can already see the grey hairs forming."

"Thanks." Joe rolled his eyes.

"Let's go grab a cocktail," she said, taking his hand.

"That sounds like a great idea. I'll let you choose."

"Mmm … I think I need a Bellini to celebrate." A cocktail made with sparkling wine was definitely called for.

"Sounds perfect to me."

Holding hands, Joe let Rhianna lead him back into the throng of music and people, and everything she envisaged her bistro to be.

And from then on, he never let her go.

EPILOGUE: PARADISE

It had been several months since Tilly and Liam's wedding. Even with Rhianna's house sale going through, and her equity received, she'd remained in Joe's apartment. That very night she'd moved into his bed and had not looked back. To wake up in Joe's arms every morning filled her with a deep joy, and she did not doubt he loved her. Joe and Rhianna were the talk of Kittiwake Cove. She was the Betty who'd 'tamed' Joe. Noah, although hurt initially, appeared on good terms with them both. Maybe he'd known deep down that Rhianna wasn't meant for him.

Now, sitting on the beach, tucked behind the rocks to shelter from the wind, Rhianna and Joe watched mad surfers in the October waters as the tide came in. Joe had already been in that morning. He'd been one of those mad morning surfers.

As it was a fine autumn day, Joe had suggested a picnic on the beach. They were sharing a bottle of sparkling wine and eating leftover scones from the bistro, as they watched the sun set, much earlier now than in the summer. The day had been warm, but a chill was forming as they huddled together under a blanket. Rhianna had a day off from the bistro. As planned, she closed for one day a week now, to enable both her and her staff to have a break. But with the October half-term soon arriving, she'd open the full seven days then.

"Rhianna," Joe said, weaving his arm around her to pull her closer.

"Yes?" She looked at him suspiciously as she sipped her wine. She hoped he wasn't going to suggest they went for a swim. No, after that dreadful evening in the summer when she'd nearly drowned, surely Joe wouldn't suggest anything of the sort.

"Shall we go for a paddle?"

Then again... Rhianna shivered. "But it's nice and warm here."

"I know, but can we go for a quick walk?" Joe had itchy feet. She might have managed to get him to settle down in the sense of commitment, but where the beach was involved, he liked to be doing something near the water.

"Oh, all right then."

He kissed her, helped her to her feet and then organised the blankets and their belongings so that a cheeky seagull didn't try rummaging for a potential meal. She frowned at him. He was taking so long.

"Come on, before I change my mind." Rhianna had started to head towards the sea, the wet sand cold between her toes.

"Patience, darling." Joe ran after her, grabbed her around the waist and kissed her passionately. "God, I love you," he said, hugging her close. "I can't believe I used to think that would be so hard to say to you."

"I love you, too."

They reached the shoreline. Rhianna couldn't bear her toes touching the water, it felt so cold. They walked along the edge, arms crossed behind each other, remaining close for warmth as they watched the surfers amongst the rough waves. There were only a few brave souls, those that could ride along the wave, and dip out of it gracefully, then paddle out for another.

Then, suddenly, to Rhianna's surprise, Joe dropped to one knee on the wet sand. She looked at him quizzically, squinting because the sun was drawing low on the horizon.

"Rhianna, with the tide and the sunset as my witnesses, will you marry me?" Joe knelt at the water's edge, hand out, a dark blue jewellery box open, and a solitaire diamond ring exposed.

Rhianna's hand flew to her mouth. She was speechless. The ring was beautiful. She wasn't expecting a proposal. Not yet.

"Take your time, it's not at all wet and cold down here," Joe said dryly, remaining in position. She could see the knee of his jeans soaking up water.

"Yes, yes, of course, you bloody fool, yes!" Caught out, just as she was about to kiss him, a wave pushed past them. Joe lost his balance and fell as Rhianna squealed at the shock of the cold shooting up her shins, drenching her jeans.

"Joe! Joe, are you okay?" She scrambled to help him up. "Oh no! What about the ring? You haven't lost it?"

He stood, jeans soaked, chuckling. His fist was clenched. He opened it up to reveal the wet blue box. "I don't care about losing the ring. I never want to lose you."

"Ah, Joe." Cupping his face with her wet, cold hands, she kissed him. They didn't care that the tide still fought past them, determined to come in. She ignored the icy water as the warmth of his tongue found hers.

Another wave rushed past, and Rhianna gave a shiver. Joe grabbed her hand and they ran out of the sea, laughing like besotted teenagers. Once on drier sand, Joe gently placed the ring on her finger and kissed her hand. "I don't want to wait any longer. I want you to be my best friend, my lover, the mother of my children, my wife."

Rhianna gazed at the man she loved so dearly. She wanted all of these things; she just hadn't wanted to rush him, fearing he'd change his mind and run a mile. The man certainly kept surprising her.

"I want all that too, Joe."

This was madness! She hadn't even been in Kittiwake Cove a year. But she'd wanted this to be her new beginning, and there wasn't a doubt in her mind. Joe was the man she wanted to spend the rest of her life with. Joe was the one who ignited her body with his touch, who lifted her heart with the slightest of smiles. Now there were no barriers between them; now all was honesty, they laughed continually, and loved and respected each other, every day.

With a smile, Joe softly pressed his lips to Rhianna's, and for a brief moment, as their mouths opened and their tongues caressed, he squeezed her body close to his.

"I promise to love you until the ocean's tides cease to turn." Joe's forehead remained touching Rhianna's. He brushed her cheek with his thumb.

"But that will never happen."

"Exactly."

COCKTAIL RECIPES

Many of my chapter titles came from *Drink Me Now: 150 Cocktails For Any Emergency* as well as some other cocktail recipe books I've acquired over the past few years, but here are a couple of recipes I thought I'd share with you:

COSMOPOLITAN
(This is the basic recipe that I tweaked for the purpose of the book for The Beach Front Cosmopolitan)

Ice cubes
1½ measures lemon vodka
4 teaspoons Triple Sec
3 teaspoons lime juice
1 measure cranberry juice
Lime slice, to decorate

Add all the ingredients into a cocktail shaker and shake. Strain into a martini glass, decorate with a slice of lime and serve.
(For a Woo Woo swap the Triple Sec for Peach Schnapps.)

SURF RIDER

Ice cubes
6 measures vodka
2 measures sweet vermouth
Juice of 1 lemon
Juice of 2 oranges
1 teaspoon of grenadine

Put 8–10 ice cubes into a cocktail shaker. Pour the vodka,
vermouth, fruit juices and grenadine over the ice and shake
until a frost forms on the outside of the shaker.
Strain immediately into two old-fashioned glasses. Serve
immediately.

STORM AT SEA

4 measures cranberry juice
2 measures pineapple juice
4 teaspoons elderflower cordial
16–20 ice cubes
3 measures Blavod Vodka

Pour the cranberry and pineapple juice and the elderflower
cordial into a cocktail shaker with half the ice cubes and shake
the mix.
Strain into two old-fashioned glasses over the remaining ice
cubes. Add the vodka slowly, which will separate briefly, and
serve immediately.

A NOTE TO THE READER

Dear Reader,

Thank you for choosing to read *Cocktails at Kittiwake Cove* and I hope you enjoyed it as much as I loved writing and researching it. (More on that in the acknowledgements!) I try to create feel-good romances the reader can immerse themselves into. We all need that escapism from time to time, and I hope my heroes, like Joe, provide that light relief.

The great thing about this book is that it inspired a series, so there are more stories to follow set in Kittiwake Cove. Next up will be Joe's cousin, Tristan.

If you enjoyed reading this book, the best way to let me know is by leaving a review on **Goodreads** and/or **Amazon**. It's also a great way to share with other readers too! And I will be eternally grateful to you.

I love hearing from readers, so please feel free to contact me on any of my social media platforms. I'd love to chat with you. You can follow me here:

Facebook / **Goodreads** / **Amazon** / **BookBub** / **Blog** / **Website** / **Instagram** / **Twitter**.

I also have a monthly newsletter that you can subscribe to **here**.

Once again, thank you. You are the reason I love to write romance.

Kind regards,

Teresa

www.teresamorgan.co.uk

Sapere Books is an exciting new publisher of brilliant fiction and popular history.

To find out more about our latest releases and our monthly bargain books visit our website: **saperebooks.com**

Printed in Great Britain
by Amazon

19604577R00183